Shawn Lamb

Shield Maiden of Eldar

Shieldmaiden
Enjoy the
Adventure,
Shawn

Allon Books

SHIELD MAIDEN OF ELDAR
by Shawn Lamb

Published by Allon Books
6829 Valley Brook Trace
Utica, Kentucky 42376-5005
www.allonbooks.com

Cover illustration by Robert Lamb
Image used under license from Shutterstock.com.

International Standard Book Number: 978-0-9964381-6-2

Other Books by Shawn Lamb

Young Adult Fantasy Fiction

ALLON – BOOK 1 – STRUGGLE FOR ALLON
ALLON – BOOK 2 – INSURRECTION
ALLON – BOOK 3 – HEIR APPARENT
ALLON – BOOK 4 – A QUESTION OF SOVEREIGNTY
ALLON – BOOK 5 – GAUNTLET
ALLON – BOOK 6 – DILEMMA
ALLON – BOOK 7 – DANGEROUS DECEPTION
ALLON – BOOK 8 – DIVIDED
ALLON – BOOK 9 – IN PLAIN SIGHT
ALLON – BOOK 10 - WAIFS

GUARDIANS OF ALLON – BOOK ONE – THE GREAT BATTLE
GUARDIANS OF ALLON – BOOK TWO – REPRIEVE
GUARDIANS OF ALLON – BOOK THREE – OVERTHROW

PARENT STUDY GUIDE FOR ALLON ~ BOOKS 1-9
ELDAR – BOOK 1 – SON OF ELDAR
ELDAR – BOOK 2 – TRADER OF ELDAR

For Young Readers – ages 8-10
Allon – The King's Children series

NECIE AND THE APPLES
TRISTINE'S DORGIRITH ADVENTURE
NIGEL'S BROKEN PROMISE

THE ACTIVITY BOOK OF ALLON

Historical Fiction

GLENCOE
THE HUGUENOT SWORD

ELDAR TERRITORIES

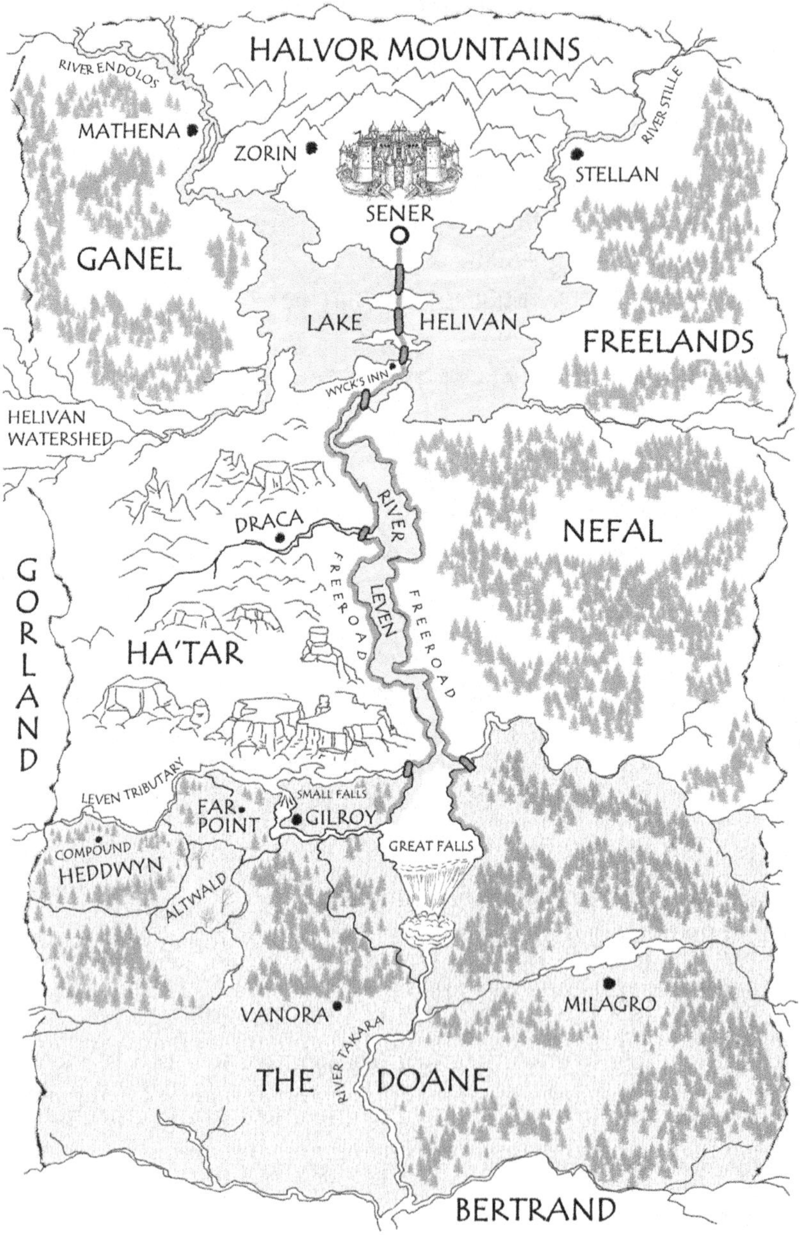

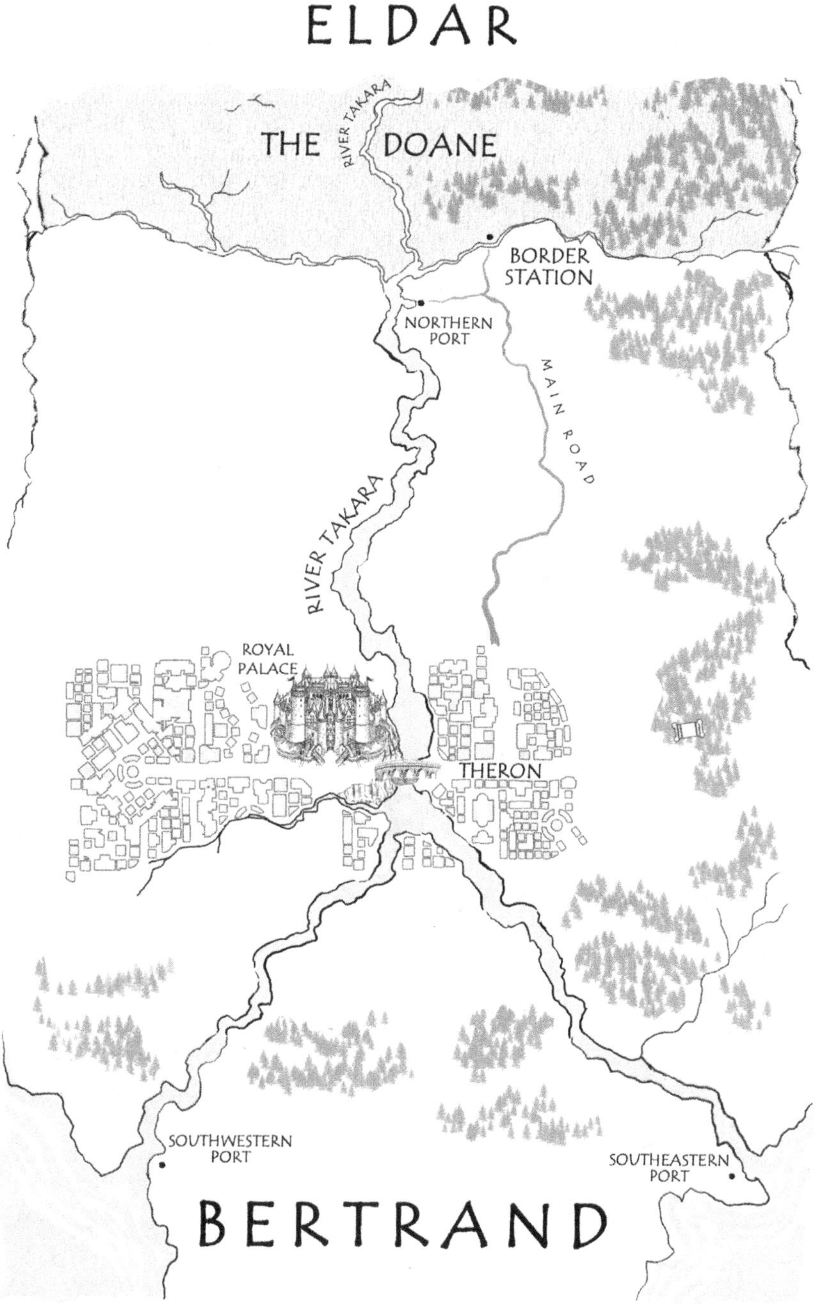
ELDAR
THE DOANE
RIVER TAKARA
BORDER STATION
NORTHERN PORT
MAIN ROAD
RIVER TAKARA
ROYAL PALACE
THERON
SOUTHWESTERN PORT
SOUTHEASTERN PORT
BERTRAND

Characters

Eldar

King Axel
Queen Alicia
Princess Lexi, sister of King Axel
Sir Gunnar
Nollen, Royal Commissary
Arctander
Lady Lorraine
Lord Ronan
Lord Cormac
Baron Irwin

Maro, Chief of Nefal
Lady Brynn, Maro's daughter
Bodil, Maro's aid
Spoor, Nefal warrior

First Ones and Animals of Eldar

Othniel, Great White Lion of Eldar
Alfgar, King of the Unicorns
Bardolf, Alpha of the White Wolves
Artair, King of the Eagles
Ajax, an eagle
Callie, female white wolf
Alydar
Sheba

Bertrand

King Rastus
Prince Felix
Princess Celeste
Vizier Cadmus
Lady Olivia
Celia, Olivia's maid
Mateo & Marius, twin sons of Cadmus

Animals

Kronos, Lord of the Buffalos
Ursus, Bear King
Spyros, Lord of the Ravens
Kyros, a raven
Zetta, a raven

Chapter 1

WEIGHING THREE THOUSAND POUNDS WITH A POWERFUL NECK, huge head, and massive razor-sharp horns, the enormous haunches of the buffalo moved with each step. Elongated canines gave the appearance of fangs with saliva dripping from them. The end of the tail resembled a mace with short thorny spikes capable of causing great injury. Thick dark brown fur rippled with movement. Patches of white covered most of the face. Despite the appearance of age, it moved with purpose and agility over the forest terrain.

Without harness or saddle, a giant being rode upon the beast's back. He wore leather and metal armor-like clothing complete with sword. A weather-beaten warrior by the look of his badly scarred face. A patch covered his left eye. His head turned from side-to-side for his good eye to survey the area. Leafing tree buds showed signs of spring.

"How much further?" he asked.

The buffalo stopped. A deep voice resonated in reply. "This far for you. Wait here. I will summon you when the others have agreed."

Once the giant dismounted, the buffalo continued for another hundred yards into a clearing. He arrived the same time as a massive bear; its reddish-brown fur highlighted by the sun's rays. The buffalo stopped. With a nod of acknowledgement, he spoke to the bear.

"Greetings, my lord Ursus. It has been a long time."

"Lord Kronus," acknowledged the bear king.

An echoing caw came from above. Ursus and Kronus watched a larger than normal raven land on a fallen log.

"Spyros," said Kronus in greeting.

"My lord Kronus. Lord Ursus," replied Spyros.

"You summoned us?" Ursus asked Spyros.

"No. I thought you did."

"Kronus?" asked Ursus.

"It is because of me you are all here." The giant boldly strode into the clearing.

Kronus snorted in anger and stomped a front hoof. "I told you to wait!"

"A Nefal!" Ursus growled and stood on powerful hindlegs.

Spyros spread his wings; his feathers ruffled. "You brought a Nefal here?" he demanded of Kronus.

"At the request of Cadmus," said the buffalo lord.

Spyros folded his wings while Ursus went back down on all fours. Ursus' voice remained wary, as he asked, "Why would Cadmus do that?"

"The time has come for Bertrand to deal with Eldar," said the giant.

"What would you know of this, Nefal?" Ursus bared his teeth.

"These scars are the result of trying to stop the Son of Eldar! What have you done since his return but continue to hide in Bertrand?"

Ursus roared with anger at the retort.

"Stay, Ursus!" Kronus commanded. When the bear king appeared reluctant to stand down, Kronus firmly said, "Cadmus seeks to stop what happened in Markita from occurring here. To do so, he needs help from us, and Nefal."

"The Nefal have caused us nothing but trouble for centuries. Give us one good reason why we should trust them!" rebuffed Ursus.

"Revenge for the death of your former comrade, Sirin," the Nefal said. Seeing he got their attention, he proceeded. "We served the gods for nearly a millennium. A single mistake notwithstanding, we can do so again."

"A costly mistake," Ursus chided.

"This an opportunity to rectify it."

The great bear stared at the Nefal. "What is your name?"

"Spoor. Son of Tolgard, chief of the Gadiks. Second-in-command to former High Chief Argus, who gave his life in battle with the Son of Eldar." His lips twitched as he spoke of Argus.

When Ursus and Spyros exchanged skeptical glances, Spoor's anger rose. "The First Ones of Eldar have become emboldened. They had the Son of Eldar destroy all the dire-buffalos and adult dragons. The Ha'tar were banished, save a few trainers to raise hatchlings in defense of Eldar. The Nefal dig in the dirt only to have crops fail, and stomachs gnaw with hunger. Our shrines reduced to rubble and left as a reminder of our humiliation!"

"What is that to us?" scoffed Spyros.

"With Sirin gone and Markita brought into submission to Eldar, the First Ones will turn their attention south. Your days are numbered if Bertrand does not act!" Spoor declared.

Kronus stepped between Spoor and the others. "Leave us to confer. And this time, wait as instructed!" The mighty buffalo made an angry snort, lowered his head, and pawed the ground as if to charge.

Spoor flinched at the intimidating action. "I will wait." He withdrew to where he originally dismounted.

"He speaks truth," Kronus said.

"We sensed a change in the wind since learning of Sirin's demise," Spyros spoke of himself and Ursus.

"How will joining with Nefal aid us against Othniel and the others? Do they even know we still exist?" asked Ursus.

"With our heads on statues how could they not suspect?" Spyros chided.

"There are common buffalo in Bertrand. Kronus is father of the dire-buffalo," countered Ursus.

"I know! Along with birds and bears," scoffed Spyros. "Yet, who else would dare impersonate gods but those with unique abilities?"

"Humans are weak-minded creatures, whose imaginations are easily manipulated by those in authority. Only the Viziers know the truth of our existence," said Kronos.

"That we are aware of," Ursus firmly stressed.

"We take care of others as needed," countered Kronus. "However, if we wish to survive and remain undetected by the First Ones, we must deal with Eldar—covertly."

"Since humans are more adept at intrigue, I assume Cadmus has a plan," said Spyros.

"It has already been set in motion," Kronus replied.

"Without consulting us?" Ursus sneered; teeth bared.

"It is in the humans' best interest to placate Eldar and lessen any unwanted attention. We are to make certain the plan succeeds. Only, if it fails, are we to act swiftly and land a decisive blow to the First Ones!"

"Sirin betrayed herself!" Spoor shouted.

"I told you to wait!" Kronus stomped his front hoof.

Spoor shrugged since he stood at the tree line. "I haven't moved. Just good ears."

Ursus stood on his hind legs to demand of Spoor, "You heard everything?"

Spoor flashed a lopsided smile due to the eye patch. "Enough to be pleased."

Spyros flew to a branch close to Spoor. "What about Sirin?"

"Pride drew her into a confrontation with men that betrayed her presence to the Son of Eldar and First Ones. Her singular effort against them failed. You would be wise to learn by her demise. Let Nefal aid the Vizier as we once did. Our strength kept the First Ones at bay."

Ursus crossed the clearing on all fours. He then stood on his hindlegs in front of Spoor. This made him head and shoulders taller. "You speak too boldly, Nefal."

Kronus joined them. "Remember, it was by Cadmus' request I brought him here."

Ursus remained standing, only in a less threatening posture. "Very well. Yet, be warned, Nefal. Another mistake, and you will not escape me."

Spoor crossed his arms over his chest and inclined his head. "I will not fail the gods, my lord Ursus."

"What reward has Cadmus promised for success?" asked Spyros.

"The return of Nefal to Bertra—"

Ursus' angry roar stopped Spoor's reply

"Peace, Ursus!" Kronus snapped.

Ursus' anger would not be stemmed. "Cadmus takes too many liberties in making such a decision without us!"

Kronus' ire rose at Ursus' stubborn persistence. "He consulted me!"

Ursus dropped to all fours. His upper lip twitched into a reluctant snarl. "Then you agree this plan will work?"

"We must try or suffer Sirin's fate."

Spyros joined in the attempt to convince Ursus. "I do not want my flock to be destroyed by the First Ones. Do you want generations of cubs wiped out?"

Ursus grunted a subdued, "No." The bear king eyed Spoor and issued a final warning. "I will be watching, Nefal." He moved back across the clearing and disappeared into the woods.

"Return to Theron. I will take Spoor to the border," Kronus told Spyros. After Spyros took flight, Kronus motioned his head for Spoor to mount.

"That went better than I expected," Spoor commented, as they left.

"Do not be so cocky. Ursus will fulfill his threat should you fail."

"Nefal cannot afford to fail. We share the same desire—to survive."

Kronus stopped. "There is a secret Cadmus entrusted to me. Only upon my approval of this meeting would it be shared with you."

"By telling me, I take it I have gained your approval."

"Do you speak Ancient Nefal?"

"Of course. It was our native tongue before appropriated by men."

Annoyed, Kronus snorted. "Ursus is right, you are too bold." He ignored Spoor's chuckle to say, "Cadmus told me the location of creatures that will aid you. But beware! One false step, and they will turn upon you!"

Chapter 2

THE BRIGHT, CRISP MORNING BROUGHT A HIVE OF ACTIVITY TO THE city's market square. Even in winter, Sener thrived with commerce. As the fortress capital of Eldar, business continued year-round. Although cold north winds still dominated the night and early mornings, signs of spring hinted at the coming of warmer days. Buds filled the tree branches in defiance of winter.

The morning chill did not deter her. Mingling with the crowds became commonplace. Taking in all the sights, sounds, and smells provided a welcome relief from the isolated life she once knew. So many different people to meet. Freelanders, Halvors, Ha'tar, Nefal, Ganels, and The Doaners all populated Sener. She felt her senses enlivened and intended to learn as much as she could about the different races and regions of her ancestral homeland.

Youthful features did not reflect her age of twenty-five. Long brown hair softly swayed in the breeze, as she moved about the square. She warmly smiled to greet the merchants. Her soft brown eyes almost gleeful. She wore a cloak made from the finest wool, while her clothes a cross between a feminine skirt over pants tucked into knee-high boots. From the belt, hung a scabbard that held a silver embossed handled dagger alongside a small purse.

"Good morning, Princess," the baker hailed from the shop door.

"Master Dayne."

"I placed aside the morning's first meat pie. Extra special, with venison."

"Tell me, did use dried apples and onions again?" she eagerly asked.

Dayne flashed a large, friendly smile. "Especially for you." He disappeared inside to retrieve the treat.

She withdrew a coin from her purse to exchange for the pie. Her face showed great pleasure at the first bite. "Master Dayne, this is delicious," she spoke with a mouthful.

"Enjoy, Princess."

She ate the meat pie while she moved along the square.

"Can't forget a drink with breakfast," said the wine merchant. He held out a small wooden cup. "Warm honey mead for this nippy morning."

She took it and sat on a bench to drink and eat. "Perfect with the pie, Master Harvey."

He grinned. "If you need more to drink, just knock." He went inside.

When finished, she left a coin on the bench beside the cup and knocked on the door. Cries of competing merchants selling wares filled the air as she resumed her trek. During the few short months in Sener, she learned which voices to heed, and those to ignore. She followed the sound of hammered metal to the swordsmith's shop.

Upon entry, she called, "Master Jodi!" She was promptly greeted by a large dog, the sight of which would make most cringe. Instead, the mastiff, eagerly wanted to be petted.

The hammering stopped. "Rendor!" he scolded the mastiff. When the dog didn't respond due to enjoying the attention, the swordsmith wryly grinned at recognizing the visitor. "Princess Lexi. I should have known. Rendor, down!"

Lexi nodded at the mastiff. It moved to lay down. "I don't mind. He's a nice dog."

"Nice? Just to you. Anyone else would turn and run."

"I came to see if my new sword is ready."

"Aye." Jodi removed a polished sword with intricate hilt and pommel. "I incorporated the royal crest." He pointed to the hilt.

"Nicely done." Lexi took the sword to test it. She made a few passes and lunges. "Excellent balance." She deftly handed it back to Jodi. "Have it sent to the castle."

"It will be there this afternoon, Princess."

Lexi continued on her course. She stopped upon seeing him with the butcher. He didn't notice her, as told by the fact he inspected some chickens in a wooden cage. With a sly grin, she carefully approached from behind. He stood, which made her reach up to place hands over his eyes. He balked then relaxed to feel the hands. He grinned beneath her hold.

"This is either a poorly planned robbery, or a princess who enjoys scampering about the marketplace."

"Oh, Nollen! It's no fun when you keep guessing rightly." She released him.

He chuckled. "You're the only one who does that to me." He stood three inches taller, with brown hair and blue eyes, and near the same age.

"Are the chickens satisfactory, sir?" asked Thad, the butcher.

"Aye. Have them, the dressed hog, and cow, sent straightway to the castle kitchen." Nollen gave Thad a handful of coins. He took Lexi's arm to leave the shop.

"You didn't wait for me this morning. I called upon Master Jodi …"

"Was Rendor chained?" asked Nollen with concern.

"No. Rendor is harmless. He only wants to be petted," she replied matter-of-fact.

"Harmless? That mastiff? I won't go anywhere near the shop unless its chained."

"Well, he's different with me. But you're avoiding the subject. You didn't wait for me."

"Sorry, I had very early business, and you were still asleep."

"With you gone, I had to sneak out," she continued her complaint.

"Why? You're hardly a prisoner." When she glared at him stricken, he immediately became regretful. I didn't mean prisoner exactly. Poor choice of words. Forgive me, Highness."

Her ire doubled. "Lexi! How many times must remind you?"

At her upset, Nollen drew Lexi into an alley away from the crowd. "I use your title in public out of respect. Same as with Axel."

"I've been called Lexi all my life. Until coming here," she complained.

"Home," he gently reminded her.

"Too you, and others. For me, it is still new and different."

He became perplexed. "I thought coming to the market and exploring the city has helped you become settled?"

"To a point." She moved away. "I'm still confided to the city!"

"We've gone to Wyckton for luncheon."

"Across a bridge," she scoffed.

He spied a stoop not far down the alley and led her to sit. "What is it you want, Lexi?"

"The same freedom you have. To come and go without restraint. To learn more about Eldar than one city. To see and sense what is beyond these walls." Her face brightened with excitement, and she seized his hands. "That's it! When you leave next week for the trading circuit, take me with you!"

"What?" he asked, surprised.

"Why not?" she eagerly continued. "Is there a reason I can't go with you?"

Nollen momentarily pondered the suggestion, only Lexi mistook his silence.

"Why hesitate? Unless you don't want to." Her anger rose.

"I didn't say that. I hadn't considered it. And you are the king's sister."

She roughly released his hands. "What difference does that make?"

"A lot. Well, maybe not to me. To others it will," he amended his words to her anger.

"So, I mean nothing to you?"

"Don't twist my words," Nollen emphatically rebuffed. "I have learned much about speaking to females these past few months because of you. One of those lessons is not to let you misquote me."

Her annoyance turned to a wry smile. "I should not have gotten angry."

"I agree. Another lesson learned, is not to argue when you're right."

His disarming smile made her laugh. "Confident arrogance."

"There you are!" said exacerbated female. A slender fifty-one-year-old woman with light blue eyes stared with annoyance at Lexi.

Lexi's frustration immediately returned. "Lorraine," she huffed.

"Lorraine," she sarcastically mimicked. Nollen became the target of Lorraine's wrath. "You shouldn't encourage her to disregard duty."

Lexi stopped Nollen from offering a dispute. "He has nothing to do with it. I happened to meet him at the butcher shop."

"I ordered meat for tonight's banquet," Nollen told Lorraine.

"Banquet?" Lexi asked, surprised.

"The Queen's birthday dinner," Lorraine sternly reminded Lexi. "Axel came looking for you after breakfast. Upon learning you were gone, he sent me to find you."

Stunned at the reminder, Lexi hurriedly told Nollen, "I must get back!"

"We will all go. I finished my errands."

Built on levels, they walked the circular streets from the lower market to the castle at the apex. Once inside the courtyard, Nollen headed for the commodities office, while Lexi and Lorraine proceeded inside the main building to the King's study.

"I need to see my broth— the king," Lexi told the guard. As she waited admittance, she saw Lorraine move across the hall. "What are you doing?" She waved Lorraine to come back.

Lorraine shook her head. "You answer to him alone."

"Princess." The guard held the door for her.

Lexi steeled herself to face Axel and boldly entered the study. He stood near the hearth with a book in hand. Eight years older, he stood six inches taller with dark hair and a neatly trimmed beard. She couldn't determine his mood in profile. From Lorraine's comment, she assumed displeased. Then he looked up. Hazel eyes fixed on her and confirmed the assumption. He slammed the book shut and placed it on the desk to confront her.

"Gunnar tells me you missed training again. Then, when I go to speak with you about preparations for Alicia's banquet this evening, and you are nowhere to be found."

"Axel ..."

His stiff raised hand silenced her. He took a deep breath to curb his temper. He guided her to sit in chairs at the hearth. A fire chased away the morning chill. "I realize this has been a difficult transition for you, so I have tried to be patient. However, you must be more diligent in study and practice."

She fought upset. "I'm trying. Truly. I just …"

"What?" he gently probed when she stopped.

With rising tears of indecision, she regarded him. "I don't know if I can make you understand. You have taken so easily to your role as king, and it suits you. More than I ever thought." She looked down to regain her composure. "I once believed I would take to this new life as readily, but in reality …" Her composure broke. She sobbed and stood. "I have gone from one prison to another!"

Confused, he rose. "You consider Sener a prison?"

Tears freely fell, as her frustration spilled forth. "It is no different than Kranston. I can't come and go, as I please. To venture anywhere in the city or even across the bridge to Wyckton, I must have a guard or companion. I snuck away this morning to be alone. I study the same lessons of etiquette and duty as when younger. Only now, forced to adhere to strict rules and bound into uncomfortably tight clothes. Have you ever worn a corset?"

Axel bit back a chuckle. "No—"

"You find it amusing?"

"I'm sorry. I didn't mean to laugh." He comforted her with a brotherly embrace. "I had no idea you felt this way." He gave her a handkerchief to wipe her eyes.

"I don't mean to sound ungrateful. I am thrilled to be away from Kranston. Gott has answered prayers to restore our family. You are king, and finally married to Alicia." Her tender smile slightly quivered.

"Tonight, we celebrate her birthday. As such, I want you to wear mother's brooch. Which is one reason I called upon you earlier."

The request caught her off-guard. "Mama's brooch?"

"You did remember to bring it in your belongings, didn't you?" he asked with a hint of concern.

"Of course. I've just not worn it before. We didn't have much to celebrate in Kranston." Her tone turned sour when speaking of Kranston.

"This is a special occasion. So, please wear it."

She shrugged and nodded; renewed vexation made her mute.

Keen to her mood change, he asked, "What else troubles you?"

She struggled to explain. "Since being here, I sense things about people and surroundings in a way I never have before. In the deepest part of my being, there is an overwhelming compulsion to experience Eldar beyond Sener. That I *must* do so. I don't fully understand why, yet unable to contain the sensations." She fought tears.

He led her back to the chairs. "I wish you had told me sooner."

"I didn't want to disappoint you," she droned.

Axel knelt and stroked her hair. "You could never do that." He lifted her chin. "Have you thought about where you would like to go?"

"Everywhere! Or at least a town or two in each Territory. To experience true freedom." Her face brightened. "And I know how. Let me go with Nollen on his trading route."

Axel sat back on his heels to regard her at the suggestion. This made Lexi cross.

"Why do men always look so hapless when given an answer?"

"I am merely considering the possibility."

"Nollen said the same," she huffed.

"You spoke to him about this?"

"This morning, when we met at the butcher shop."

He scowled and moved to the opposite chair. "I would have preferred you came to me before approaching him."

"Why should my talking to Nollen make you angry?"

"I'm not angry. There are considerations."

"Such as?" she demanded.

"Your welfare. The route. Communication. Protection …"

"I can protect myself. I am the Shield Maiden!" Annoyed, she stood. "I just spoke of restrictions, and now you want to place conditions on me seeing Eldar with Nollen. Did you hear nothing I said?" Overcome, she fled from the study.

Lexi ran as far as she could until out of breath from angry tears and exertion. She reached an isolated corner of the rear courtyard. This became her place of retreat and solace.

So much had changed. Although a princess, title and rank meant little in the hidden fortress of Kranston. Born there, she only knew Eldar through tales, lore, and legend. Raised on history and heritage regarding the two-hundred-year absence of her family, everything seemed abstract. Reality began when Axel and Gunnar left to fulfill prophecy.

For three years, those left behind waited, prayed, worried, and wondered; did they succeed? or die trying? During that time, she and Alicia kept constant company to bolster each other. When Gunnar returned with Nollen, hearts and spirits soared at the news her family had been restored. What exactly that meant for her, remained unclear.

The journey from the Black Mountains through Markita proved more hazardous than anyone imagined. Fearlessly, Nollen led them, and nearly died twice. Gunnar bares the scar of trial by combat to free them from the Markitans and the false goddess, Sirin.

Finally, safe in Eldar, she rejoiced at the wedding of Axel and Alicia. Their long-await marriage wonderfully celebrated throughout the kingdom. During the five months in Sener, she struggled with what her royal title princess and duty as Shield Maiden truly meant. Imagination based upon tales and academic rhetoric of ancient practices fell short of preparing her for reality. Still, a deep awareness grew with each passing day. She began to feel smothered by restrictions. The peace and freedom she longed for eluded her and made more intolerable by the awakening of her senses. How can she make Axel understand the strong compulsion to explore Eldar?

"Lexi."

She scowled when Lorraine sat beside her. "Just leave me alone."

"That is the last thing you need." She tenderly stroked Lexi's hair.

Lexi responded by leaning against Lorraine. "Why are men so stubborn to hear what we say? Axel reacted the same as Nollen when I suggested joining Nollen on the trading circuit so I can experience Eldar."

"Did they outright refuse?"

"No. Both became silent. I had to prod them for an answer."

Lorraine grinned with seasoned understanding. "Men solve problems. When presented an issue, they give it due consideration. Hence, the silence." She tilted Lexi's head to look at her. "If you push too hard, they won't answer the way you want. Rather allow them time to come around to your suggestion."

Curious, and a bit uncertain, Lexi sat up. "You mean manipulation?"

"No! That makes it worse. Allow them to be men. I did so with Waldo."

"And now Gunnar?" Lexi tried to curb a smile.

Lorraine laughed. "In a different way. Waldo didn't take much convincing. However, I still allowed him to be himself when presented with a problem. Gunnar is very different. Stronger, opinionated, yet with the same masculine tendencies. It simply takes more time and patience." She moved to fully face Lexi. "Axel isn't just your brother; he is also king." She softly touched Lexi's cheek. "Unlike Kranston, here in Eldar ,you are vulnerable to dangers and machinations unknown before. He must consider everything. Be patient."

Lexi pondered the advice. "Maybe I can ask Nollen to speak with him. Axel is inclined to listen to him."

"To use Nollen, would be manipulation," Lorraine cautioned. She then smiled in remembrance. "Being young, Nollen has extraordinary reasoning."

"While blind to feelings," Lexi groused.

"Some men do take a little longer. Once Nollen is resolved in mind, he is decisive in action. Sirin proved that." She noticed Lexi's forlorn expression. "Is Miska when you fell in love with him?"

Lexi nodded. "He didn't know about me or Alicia, yet willingly went in our place to face Sirin, and almost died."

"Men protect. Don't begrudge that."

"I'm not helpless," Lexi said in mild dispute.

"None of us are. They taught us self-defense to strengthen us, so we can work together. Not in opposition."

"Couldn't tell that by the way you and Gunnar used to react to each other."

"Indeed," Lorraine soberly admitted. "Seeing the same clash of wills happen with you and Nollen, helped us to change."

The chapel bell sounded the time.

"Come." Lorraine tugged Lexi to her feet. "We have much to do before the banquet."

Chapter 3

IN THE QUEEN'S PRIVATE CHAMBER, ALICIA STOOD BEFORE A full-length mirror. Her blond hair elegantly styled to compliment the regal blue and gold gown. Her maid helped with preparation. Alicia gasped and flinched when Nettie pulled the lace.

"Not so tight!" she scolded.

"Sorry, Majesty." Nettie loosened the lace. "Is that better?"

Alicia held her chest and took a breath. "Aye." Hearing a knock at the door, she waved for Nettie to answer it.

"Lady Lorraine and Princess Lexi, Majesty."

"You look lovely," Lorraine said.

"As do you. Magenta and silver suits you well." Alicia smiled and held out her hands for Lexi. "I know you dislike corsets, but you are stunning."

Lexi shyly smiled. She plucked the full skirt of a midnight blue brocade gown with silver accents. "It is beautiful material. I'm simply having difficulty wearing such clothes."

Alicia giggled. "So am I. Ah! You remembered the brooch."

"Aye. Not sure why Axel wanted me to wear it." Lexi gently felt it. Intricate silver knotting surrounded carvings of a wolf, eagle, and unicorn. Ruby chips served at eyes for each animal. "I suppose to have a part of Mama enjoy the celebration."

"She would be proud of the woman you've become," Lorraine offered encouragement.

"I'd like to think so."

"The King!" Nettie curtsied.

Axel wore the finest brocade suit to coordinate with Alicia. Gunnar accompanied him, fully attired in his formal First Knight uniform complete with the royal crest. More gray invaded his brown hair. The surgeon's excellent skills kept the battle scar to a thin line that ran from above Gunnar's left eye and halfway down his cheek. Fortunately, the injury didn't mar his vision. If anything, it gave the distinguished clean-shaven knight a more imposing battle-hardened persona.

Axel widely smiled. "My three favorite women. Even after months, it is a pleasure to see all of you so finely dressed."

"Some of us are still getting accustomed to it." Alicia elbowed Lexi, to which Lexi rolled her eyes in a sarcastic reaction.

His smile turned tender upon sight of the brooch. "The last time Mama wore it was at your dedication."

"I don't remember."

"Of course not, you were just an infant. Even in exile, we kept the old tradition of dedicating each royal child to Gott. Thank you for wearing it tonight." Axel kissed Lexi's cheek. "Time to join the festivities." He offered his left arm to Alicia, and right to Lexi.

Lorraine walked beside Gunnar to follow the royal family. She didn't take hold of his arm, should defense be necessary. They exchanged private smiles of greeting.

In the Great Hall, servants attended the guests. High Table stood on a platform. Each of the Six Territories had a table arranged in accordance to rank and position. To right side of High Table came the Ganels, the Halvor Mountains, then Ha'tar. To the left of High Table were The Doane, Freelands, then Nefal.

The Ganels assumed the place of honor since their leader, Lord Ronan, served as First Minister. They were tall, elegant, ancient people with long flowing hair. Throughout history, the Ganels acted as faithful keepers of the University of Wisdom and Knowledge. Lord Ronan's black flawless hair was pulled back in a ponytail. Ganel men often styled their hair this way for formal occasions, while the women pampered the flowing locks with curls and jewels. Newly married, Baron Irwin, and his wife, joined Lord Ronan. Irwin served as armory quartermaster. He and his wife were blond headed. The other Ganel, Lord Cormac, sat beside his wife, Jenna. They matched each other in coloring with brown hair. Cormac used his expertise to oversee the royal archives and library.

Seated with the Ganels, was Ambassador Dynos of Bertrand. His brooding countenance of tanned skin, black hair, and dark eyes were in marked contrast to the Ganels. His elaborate attire made of rich embroidered fabrics layered over each other, so it appeared as a skirt with outer cloak down to the floor. He wore a round cap of intricately embroidered material and fur.

The Halvor Mountain table stood beside the Ganels. Mortals of this Territory sent Mayor Lorne, his daughter, son-in-law, and high sheriff. At the last table on the right side, sat the Ha'tar chief Myn, his wife, and adult sons. Olive skin, dark eyes and hair, showed the Ha'tar were not native to Eldar like the humans of Halvor, The Doane, and Freelands. As dragon breeders and riders, the apparel reflected their proud heritage of nature and dragons. Even formal clothes incorporated these qualities.

Across from the Ganels, on the left side of the Hall, stood the table reserved for the High Priest Arctander. This also served to represent The Doane, Arctander's home Territory. He moved slowly due to age, while the heavy robes of office added to the impediment. Nollen aided his grandfather to his seat. As Royal Commissary, Nollen wore a brocade suit of light gray and dark blue. Although, not officially of nobility, his office gave him status to indulge on occasion. He provided his sister Ida, and her husband Jarred, with suitable clothes for the evening. Also, at the table were the Territorial representatives, Governor Ebert and his wife, Lady Blythe, Nollen's cousin.

Next came the Freelands, home to Gunnar. The Territory sent Governor Gorman, his wife, and eldest son. General Mather joined his Freelander companions. At the final table, sat Nefal, giants with the renowned strength of fierce warriors. However, they suffered tremendous losses for aligning with Javan against Axel. Although their population diminished, their strength had not abated. Ceremonial attire held hints of past glory. Like the Ha'tar, Nefal came later to Eldar. Lord Maro wore a chieftain's headdress and an elaborate robe over his leather jerkin. No one could guess Maro's age. Common knowledge suggested he witnessed three Electors spanning almost seventy years. His daughter, Brynn, accompanied him. An imposing figure, with little femineity to her demeanor despite the womanly aspect of her clothing. Bodil, Maro's assistant, also joined them.

Territorial representatives were not the only ones in the Hall. Othniel, the Great White Lion of Eldar lay beside high table. At the opposite end of the table sat Bardolf, alpha of Eldar's White Wolves. With Nollen came Cassie, a white she-wolf. Even after their adventure in Markita, Cassie chose to remain with Nollen rather than return to the Halvor pack.

All rose when the herald announced the royal couple, Princess Lexi, First Knight Sir Gunnar and Lady Lorraine. Alicia sat to the right of Axel, Gunnar to the King's left. Lexi sat beside Alicia with Lorraine next to Gunnar. Axel held the chair for Alicia. Once she sat, he signaled those gathered to join him in sitting.

"High Reverend, will you do the honor," Axel said to Arctander.

Arctander rose and spoke a blessing on the gathering. When finished, servants brought dinner for the King, Queen, and royal guests. In the balcony, musicians played soothing music. Once everyone had plates and filled tankards, Axel motioned to the herald, who in turn, called for attention. Axel rose.

"Tonight, we celebrate the Queen's birthday. For this event, we welcome Bertrandian Ambassador Dynos. Although your arrival unexpected, we thank you for sharing in this celebrated occasion."

Dynos stood to graciously bow. His Eldarian heavily accented. "Forgive me for not coming sooner. News of Your Majesty's wedding delayed in reaching King Rastus, who immediately dispatched me with a gift."

"We are delighted by the gift, and bid you enjoy our hospitality."

Dynos again bowed before he sat.

Axel continued, "I cannot adequately describe my happiness to celebrate this particular day." He proudly smiled at Alicia. "Not only am I overjoyed to have my love, but it is also with great pleasure to announce the Queen is expecting. An heir is soon to be born."

The stunning news brought applause of men and Ganels banging on the table. The Ha'tar and Nefal politely joined it. Gleeful, Lexi seized Alicia's hand. Lorraine looked down the table to speak hearty congratulations. Gunnar proudly smiled at the announcement.

Ronan rose with tankard in hand. "Sire, allow me to offer a toast." When Axel nodded, he proceeded. "The blessings of Gott be upon our gracious Queen and noble King. May the character of the future heir be a combination of beauty and wisdom. To Gott, to Eldar!" He held the tankard high in salute.

Everyone rose with tankards in hand to repeat, "To Gott, to Eldar!"

"Thank you, my Lord Ronan. Now, enjoy the evening." Axel sat.

"Why didn't you tell me sooner?" Lexi asked Alicia with giddy excitement.

"And spoil the surprise?"

"I'm good at keeping secrets." Lexi laughed and hugged Alicia.

"Now, you know why Axel asked you to wear the brooch."

Tears welled in Lexi's eyes, as regarded the brooch. "An early dedication."

"Aye. Don't cry, or you'll make me cry. My emotions are more sensitive now," Alicia lightly scolded Lexi. Both laughed.

As she resumed eating, Lexi caught Nollen gaze. She blushed when he held up a tankard in a private salute.

Conversation buzzed about the hall. Music continued to play. When the meal concluded, the music gave way to acrobats and jugglers. A local troupe of actors performed a short comedy to the riotous laughter of all. Dancing followed the entertainment. As custom, the King and Queen led the first dance. Lexi sat while Gunnar, Lorraine, and other guests joined the royal couple. After the initial dance, Axel and Alicia resumed their seat before the start of the next one.

"I think my dancing days are done for a while. The baby is already making me short of breath," Alicia told Axel, as she held her belly.

"Then we shall enjoy watching others." He kissed her hand.

"You can dance with Lexi. She needs the practice." Alicia grinned.

In playful banter, Lexi replied, "I have been practicing with—"

"Sire, may I request the next dance with the Princess?" Nollen stood before the table.

Lexi spoke before Axel. "With pleasure." She came around the table to take his hand.

"She didn't dance at our wedding," Axel commented to Alicia.

"Neither did I. We only knew the old folk dances brought to Kranston."

Axel sent an inquisitive sideways glance to Gunnar.

"I didn't teach her," Gunnar answer the silent question.

Alicia leaned close Axel. "I believe she dances with her practice partner. They move so easily together."

"I didn't know Nollen could dance either."

Lorraine's giggle drew attention. "I encouraged them to take lessons from Master Tomas. I might even consider enlisting his aid for my husband. My toes need mercy from his feet."

Gunnar retorted in a good-natured manner. "I thought swordplay would help with coordination for dancing, since I move in response to action. However, timing movement with the rhythm of music …" He shook head, chuckled, and took a drink.

Axel laughed so hard, he fought to catch his breath. He calmed down enough to watch Lexi and Nollen. Amusement turned to pleasant consideration. The sight brought to mind his earlier conversation with Lexi. He leaned close to Alicia. "We need to speak later."

Curious at the statement, she asked, "A serious matter?"

"A matter that needs a woman's opinion."

When the dance ended, Nollen and Lexi remained on the floor. Alicia motioned to the musician. Soon, a lively familiar tune echoed in the hall.

"The Landler. Did you request it for tonight?" Axel asked Alicia.

She sweetly smiled. "I thought we could incorporate the old folk tunes with courtly dances. No need to be formal all the time."

Axel enthusiastically tapped out the beat on the tabletop. The dance involved participants clapping hands, and stomping feet at certain intervals. He saw Lexi laugh when Nollen got turned around. She pointed him in the right direction. Nollen sly grin made Axel speak to Alicia.

"He did that on purpose."

"I remember a certain youth did the same when we first learned the Landler. You tripped so I wouldn't feel bad for missing steps."

At the conclusion of the dance, Nollen escorted Lexi back to high table. Both breathed hard from exertion and laughter.

"Thank you for the honor of your company, Princess," he respectfully spoke.

"Lexi ...," she began to correct him when Axel coughed. At her brother's reminder, she assumed a formal posture. "My pleasure, Master Nollen." She gracefully sat.

Nollen bowed and withdrew.

Lexi brought the tankard to her lips to hide her words from view. "I wish there weren't so many rules of etiquette," she complained to Alicia.

"There is more freedom here than in Kranston or Markita," Alicia replied.

"If you say so," Lexi muttered into the tankard.

Axel didn't hear the rough comment as told by his casual tone. "You and Nollen dance very well together."

Lexi grinned, yet short-lived, as she squirmed and pulled at the bodice. "At times the confinement made it hard to breathe."

"Gently." Alicia touched Lexi's hand. Her gesture met with a sigh of resignation from Lexi. Suddenly overcome with fatigue, Alicia fought a yawn that Axel noticed.

"Too much activity?" he asked.

"I'm afraid, I weary easily these days."

Axel's rising diverted attention. Dancing and music ceased.

"The Queen is fatigued, so we shall retire. Continue to enjoy the evening." He held her arm to leave the Hall.

On route to the royal chamber, Alicia yawned several times. Axel dismissed Nettie. To Alicia's curiosity, he said, "I won't keep you up long."

"Good. We can speak while you help me get out of this heavy dress."

When Alicia turned her back to him, Axel quizzically regarded the lace. Again, the image reminded him of the earlier conversation.

She glanced over her shoulder. "You have unlaced a dress before." She held her hands against her body in preparation of the loosening lace.

He searched for the ends to begin. "A bodice is really tight, isn't it?"

"Aye. The object is to have it meet the corset. Ah!" She sighed with relief, and let the dress fall to step out. Underneath she wore a corset, under skirt, and shift. "Now, the corset, please." When she felt him untie the lace, she asked, "What is it you want to discuss?"

Axel's brows leveled in consideration. "Why do women wear so many constricting layers for fashion?"

She laughed. "I don't know. Mistress Mogens says it is tradition." She removed the corset, leaving on the shift and skirt. She rubbed her belly. "Feels much better. I will reconsider what I wear as the child grows."

He drew her to the sitting area of the chamber. "Fashion is what I want to discuss."

"Since when has fashion interested you?" she asked with a light laugh.

"Not me, women's clothes. Corsets and bodices. Lexi complained about them earlier."

"So, our discussion is about Lexi?"

"Aye. She was in tears."

"About corsets?"

"No, freedom from constriction. She mentioned the corset as an example."

"You best start at the beginning."

"Earlier this morning, Gunnar told me she has been derelict in training. When I asked her about it, she burst into tears and compared Sener to a prison—like Kranston. No freedom to go where she wants or do what she wants. I had no idea she felt that way."

Alicia gently touched his face. "My dearest, Lexi is not like us. She is a free spirit."

"Aye, father tried to corral it when younger, alas I don't know how to…" Regret made him stop.

"After you and Gunnar left, I sensed a change in her. With the fulfillment of prophecy on the horizon, she threw herself into learning about the Shield Maiden. She read the old manuscripts, asked endless questions, and practiced hours a day with the sword, and self-defense. When Nollen arrived with Gunnar, she tested him, watched him closely. She helped fight off predators and the Markitans during the journey. All in hopes of being free," she emphasized.

"That is why I have been patient during this transition. To give her time before speaking about her future as the Shield Maiden. Unfortunately, she is not inclined to listen."

Alicia briefly thought before asking, "Do you remember the day you learned the truth about your role in prophecy? How hard it struck you?"

"Aye. You heard me reassure father on his death bed. I only told Gunnar shortly before it happened. I don't believe Lexi could have accepted what it required of me after losing our parents. She was just a teenager," he said with woeful remembrance.

Alicia gently turned Axel's head to look him in the eye. "With that discovery, you became bound to a destiny. No longer able to do act in your own will. Lexi did the same with the Shield Maiden to protect me until we became reunited. However," she stressed, "she believes her task is done, and is she searching to find her place in the world."

"You know that isn't true. Her role as Shield Maiden is hardly begun."

"Aye. She is beginning to sense things. Heightened intuition."

"She mentioned it this morning. Again, how can I tell her when she feels trapped?"

"She must learn it for herself, and not have it forced upon her."

Axel nodded with a partial frown of consideration. "How is the issue? She made a suggestion, which is why I need your opinion. She wants to go with Nollen on the trading circuit to explore Eldar. Yet, I wonder if I should let her go?"

"You trusted Nollen to bring us back. Can you not trust him to watch out for her in Eldar?"

"This isn't about trusting Nollen, which I do completely. Despite her awakening feelings, or perhaps, because of it, I hesitate. The past three years have required much effort and energy to quell unrest and secure each Territory to bring a peace Eldar hasn't known in centuries. Foreign diplomacy, trade issues, agricultural problems beyond anything I thought past prophecy." He smiled and placed a hand on her belly. "Now, we are expecting an heir. I must keep firm hold on what has been established and be prepared for whatever may come. As king, allowing my sister to travel the country in an untrained state is a bit unnerving. That is why I need your opinion. If anyone who knows Lexi best, it is you."

She smiled with reassurance. "Lexi loves and admires you. She is not ignorant of what has been accomplished. Despite naivete with the world, you can't restrict her forever, and certainly not out of fear. She is twenty-five years old. It is time for her to experience life in ways she couldn't in Kranston. To allow Gott to teach her, whether by mistakes, bad choices, or right choices. To prepare her to assume her role, you must let her go."

"I will prayerfully consider your advice." He kissed her lips. He felt her yawn. "To bed."

Axel went to the private chapel adjacent to their chamber. He stared at the small altar where candles and incense burned. Conversations with Lexi and Alicia replayed in his mind. Both women spoke earnestly of restriction and freedom in ways he never considered. Alicia keenly described Lexi's different nature. Visions of childhood came before his mind's eye. He was eight years old when his mother gave birth. He hoped for a brother, but the moment he saw his infant sister, he loved her.

Like all siblings, times of tension arose, more due to their contrasting natures and age gap. While being groomed for his position, she constantly interrupted his training or lessons. How does one become angry with the innocence of a small child? By the time he reached the age of manhood, thirteen, she began formal lessons at age five. That year, their mother died. Fortunately, other women in Kranston helped with Lexi. Still, the incident made him even more tolerant of her antics. Ten years later, their father passed away. At age twenty-three, he became solely responsible for his fifteen-year-old sister. As a young adult, he could neither act as a strict parental figure, nor domineering older brother. He tried to strike a balance, until seven years later, he left to fulfill his destiny. From Alicia's narrative, Lexi matured during his three-year absence.

"Perhaps it is time I treated her like an adult," he told himself.

His mind drifted to Lexi's request of accompanying Nollen joined with Alicia's question: *You trusted Nollen to bring us back. Can you not trust him to watch out for Lexi in Eldar?*

Irony struck him. Nollen was the same age as when he became responsible for Lexi. Over the past few years, Nollen also matured in faith and fortitude. While Gunnar expressed sentiments of fatherly affection for Nollen, Axel inwardly admitted brotherly love for the stalwart trader. A King could not publicly declare favoritism, though some complained of it when he appointed Nollen as Royal Commissary. However, Nollen's shrewdness with contracts and treaties stifled the idle gossip.

Only one more conversation could help the decision. Coming to that conclusion, and satisfied in prayerful consideration, Axel retired.

Chapter 4

When staying at Sener Castle during the winter, Nollen occupied an apartment in the guest wing. The suite divided into several areas, a bed chamber, dressing area, toilet, and small sitting area with a desk for working. He finished dressing for the day just as the first rays of morning filtered through the curtain. Being in charge of commodities for the royal household, often required late nights and early mornings. A page arrived to inform him of the King's summons. Not uncommon, since Axel also rose early. Breakfast would have to wait.

Nollen fought a yawn as arrived at the King's study. He nodded to the guard then entered after receiving permission. "You sent for me, Sire?"

Axel cocked a grin. "You look as tired as I feel. When did you retire?"

"Around one o'clock. After the Ganels and Freelanders finished playing fuddling cup. I never knew Ganels could drink so much. They consumed all the mead! Though not surprised they won by solving the puzzle. Dynos was greatly intrigued by the friendly competition. Apparently, Bertrandians aren't gracious losers." Nollen covered his mouth to hide a yawn.

Axel laughed. "Join me for breakfast." He guided Nollen to a table filled with food. After a short prayer, they began to eat. "My compliments on the meal selection last night."

Nollen swallowed before replying. "Cook chose the menu, I simply acquired what was necessary. Still, since awarded the contract, Thad manages to get the best quality meat and fowl. Harvey always has the finest selection of wine and mead. In the past, he supplied me with the best when needed for a special trade."

"Speaking of trade, what do you think of Dynos' arrival?"

"I don't doubt the slowness of news. However, with Javan's trade agreement due to expire later this year, he came to get a sense of you. Bertrand greatly profited through trade with the Electors."

Axel nodded. "I assume you have begun giving it consideration?"

"Of course, yet," Nollen began with a cautious pause, "for years there have been rumors of a black market and smuggling of illegal goods in Bertrand."

"What?" Axel snapped.

"Nothing has been proven, though many speculated. Including my father. With five major ports, Bertrand is a hub for exporting and importing goods, and not always legal. Being one of four charters, Far Point often received requests from the Electors. Whenever we could, we tried discover the origin of the merchandise."

"Naturally, you had to fulfill those requests regardless of suspicions."

"Aye. More research is needed before we proceed with any negotiations."

Thoughtful, Axel stroked his beard. "Cormac expressed similar sentiments of caution since he found nothing in the royal archives for guidance. Although, he believes some entries were altered, even removed. A few pages torn from several official books. He leaves today for Mathena to explore the university library. He hopes to find unaltered information."

"Good. Bertrandian traders seek wealth over equity. Every time I tried to make a deal more favorable to Eldar, they invoked Javan's agreement. Many unscrupulous suggestions and items. Unfortunately, I had no choice or risk discovery and endanger the Brethren." Nollen grew somber in recollection of his former clandestine activity to shield those faithful to prophecy regarding the Son of Eldar.

Keen to the reason for Nollen's sobriety, Axel firmly clasped the young man's arm. He spoke with reassurance. "You *shall* have the choice to refuse anything detrimental to Eldar."

Nollen grinned and resumed eating.

"When do you leave for the circuit?"

Nollen swallowed before answering. "Next week."

"The normal route?"

Nollen nodded since he ate.

"Cormac should have information by the time you reach Mathena. Take what time you need for consultation." Axel glanced circumspectly at Nollen. "Lexi told me she spoke to you about joining you."

"Aye," Nollen said warily. He kept close eye on Axel.

Axel smiled, warm and friendly. "Relax. It is why I asked you to breakfast. What did you think of her request? Answer honestly."

Nollen took a long drink since the topic caught him off guard. He could never fool Axel. However, he hoped to gain time to process the discussion with Lexi while getting a sense of Axel's demeanor. "Upon return from our brief discussion, I became busy with last minute arrangements for the banquet," he spoke discreetly.

"I gave it prayerful consideration since Lexi is having difficulty adjusting to life here."

"She frequently speaks of it."

Axel perked up. "Ah! How so?"

To this question, Nollen could answer honestly, yet still with careful wording. "She believed leaving Kranston meant freedom. Even on the journey, I tried to temper that belief with reality. I understand living in daily fear of discovery. It's difficult feeling like a prisoner in one's own home and business. Of course, I could travel beyond the walls of Far Point. Yet, the sense of uncertainty never left. Until you arrived, and our victory. For the first time in my life, I know peace." His tone changed from hesitant to poignant by the end.

Axel stopped eating to regard Nollen during the reply. The long moment of direct eye contact made Nollen squirm.

"Sire?" When no immediate reply, he ventured, "Axel?"

"What are your thoughts about Lexi's request?"

Again, out of respect, he answered tactfully. "I am not opposed. Still, there are many considerations not present when leaving Kranston. Being sister of the King, for one."

Axel chuckled. "She has always been my sister. Location doesn't change that." The laughter faded to disappointment. "Sad a title does." He leaned on the table. "She expressed the same sentiments about fear and freedom yesterday. I regret, I didn't fully realize the depth of her struggle until she declared Sener a prison like Kranston." A tone of dejection crept in when he sat back to continue. "I have tried to be patient. Allow her free roam of the city. Even go with you or Lorraine to Wyckton." He heaved a hapless shrug. "Alas, I am at loss of how else to help her."

Sincerity from Axel made Nollen flush with embarrassment. "I confess, I haven't been completely honest, as you asked. I fought distraction all day yesterday thinking about her joining me."

Axel's only reaction came in a raised eyebrow to the admission.

At the parental expression, Nollen fumbled over his words. "I didn't want to offend you, both as king and her brother."

Axel began to chuckle, then louder, until a good belly laugh. Nollen watched with befuddlement. Axel took several moments to calm down. "My dear young friend, do not think me ignorant of certain feelings you are trying hard to conceal."

Nollen blushed with embarrassment. "She is of royal blood. I am a mere trader. I would not dare to presume."

"Which is why I trust you. Yet do not speak so basely with the label *mere trader.* You are much more than your station."

Nollen's lips quivered at the statement. "You helped make me what I am today," he spoke with deep appreciation.

Axel smiled. "Gott did that. I simply lent a hand. Now, let us finish breakfast, and get on with the day's business. I shall speak with Lexi."

With fatigue replaced by anticipation, Nollen briskly exited the main building. He could have walked the interior halls to the commodities office, but he risked the possibility of encountering Lexi. He respected Axel's offer to tell her. An impulsive smile crossed his lips at thought of her reaction. His preoccupation became interrupted at the sounds of shouting and harness. The Nefal made ready to leave. With dire-buffaloes gone, they rode draft horses, the only other animal capable of bearing their size and weight. Curious to the early departure, Nollen changed course.

"Good morning, my lord Maro. Lady Brynn," he cordially greeted.

Maro sneered and grunted in reply.

"May I ask why you are leaving so soon? Did you find the seeds unacceptable?" Nollen continued in gracious manner.

At Maro's deepening sneer, Brynn spoke. "The seeds will help replenish those lost to the plight." She patted a large sack on the horse. "Matters at home require our return."

"If there is any problem with the planting, please send word for assistance."

Maro gave a short nod and mumbled thanks.

"Gott speed." Nollen made the Nefal sign for greeting and parting.

Brynn returned the gesture.

"Nollen!" Lexi called. She wore day clothes and a cloak.

He hastily moved from the Nefal to meet Lexi. "Highness," he spoke loudly for the benefit of those in the courtyard.

She ignored the correct address. "Good! You haven't left."

He slightly balked. "Not for a while yet."

"Then you are going to market today?"

He smiled in relief. "No ... I mean, aye, market. Later."

The discussion paused when the Nefal rode past. Maro narrowly glared at Nollen. His focus passed to Lexi, where it lingered before Brynn snapped his name. Nollen guardedly watched them ride through the gate. His attention didn't change until Lexi gripped his arm.

"The Nefal make me nervous," she said.

He flashed a reassuring smile. "A few are full of bluster for intimidation. Many are nice." He changed topics. "Have you seen Axel this morning?"

"No. Why?"

"To talk more about becoming an aunt," he offered as quick excuse.

"Princess!" called Gunnar in a tone of displeasure as he approached.

Lexi sighed, to which Nollen said, "Skipping lessons again?"

Gunnar's expression matched his voice. "Once a week isn't helpful."

"I have a lifetime of practice. A missed session will hardly undue that. We," Lexi linked arms with Nollen, "are leaving for town."

"Eh, no, we're not," Nollen said in halting dispute. Her anger made him add, "I have business from last night. Hence, why I will go later to market." He removed her hand to hold out to Gunnar. "Go practice, then speak to Axel about becoming an aunt." He didn't wait for her reaction, rather headed for the outer door to the commodities office.

The large apartment consisted of eight individual desks for assistants, his private office, and various secured locations for safes and storage of precious items. Being early morning after a royal banquet, the staff reported an hour later than normal. The only person in the room was Sir Hastins. A shrewd older nobleman, he took over the duties of Commissary when Nollen left for the trading circuit.

"Morning, Sir Hastins. What business today?"

Hastins glanced up from reading papers "Ambassador Dynos sent a list of Bertrandian terms for you to consider." He gave them to Nollen.

Nollen huffed an ironic laugh. "We knew the real reason for his arrival." He paused in looking at the papers. "Sir Hastins, were you here during the negotiations of Javan's agreement with Bertrand?"

"Alas, no. Or should I say, grateful I was not. Gorman requested my return to the Freelands, which was granted. I gladly went!"

Nollen indicated the terms. "There will be no agreement until after the circuit. Anything else?"

"The usual need to replenish the larder after the banquet."

"I don't know if Harvey has any seasonal mead left. The Ganels drank it all last night."

Hastins laughed. "I heard they won. Gorman woke with a tremendous headache."

Nollen sarcastically grinned. "Freeland news travels fast."

"We love a good game, just hate to lose."

"Now, I understand Gunnar's attitude. When Gibly arrives, send him to fetch a list from Cook and Butler about what is needed." Nollen entered his office to begin work.

From the study window, Axel witnessed everything that happened in the courtyard with Nollen, the Nefal, and Lexi with Gunnar. The final decision required speaking to one more person. His arrival made Axel leave the window.

"You sent for me, Sire?" Cormac appeared alert and normal. No sign of drinking or staying up past midnight. In fact, he wore traveling clothes.

Axel wryly surveyed the Ganel. "I must say, when Nollen told me about fuddling cup, I expected to see fatigue or at least blood-shot eyes. It appears the myth is true, Ganels can't get drunk."

Cormac laughed. His wry humor matched Axel. "It takes a great deal more to affect us than mead. Is there a reason you wanted to see me, beside fuddling cup? Jenna and I are preparing to leave."

"Aye, and your departure is a factor." Axel motioned to the table used earlier for breakfast, yet now cleared of plates. They sat. "No doubt, you have noticed Lexi's difficulty in adjusting to life here. After various conversations, I'm at the point of making a decision regarding how to help her. The last piece deals with her capacity as Shield Maiden."

"Mathena is the best place to complete her training."

"The questions is how and when? She is totally unfamiliar with Eldar outside of Sener. She even considers herself a prisoner unable to freely explore, which translates into resentment of what she has already learned. However, her senses are becoming heightened, more sensitive, and intuitive."

Cormac's expression showed understanding. "Sounds like Gott is awakening her needed discernment."

"Aye. She doesn't yet understand what that means. Multiple times I tried to broach the subject of her duty as Shield Maiden, but she refuses to listen." Axel swallowed back some discomposure. "There are times our age difference interferes. She sees me as a parent rather than a brother." He noticed the way Cormac regarded him. "I don't mean to keep you, so I will come to the point. She made a request, which I am inclined to agree, to accompany Nollen on his circuit, which will bring her to Mathena."

"When she arrives, you want me to gauge if she is ready for training."

"Exactly! That is why I wanted to speak with you before you left.

Cormac kindly said, "Consider it done, Sire. Like myself, Jenna is well versed in that part of our history. While I continue with the Bertrandian research, she will engage Lexi."

"Excellent! Thank you."

Lexi half-heartedly participated in the sparing match with Gunnar. Annoyed by her attitude, he stopped. "You must put forth the effort."

"Why? There are soldiers everywhere. I can't leave the castle without at least one."

"That is not an excuse."

Lexi sat on a bench. She used a towel to wipe the small amount of sweat from her face.

Gunnar grew sympathetic. "I understand how difficult this—"

"No, you don't! So, stop pretending."

His ire rose at the rebuff. "The only one pretending is you! As witnessed by your indifference to anything required."

Pricked, she stood to confront him. "How dare you?"

"I dare because I know you as well as I do your brother."

"Do not compare me to Axel!" she hotly warned.

He shook his head. "The only comparison is the same royal blood. It is time to start acting like it."

Unable to speak due to hurtful anger, Lexi snatched her cloak and left the armory. Outside, she peeked over her shoulder. Gunnar didn't pursue. She donned her cloak and headed for the main gate.

"Princess!" A page ran after her. "The King wishes to see you."

Lexi's shoulders sagged in visible frustration. She returned to the study where Axel sat at his desk. "You wanted to see me?" she asked, tersely.

Axel momentarily regarded her before he placed aside the quill pen to stand. He waved her to the chairs at the hearth. He sat after she had taken a seat. "Lexi, …"

She raised a quick hand to interrupted him. "Do not say you understand. I have heard that placating phrase too many times."

"No, I don't. I can't since our attitudes and natures are different. Yet, that is not what I was about to say."

The confession placed her more at ease. "What then?"

"I have reached a decision about your request."

Moved by anticipation, she sat perched on the chair. "And?"

"You have this week to prepare for depart —" He didn't finish when she jumped up and threw her arms around his neck.

"Thank you! Thank you!" She kissed his cheek and ran toward the door. She paused to say, "I can't think of where to go first."

"You will follow Nollen's route."

She ran through the halls to the commodities apartment, now a buzz with activity. She burst into Nollen's office. He and Hastins were in conference with two other assistants and startled by the blustery entrance.

"Lexi ... Highness," Nollen corrected.

Oblivious to the disturbance, she announced, "He said I can go!"

Briefly stunned, Nollen partly stuttered, "Wonderful."

"Aye! It is. I finally get to see Eldar!"

Nollen sent a prompting glance to Hastins. The latter left with the assistants. "There is much to do before we leave. At least for me." He picked up papers.

"Oh!" she said with realization. "I'm sorry. I was so excited, I had to tell you."

He smiled. "In truth, I knew he would agree after breakfast this morning."

"You spoke to him about it?"

"Aye. Since you told him about me, he wanted my opinion."

She warmly gazed at him. "You convinced him to let me go?"

"Maybe some," he modestly said. "He spent time in prayerful consideration. Which is a good thing when making such a decision."

She took his hand. "Thank you. I won't be any trouble. I promise."

"After our last journey, trouble should be the least of our worries. At least, that kind," he joked.

She laughed. "Again, thank you. I will let you get back to work."

As she left, Sir Hastins returned. "The King is preparing for an audience with Dynos and requests your presence."

Nollen scowled. "Bertrandians are not patient people. But, we won't be rushed."

He picked up a floppy leather document case and left the commissary. He took the route through the hallways. He walked at a more leisurely pace than Lexi. Axel sat at the desk reading a book when he arrived. "Glad to see I arrived before Dynos."

"I made certain of that. Have you studied the list?"

"I just received it this morning." Nollen withdrew it from the leather case. "Most are standard items. With the exception of the free trade provision. That might have been the agreement with the Electors, but I wouldn't advise it."

"Agreed. I wanted you here for the first round of discussions." Axel rose and signaled the guard. "Fetch Ambassador Dynos."

When Dynos emerged from the antechamber, he bowed to Axel. "Live forever, most gracious King Axel," he made the Bertrandian obeisance.

"Ambassador Dynos. You have met Commissary Nollen." Axel indicated Nollen, who stood respectfully behind him to observe.

"Yah. Last night. A most wonderous banquet, Majesty. I offer the blessing of the gods to your most gracious queen."

Axel stiffened at the statement. "Eldar has one god, Ambassador."

"I meant no offense, Majesty."

"There have been many changes since your last visit."

"Yah. King Rastus wishes to remain on good terms with Eldar. As such, I presented terms for new negotiations."

"Those terms shall be given proper consideration by myself, my ministers, and Commissary Nollen. His expertise in trading should be known in Bertrand."

A brief expression of objection crossed Dynos' face when Axel referenced Nollen. Ever the poised diplomat, he quickly masked his displeasure. "His reputation is known."

"Your tone suggests disapproval," Axel sternly said.

"Ascertaining what changes mean for our relationship, takes time, Majesty. The Commissary's reputation is based upon private transactions rather than official negotiations between our kingdoms."

Axel's glance told Nollen he was at liberty to speak.

"Ascertaining changes works both ways, Ambassador. To begin, you make an erroneous assumption that I engaged in private endeavors. Far Point was one of four trading posts under charter by the Electors. Thus, my trades were officially sanctioned. As for my current position, I have already negotiated trade agreements with Markita and Gorland."

This time, Dynos couldn't conceal his surprised annoyance at the rebuff. "I stand corrected." He made the Bertrandian salute in deference. "Commissary."

"Enjoy our hospitality while we consider the terms before further discussions," said Axel.

Dynos bowed at the dismissal.

When the door closed, Axel clapped Nollen's shoulder. "Well done."

"For now. I need to consult the archives about past agreements."

Axel tried unsuccessfully to still a teasing laugh. "Mathena is now on a tour circuit."

Nollen chuckled. "She's so excited, she rushed into the office to tell me you agreed."

"No doubt." Axel's smile showed gratitude. "Again, thank you."

Chapter 5

THERON, THE SPRAWLING CAPITAL OF BERTRAND, SPANNED BOTH banks of the Takara river that it shared with its northern neighbor, Eldar. For one hundred miles Takara continued from the border to Theron. Just beyond the capital, the mighty river split into two smaller rivers: Quitin and Starvos. River access provided easy travel and trade. Surrounded by lush, fertile farmland, made an ideal location for the city to thrive.

Bold architecture of soaring columns with intricately carved archways and windows told of Theron's wealthy heritage. Large edifices and statues of Bertrand's heroes and gods dominated the major buildings. Workers diligently maintained the cobblestone streets to accommodate the continuous flow of traffic.

Built on the highest peak nearest the river, the King's palace overlooked both Theron and Takara. Sheer cliffs of the river, served as the back wall. Dark gray slate capped the domed roofs of white marble buildings. One building in the large complex, belonged to the Vizier. Second only in power to the King, Cadmus enriched his position beyond his predecessors. He raised the splendor of his villa to match the royal palace with carved columns overlayed in gold and silver. Colorful mosaic tiles covered the ceilings and floors. The painted walls contained flecks of gold leaf that sparkled in the daylight and gave a warm glow in evening lamplight. A new white veined marble fountain provided serenity in the private courtyard.

Forty-five years old, Cadmus carried himself with pride and dignity equal to his station. From beneath the cranberry-colored embroidered cap were strains of salt and pepper hair. Hazel eyes shone with intelligence and a quick wit. Over his sand-color tunic intricately embroidered with red and black thread, he wore a cranberry robe that matched the hat. More elaborate designs on the robe signified his high status.

He crossed the courtyard to his office. Inside, the cawing of a large raven greeted him. The bird perched on a stand specifically made for it. The raven flapped its wing and cocked head toward the door. A very tall, cloaked individual stood in the archway of the opened garden terrace door. The being's bulk filled the threshold.

"Your presence has upset Spyros," Cadmus chided. He stroked the raven's head to help calm the bird. "Are you here by coincidence or did you receive my message?"

The giant turned and lowered the hood. Spoor. "Your message. However, I bring news which might change the plan."

"A little late. Dynos went to Sener to present our trade terms."

"Those terms will mean nothing without Nefal backing."

With cool indifference, Cadmus made himself comfortable at his desk. "Times are different. The days of Nefal dominance are over."

"Not if we keep to the plan."

Cadmus' steely eyes focused on Spoor. "You ask much of Bertrand."

Spoor's angry sneer made his patch more intimidating. "For centuries, Nefal protected your northern border. Our strength kept you humans safe. Then, after we secured our place in Eldar, we made certain the Electors favored Bertrand with generous terms." He spread his arms. "Theron would not be what it is today without us. Do not forget that."

Livid at the stern reminder, Cadmus stood. "You forget to whom you speak! As Vizier, I know the secrets of the gods. And the Nefal."

At Spyros' angry caw, Cadmus moved around the desk to confront Spoor. He waved his hands together as he mumbled words. Gray mist form between the palms than transformed into images of sky, earth, Nefal, and other beings locked in confrontation.

Cadmus' words came laced with ridicule. "Your kind punished for failure to serve the gods. Driven by greed of conquest, and lust for power, believed you could seize the heavens." He clapped his hands, and images turned to dust that evaporated. Spyros settled on the perch.

The glare of Spoor's good eye betrayed the fury beneath. It took great restraint for him to speak. "We may have lost our exalted position, but not our strength or cunning. If not for us, Bertrand would still be a poor kingdom easily controlled by others. Nor has it any bearing on the future should Eldar cease trade. For all your knowledge of the gods, you still need us."

Cadmus returned Spoor's stare in a battle of wills. "The news!" he snapped.

"Axel is married and his queen with child."

"The child is news. Word of the wedding reached us in time to eliminate the proposal of a royal marriage from the terms."

"There is his sister. Lexi."

"Yah," Cadmus mused, intrigued. "Rastus may now be more agreeable to my original suggestion." A satisfied smile appeared, as he continued. "Once more allowing me to pursue my own interest in Celeste."

"Changing the plan would not be advisable," chided Spoor.

"I have no intention of changing it. One way or another, Eldar will be allied with us. Too much is at stake for it not to happen."

"You need Nefal aid to succeed!"

Cadmus' initial sneer at the snide comment turned into a sly grin. "Serve me well, and you may return to Bertrand. Thus, benefiting all." He picked up a bell on his desk to ring.

From another room two young men in their early twenties entered. Strikingly similar in feature with dark beards and dark eyes. They wore long black embroidered surcoats complete with leather belt and ornate short swords. The leather boots matched the belt. The black cloaks had a hood over which they wore fur-trimmed caps.

"Mateo and Marius. Twins, if you couldn't tell," Cadmus introduced them.

Spoor shrugged with indifference. "I pay no attention to human appearances."

"You better, since they will help execute your part of the plan."

Spoor's one good eye studied the brothers. They didn't shrink from his intense regard. "You have no fear. That is good," he said with approval.

"Of course not. They are my sons, and well educated in Bertrandian history concerning the Nefal," Cadmus proudly spoke. "Now, all of you, leave unobserved."

Mateo and Marius silently returned through the door they entered.

Cadmus turned his back to Spoor in an obvious move of dismissal. He crossed to stand before a wall map displaying the known kingdoms, Eldar, Markita, Gorland, Bertrand, Niran, and Walerian. The latter two countries flanked Bertrand, and all three countries ended at the Bothin Sea. His eyes focused on the northern border with Eldar. He ignored Spoor's annoyed grunt, nor did he move when the door slammed shut.

"The scope of the plan is well thought out. However, the Nefal is not to be trusted," Spyros spoke.

Cadmus casually looked at the raven. "I don't. That is why I am sending my sons."

Spyros made the short flight from the perch to the desk. "Mateo is willing. Yet I sense hesitation in Marius."

"Marius is his mother's son," scoffed Cadmus.

"Romia served us with a devoted heart. Within Marius, there is conflict."

"Mateo prods him. He will act accordingly."

"One of the Ancient Flock will follow to assure the plan is executed. My fellow gods will not be pleased with failure." Spyros made a deafening caw that caused Cadmus to cringe.

"It will be as you say!" Cadmus painfully insisted.

Spyros flew out the terrace door. Cadmus took several moments to recover from Spyros' rebuke. He didn't realize someone knocked on the main door until he heard his title called.

"Come."

The male servant knelt with head bowed to the floor. "Vizier, the King summons you."

Cadmus soothed his outer garments. "Where?"

"The private drawing room." He remained on his knees, as Cadmus passed.

The fragrance of spring blossoms and lively bird songs made a pleasant day for crossing the expansive courtyard. Servants and soldiers deeply bowed to Cadmus. Guards opened the massive ornate wooden doors to allow admittance to the palace. Although, Cadmus' decorating exceeded those before him, the Vizier's residence still paled in comparison to the splendid magnificence of the palace. Impressive marble, gold, jewels, mosaic tiles, and lavish furnishings spoke of enormous wealth. At the door to the drawing room, he briefly paused for a guard to announce him.

At age sixty, Rastus looked much older. His white, thinning hair covered by a brocade hat with an ostrich feather brim. Even his regal tunic and robe exceeded Cadmus. Extra material needed to amass his girth. He sat in a plush cushioned chair before a massive marble hearth. Being early spring, a modest fire warmed the room. His son and daughter joined him in the drawing room.

Age thirty-five, Prince Felix resembled a younger version of Rastus with dark brown hair and brown eyes. He wore clothes nearly identical in color and richness of his father.

Six years younger than Felix, Princess Celeste shared in the family traits. Long chestnut tresses curled and fashioned with pearl combs and jeweled headdress. Her green eyes shaped like those of her brother and father. Over her high-waisted brocade silk dress, hung a matching robe. She sat at a mahogany frame with a stretched canvas for needlepoint. She caught sight of the door opening, her father and Felix unaware of Cadmus' arrival. The Vizier's suggestive smile made her squirm and return to the needlepoint.

Cadmus assumed a casual air to speak. "You summoned me, Sire?"

"Ah, Cadmus. Any word from Dynos?"

"No, Sire. Barely three weeks have passed. Just time enough to reach Sener, and perhaps, begin preliminary discussions."

"We need a sense of Axel!" Rastus snapped.

"You should have heeded my advice and sent for Nollen of Far Point before dispatching Dynos with terms," Felix argued.

"He is now Royal Commissary, not a simple outpost trader. He needs Axel's permission to engage in such negotiations," Cadmus countered.

"He still runs Far Point. It could be a personal visit."

Rastus grabbed Felix's arm. "I appreciate your reminder."

Felix jerked away. At Celeste's glare, he tempered a reply. "I merely want to allay your worry about Axel," he told Rastus.

"Too much has changed. It is a wonder he did not void Javan's treaty immediately," complained Rastus.

"Internal stability required his attention before any foreign considerations, Sire," said Cadmus.

"Tell that to Markita!"

"Montre captured his people," Felix chided. "We are simply offering terms of trade. By dealing forthrightly, we can avoid arousing his anger."

"With the Electors gone, we can no longer rely on our past agreements. That is the stark example of Markita!" Rastus harshly countered.

"An interesting piece of information has come to my attention that may help us." Cadmus' gaze passed between Celeste and Felix.

"How?" Felix asked, guarded.

"The marriage proposal can be reintroduced—"

"Axel is married! I will be queen not a concubine," Celeste protested.

Cadmus flashed a tolerant smile. "My original suggestion of his sister." His eyes fixed on Felix.

"Yah!" Rastus used the chair arms to push himself up and chide Felix. "No objection this time! It is your duty to marry and produce an heir."

Felix bit back a reply as Rastus spoke eagerly to Cadmus.

"Compose an official letter amending the terms for Dynos to present Axel. I want it within the hour for immediate dispatch."

Speed of the decision caught Felix off-guard. "Isn't that a bit hasty? After all, what do we know of her?"

"What is there to know? She is the sister of a king. That is enough," Rastus dismissively said. "Go! Shoo. Shoo." He waved at Cadmus.

At Felix's heightened frustration, Celeste left the needlework to approach Rastus. "Da. Is it really necessary to act so swiftly? To ally with Eldar by marriage?"

"Royal alliances by marriage are commonplace. They provide stability and security by forming good relations with other kingdoms."

"Give Dynos time to negotiate before resorting to marriage," Felix urged.

"Why are you so opposed to fulfilling your duty as heir?" demanded Rastus.

"I simply want to know the woman before I commit."

"I did not know your mother until our wedding day. The same as my father, and his father." Rastus waved a finger at Felix. "You will do the same. It is your duty!" He left in a huff.

Felix plopped in the chair. Celeste knelt beside him. "You must tell him," She said.

"How?"

"The direct way is always best."

That I secretly married and have a child?" he spoke in a horse whisper.

"No, that you love another woman. The rest can come once you have won him over."

"It is not as simple as you suggest."

She seized his hand. "Cadmus is writing the letter now. Then Da will dispatch it. You don't have much time."

"I have at least a month before receiving an answer. Providing Axel agrees."

"If you wait too long, Axel will take it as a great insult, while Da furious."

Angry, he leaned forward, yet kept his voice low. "It is Cadmus I fear not Da. I won't risk their lives! I will take my chances and wait." He hastened from the room.

Chapter 6

ON THE HIGHEST ROOF OF THE ROYAL COMPLEX, SPYROS WAITED. Another raven descended from the sky to land beside him. The raven bowed his head and spoke in a male voice, "Mighty, Spyros."

"Kyros." Spyros peered down at the courtyard. Mateo and Marius rode from the complex. "The Vizier's twins are joining a Nefal name Spoor to help execute the plan. Make certain they succeed."

"I saw a Nefal with a harpy yesterday."

"A harpy in Bertrand, and you did not alert me?" demanded Spyros.

"There were also two jackals—"

Spyros' angry caw made Kyros lose balance and nearly fall from the roof. "Of all my hatchlings, you were to be the example!"

"I wanted to learn the reason beforehand. Forgive me."

"I told Cadmus the Nefal could not be trusted. This proves it. Follow the twins, yet also inform Ursus so he can handle the jackals, if necessary."

Kyros shook his feathers, and his voice betrayed nervousness. "The last time I encountered Ursus, he tried to kill me."

"You made the mistake of poking the bear king."

"He raided our nest! Zeta could not produce eggs for over a year."

"Tell Ursus I sent you on an errand involving Nefal. He will listen. Though what he does afterwards, is your problem. Now, go!"

Kyros took off. From high above, he spied the twins as they rode through the crowd. It would take a while to navigate the bustling city street and pass through the northern gate. No doubt, they would travel the main road while in Bertrand. Kyros made a few circles to bring his flight path out of sight from the royal complex. Once safe from Spyros' observation, he headed north as quickly as his wings could carry him.

Kyros used upper wind currents to aid his hasty divergence. Though not an errand he wanted, he could not afford to fail. Deep into the wilderness, he flew. Keen eyes searched the ground below. When he reached the vicinity of his last encounter with Ursus, his caws echoed over the forest. He repeated the call four times, with pauses between to await an answer. Finally, he heard the roar of a bear. He altered course to spy the responder. In a small clearing, he spotted the bear king.

Cautious, Kyros landed on a branch across from Ursus. Twelve feet off the ground should be safe enough to avoid a direct encounter. "I come at the request of my father, Spyros the Mighty. Will you hear me, Lord Ursus?"

Ursus did not respond. Instead, his enormous haunches moved with each step to cross the clearing. He stopped at the base of the tree and stood on his hind legs. He bared his teeth.

Kyros backed away since Ursus' height nearly reached the branch upon which he perched. "I come in peace!" he anxiously clamored.

"I will hear you, fledgling," Ursus' deep voice spoke with forced tolerance. "What says Spyros that he risks sending you after last time?"

"There is a Nefal in Bertrand—"

"I know."

Kyros ignored the interruption to proceed. "With it, are a harpy and two jackals—"

Ursus' might roar made Kyros flap and caw with fear. "Stay, fledgling." Ursus sat to assume a non-threatening posture. "What does Spyros want?"

"For you to watch the Nefal. The plan is in motion."

Ursus scoffed a laugh. "I have been watching. However, I saw no harpy or jackals."

"I am the one who sighted them with the Nefal. Deep in the woods, cleverly hidden from ground view."

"I would smell jackals," Ursus insisted. His teeth fully bared.

"I do not insult you, Lord Ursus!" Kyros hastily spoke. "Sighted or smelled does not change their unwanted presence in Bertrand."

"Indeed," Ursus agreed. "Anything else?"

"The Nefal is not alone. Cadmus sent the twins to ensure he fulfills his part. Spyros wants you to make certain the jackals are not a threat to Bertrand. If they are, kill them."

"I would rather kill the First Ones."

"I have discharged my duty." Kyros took off.

The further he flew from the wilderness, the safer he felt. Not that a bear threatened him when airborne, he simply needed distance to recover from the unpleasant task of dealing with Ursus. The easiest part of his assignment would be following the twins. Humans rarely had the sense to interpret the behavior of nature. Once they join the Nefal, things will change. Harpys were ancient enemies of ravens.

Because of the distance traveled to speak with Ursus, Kyros didn't find the twins until twilight. They camped a short way off the road. Suddenly, he heard a distinct shrill very close. He banked to avoid the harpy's attack. Being smaller and more agile, Kyros juked, looped, and dove in various directions to elude the harpy. At one point, it got so close, it snapped off one of his fantail feathers.

Another raven's caw came a split second before it dove out of the blinding setting sun. It violently snatched a harpy's crown feather in its talons, which threw the harpy off course. This gave Kyros the chance to escape. He climbed to join the newly arrived raven. Despite the size disadvantage, two against one sent the harpy retreating.

Weary and wounded, Kyros headed for the shelter of a nearby grove. "Zeta, what are you doing here?" he chided when she landed beside him.

"Are you badly hurt?" she asked.

"A tail feather. Other than that, I'm very tired. What are you doing here?" Kyros stressed the question a second time.

"I observed your exchange with Spyros. And no, he did not see me," she answered in anticipation of his question. "Yet, I lost you after leaving the city. Where did you go?"

He needed to be discrete. The encounter with Ursus traumatized her. "An errand for Spyros. With that done, I am to follow the Nefal and twins."

Zeta looked down toward the camp. "The harpy is with them."

Kyros bobbed his head. "I know. But the plan is important."

"Why? We have never known the First Ones nor been to Eldar. What is it to us?"

"My father commands it! If I am to lead the flock someday, I must obey."

Zeta moved closer to Kyros and lowered her voice. "There are many who do not agree with Spyros. They question centuries-old grudges that no longer impact the flock."

Kyros hopped down the branch from Zeta. She followed. "Kyros, we have the whole sky of Bertrand to ourselves. We fly without fear of eagles or harpys. Why jeopardize that?"

"You don't know what you're saying," he half-heartedly chided.

"Maybe not. Though I just saved you from a harpy. Is that what you want for our fledglings? For the flock? To be on guard whenever we take to the skies? A leader thinks beyond blind obedience to the good of all."

"Enough, Zeta! Return to the nest!" Kyros ruffled his feathers.

The rebuke and hostile act made Zeta back away. Without another word, she flew off.

Kyros settled in for observation. He felt a stab of guilt at being gruff with Zeta. Their first hatchlings since Ursus only left the nest last week. He couldn't think about that now. He had a task that demanded full attention.

Chapter 7

EXCITEMENT KEPT LEXI FROM SLEEPING. BY LAMPLIGHT, SHE GAZED at herself in the mirror. Alicia ordered traveling clothes made from leather and wool. Pants suited her more than dresses. One thing Axel insisted on incorporating was a hidden dagger sheath in her right boot. Since the boots came to her knees, she didn't need to reach down too far. Of course, she wore her new sword. She fiddled with her hair. Totally braided, partially braided, or completely loose? She finally braided it since that proved to be the quickest style. She packed her saddle bags according to Nollen's instructions.

When the first rays of dawn peeked through the drapes, Lexi donned the cloak and snatched the saddle bags. If she hurried, maybe she could reach the stables before Nollen. No luck. He finished saddling Alydar, his faithful former unicorn mount since Markita. Beside the fence, lay Callie. The she-wolf rose when Lexi arrived.

"Good morning, Princess."

"Callie. Alydar. Nollen."

"Good morning," Nollen replied.

Lexi placed the bags behind the saddle of a dun-colored mare with black mane and tail. "Sami." She patted the mare's neck. She noticed Joslin. "Is Gunnar joining us?"

"Aye. He and Lorraine are coming."

"Lorraine too?" she asked with disappointment.

He grinned. "We thought you might want to join them for a visit to Kean and his family while I conduct business in Stellan."

Her annoyance quickly turned to joy. "Oh, aye! I haven't seen them since the wedding. But there are only three horses."

"Good morning." Axel wore a cloak against the morning chill. A servant stood behind him and held a large oblong carved wooden box. He saw Lexi's gleeful expression. "Excited?"

"I get to ride Sami further than Wyckton," she eagerly replied.

Axel chuckled at her enthusiasm then turned his attention to Nollen. "I have a gift for you." He waved the servant forward and took the box to give Nollen.

"What is this?"

"You didn't think I would forget *your* birthday, did you?"

"No, but I'm usually on the circuit."

"Exactly, why I'm giving it to you now. To help with this year's tour."

"Your birthday? How old are you?" asked Lexi, pleasantly intrigued.

"Twenty-four, but not for a couple of weeks." Nollen placed the box on a bench to open the lid. On top of the interior felt lining lay a new crossbow of polished yew wood with steel prod and ornate carvings flecked with gold leaf. Speechless, he picked it up.

Axel's smile widened at the reaction. "I assume you like it."

"Aye!" Nollen aimed the bow then cocked it to feel the weight. "Wonderful balance. I've never seen one so handsome. Almost a shame to use it." He pulled the old crossbow from the saddle holder to replace it with the new one. "This will help with hunting and defense." He gave the old bow to Lexi. "Put it in the holder I added to your saddle."

"Only not on Sami." Axel took the crossbow from Lexi. He placed two fingers in the mouth to whistle. There came a whinny reply, as a horse trotted from the stables to Axel. A beautiful light sorrel mare with white mane and tail, and handsomely saddled for travel.

At sight of her, Alydar lifted his head, his ears straight up. He made a grunt whinny. The mare responded with soft grunting, to which Alydar resumed a natural posture.

"You need a dependable mount for such a long journey since Sami is for Lorraine. Her name is Sheba," Axel explained. He put the crossbow in the saddle sheath.

"She's beautiful!" Lexi stroked the mare's neck.

Gunnar and Lorraine arrived. He wore both sword and dagger, while Lorraine had a dagger on her belt. Gunnar observed the brightening sky. "Fine day for a ride," he commented.

"Nollen told me about the visit to Kean. It's a grand idea," Lexi cheered. "Axel gave me a new horse." She patted Sheba.

Gunnar laughed at her excitement before he spoke to Nollen. "This is for you, lad." He gave Nollen a cloth wrapped item. "Can't have a new crossbow without a quiver."

"Happy birthday from both of us." Lorraine hugged Nollen.

Nollen removed the cloth to see an expensive leather quiver with embossing that matched the crossbow carving. "Thank you."

"Am I the only one who didn't know about your birthday?" asked Lexi.

"Apparently, more people knew than I realized." Nollen switched the arrows from the old quiver to the new one.

"Now that everyone is assembled, let us pray." Axel stood with palms opened and head bowed. "Gracious Gott, we commit this journey to your care. Protect them as they travel. Give Nollen wisdom and insight in his business dealings. May Lexi experience and learn what is needed to become settled in spirit. Allow her to see you at work in Eldar. Return them safely to us when all is complete. Amen."

Lexi hugged Axel. "Thank you. Tell Alicia I will miss her."

"She wanted to see you off, but the child isn't too agreeable this morning." Axel held her shoulders. "One thing you must do, is keep your identity confidential. It is best people do not know you are my sister."

"Why?"

"You complain about a title. The moment you ride through the gate, you are again Lexi." When she smiled in agreement, he kissed her forehead. "Gott's speed."

Outside the postern gate, Callie took the lead. Lexi rode beside Nollen. Gunnar and Lorraine followed.

Lexi turned slightly in the saddle to ask Gunnar, "Where do they live?"

"An hour northwest of Stellan in the Freelands."

"Stellan is the capital of the Freelands. I studied the maps," she sarcastically said. "How long will it take to get there?"

"Two long days, which includes crossing the River Stille."

"That's why we left at dawn," added Nollen. "Sometimes, I leave earlier to reach a certain destination before dark. Fortunately, there is an inn near the bridge where we'll spend the night."

"I have missed Kean and Brita," Lexi said with fondness.

"I thought as much, which is why I suggested to begin your exploration of Eldar by visiting close friends," said Gunnar with a knowing smile.

"You and your family have been a great blessing to me and Axel."

"The feeling is mutual." Gunnar grew thoughtful with reminiscing. "After being together so long, everyone from Kranston is family."

Lorraine reached over to take his hand. "You're finally going home."

"Aye," he said a bit wary.

Curious at his somber response, Lexi asked, "Why haven't you visited them before now?"

An unusual hint of uncertainty crept into Gunnar's voice and expression. "Not exactly sure what to expect after nearly four decades. I was a lad of ten when we were forced to flee."

"All of us going together is a bolster for him," Lorraine told Lexi.

"Woman," Gunnar grunted and snatched his hand away.

"Don't get testy," Lorraine rebuffed. "It took much convincing from me and Nollen for you to agree."

Gunnar squirmed in the saddle. "I'm not afraid, if that is what you're implying."

"Nothing of the sort," Nollen interjected. "There comes a time we must face our past. Something I know about." He looked directly at Gunnar.

The older knight's expression softened. "Aye, lad."

Silence fell as they continued. Lexi's eager gaze took in the scenic countryside. Shortly, she squirmed with some discomfort.

"Something wrong?" asked Nollen.

"My stomach is reminding me that I haven't eaten since last night."

"Did you remember to pack a day's provisions?"

"Aye, but ..." she looked at the saddle horn. "I forgot a flask."

Nollen removed one of two flasks from his saddle horn. "I brought a second just in case. Only, you won't find kirsch," he teased when she took it.

Gunnar and Lorraine laughed at the joke regarding the powerful liquor Lexi used to test Nollen when he arrived at Kranston.

"You should thank me for acquiring a taste for it," Lexi countered.

Nollen grinned. "Hard to find in Eldar. Except where we're going."

The rest of the day passed between periods of lengthy conversation to answering Lexi's questions about plants and animals, and riding in silence. During those quiet times, Lexi studied the landscape. Twice, they walked the horses to stretch their legs. At midday, they stopped beside a creek to rest and eat lunch.

Lexi lay on the grass to stare at the sky. For the first time since arriving in Eldar, she left Sener completely behind. "Freedom."

The others made no comment to her statement. Instead, Nollen said, "Don't fall asleep. We still have a long ride ahead of us."

Shortly after twilight, they reached the inn. The location proved prosperous since the bridge connected the Freelands to the Halvor Mountains and the road to Sener. At the corral, Nollen instructed the groom about the care of the horses. They each took their bags, while Lexi and Nollen also carried their crossbows. Inside, the smell of food and noise bombarded their senses. Almost immediately, a middle-aged woman greeted them.

"Master Nollen. We reckoned it about time for you to arrive."

"Helga. Food and two rooms." Nollen led the others to a table. "You and Lorraine will share a room tonight," he told Lexi.

"Break up a married couple?"

"We aren't sharing a room. In fact, we will have separate quarters during the journey."

She grew flustered, yet asked, "Will they know you everywhere we go?"

Nollen waited to reply since Helga brought tankards and a pitcher. "Aye. This is the fourth year. I start in the Freelands then double-back to the Halvor Mountains, continue through Ganel, The Doane, and finally Nefal. Keeping to a schedule is helpful in maintaining contacts and encouraging trade."

"Why not just end in the Freelands instead of backtracking?"

"Because of me." Gunnar flashed a smile, which confused Lexi. "I convinced Nollen to begin with the Freelands."

"That's it? Nothing more intriguing?"

Nollen laughed. "Intriguing? This is business. Sometimes boring, often tedious."

Lexi blushed. "I meant a more interesting reason."

Nollen and Gunnar ate to conceal further amusement.

"No need to embarrass the poor girl," Lorraine lightly scolded them.

Lexi smirked as she spoke to Lorraine. "Don't worry. I'll find a bottle of kirsch in Stellan and put it in his food when he least expects it."

Nollen nearly choked for laughing. He took a drink to recover.

Late the following afternoon, they arrived at Kean's farm. One of Arnie's teenage sons alerted the family. Arnie ceased chopping wood while Kean left the ox and plow. Being Gunnar's older brother by six years, Kean bore his age with robust vigor. He greeted Gunnar in a bear hug. His wife, Brita, showered Gunnar and Lorraine with hugs and kisses. Arnie's wife, Giselle, and children joined in the reunion. They warmly embraced Lexi, and heartily welcomed Nollen.

"Eb, take their belongings to the guest rooms. Hans, tend the horses," Arnie instructed the teenagers.

"Where will you sleep?" asked Lexi.

"Our house is up the road." Arnie pointed to a distant structure.

Gunnar noticed the plow. "You have an ox."

"Along with a cow, work horse, rooster, and some chickens. Gorman and Axel have been generous. We expected Nollen, but no one else."

"I have seeds." Nollen took off a heavy sack from behind the saddle. "Mostly wheat, but also, cabbage, potatoes, beets, and carrots."

"Wonderful." Kean accepted the sack. "The fields should be ready in a couple of days."

"Come refresh yourselves." Brita took Lexi's arm to enter the house. "My dear, it is so good see you." She hugged Lexi again.

"I have longed to visit and see your new home."

Kean fetched tankards from the sideboard while Giselle took the cloaks. "Well, it's not actually new."

Gunnar wandered the room. "It doesn't look the same."

"We made repairs." Kean handed each a tankard of ale. He explained to Lorraine and Lexi, "Through the efforts of others, and Gott's mercy, this main house was not destroyed, though it suffered decades of neglect. Other buildings were torn down."

"We lived here to help with the repairs and restore the guest house until it became habitable for my family," said Arnie.

"We plan on starting on another house shortly." Kean smiled at Gunnar.

"Oma and Papa's?" Gunnar asked with anticipation.

"For you and Lorraine. Should you decide to retire."

Stunned, Gunnar stared at Kean. "I don't know what to say."

"This is your home as well."

Lorraine held Gunnar's arm. "Now, you see why we were so eager to convince you?" She spoke of herself and Nollen.

"You knew?" Gunnar's astonished glance shifted between Lorraine and Nollen.

"How do you think we get supplies?" Arnie motioned to Nollen.

"Lad, I …," began a humbled Gunnar.

In a gesture of modesty, Nollen shook his head and waved a hand. "I merely follow instructions and facilitate acquisition."

Kean raised his tankard in a brotherly salute. "To being home."

The men discussed crops, livestock, and trading. Lexi and Lorraine joined Giselle and Brita to help prepare supper. Hearing the women laugh brought a pause to the conversation.

"Lexi's been greatly missed," Kean said.

"Adjustment takes time," Gunnar droned.

"You're being cagey. How has she done in Sener?"

"It's been difficult," Gunnar tactfully admitted. "Alicia is doing wonderfully well. And is with child." He spoke the last sentence loud enough for the women to hear.

"What? Alicia with child?" Brita replied, happily.

"This calls for kirsch!" Kean fetched a bottle of the rare liquor.

"Before supper?" Brita asked.

"Woman, this is calls for a toast! A royal heir is to be born in Eldar after two centuries." Once the glasses were filled, Kean held up his to make a toast. "Gott's blessing upon the King, Queen, and royal heir. May the child be full of grace and wisdom."

The clanked glasses together in salute and drank.

"You're going to be an aunt!" Giselle cheered to Lexi.

"Aye, though unsure exactly what that means."

"Once you see that precious face, you will know."

Lexi smiled at Giselle's enthusiasm. "I have seen babies before."

"This is different. A blood connection. Child of your brother," Giselle kindly said. "You will understand soon enough."

"We need to finish supper," Brita said. The women complied.

"Smells like venison," said Nollen.

"Game is more plentiful here than at Kranston," said Hans.

Kean shook a grandfatherly finger at Hans. "You and Eb cannot favor hunting over plowing."

"With the seeds I brought, this can once again be a prosperous farm," said Nollen.

The comment brought forth a series of childhood stories from Kean and Gunnar. Nollen, Arnie, Eb, and Hans enjoyed listening and laughing.

At one point, Nollen fought to catch his breath due to merriment at one of Kean's more amusing stories.

"Gunnar hid in the hay loft for three days. Every time Jann or I brought him food, we exaggerated how angry father was that Gunnar lost his prize bull."

"Not lost. It accidently got away." Gunnar joined in the fun. His speech told he had a bit too much kirsch. "As a scared nine-year-old, I believe them until Mama discovered me and said the bull had been found while I was in hiding. Gad!" he said with sudden thought. "That was forty years ago. I'm old." He poured more kirsch into his tankard.

"Too old to see the foundation before supper?" asked Kean.

Gunnar paused in drinking. "The foundation is laid?"

Kean took the glass from Gunnar and pulled him to his feet. "Lorraine. Lexi."

Curious, the women followed the men outside. They crossed the cart path and passed the barn to the other side of a large corral.

Gunnar stopped in his tracks to stare at the outlined foundation. Unexpected tears swelled. "It's as if I can see their house."

"It might not be as large," said Kean.

Gunnar walked the outline. "That doesn't matter." He glanced back to the main house, the guest house, and the foundation. "I never thought to see any of this again." He wiped away tears. Lorraine hugged him.

"We hope to have it finished by the fall," said Kean. "The furnishings will be for you and Lorraine to choose."

Lexi sniffled back tears of joy, as she came on the other side to hug Gunnar. Not often did the stalwart knight display such tender feelings.

"Supper!" Brita shouted from the main house.

They shared stories, laughter, and memories late into the night. When Lexi finally retired, she lay in bed and stared out the window. Stars filled the clear night sky. Her heart overflowed with joy and a sense of belonging not experienced in Sener. She couldn't fault Axel or Alicia for her inability to assimilate. They exhibited great patience. Gunnar believed maintaining the same structure as in Kranston, could help during transition. Like always, Lorraine listened and provided counsel. The one person who didn't coddle her, was Nollen. True, he publicly showed respect due to her royal station, yet was forthright when dealing person-to-person. Their journey together was just beginning. For tonight, the warmth of fellowship gave way to a peaceful sleep.

Chapter 8

THE FOLLOWING MORNING, LEXI ARRIVED IN THE KITCHEN TO hear Nollen speak to Kean, Gunnar, and Arnie. Lorraine helped Brita with breakfast. Lexi silently joined the women while she listened to Nollen.

"Researching the royal archives, I discovered your family's farm once held a high place among those given a royal grant for agriculture. In fact, your ancestor, Sir Obed, served as the head of the agricultural guild before the coup. Axel wants to issue another such grant, yet I advised against it … for now," Nollen stressed when Kean went to object. "Favoritism must be avoided. However, the seeds are the highest quality found in the royal granary. This year's harvest should produce a great enough yield that no one will object to your family once again providing for the King's table."

"I told you he's a shrewd one," Gunnar commented to Kean.

"Our journey here proved that," Arnie said.

Kean simply nodded, more interested in talking crops with Nollen. "We once had cherry trees to produce kirsch. Papa managed to bring a few saplings we planted in the orchard at Kranston. Is there any way to get a dozen saplings? Perhaps trade for them?"

"It can take five to ten years to produce fruit," said Gunnar.

"In the meantime, we can rebuild the fermenting barn and purchase or barter for local cherries," Kean countered.

"I'll see what can be done when I go to Stellan today," said Nollen.

The statement disturbed Lexi. "We're leaving already?"

Her harshness caught Nollen off-guard. "No. Agreements take days. I thought you would remain here while I tend to business."

She relaxed. "Aye."

Nollen left for Stellan right after breakfast, so Lexi joined the women in various projects. The men prepared the field for wheat while Eb and Hans repaired the chicken coop, chopped wood, and fetched water. The cool morning turned into a pleasant spring day for such labor. The younger children scampered about the farm. Trying to corral them for a task proved more difficult than at Kranston.

Lexi became short of breath from chasing them. She pulled up alongside Giselle, who hoed the house garden. "I don't remember them having this much energy." She spoke between breaths of recovery.

"There are no walls or prohibitions. What lies before them is open space." Giselle motioned to the land. "Even the boys and Arnie revel in the ability to hunt unafraid." She leaned on the hoe to stare west. "Watching the sun rise and set is even different."

"Freedom," said Lexi.

"Aye. Something we never thought to experience. Each night, we thank Gott for it, and embrace the next day with appreciation. The work needed to bring back the farm is done with love and enthusiasm I cannot even describe."

"No need. It is self-evident. There is a sense of peace and contentment … unlike Kranston." A tone of complaint crept into Lexi's voice, which made Giselle curious. She hastily added, "Not that there wasn't unity then. Just different …" Frustration made her stop.

"I understand," began Giselle kindly. "We often discuss the contrasts between here and Kranston." She touched Lexi's shoulder to get her full attention. "Nothing has been lost to us. Instead, the bond has deepened, as we gain a greater appreciation for Gott and each other because of our past. Now, since I lost my helper, plant the carrot seeds while I hoe." She went back to work. "How is Alicia? Is she experiencing morning sickness?"

"No, at least she hasn't complained."

"She rarely does."

"Aye. She is well settled in Sener."

Giselle paused at hearing annoyance. "You haven't?"

Lexi shrugged, as she focused on planting.

"Why?"

"I don't know. It's not like here. Open, comfortable. Rather stuffy and cold. Well, court etiquette. Axel has changed too."

"He's king. Did you expect him to remain the same?"

Again, Lexi shrugged. She covered the seeds with dirt as she went.

"Does he behave differently towards you?"

"No!" Lexi quickly insisted. "He's still Axel in that respect."

Giselle stopped hoeing. "Does that trouble you?"

"No. Why should it?"

"You sound resentful."

Lexi sighed and sat on the stump of a tree cut down for planting. "Not resentful. Frustrated."

Giselle joined Lexi. "Why?"

"During my short time here, I sense the peace, contentment, and appreciation you mentioned. Sener is cold, impersonal. Oh, the people are welcoming and hospitable when I visit the marketplace, but to them I am a princess, not Lexi."

"You were born a princess."

"You don't understand! The freedom I thought to find is devoid in Sener."

"I find that surprising. Especially knowing Axel and Alicia."

"Not them! The city. The castle. The lifestyle is so drastically different." Exasperation made her words come fast and furious. "No matter how hard I try, I don't fit in. Neither Axel nor Alicia understands. Though, Gott bless them, they try. I'm grateful Axel agreed to this journey. I needed to get away. To experience a sense of true freedom. To consider the direction of my life." When Lexi wiped the tears from her cheeks, Giselle embraced her.

"Axel loves you. So does Alicia. We love you." Giselle kissed Lexi's head. "Put aside all fear and rest. Gott will show you what you need."

Later, in the afternoon, prior to supper, Lexi saw Nollen in the corral where he unsaddled Alydar. She leaned on the rail to speak. "How was trading?"

"Marginal, but that is normal for the first day. I'll make more headway tomorrow. How was your day?" He left the corral carrying his crossbow, quiver, and saddlebags.

"Fun, actually. I hadn't realized how much I missed planting crops."

He chuckled. "I'm going to clean up for supper. Unless everyone has eaten?"

"No. It will be ready soon."

"Good. I'm hungry." He headed for the house.

Alydar and Sheba came to greet Lexi. She stroked Sheba's blaze. "Such a beautiful horse. I have never seen your coloring before. Almost copper with white contrast. You are much more agreeable to ride than Sami. Only don't tell her I said that." She then scratched Alydar's cheek. "Noble Alydar. I share Nollen's disappointment that you can no longer speak. You gave such wisdom." She placed her forehead against his muzzle. "I could use some now."

Alydar softly grunted.

"Humans can also offer wisdom." Gunnar held two cups.

Alydar tossed his head in a nod. He and Sheba moved off.

"Cider." Gunnar gave Lexi a cup. He leaned against the fence. "You are not the only one at a crossroad in life."

"I know. I witnessed your reaction to the house." She used the cup to motion toward the foundation. "Will you really leave Axel for retirement?"

He flashed a tender smile. "That is a question I continually ask myself. Especially since this." He pointed to the facial scar. "Though my dedication to him will never waver, reflexes slow with age. Gott's grace kept it from being worse."

She gripped his arm. "You would be greatly missed."

"Sener is only a two-day ride. Visiting works both ways."

"I would be here frequently."

"However, the decision is not yet made. It won't be without speaking to Axel."

Lexi stared at the western skyline. "Giselle is right. The sunsets are different, though just as beautiful."

"Supper!" Lorraine called from the threshold.

For three more days, Lexi helped at the farm while Nollen went to Stellan. They spent the evenings in merry conversation, friendly competition between the men, and mending or sewing for the women. At night, Lexi retired, happy and satisfied.

Very early on the fifth morning, Lexi quietly slipped out of the house. Fully dressed, she went to chicken coop that faced east. The first grey light of day broke over the horizon. She forgot a cloak. A brisk breeze made her fold her arms for warmth. She flinched in surprise when someone placed a cloak over her shoulder; Nollen, fully dressed, including a cloak.

"Sorry. I saw you leave and thought you might get cold."

"Thank you." She closed the clasp.

"Why are you up so early?"

"All my life I watched the sunset, rarely a sunrise. The ending of a day, but not the beginning," she spoke in a tone of thoughtfulness.

Nollen regarded her more than the dawn. "What do you see?"

Her eyes fixed on the sunrise. "Life. Renewed hope."

"Interesting." He studied the horizon. "For years, we feared the rising and setting."

"Why?" she asked with concern.

"Black Jackals came out at night while harpys dominated the day. Dawn and twilight were the favored times for hunting. Useful tools of the enemy." His brows leveled in disturbed recollection.

She touched his arm. "They are gone."

He grinned at her consolation. "Aye. Now, I use the sun as a time for travel." He picked up his saddlebags, quiver, and crossbow.

She hadn't noticed them on the ground beside him. "Stellan? Or are we leaving?"

"Stellan. Tomorrow we leave." He saw her frown. "Have you changed your mind about the journey?"

"No. I will miss the farm."

"It's not as if you can't come back for a visit," he teased.

"True." She escorted him to the corral. "Any news on the cherry trees?"

A clever gleam rose in his eyes. "I may have something later." He placed a finger to his lips and winked. "The others are awake. Remember," he made the silent sign again.

Later in the morning, a brief rain shower spoiled the younger children's attempt to gather the eggs. Other chores continued uninterrupted. With the seed planting complete, work on the house for Gunnar and Lorraine became the day's focus for the men.

After luncheon, they left the main house intent on returning to construction when the sounds of harness and horses caught attention. Nollen rode ahead of two wagons. A dozen men walked beside the wagons.

"That's a tree!" said Hans about the object in the first wagon.

"A rather big tree." Kean moved to view the second wagon. "Saplings." He, Gunnar, Arnie, and the boys hurried to greet Nollen. "What is this?"

"A cherry tree. Six years old and producing fruit. Plus, four saplings. Two more mature trees will be delivered next week."

"How did you manage that?" asked Kean, astonished.

"Gorman's cousin, Lord Philbert, is building a new house, and the cherry trees were in the way. So, instead of destroying them, I convinced him to let me move them here."

Gunnar heartily laughed and slapped Nollen's leg. "Lad, you never cease to amaze me."

"At what cost?" asked Kean, now concerned.

"Where should we plant them?" a man asked.

"Arnie, show them the old orchard," Kean instructed. He took hold of Alydar's bridle to speak confidential to Nollen. "Tell me the amount, and I will reimburse you."

"There is no cost. Well," Nollen admitted to Kean's contrary gaze, "for the trees. I paid the workers. A business expense of the crown. I needed them to load three wagons for transport to Sener. A few pennies more, and they agreed to plant the trees."

Kean held back his emotions. "Your generosity is overwhelming. I cannot …"

Nollen held Kean's shoulder. "Send me the first bottle of kirsch. That will be enough."

While Kean headed for the orchard, Nollen steered Alydar to the corral. Gunnar accompanied him. By now, the women saw the trees. Giselle, Brita, and Lorraine joined Kean and Arnie at the orchard. Lexi knowingly smiled at Nollen. He winked at her before he unsaddled Alydar, and she went to join the others.

"Why do I suspect that Lexi knew your plan?" asked Gunnar with suspicion. When Nollen simply chuckled, Gunnar said, "She told me about leaving tomorrow."

Nollen brushed Alydar. "My business is concluded. Time to head for Zorin. When do you and Lorraine plan to leave? Or will you stay?" Gunnar hesitated to answer, which made Nollen pause in grooming. "You are just as reluctant to leave as Lexi. The reason is obvious." He used the brush to motion to the construction.

Gunnar fondly regarded the house and land. "This place holds so many memories." His focus came to rest on Nollen. "Lad, I grow old and slow.

"Kean is older. And if his abilities are any indication of slowing down, you have nothing to worry about."

Gunnar stopped Nollen from returning to Alydar. "Kean isn't a knight. For me, being slow can get people killed."

The seriousness concerned Nollen. "Have you spoken to Axel about this?"

"Not yet. I want my mind settled first. If you return to Sener before me, say nothing."

"Of course. But my earlier return is doubtful since I am on circuit."

The answer pleased Gunnar. He took the brush from Nollen and placed it aside. "Come. There is a tradition in our family to dedicate a newly planted tree."

With all the men working together, planting took an hour. The women brought refreshment at the completion of the task. After the workers left, Kean took a bottle of kirsch from Brita.

"This tree is one more sign of a new beginning. As such, we dedicate it to Gott." Kean carefully began pouring kirsch onto the roots as he continued speaking. "From its first fruits comes a sweet offering. May Gott bless it with a plenteous harvest for people to enjoy, fruit to eat, and kirsch to gladden the heart. May its shade provide a respite for the weary. Its branches a shelter for birds and animals." He stopped pouring. "As long as it blooms, we shall remember this day in gratitude to Gott, and our friend, by whose hand it was delivered. To you, Nollen." He saluted and took a drink from the bottle then handed it to Nollen for him to drink. Kean happily announced, "Tonight, we celebrate, and send you off in the morning with a blessing."

Lexi took hold of Nollen's arm for the walk back to the house. "You're a good man, Nollen of Far Point. I look forward to seeing what else you do to help people."

Chapter 9

Zorin, the capital city of the Halvor Territory, was located just south of the foothills leading into the Halvor Mountain Range. The Halvorians proved most gracious in hospitality, and willing to make trade deals. After spending a few days there, Nollen and Lexi headed west for Ganel Territory.

On the second day of the journey, they took a break from riding to walk the horses through a blooming meadow. Lexi gazed north to the mountains. Snow remained on the highest peaks. "I hadn't realized how much I missed the mountains."

"I have never ventured into the Halvors. There are tales of terrifying creatures that roam the mountains," Nollen commented.

"Those creatures are long gone," said Callie. The she-wolf walked between them.

"Have you seen any?" asked Lexi.

"No, before my time. I too only know of them by reputation. Alydar could have answered you better."

Alydar whinnied and chomped in affirmation.

Nollen stroked Alydar's neck. "Were the creatures feared by the First Ones?"

Alydar again whinnied and tossed his head in affirmative.

"I faced a few of those before."

Alydar grunted, chomped at the bit, and nudged Nollen.

"I think he is scolding you for being overconfident," Lexi teased. Alydar nodded. Even Sheba made a horse sound for amusement. "She finds it funny, too."

Nollen spotted a few boulders in the meadow near a stream. "There's a good place for lunch." He grabbed his saddlebag. He and Lexi sat on a boulder. Alydar and Sheba drank from the stream then grazed on the spring grass.

"Hold the bread while I cut the apple and sausage." Nollen gave Lexi two small flat loaves. Once cut, he placed slices of apple and sausage on each loaf, which could be folded for ease of eating. "Wait," he said when she held one out to him. He reached into the bag to pull out a jar. "Highland mustard. Made from the seeds of a bush that only grows in the Halvor foothills. Lucky, I could secure a jar."

"Mustard with apple?"

"Made with a touch of honey to compliment the sausage and apple." He used his knife to carefully spread the mustard. He gently wiped the blade with a finger to enjoy the excess before he placed it aside. "Try a bite."

Lexi's eyes grew wide with delight. "This is delicious!" she said with a mouthful. "Each new taste and dish bring greater appreciation of why Axel made you Royal Commissary."

"Thank you. However, I can't take all the credit. I learned much from my father, grandfather, and Jonas." He sighed with sobriety at the mention of Jonas. "I still miss him. Things have been hard for Sharla and the boys."

Callie sat and placed a paw on Nollen's lap. "You honor him by using what he taught."

Nollen patted Callie's head in gratitude. He turned at Lexi's touch and grinned at her sympathy. "Let's finish eating so we can reach Mathena by nightfall."

He refilled his flask before placing it on the saddle. He noticed Lexi crouch down and carefully reach her hand toward a rabbit. She spoke in a soft voice. Amused, he leaned on the saddle to watch. The rabbit inched close enough to sniff her hand, and even allowed her to stroke its head.

"I've never seen a rabbit willingly come so close."

Her movement to his speech startled the rabbit. It hopped away. "You scared it."

"Normally, I would set a trap to eat it."

"I told it not to be afraid, and it wasn't. Even let me pet it. Although, it didn't reply."

Nollen heartily laughed. "Not all animals talk."

She flushed with embarrassment. "How do you know which ones can or can't?"

He had difficulty calming down from merriment. Alydar did another admonishing snort. "Sorry. It was funny," Nollen said to Alydar.

Callie explained. "Only the First Ones are blessed with speech. Wolves, unicorns, eagles, ravens, bears, and lions. We were created to protect Eldar. The rest of nature is silent—in regard to speaking with humans."

"I have never seen a bear or raven," began Nollen. "Although, I heard tales of bears inhabiting the mountains, and stories about elusive ravens. Crows constantly cause problems."

Lexi flinched with discomfort and asked Callie, "You said lions. I only know Othniel."

Callie ears laid back to display sorrow. "He is the last. Many were slain in the battle to try and stop Oleg's downfall. The same with the bears, yet some are believed to have fled when seriously wounded. With defeat near, Bardolf and Alfgar convinced Othniel to withdraw because of his importance. Over the centuries, lions, and wolves were hunted at the direction of the Electors. My pack, the Halvor Wolves, hid deep in the mountains while Bardolf took his pack to The Doane to watch over Nollen's ancestors."

"Bardolf knew back then?" asked Nollen in surprise.

"All the First Ones knew Oleg divided the Six Treasures between the remaining priests for safekeeping. Alfgar remained in Ganel, the eagles guarded the Halvors and Freelands. None dare venture into Ha'tar or Nefal because of the dragons, harpys, and black jackals. What became of the first ravens after the battle, no one knows."

"Were harpys and jackals created after the First Ones?" asked Lexi.

"No. They came with the invaders, just like the dragons," Callie chided.

This time, Lexi visibly shivered and rubbed her arms to ward off the sudden chill.

"What's wrong?" asked Nollen with concern.

She shook her head with uncertainty. "I'm not sure. I feel cold uneasiness when speaking of harpys, jackals, and ravens. Not something I sense with other animals. Yet, Callie said ravens helped protect Eldar."

"You sense other animals? How?" Nollen asked, curious.

Uncertain, Lexi shrugged. "I don't know. Lately, I sense many things I can't fully explain."

Nollen reached over to take her hand. "Don't let it unsettle you. Some answers take time. I learned that from my grandfather." He gathered the reins to mount. "We need to pick up the pace to cross the causeway before nightfall."

Several hours passed in silence. They switched between galloping and walking the horses, though remained in the saddle. At the slower gaits, Lexi took in the magnificent surroundings of Halvor. The vastness of the region exceeded Kranston a hundredfold. During the quieter times, her mind reflected on the journey. Nollen tried to encourage her with his council of waiting for answers, yet the sensations grew stronger. Good and pleasant, or cold and disturbing, she keenly felt everything. On this trip, she sensed the land along with the people. She reveled in delight at the changes in Kean and his family. To see their heritage restored, warmed her heart.

In Zorin, she experienced the kindness of strangers. Of course, Mayor Loren knew her identity from his visits to Sener. He respected the desire for anonymity, thus introduced her as Nollen's traveling companion and fellow trader. Now, they headed for Mathena, home of the Ganels, and the noble unicorns. The thought made her regard Alydar, as they rode side-by-side for a walking period.

"I wish Alydar could speak again. I would ask how he feels about returning to Ganel, land of the unicorns," she said.

Alydar made several noises. Nollen patted Alydar's neck. "He is proud of his herd. A most noble animal, who I am honored to call friend."

Lexi gasped in astonishment. "What is that? Above the trees."

"The causeway to Mathena. We will use it to cross the Endelos River to the main gate. Around that bend, everything will come into view," Nollen replied.

Lexi watched the horizon in anticipation. Her mouth dropped opened in wordless wonder at the colossal aqueduct. Water cascaded from the upper elevation of the river to continue south. Small figures of human, horses, and wagons appeared near, and on, the aqueduct. The enormous city of Mathena sparkled with crystalline brilliance. The walls stretched along a plateau beyond the aqueduct. Ornate arches, and decorated roofs told of different levels that spiraled up to the apex.

Nollen watched Lexi's reaction. "Like Sener, the castle is at the top. Lord Ronan's home, when he comes to Mathena. Lord Cormac's residence is near the castle. We will stay with him."

By late afternoon, they reached the smaller bridge that crossed to the isthmus, which divided the river between Ganel and Halvor. This helped to keep the incline of the aqueduct from being too steep.

"I will not join you in Mathena," said Callie.

"Why?" asked Lexi.

"Let's just say, I prefer the forest." Callie trotted off.

The aqueduct served as the main water supply to Mathena with channels on either side of the causeway. A wrought iron fence separated the channels from the traffic. The thoroughfare proved large enough to accommodate wagons and riders even riding three across.

Due to traffic noise, Nollen leaned toward Lexi to speak in a loud voice. "We left Mathena this way for the final confrontation at Sener. That is when I learned something I never expected of Gunnar. He's afraid of heights."

She laughed. "I knew that. Even at Kranston, he never got too close to the western edge, and found ways to avoid standing lookout on the rampart.

"Come to think of it, he did stay back when I surveyed the route from Kranston."

Nearing the gate, Nollen nodded to the watchmen. In turn, they saluted him.

"You are well known," Lexi wryly comment.

Nollen led the way through winding street up to various levels. It took almost an hour to reach the apex. By then, the soft hues of daylight faded. Nollen pointed out the castle when he steered Alydar down an adjacent street. He stopped before a grand city home with an enclosed courtyard. He dismounted and rang a bell. Shortly, two Ganel grooms appeared.

"Master Nollen, welcome."

"Ivor." Nollen took his saddlebags and crossbow. He waited for Lexi to retrieve her bags and weapons. "Treat them well," he instructed Ivor. He pushed open the door, which led to a smaller courtyard.

Another Ganel greeted them. This one had rank, as told by his clothes. "Master Nollen, Lord Cormac is expecting you. He is in the drawing room. I will take your things to the rooms."

Cormac sat before the hearth reading. Jenna worked on needlepoint. "My lord. My lady." Nollen bowed.

"Nollen. Lexi. Welcome." Cormac set the book aside. "I assume you have not yet dined."

"No, we came straightway," replied Nollen.

"Excellent. Dinner will be in an hour. Refresh yourselves until then."

Lexi flushed with mild embarrassment. "I brought nothing but traveling clothes."

Jenna sweetly smiled. "I can help with that." She took Lexi's arm to leave.

Later, Nollen arrived in the private dining room, refreshed and wearing fresh clothes. Cormac stood at the sideboard where he poured a reddish liquid from a decanter. He gave Nollen a glass.

"I came across some information about Bertrand that you will find interesting. May require more research, but a start," said Cormac.

Nollen swallowed a sip. "After I conclude the annual business, I can give it my full attention." He smacked his lips and admired the glass. "Not until after the banquet, did I understand what Alicia meant about this being helpful. She said it calmed morning sickness."

Lexi and Jenna arrived. For the first time since leaving Sener, Lexi wore a lavender gown with dark purple accents, and her hair styled. Nollen raised the glass in salute. She bashfully blushed at the gesture.

"You too wear different clothes," she said.

"The guest wardrobes are filled with clothes to accommodate any occasion."

"So, I have learned."

Cormac gave Lexi and Jenna filled glassed. "Ganel sherry," he told Lexi. "Shall we sit? He held the chair for Jenna while Nollen did the same for Lexi. After a blessing, Cormac rang for the meal to be served.

Lexi observed the food. "Although I know Ganels refuse to eat meat, I do not recall having Ganel cuisine at Sener."

"You will be surprised by the wonderful tastes and textures," Nollen said.

"Thank you," Cormac said. "Ganels enjoy dining as much as anyone. One of our joys is to take the bounty Gott provides and make them pleasurable for eating."

Lexi eagerly tasted the various dishes. "These are delicious. At Kranston, we were limited in what we could grow or trap. Being at high altitude, wheat was impossible to grow, so we used oats and potatoes for bread. In winter, we relied on dried meats, sausage, and root vegetables." Realizing what she said, she spoke apologetically, "No disrespect intended by mentioning meat."

Cormac kindly replied, "No offense taken. We understand dietary preferences."

"Please, tell us more about Kranston. We only know about it from legend," said Jenna.

"Legend is what kept it secret. Along with a constant shroud of fog. At least, that is what it appeared like to outsiders. On most days, we could see very clearly. It offered a spectacular view of, well, Markita." A fond look appeared, as Lexi continued. "I enjoyed watching the sunsets. Looking west, I often wondered what Eldar was like. Would I ever see it? The reality of that possibility grew with Axel's departure. Of course, we didn't know what happened until Gunnar returned with Nollen."

"Now, that you are here in Eldar, has it met expectations?" asked Jenna.

Lexi paused in eating for a moment of consideration. "It is still surreal in many ways. My ancestral home, yet foreign."

Cormac and Jenna appeared thoughtful at the answer, so Nollen interjected. "Which is why Lexi is joining me on the circuit. To see Eldar in all its diversity and beauty."

His intervention gave Lexi time to recover; her smile genuine. "I have already seen the Freelands and Halvors, which are definitely more majestic than the Black Mountains. I look forward to learning about Ganel."

Cormac and Jenna return to a congenial demeanor. "Jenna will serve as your guide to Ganel society. I must help Nollen with business." He raised his glass to Lexi.

Chapter 10

IN THE GUEST QUARTERS AT SENER CASTLE, DYNOS REVIEWED THE new instructions from Rastus. Since Nollen's departure, Lord Ronan tried to accommodate him, but their discussions yielded little results. True, the old agreement with Javan did not expire until the end of the year. However, the earlier discussions began, the better for Bertrand. He compared the new order with the original. Most remained the same, with a few heftier items added should Axel agree to the major change—marriage between Princess Lexi and Prince Felix. He heard rumors that the Princess had left Sener to visit friends. Of course, her absence didn't matter in presenting the new terms. The ultimate decision lay with the King. The only way to know Axel's mind is to present the new provision to Lord Ronan.

Dynos placed the papers in a leather folder and tied it closed. He finished donning his formal attire before heading to Ronan's office. All the while, he kept bolstering his self-confidence with past success in negotiations. Still, the one glaring failure kept invading his thoughts. He couldn't let that fact interfere.

He entered the antechamber where he briefly spoke to Ronan's secretary; a standoffish, older Ganel with long grey hair and arrogant gleam in his eyes. He simply nodded at the requested audience. While Dynos waited, he considered the unique races that populated Eldar. Ganels, Ha'tar, Nefal, and humans. His consideration didn't last long when the Ganel returned.

"Lord Ronan will see you." He escorted Dynos into the primary office.

Ronan gazed out a window with his hands clasped behind his back. Only his profile visible in a posture which suggested tolerance.

Dynos offered the Bertrand bow and salute. "Thank you for agreeing to speak with me on such short notice."

Ronan just turned his head toward Dynos. "Lyron told me it is important."

"My lord King Rastus sent a new proposal. Before presenting it to His Majesty King Axel, I value your opinion on the addition."

Ronan fully turned to face Dynos. "As I told you last time, final negotiations must wait for the Commissary's return. I know, Sir Hastins supplied a list of available items."

"This is not something for the Commissary's consideration."

The statement brought Ronan from the window to confront Dynos. "How so?"

"Please, read the communiqué." He withdrew the formal letter from the folder.

Ronan read with stoic features that quickly turned to incredulity.

Dynos steeled himself against the reaction. "Your opinion, my lord?"

"A bold and stunning request under the circumstances, Ambassador!"

"King Rastus hopes that the offer of his son to wed King Axel's sister will be taken as a sign of goodwill," Dynos offered in hasty explanation.

"Or make amends for your failure to secure a bride for Bertrand's heir!"

Dynos' eyes widened in shock.

The reaction not lost on Ronan, who continued his rebuke. "Do you believe Eldar would go blindly into negotiations with a former ally of the Electors?"

With wounded pride, Dynos gathered his composure. "Bertrand never offered a royal marriage to any Elector! We would not pollute our sacred line with imposters. The heritage of our kings is unbroken and predates Eldar. It is you, who should be honored by this offer."

Ronan's anger nearly crumpled the paper. Dynos snatched it away before serious damage done. Ignoring protocol, Dynos marched from the office to his quarters. He tossed the folder on the bed. He muttered angry words in Bertrandian. His failure came back to haunt him and could end an important negotiation before it began! He could not allow it. He quickly sat at the desk and composed two letters. In the first he wrote:

Vizier Cadmus,

Due to recent developments regarding Rastus' latest request, I feel I must implement the alternative we discussed prior to my departure. One way or another, Bertrand will benefit from an alliance with Eldar.

Your Obedient Servant,
Dynos.

The second letter contain only these words:

Execute immediately! Quarry on move.
D

He double sealed both letters as an official document then summoned the Bertrandian messenger with instructions for immediate dispatch.

Ronan regained his temper before he called upon Axel. Unfortunately, the King kept company with the Queen, Lady Lorraine, and Sir Gunnar in the private salon. The couple returned yesterday from their visit to the Freelands. This could not wait.

Ronan entered to the sound of laughter and humorous voices. No matter when or where, the news would come as a great shock. For the sake of Alicia and Lorraine, he forced a pleasant expression. "Sire. Majesty. My lord and lady." He bowed.

"Ronan," cheered Axel in merriment. "Join us. Lorraine and Gunnar are telling of their visit to the family farm."

Ronan made a polite decline. "I'm afraid my coming is not for enjoyment, Sire."

Though visibly disappointed, Axel nodded with understanding. He told Alicia and Lorraine, "Duty of a monarch is never done. Excuse me."

"Sir Gunnar, also," Ronan added.

Once in an adjacent room, Ronan tried to find words to broach the subject. "Forgive the intrusion, but I had to speak with you before Dynos."

"I appreciate you dealing with him during Nollen's absence. Gott knows he is a handful." Axel wryly chuckled.

"The latest development is outside of Nollen's expertise."

Gunnar observed Ronan's uneasiness. "Which deeply disturbs you."

"Aye. Rastus sent Dynos a new offer to present … There is no easy way to say it other than direct. A royal marriage between his son, Felix and Lexi."

Axel's joviality instantly changed to indignation with narrow eyes and flexed jowls.

"I made certain Dynos understood it is a bold request," Ronan hastily said. "Again, I wanted to tell you before he could."

Gunnar's warning grip on his arm, made Axel restrain his temper. "Inform Ambassador Dynos, I will not speak to him on this matter until I have given it prayerful consideration. Until then, he is to remain in his apartment. Meals, and all other necessities, will be brought to him."

"Sire, he might consider such undue restrictions—" began Ronan in dispute when Axel raised a hand to stop further speech.

Axel softened his tone. "Forgive me, the anger is not directed at you. Quite the contrary. I appreciate your efforts with Dynos. I sense something beyond this offer, which troubles me. I must discern the source before we proceed further."

"It could be the same uneasiness we Ganels experienced when Dynos arrived. What drove Cormac to the archives."

Axel stroked his beard. "Nollen will research past agreements with Bertrand when he reaches Mathena. Hopefully, he and Cormac will discover the answer."

"We don't know when Nollen will arrive nor how long he needs. Ronan may be right about Dynos. You can't keep him confined for too long," said Gunnar.

"Dispatch a shield owl to Cormac, and inquire about Nollen's arrival," Axel told Gunnar.

"Should I mention this—?"

"No! I want nothing to interfere with Lexi's journey. This is too important for her. And Nollen."

Gunnar clapped his sword in acknowledgement. "Consider it done."

Axel gave Ronan a friendly pat on the shoulder. "I do not envy you speaking to Dynos."

"My sworn duty is to you and Eldar. Any personal feelings in the execution of that duty, is negligible."

"Those feelings have served well."

Ronan slyly grinned. "I would tell you if it is necessary."

"I depend upon it. Now, to consider what I tell Alicia and Lorraine."

"The truth. Women have an uncanny intuition about marriage."

Axel laughed in a teasing manner. "Is that why you are still single?"

Ronan's expression held a mischievous hint. "Not for long."

"Oh, ho! There is someone?"

"We wait for the spring, when the flowers are in bloom to grace the wedding with Gott's creation. All Ganels marry in Spring and Summer. Men do so throughout the year."

"For us, the season doesn't matter, as Gott blesses each union."

"True. We simply enjoy the bounty of nature to remind us of life."

Axel returned the mischievous grin. "You're stalling."

Ronan changed his demeanor in the walk from the royal wing to the guest quarters. Along the way, he called for the captain of the guard. He could not fault Axel for the order. If he had a sister, he might consider doing the same. Her future, and the that of the kingdom's foreign relation, rested on the decision. Which is more important? The consequences and scenarios of either choice were deeply troubling.

He made a sharp rap on the door. "Ambassador Dynos!"

When Dynos appeared in the threshold, he noticed the guards with Ronan. "Am I arrested?"

"No. However, until His Majesty decides upon the matter of this latest request, you are to remain in these quarters. Should you require anything, inform Captain Erhard for prompt compliance."

Dynos received the answer with grim reservation. "Confinement. I thought better of this King than the Electors."

Ronan's ire flared. "The unprecedented move by Bertrand is to blame! There is not even a basic relation between our countries, yet you seek a privileged alliance by royal marriage. Take care not to further provoke Eldar." He waved at Erhard, who jerked the door closed to shut in Dynos. "Captain, he is not to step one foot out this door! Any trouble, tell me."

Chapter 11

IN THE MIDDLE OF NEFAL TERRITORY, STOOD THE ONCE PROUD CITY of Ogun. Alliance with the Electors cost the Nefal dearly. Many stone buildings lay in ruins. Only half the remaining homes were occupied. Slowly the city recovered with commerce. Still, the Nefal went humbly about their daily business.

Inside a recently built home of stone and timber, Maro sat at the kitchen table for supper. Bodil waited on him while Brynn joined her father in eating. Once finished, Maro shoved the plate away. When he rose, so did Brynn, despite food remaining on her plate. Maro took the tankard and left. Brynn and Bodil dutifully followed him to the living room.

Maro sneered when he discovered someone sitting in his cushioned chair before the fire. He saw the back of the individual's head. "Who?"

The Nefal stood and faced the chief.

"Spoor?"

"What is left of me."

Brynn and Bodil mirrored Maro's surprise. "How did you survive? We heard all were killed," said Brynn.

"Being killed in battle would have been preferable to those executed."

Recovered from the momentary shock, Maro grew impatient. "That is not an answer." He pushed past Spoor to take a seat in the chair.

"They left me for dead. I woke up the next day in a pile of Nefal bodies. I managed to crawl away and waited until nightfall to escape."

"Doubtful you could see any better at night with that wound," grumbled Maro.

"I either stumbled my way in the dark or stayed to be executed."

"Where have you been these past few years?" Brynn asked.

"First recovering, then hiding. Disgusted by what has become of Nefal!"

"We are lucky to be alive," Maro countered with a tone of dejection.

"You call this lucky? Everything sacred destroyed, and the rubble left to remind us of a humiliating defeat?" When Maro faced the hearth, Spoor continued. "The old and weak may consider it lucky, but not warriors."

"There are no more warriors!" Maro roughly snapped.

"So, you beg, plead, and bargain with men for a meager existence? We live in shame. Our temple in ruins. Spears used to till the ground. These hands are made for war not farming."

"Take care, Spoor," Brynn warned.

Maro stood to confront Spoor. "What do you expect us to do? We have no more homeland. We abandoned that when we came to Eldar in support of Lorcan's coup!"

"I have a plan to give us back our dignity. To bring Axel to his knees!" Spoor clenched his fist in Maro's face.

"Rebellion? Are you mad? Get out!" Maro abruptly waved.

Spoor didn't move. The left side of his face twisted in a warped smile. "We do not need rebellion. Men are sentimental weaklings. Strike at Axel's heart, and he will crumble."

"You underestimate the Son of Eldar. Same as Argus did."

Irate at the reminder, Spoor lashed out. "I was at Sener that day! Argus sacrificed himself to protect others."

"What you suggest is dangerous!"

"More dangerous than continuing to neglect our gods?"

"The gods expelled us." Maro scowled and took a long drink.

"Spoor is right," began Bodil. "We might have suffered for neglect, but Axel defiled our gods when he ordered the temple and other sacred buildings destroyed."

Maro's resistance waivered. "We have no resources for rebellion."

"We need none. At least none that can be traced back to Nefal." Spoor's lopsided smile again appeared. "There are allies, who also wish revenge and are willing to help."

Maro sarcastically laughed. "The majority of Ha'tar are gone. Only a group smaller than us remain to train dragons for defense."

"At least, they had a homeland to go back to," Bodil chided.

Spoor made a whistle. From a far back corner of the room, a cloaked hunched figure advanced. Spoor pushed back the hood to reveal a creature part man, part troll dressed in primitive clothes of animal skins and leather. The helmet made from animal hide had slits over the eyes. Its nose flattened and mouth overly large with pointy teeth. It reeked of decay.

Maro, Brynn, and Bodil recoiled at the stench.

"What is that cursed creature doing here?" demanded Maro.

"The Cursians are our allies," replied Spoor.

"I am Borka. The Son of Eldar killed my brother when he trespassed Altwald. We will do whatever the Nefal ask to take revenge!" He spoke with some difficulty in breathing.

"My lord, I have served you faithfully, so I beg you to hear me," Bodil began. "As smallest of my family, I was groomed for matters other than war. First your apprentice, now your aid. I lost my father, brothers, and an uncle that day. Since then, I have petitioned the gods to restore our honor. The means may not be to our liking, but this may be the answer!" His fervency grew. "Our people are dying! In here!" He tapped his chest. "Their spirit is trampled. There is little hope past scratching in the dirt to grow food or raise hogs to feed the fat bellies of men!"

Borka joined the argument. "Nefal at least have homes, land, and light! Oleg's curse confined us to a dark forest with few creatures to feed our offspring. Since the Son of Eldar's coronation, Altwald is dying. The trees and plants wither, which make the animals of darkness leave. My people starve. A few have ventured beyond Altwald in search of food. None returned. Whether killed by men or victims of the curse, we do not know." He motioned up to Spoor. "Lord Spoor saved me from men when I tried to hunt outside Altwald. Each day I remain outside, my energy drains." Distress manifested on his face and labored breathing.

"Then why come here?" asked Brynn.

"For my life, I am duty bound to Lord Spoor until the debt is paid. Yet more, if it will help the Cursians survive."

"I did so with stealth. No one saw me." Spoor spoke with assurance at the visible concern of his fellow Nefal.

Weary from standing, Maro sat.

"Da?" asked Brynn.

Maro sighed with resignation. "They make good argument. I have lived under seven Electors. In those days, Nefal were feared." He sternly glared at Spoor. "If your plan is not well thought out, I will gut you here and now rather than see Nefal totally disgraced."

An hour later, Bodil left with Spoor. Maro paced with his head bent and brows etched in disturbed consideration.

With trepidation, Brynn asked, "Why did you agree to Spoor's plan?"

He waved her close. His low voice thick with warning. "Spoor's return is deeply concerning. He remains respected and feared among the populous. Bodil is proof of that. If his talk of rebellion spreads past these walls, the consequences will be deadly for Nefal."

"The same if he fails!"

With heavy sobriety, he spoke. "You must be my eyes and ears with Spoor. Try to mitigate the consequences while I work with others to undermine his influence."

"Why not send word of this to Axel?"

Irked by the suggestion, he rebuffed, "Nefal do not betray our own!"

"You sound as prideful as Spoor." She recoiled at his slap across her face. She fought tears. "Forgive me, Da." She flinched in defense when he reached for her. This time, he held her shoulder.

"Daughter," he began formally. "The time will come when I am gathered to the gods, and you will be chief. The law and code of the Nefal must be honored above all else. Go. Find Spoor and Bodil."

Brynn made a short bow. Nearly four years ago, her world changed. Now, it could change again. The rebuffing of her suggestion to inform Axel, left few options. Of paramount importance was how to stop Spoor. Preoccupied by thoughts, she didn't realize where she walked until she heard riotous laughter. She reached the seedier side of Ogun where old warriors and derelicts congregated. More laughter, and a raised voice.

"Spoor," she said in recognition. Conversation stopped when she entered. All eyes turned in her direction. A quick survey showed no other female present. Bodil, three Nefal, and Borka sat at a table with Spoor.

Bodil quickly rose to meet her. "Brynn! You should not be here."

"Why not?" She pushed past him to approach Spoor. "No doubt, you came here looking for recruits. I volunteer."

Spoor stood a few inches taller, thus stared down at her. "I thought Maro disliked my plan. Why go against him?"

"He is old. Thus, leery of anything. Especially something so bold."

"You are not?"

Her glance shifted to the others. "I will be the next chief. If any plan is launched, it will be with my help. Or I will convince my father to bury you."

The Nefal men grumbled at her brashness. Spoor's scowl made his marred face menacing. "You challenge me?"

"No! You challenge my father, and in turn, me."

When Spoor went to strike, Brynn ducked and kneed him in the groin. He rocked back but remained on his feet. She whipped out her dagger to hold up to his face.

"Come at me again, and I will add to your scars."

"Maro taught you well. Put up your blade. You can join us."

"She cannot be trusted," Bodil whispered to Spoor.

"I have never trusted a female. However, they are useful."

Brynn heard yet made no remark or other noticeable indication. Spoor gave in too easily. She would watch her back from now on.

Chapter 12

FOR THREE DAYS, LEXI ACCOMPANIED JENNA ON A TOUR OF Mathena. The Ganels excelled in every area of creativity. They danced with fluid movements to haunting melodies or lively folk music. Art flourished in the city. Pottery, colored glassmaking, intricate ironworks, skillfully crafted woodwork and furniture, even delicate silver and goldsmithing jewelry. All aspects of life incorporated nature.

Although master craftsmen, and willing to share their expertise, the Ganels did so with a self-possessed nature. This came in marked contrast to the gregariousness of Freelanders and Halvorians. As an agricultural region, the Freelanders fit the name of their region, freely giving of their time and sustenance. To the Halvorian Highlanders, hospitality meant life in such a harsh environment. They gave while asking for nothing in return.

After luncheon at a local inn, Jenna took Lexi down an adjacent street. She pointed to a sign over an apothecary shop. "You will find this place very interesting."

"I have found everything interesting," replied Lexi.

"Take heed. Master Alwyn is very old and eccentric, even for a Ganel."

Bells in the threshold rang when pushed by the door to announce entry. Lexi surveyed the interior. Positioned under a window opened to the street, stood a table with a chair on either side. Two sets of scales, a mortar, pestle, block for cutting, and wooden bar with assorted knives were arranged on the table. Along the two side walls, various crocks, jars, and brown glass bottles filled floor-to-ceiling shelves. Directly in front of them stood the counter. A large chest with numerous small drawers dominated a wall behind the counter. Opposite the chest, were more built-in shelves and cubby-holes that contained slips of paper. A walkway between the chest and cubby led further back into the shop. From the ceiling, hung metal racks filled with plants and flowers in different stages of drying. A plethora of scents bombarded the nostrils.

"Master Alwyn. I brought a guest to meet you."

They heard grumbling along with the scraping of furniture. Through the walkway came Alwyn. His long white hair still healthy and supple. He walked slightly bent at the shoulders. The wrinkle-lined face betrayed years of long life. He paused at the counter to regard them, especially Lexi.

She stared into ancient eyes. "I know you. How is that possible?" she spoke in wonder.

His eyes narrowed with concertation. His unspoken question obvious.

Jenna fought a smile to at the exchange then made the introductions. "Master Alwyn. This is Lexi. Sister of the Son of Eldar."

Lexi began to dispute the use of Axel's prophetic title when Alwyn's eyes widened with excitement. He moved quickly around the counter and seized her face between his hands. His piercing blue eyes made the sense of familiarity deepen though she could not move or speak due to his hold.

"You are the Shield Maiden. That is why you feel connected," he said with delight. "Why did you not bring her to me sooner?" He chided Jenna, though he still held Lexi. "You have much to learn, dear one. We shall start with the basics." He released her to disappear into the back.

"I don't understand," Lexi whispered to Jenna, disconcerted.

"Simply listen. Do not be afraid." Jenna softly smiled with reassurance.

"I have faced more dangers than an old man. Just confused."

Alwyn reappeared carrying a tray with two jars, a crock, and measuring spoons. "Come, come, come." He nodded toward the table. Lexi sat opposite him. He studiously regarded her. "Five and twenty, I reckon your human age. A little old to start, but we do what we must."

Jenna carefully shook her head when Lexi sent her an inquiring glance. She motioned Lexi's attention back to Alwyn, as he arranged everything from the tray onto the table.

"Nature is filled with all we need to live, to grow, and to heal. These," he touched each vessel, "are for healing. The most important ingredients you will need." He opened each to take out a piece of the plant to place on the table. "Goldenseal helps to stave off infection. Very important. Comfrey, for pain, and yarrow for swelling. Memorize them."

"I already know some remedies for wounds, bites, and burns."

His seizure of her arm startled her while his intensity, alarming. "These are what the Shield Maiden uses! Others might not work as well."

"I'm sure she will remember," Jenna intervened.

Alwyn frowned at the interruption. "I will show you how to mix them. The proportions must be precise. Watch closely."

Even though Lexi mimicked Alwyn exactly in preparation of the poultice, he made her repeat the process until satisfied.

"Good. Now for internal." He left the table.

Lexi tugged on Jenna's sleeve, so she bent over. "Why are we doing this?"

"I shall explain later."

Alwyn returned with three more crocks. He huffed when he sat.

"Take a moment to catch your breath," Lexi suggested.

"You are kind. A trait the Shield Maiden should exhibit toward all, save the enemy. To them, fierceness must mark your character." He leaned forward. "Never show weakness or fear to the enemy. Remember that."

"I will."

He continued the instruction. "Ginger, skullcap, and feverfew. All can be used individually, but potent when combined to help with fever and infection. Observe, and memorize the amounts."

Again, Lexi repeated the preparation until Alwyn was satisfied. He sat back with a very weary sigh. Jenna held his shoulder.

"Our visit has exhausted you."

"No, no, no." He waved her aside. "There is much she must learn."

"She shall," insisted Jenna. "To that end, Cormac and I are agreed."

Alwyn momentarily stared at Jenna. "Aye." He patted her hand, which remained on his shoulder. "Heed what they say. Gott is with you, Shield Maiden, same as your brother."

Lexi kindly smiled. "Thank you for the lessons."

Alwyn nudged Jenna's arm. "There are small sacks on the counter. Fill them with the preparations." To Lexi, "Remember which is which." He sighed. "I need sleep." He shuffled behind the counter to disappear in the back of the shop.

Outside, Lexi confronted Jenna. "Tell me what that was all about."

Jenna linked arms with Lexi. "There is more to being a Shield Maiden than wielding a sword. Your sense of familiarity with Alwyn shows the awakening of discernment and bond with all that is Eldar. Traits Gott gifts the Shield Maiden for her great task."

"I thought the Shield Maiden just protected the queen." Lexi spoke with thoughtful unction.

"The duty goes well beyond that. As such, training is important. This," she looked over her shoulder to shop, as they walked away, "is just the beginning of what instruction awaits you. To hone your skills and interpret discernment, while strengthening the bond between you and Eldar."

Lexi stopped. "I'm not in Mathena for training! I travel with Nollen to see Eldar."

Jenna again took Lexi's arm to draw her into the shadow of an alleyway. "After the journey is soon enough. Now, please, let us enjoy the rest of the day. Tonight, Cormac and I shall fully explain."

The afternoon of visiting more places passed in a blur, as Lexi's mind wandered back to the encounter with Alwyn. Since leaving Sener, her senses became heightened to the point where she had difficulty masking any reaction. People, nature, sights, sounds, smells all seem to bombard her. She hoped the explanation would help to understand the growing sensations.

Upon returning home, the women found Nollen and Cormac laughing.

"Something must be very amusing," Jenna said.

"Ah! You have returned," said Cormac, amusement still evident in his smile. "Did you enjoy the outing today?" he asked Lexi.

"I think so. Although I remain puzzled about our visit to the apothecary." She shot Jenna a prompting glance.

"What was so unusual about that?" Nollen innocently asked.

"Something to be explained after dinner," Jenna answered.

During the meal, Nollen related several humorous anecdotes from the day's trading, which made Jenna and Cormac laugh. Lexi barely smiled; her mind too preoccupied to give her full attention. She caught Nollen's curious glance. Her genuine smile short-lived.

When they retired to the private parlor, Lexi gave voice to her preoccupation. "I hope now is the time to explain how and why I knew Master Alwyn. And what he meant about my position as Shield Maiden."

"You sensed a connection?" asked Cormac, intrigued.

"Before I made the introductions," Jenna answered with emphasis.

Cormac nodded. "Axel mentioned her growing awareness."

"Axel?" Lexi began the same time Nollen asked Cormac.

"Would that awareness include animals?"

Cormac became intrigued by Nollen's the question. "Indeed. Have you witnessed …?"

At being ignored, Lexi grew insisted. "Never mind the animals. Does Axel know about Master Alwyn? Is that why we went to the apothecary?"

Cormac cocked a wry grin at the terse questions. "You have the same demanding tone and expression when Axel's patience is done."

"That should hardly be surprising."

"Be seated. To hear the explanation," Cormac said when she hesitated.

Lexi sat with fixed expression. Nollen stood beside her, visibly curious.

Cormac began; "Many centuries ago, before men came to Eldar, Ganels lived in harmony with nature. We possess knowledge passed down from Gott and the First Ones. When Gott allowed men to join us, tension naturally arose at the initial meeting. Of course, we would not dispute Gott, and sought to soothe over relations. We opened our university to those among men with unique skills and abilities that could be enriched. Priests, apothecaries, scientists, mathematicians, and princes benefited from Ganel instruction."

Cormac paused to take a drink. "Being so close in daily study, a Ganel princess fell in love with a prince of men. Their love ran so deep, that each convinced their parents such a union would benefit both races. For men, the advantages were obvious. For the Ganels, it meant losing a most important member of our royal family. The one entrusted with Arkin, the eternal sword of truth to protect our Queen and Territory."

"She sounds like a Shield Maiden," said Lexi.

"Indeed. Princess Sarina was our Shield Maiden. She married Prince Hagen, and the line of Oleg began."

"My family," Lexi murmured with astonishment.

Cormac positioned a footstool to sit in front of Lexi. "Sarina passed down the duties of Shield Maiden to her eldest daughter, beginning a tradition that now comes to you."

Lexi tried to comprehend the stunning disclosure. "By your earlier statement, I assume Axel knows."

"Of course. He has tried to be patient and offer encouragement during your transition. Unfortunately, you have been unwilling to listen."

"I didn't know about Sarina. Just the legend of the Shield Maiden. If I had …"

Nollen sat to hold Lexi, as tears of regret choked her words.

Jenna reached over the back of the sofa to gently stroke Lexi's head. "It is not too late."

Lexi wiped away the tears. "Where do I begin?"

"You started in Kranston, with basic instructions from Axel and Gunnar," said Cormac. "Let me ask you a question. When did your sense of awareness take hold?"

Lexi briefly considered. "I have always been aware of my surroundings. As a child, I called it a *hunch*. The only term that seemed appropriate."

"Has the hunch become more acute recently?"

Lexi's brows knitted in recollection. "Aye. At Sener, it became more frequent. I knew no one upon arrival yet became aware of who to avoid and who to trust when wandering the city. During this journey, there have been times I felt overwhelmed by sensations. Especially here in Mathena."

"Don't forget the animals," added Nollen, who then told Cormac and Jenna, "A fierce mastiff becomes a puppy wanting attention, while a wild rabbit comes to her for petting."

"Interesting." Cormac lifted Lexi's chin till their eye met. "Gott gifts the Shield Maiden with keen insight of individuals, nature, and discernment regarding situations. Until one is fully trained, it can be overwhelming. Training will help interpret those sensations, and judge when to act or not act. That is best done here in Mathena, where it all began with Sarina."

Lexi spoke with indecision. "But I journey with Nollen to see Eldar."

"I can continue alone. I've done it before," Nollen graciously said.

Cormac kindly spoke. "Proceed with the journey. Although a Shield Maiden's priority is the Queen, her broader duty is to Eldar. Learn by sight, and sense the provinces, races, and creatures."

"That is the main reason for this journey," Nollen's comment interrupted Cormac.

The Ganel lord continued to Lexi; his tone confident. "Once you have finished, you will want to come back." He nodded to Jenna.

She briefly left and returned with a small black velvet box. She knelt before the sofa to open the lid to reveal an ornately crafted silver amulet with brilliant ruby in the center. "Volker. The Shield Maiden's amulet. The ruby was gifted to Serena by the eagles, taken from deep within the Halvor Mountains. The unicorns empowered it to sense the presence of evil. It glows in warning. Othniel's roar made it indestructible. Even a broadsword will not leave a scratch. The chain forged by Ganel's most renowned silversmith with the strongest metal from the Halvors. We kept it safe since the overthrow." Jenna placed it around Lexi's neck.

"That could explain your sensitivity to animals," Nollen told Lexi.

She regarded Volker. "What are the symbols around the edge?"

"Ancient Ganel. These are words the Shield Maiden speaks when facing the enemy." At Lexi's quizzical look, Jenna to interpret the words. "By Gott's power, I defend Eldar."

"What happens after I say the words?" she asked in anticipation.

"Your discernment will dictate how to use your skills in defense."

"Nothing else? No unnatural powers?"

"Gott will strengthen you to do what is needed at the time. The form is unknown. However," Cormac stressed, "As you acquire knowledge, and increase your skills, wisdom will grow, and guide you on when to act. The most important aspect is faith." He tapped on the amulet. "This is a tool, the same as Arkin, and even the sensations. What determines success or failure, is in your heart, and mind." He pointed to her head and chest. "When you leave Mathena, conceal Volker beneath the collar. This way, you can feel the warmth and begin to learn how to determine the danger before the glow. Eventually, feelings and Volker will become one."

"Is it never to be worn outside?"

"Upon presentation as Shield Maiden, Volker is revealed to the world."

Lexi again admired Volker. "How long will that take? Years?"

"Time in the form of days or years are meaningless to Ganels. Our lifespan is eight hundred to twelve hundred of your years. Sarina lived a thousand years and saw many generations of her offspring. She died seventy years before Oleg's birth. The Ganel blood in you is as fresh today, as when she lived."

Though tentative, Lexi asked, "How old are you?"

Cormac grinned. "Slightly over two hundred."

"Does that make you younger than me?" asked Nollen, amused.

Cormac laughed. "Do not try to equate year for year. My experience far exceeds you. Now, I think we have answered enough questions for one night. Tomorrow, we visit the university. Nollen and I to research Bertrand, while you and Jenna to read up on history."

Chapter 13

NO MATTER WHERE HE SLEPT, NOLLEN ROSE BEFORE DAWN. When in Sener, he joined his grandfather in morning prayer before breakfast. A family habit since childhood. At Far Point, he sat outside to watch the sunrise and personal meditation.

In Mathena, wealthy Ganels dedicated a room in their homes for a chapel. Nollen always stayed at Cormac's house whether the Ganel lord was there or not. To his mild surprise, Lexi sat on the front bench before the small altar.

"Good morning." He spoke in a quiet voice so as not to startle her. Didn't work.

"Oh! I didn't hear you."

"I tried not to scare you." He sat beside her.

"My meditation went deeper than I expected."

"How long have you been here?"

She shrugged with uncertainty. "What time is it?"

"Around five thirty. Close to dawn." When she bit her lip, he held her hand. "Are you upset about what they told you last night?"

She lifted Volker to gaze at it in consideration. "Learning the importance of my duty, and family history, was surprising." She released Volker to drop back against her chest. "More disturbing, is realizing how I allowed disappointment to turn into frustration, with Axel as the main target for venting. In my mind, I made Eldar a utopia of freedom. Reality has shown the truth of my ignorance. Even then, I didn't want to accept my mistaken perception, which increased my frustration." She blinked back rising tears. "No matter how cruel I behaved, Axel patiently endured."

She lifted Volker again. "Now, I understand why. I needed to discover my destiny because I would not have believed it if he told me."

"I learned that Axel's patience is born out of love and concern." Nollen's tone grew reminiscent. "When he and Gunnar first arrived at Far Point, I became angry upon learning my parents sent the medallion. It costs their lives. Despite that, duty compelled me to aid Axel. Little did I realize how it would impact on my life." He pursed his lips to contain a sudden rise of emotion. "It was as if he knew the guilt and pain I held inside because of their deaths. His concern wouldn't let me wallow in it. He confronted me, comforted me, and called me friend. He trusted me at the most crucial time. After I blew the horn, it disintegrated in my hands. I wept because I believed I failed him. Victory seemed impossible. Only by Gott's grace did it happen."

Lexi held Nollen's arm and leaned her head against his shoulder. "You're right about Axel. He indulged me as child, and I took him for granted. Even after our parents died, I tested his patience. When he left for Eldar, guilt drove me to learn what I could about the legend of the Shield Maiden. I read what few old parchments were saved and pressed the elders with questions. I thought if I became proficient in such knowledge, he would be proud of me. Then coming here, I resisted and disappointed him …" She wept.

Nollen used his sleeve to gently wipe her tears. "No. He is proud of you. What you need to do now, is what I did then—release guilt and embrace your heritage."

She smiled with tears glistening her eyes. "Thank you for letting me join you."

"My pleasure." He stroked her cheek. Naturally drawn together, they kissed. After a moment, he broke off. "I shouldn't have done that."

"Why? I liked it."

"You are the king's sister. He trusts me with your life. I won't compromise that."

Lexi fought hurt. "Are you ashamed of having feelings for me?"

"No! I don't want to jeopardize our relationship. I mean … this isn't coming out right." He held her hands. "I won't deny what just happened, nor that I have feelings for you. Yet, I promised Axel to keep you safe. Help me keep that promise, and once we return …" Her fingers on his lips stopped speech.

"You are a good man, Nollen of Far Point. I would do nothing to change that."

In grateful relief, he kissed her hands. "I see by the light outside, it's past dawn. We should find out if Jenna and Cormac are awake. There is much to do today."

Vastness of the university library dwarfed even the tallest Ganel. Thousands upon thousands of books, ledgers, and parchments filled the multiple levels that encircled the main hall. Massive stained-glass windows divided bookcases at evenly spaced intervals of ten rows. These windows started on the second level and rose to just beneath the vaulted ceiling joists. On the main floor, smaller, less grandiose windows allowed in light at the same interval.

Large ornate pillars held up the various levels while impressive ironwork railings spanned the distance between the pillars. On the main floor, long tables capable of seating twelve were arranged to keep from overcrowding. On the upper levels, smaller tables accommodated four due to limited floor space. Also, on the main level, were alcoves for private study.

Nollen sat an individual alcove table with books scattered before him. Some were open, others closed. With great concentration, he read from the book directly in front of him. Cormac stood at the entry to the alcove and flipped through a book.

"You said the pages torn from the ledges in Sener dealt with Bertrand. I'm hard-pressed to find exactly what is missing." Nollen motioned to the books.

"I think I have. Do you speak and read Bertrandian?"

"Aye. More fluently than Markitan due to its proximity to Far Point." Cormac set the book in front of him. Nollen's eyes glowered in anger at the indicated entry. "So, it is true! Black markets."

"Shhhh!" Cormac warned at the raised voice.

Nollen lowered his tone. "How did you come by this book?"

"Before the Electors, Bertrandian nobles and scholars occasionally came here to study. As gifts, they donated books to the library. This ... well, is an unofficial donation."

Nollen cast a wry glance to Cormac. "Unauthorized or obtained by other means?"

Cormac heaved an inconsequential shrug. "Either way, it contains information we need." He indicated a place on the page. "Compare the list of items to trade agreements with the Electors then, and now."

Nollen grabbed the paper provided by Dynos. It took a moment to make the comparison. He frowned with disgust. "This confirms what my father believed about shady deals he was forced to make. And I had to continue."

"Based upon this information, there can be no agreement."

Nollen slapped the Bertrandian paper. "Dynos will vehemently deny it."

"If he, Rastus, or Cadmus know. This book predates the Electors, the black markets may no longer exist."

Nollen's brows leveled, as eyes shifted between the book and Dynos' paper. "These items are almost exactly the same, which makes ignorance and obsolescence suspect. In my experience, Bertrandian traders always look for an edge to outwit the competition."

Cormac sat on the corner of the table to tap the book page. "They have effectively used it for centuries."

With a sly tone, Nollen said, "Now that we know their sordid past, I need to figure out how to use it to our advantage. Preferably, without starting a war."

"Axel must be told."

"Naturally. I will send a dispatch before we leave for Ha'tar. Fortunately, we have until the end of the year to formulate a strategy."

"Nollen!" Lexi called a split second before she appeared in the alcove.

Hearing his name, he shoved the Bertrandian paper into the book to mark the place, and slammed it shut. He assumed a neutral posture.

"I found a book about Sarina, her position as Shield Maiden, and even her marriage to Hagen." Excited, Lexi set the book down to show Nollen.

"Did you doubt my retelling?" Cormac teased.

"No, my lord." His good-natured laugh made her flush with embarrassment.

"Ganels have a dry sense of humor," Nollen told Lexi.

"So, I'm learning," she bantered.

"Oh, I do hope you learn more than that," Cormac continued in his humor.

She giggled. "This place is incredible! Have you been here before?" she asked Nollen.

"I spend at least a day here each time I visit. I think a person could devote a lifetime to exploring this place and not exhaust the resources."

Cormac cocked a grin. "Certainly not a man's lifetime."

Jenna arrived. "Here you are," she said to Lexi.

"I came to show Nollen." Lexi picked up the book. "Where to next?"

"The armory museum."

"Ladies," Cormac's address delayed departure. "We shall be leaving on business and rejoin you for dinner." He made certain the women were out of earshot before speaking. "I shall make arrangements with the librarian to take the book with us."

Nollen reread the entry. His initial disturbance deepened. However, the discovery also clarified his interaction with Bertrandians. He didn't have time for further consideration when Cormac returned to report success. With book in hand, they left.

"I assume by business you mean the dispatch," Nollen commented. They walked the short distance from the university to Cormac's residence.

"For the most part. While you compose it, I want to compare this with the books I brought from the royal archives." Cormac's voice hinted at a further disturbance.

"Is there something else of concern?"

"Again, I want to learn more before speaking."

Although armed with the new information to counter Bertrand's demands, Nollen had difficulty composing the letter. Which topic? Bertrand or Lexi? Thoughts of Lexi invaded his mind since their shared kiss. Even at the library, he fought to stay focused. With Dynos at Sener, it had to be Bertrand. Determination gave way to a flow of words. He sealed the letter with his stamp of office and dispatched it by way of Cormac's trusted courier.

Meanwhile, at the university armory, Jenna and Lexi toured the room. Weapons of all kinds lined the walls and racks. Elegantly crafted swords, axes, pikes, shields, crossbows, and long bows were all on display.

"The armory at Sener has nothing like these. They look new," said Lexi in awe.

Jenna lightly laughed. "Some of them are a thousand years old."

"Really?" Lexi lightly touched a sword with an elaborate hilt and pommel.

"Aye. You may try it if you wish."

Lexi drew the sword from the rack. She took several swings and tested the balance.

A male Ganel rushed over. "Put that back! You cannot ..." His speech stopped when Lexi turned, and he saw the amulet. "Volker?" His wide-eyed gaze shifted to Jenna.

"This is Lexi, sister to the Son of Eldar."

"Shield Maiden." He crossed his arm in a x-shape over his chest and bowed. "That sword belonged to King Hagen, your ancestor."

"The craftsmanship speaks to its nobility."

"There is one that has been waiting for you, Shield Maiden."

"So, I have been told." When he motioned to take Hagen's sword, she deftly turned it to hand him by the hilt.

Once in an antechamber, he locked the door. At the far back wall, he waved his hand over an image carved in the wood paneling. Lexi flinched when a large panel slid open to reveal a room. Upon entrance, he pulled a small lever and four wall lanterns lit.

Lexi became mesmerized at the sight of silver armor augmented with red leather, a crested shield, and ... "Arkin," she murmured. The sword hung beside the armor. The hilt matched the amulet of silver with polished rose marble. Another ruby fixed to the center of the cross guard. She took the sword in both hands. "It's so light."

"Yet strong enough to match any blade," said the curator. "What was damaged during the coup has been restored, awaiting the Shield Maiden's return."

Lexi's eyes took in every detail of the armor, shield, and Arkin. She noticed a vacant circle in the red leather over the left breast. "Is something missing?"

"Aye. The Shield Maiden's badge," replied the curator.

Lexi's fingers traced the circle. "Lost or destroyed?"

"No one knows. It has been missing since Oleg's coup."

"I am not ready to do it justice," Lexi spoke in reverence.

"You will, after training. It is your destiny," said Jenna with certainty.

Lexi raised Arkin to admire the blade. After a moment, she handed it to the curator. "Keep it safe until I am ready." She paused by the locked door to watch the curator close the secret panel. "Until now, I believed only Axel had a destiny. I have much to consider."

Chapter 14

FOR FIVE DAYS, NOLLEN AND LEXI TRAVELED THE MAIN HIGHWAY south from Mathena toward the border with Ha'tar. Each night they spent at an inn with separate rooms. Throughout the journey, Lexi told Nollen of her experience exploring Mathena. Her words flowed with excitement of learning something new. She found Nollen much easier to speak with than Axel. He willingly listened and did not correct her when she repeated a story or considered a different aspect of an issue. Even during lengthy verbal consideration, she took notice of his attitude and action. At times, he gently tempered her enthusiasm with personal accounts of past events. Rather than finding this irksome, she weighed his tales against what she learned. After all, he experienced more of life than she. He also knew Eldar intimately. Axel relied on Nollen's expertise.

On the sixth morning, Lexi viewed the blooming forests and meadows with a pleasant smile. "There is a serene sense of beauty and peace in Ganel, more than either Halvor or the Freelands. Those are lovely territories. It is as if, the land reflects those living there."

Nollen's grin at her comment faded to a sneer. "You will find Ha'tar bleak and void."

"Why?"

"Dragons prefer rocky places of habitation. Draca, and other cities along the Leven River, are more lush. Although, that is relative to the landscape."

"You sound as if you don't like the Ha'tar."

"They added to the difficulty of life in The Doane. Those nearest the border, became victims of constant raids by dragon riders. This included Far Point and Gilroy." Her sympathetic gaze made him modify his harsh attitude. "Things have improved since the majority of Ha'tar left Eldar. Those remaining are more agreeable."

"Have you business in Draca?"

"No. We are passing through."

His curtness bothered her. "Why not trade with them like the rest?"

Nollen made a deep, purposeful sigh before he replied. "There is really nothing of value to trade past the need of the dragons for defense. The land yields no useable crops, nor natural resources to encourage smithing or craftsmen. Their whole society centers around dragons."

Silence fell, deep and unsettling, as she considered his gruff description of Ha'tar. This was the first time during the journey he spoke with a harsh attitude about a Territory. She had more questions yet thought best not to press him. Recent history still disturbed him.

The closer they came to Ha'tar, the road became less traveled. Finally, at Helivan's Watershed, Nollen drew rein. To the right, stood a tall stone inscribed with a rune, while in front, a bridge over the watershed.

"Why have we stopped?" asked Lexi.

"This bridge used to be hidden. One had to know the secret to cross. This rune, and another on the far side, were key. Too weak from wounds and illness to do it, I instructed Axel on how to raise and lower the bridge."

"What?" she asked, disturbed.

"I became wounded when we fled Gorland border guards. I fell off Gilen and landed in the shallows. Back then, the Unicorns poisoned the water to protect Ganel. The only safe passage was over the bridge. Once we crossed, Alfgar arrived. He healed me using Unicorn magic. I would have died otherwise."

Alydar snorted and pranced in place. He pulled at the bit and tossed his head in excitement. Sheba also chomped on the bit and pranced in place.

"What's wrong, girl?" asked Lexi, concerned.

"There is nothing wrong." The voice preceded an emergence from the forest. A magnificent white unicorn with silver horn appeared. Callie accompanied him.

"Alfgar," said Nollen in greeting.

Alydar lowered his head in bow to Alfgar. Sheba also acknowledged the Unicorn King. Alfgar grunted and snorted, as he came muzzle to muzzle with Alydar. Alfgar similarly greeted Sheba. He then arched his neck in an elegant nod to Lexi

"Greetings, Shield Maiden."

"It is an honor to see you again, Lord Alfgar."

Alydar again pulled at the bridle to grunt and chomp. Alfgar replied in kind.

Lexi's smile held a hint of forlorn reminisce. "I miss hearing Alydar speak. He had such a pleasant, reassuring voice."

"You wish it again, Shield Maiden?" asked Alfgar.

"If it were possible. He lost so much to save me and the others." She regarded Alydar with affectionate sympathy.

Alydar turned his head to Lexi and continued in horse noises.

"He would gladly do it again to bring home the Shield Maiden," said Alfgar.

Nollen stroked Alydar's neck. "We have much to thank you for, my friend."

"Do you also miss his speech, Nollen of Far Point?" asked Alfgar.

"Very much. He has come to mean a great deal to me." Nollen played with Alydar's mane.

Alfgar loudly whinnied, reared, and tossed his head. When his front hooves hit the ground, his silver horn struck the star on Alydar's forehead. The jolt made Alydar tremble and Nollen rock in the saddle. Alydar breathed hard from the encounter. Nollen also took a moment to recover.

Lexi fought to steady a startled Sheba. "Nollen?"

"They are unharmed," Alfgar spoke with reassurance. "Is that so, brother?"

Alydar's lips chomped first with horse noises then, "It is so."

Lexi and Nollen were dumbstruck. "You can talk again?" Nollen asked.

"Well, it wasn't Callie," Alydar sarcastically replied.

Sheba laughed in a human sounding way. She turned her head to Alydar. "You always had a droll sense of humor."

Again, Lexi and Nollen balked in surprise. "Sheba? I thought horses couldn't talk," said Lexi, confused.

"I am a Unicorn."

"Did you lose your horn like Alydar?"

Sheba shook her head. "No, it is hidden. And will remain so until you are trained and formally revealed as The Shield Maiden."

Alfgar took up the explanation. "Since Sarina, Shield Maidens have ridden Unicorns. A joining of nature and humans. Sheba is the last foal of my beloved Teva."

"Your daughter, then," said Nollen.

"In human terms."

"And my niece," said Alydar. "I recognized her immediately in Sener."

Alfgar's voice turned sober. "Beware of the way through Ha'tar. A foreboding sense has settled on the Territory. What that means, I do not know."

"We have no plans of staying, only passing through," said Nollen, firmly.

"Do so quickly. Gott's speed." Alfgar disappeared into the forest.

Callie remained. "I shall cross first and scout ahead."

"It's too narrow to cross together." Nollen waved Lexi to follow Callie.

After they climbed the far bank, the landscape dramatically changed. The lushness of Ganel, and the watershed, gave way to desolate rockiness.

Lexi shifted uneasily in the saddle at the stark difference. "How can people live here?" she asked in breathy disturbance.

"I often wonder that myself," said Nollen.

"You said dragons prefer such places, though not the reason why."

He shrugged. "I'm not exactly sure. I know they give birth in caves and remain until the young can fly. Sometimes Ha'tar breeders raid the caves and steal eggs to raise for riding."

"Less places for predators to hide," said Alydar. "Dragons only lay an egg every twenty years, thus fiercely protective."

"Explains why there are no other predators in the Territory," said Nollen.

"How long will it take to cross Ha'tar?" asked Lexi.

"Four nights."

Lexi visibly shivered as she regarded the landscape. An unnamed dread formed in the pit of her being and threatened to envelope her. The harrowing sensation only lasted a moment before she heard Nollen speak again.

"No need to fear. It's not as dangerous as it used to be."

"We could have taken a ferry from Mathena to The Doane," Alydar said.

"That would defeat the purpose of the Shield Maiden exploring all Territories and learning about various groups." Nollen wryly grinned at Lexi.

The brief conversation gave her enough time to draw herself from the dreary impression. "I'm not afraid. Merely struck by the stark difference from Ganel."

"I sensed your fear," disputed Sheba.

Lexi frowned in discovery. "Maybe a little."

"Do not underestimate your feelings. They can serve you well. What you must do, is learn to determine reality from illusion."

"Lord Cormac told me the same. The problem is making the distinction."

"I will ask a question yet consider before replying. Was your fear based upon something you sensed, or from what was said about Ha'tar?"

Lexi made a wry huff. "I don't need to think. A deep sense of dread struck me upon sight of the land. What Nollen and Alfgar said may have prepared me, but not for the intensity of what I felt."

Sheba nodded. "Good. That is what I meant by determination. The sense of discernment is a gift Gott grants the Shield Maiden."

Lexi touched Volker, which she wore tucked beneath the collar of her doublet. "Lord Cormac said the ruby glows when evil is near."

"He also said, that with training, wisdom will grow, and guide you on how and when to act," Nollen reminded her. "A heightened sensation is one of those elements."

"You too have a keen awareness of danger."

"Forged over a lifetime, not natural instinct. Though some may think that way now due to my experience," he countered. "This is your first trip to Ha'tar, yet you sensed its coldness. In fact, you express sentiments about each Territory I never considered, or even felt." Nollen's tone changed to reminiscing. "When I was thirteen, my father brought me through Ha'tar for the first time. I became curious to see where dragons lived and ignored caution. I acted reckless, and he became injured. Nothing serious. A badly twisted ankle, thank Gott. It taught me a valuable lesson of observation and to interpret what I see. Although feelings of caution and alertness began to accompany the visuals; again, learned, not intuitive."

Lexi considered his words. "So, in essence, I must do the opposite. Interpret my feelings about what I see, and act accordingly."

"Evil is not always seen before it arrives," Alydar cautiously warned.

"I learned that with Sirin," groused Nollen.

"Gott it only caused injury and nothing worse," Lexi said with unction.

Nollen faced forward, his jowls tight and hands clenched the reins.

His reaction caused her to regret her words. "I seem to be saying things that upset you."

With Nollen unable to reply, Alydar spoke. "It is not your fault. Even minor injury suffered by evil leaves a lasting impression."

"Aye," Nollen agreed in a low somber voice.

Despite the reassurance, Lexi became lost in thought about all that happened in Mathena, and the sensation of Ha'tar. Several times, she touched the neck of her doublet for Volker. For all his self-deprecation, Nollen learned well the lessons of youth to become a seasoned man of trade and pathfinding. Traits she once mocked. Now, she faced similar training to harness a whirlwind of thoughts and feelings stirred by the Ganel visit. Preoccupied, she let Sheba follow Alydar. Not until they stopped, did she realize twilight had fallen and what lay before them.

"It's a cave."

"Our shelter for tonight." Nollen dismounted to lead Alydar inside.

Lexi followed on foot with Sheba. "Not an inn?"

"The few Ha'tar inns are located in Draca, which is the only inhabited city left. But we don't want to go there."

"A dragon cave is safer?"

"There is no scent of a dragon," said Callie.

"This is why we gathered firewood in Ganel and bought ample supplies in the last town before crossing." Nollen removed his bedroll in which he placed firewood. "We'll use my wood to cook food tonight, eat cold rations tomorrow, then your wood to cook another meal. We end with cold rations on the final night. After that, Ida will prepare us a feast."

Lexi joined him at the fire site. "I look forward to seeing Far Point."

He lit the dry wood. "I hope you won't be disappointed. It's a simple trading post." He fetched his saddlebag and took out the provisions. "Cut the bacon into pieces. I'll do the same with potatoes and onions."

She removed her gloves to follow instructions. "Far Point is your home."

He paused in cutting the vegetables. A thoughtful expression appeared. "Actually, I don't have a home any longer."

"What do you mean? You were born there."

"As the eldest, ownership passed to Ida. I split my time between Far Point, Sener, and traveling. Not that I resent it. No. Your reference to Far Point as my home simply made me realize I no longer have a home—in the permanent sense."

"Do you want one?" She put the cut bacon pieces in the skillet.

He added the onions and potatoes. "Of course, but I haven't considered it with all the upheaval of the past few years. Though, I admit, when visiting Kean's farm and seeing Gunnar's emotion of being home, it stirred thoughts of settling down."

"I felt a peace and freedom at farm, which eludes me in Sener."

Nollen turned the food, as it began to sizzle in the skillet. "How so?"

"Peace of being among friends with the freedom to do what I want without restraint."

"Sound like you have a wrong idea of freedom."

Lexi scoffed with anger. "How can you say that?"

"Take no offense. I understand your frustration at all the changes. I felt the same not long ago. Since then, I learned that freedom does not mean a lack of responsibility. Rather, to go about life without fear. Kean and his family farm without worry of discovery. We travel Eldar free from anxiety of the Electors. Soothe, everyone now goes about their daily lives of chores and duties unhindered."

"I have not thought of it in those terms." She went between blowing on her hands, to warming them over the fire, as the night grew colder.

"Put your gloves back on."

"It only helps a little. My hands get very cold in cooler weather, especially fall and winter."

"I don't recall you mentioning that before."

"We had other things to worry about. It's something I deal with," she said in causal reply. "Where is Callie?"

"Hunting for her dinner."

"Is there anything around here to hunt?"

"A rodent or two." Nollen set the skillet on the ground so both could eat. By the time they finished, Callie returned. "Were you successful?"

Callie grunted as she laid down. "One mouse."

Nollen reached behind him for two thick slices of uncooked bacon. "I saved these for you." Callie licked his face before she took the bacon to eat. "You sleep. I'll take the first watch," he told Lexi.

"No need. We will keep watch while you both sleep," Alydar said.

"Habit." Nollen wrapped his cloak around him and sat back against the cave wall. When Callie moved beside him, he whispered to her. He smiled at Lexi's perplexity when Callie laid beside her. "To help keep you warm."

Chapter 15

LAMPS AND FIRELIGHT ILLUMINATED THE KING'S STUDY. NIGHT had fallen ninety minutes earlier, the length of time Axel sat before the hearth listening to Cormac tell of Lexi's visit to Mathena. A few times he smiled during the narrative yet made no comment. Gunnar and Ronan were also present, with Gunnar asking questions. When Cormac mentioned the University, and Lexi's excitement at discovering Arkin, Axel laughed with joy.

"Indeed, Sire. The visit awakened her to the possibilities of what lies ahead in her position as Shield Maiden. Which is why I brought Arkin and her armor." Cormac picked up the fabled sword that lay on the table beside his official traveling satchel and a large, wrapped bundle. "Since she will return here before Mathena, and more willing to listen to you." He held the sword out to Axel, who rose to accept it.

"A fine sword," said Axel with admiration. "This news exceeds my expectations."

"I wish all the news I bring did so."

The change in tone to sober, made Axel curious. "Oh?"

"It concerns the other matter for which I returned to Mathena."

"Ah! Nollen's letter told me how black markets are rampant in Bertrand, and most of the goods traded with the Electors were illegal. A topic we will address in negotiations."

"That is what we knew at the time. Since their departure, I found more disturbing information," Cormac said with circumspect harshness.

Axel's brows level in concerned puzzlement. He placed Akin on table. "How so?"

"Dynos lied. Bertrand did offer a royal marriage to Elector Konrad. Which was readily accepted in an effort to legitimize his claim of becoming *King Forever*. Allow me to finish, Sire," Cormac hastily said when Axel's ire rose. "Konrad lavished Bertrand with generous trading terms to receive his bride. Including a free trade agreement with preferential treatment. This established a precedent for the following Electors in regard to Bertrandian goods."

"Tying the hands of Nollen and others with trade charters," chided Axel.

"Aye. After the wedding, the Bertrandian ambassador convinced Konrad that since he married into royalty, a regency needed to be established in the event something dreadful should happen to him."

"Meaning his death," said Gunnar.

Cormac nodded and elaborated. "Konrad's first minister, Lord Godfrey, a Ganel, advised against the regency. However, Konrad felt so certain of becoming King Forever, that he ordered Godfrey to draw up the legal document. Konrad suddenly and mysteriously died three weeks after the birth of his son, Kristoff. Medea became regent. Godfrey died two months after Konrad. Also, under suspicious circumstances."

Ronan keenly listened; his curiosity peaked. "I remember Godfrey from studying our history but recall nothing about a royal marriage of an Elector. Where did you find this information?"

"It took days of research with the entire staff at the university. They found this buried in the vault under musty papers." Cormac carefully withdrew an old leather book from his pouch. "Godfrey's personal journal. He suspected Medea poisoned Konrad to gain the regency. More importantly, he discovered she was not of royal blood as claimed."

Axel, Ronan, and Gunnar harshly reacted to the statement. "What?" thundered Axel.

Cormac gently opened the journal. "Godfrey managed to intercept several correspondences between Medea and Vizier Perine." He displayed the page where faded pieces of paper were pressed together. "Fragments of Godfrey's copies are all that remain." He carefully removed pieces of very old paper. "However, he speaks of secretly dispatching this journal along with the copies he made of the letters to Mathena. This was the last entry before he died."

"At least, he succeeded in the dispatch since you found it at University," Ronan said.

"The journal and torn pieces of copied evidence," groused Gunnar.

"Ganels do not lie," Cormac firmly said.

"I did not mean to imply lying. Rather disappointment about the degraded state of the copies."

"It does not lessen the truth of what Godfrey discovered."

Axel thoughtfully listened. "No, it does not. In fact, Medea's actions confirm Godfrey's suspicions. She ordered Konrad and Godfrey killed, and proclaimed regent before anyone learned the truth. Only unaware of Godfrey's journal and secret dispatch. Gott preserved it for us to discover."

"Indeed, Sire," agreed Cormac.

"Any further details about Medea's real lineage?" asked Gunnar.

Cormac shook his head. "Not completely. She is believed to have been of high nobility, just not royal. This was done to gain access to Eldar's wealth and capitalize on favored trade."

"'Bertrandians seek wealth over equity," Axel murmured in recollection. "According to Nollen," he said to inquiring eyes.

"This proves it," said Gunnar.

Axel paced the chamber. The others watched and waited. After a few moments, Gunnar broke the tense silence.

"What about Dynos? We can't keep him confined much longer."

"Confronting him about an age-old lie regarding royal marriage might not be a good idea," cautioned Cormac.

"Trade is out of question!" Gunnar vehemently insisted.

Cormac held up Godfrey's journal. "We use the black markets as leverage."

"Cormac is right," said Ronan. "Information about Medea gives us a major advantage. Though limited to a one-time use, and only when absolutely necessary. Should knowledge of the black markets ultimately fail."

Despite the well-reasoned argument, Gunnar asked, "Sire? Your thoughts?"

Axel paused in his circuit of the room to tell Ronan, "Bring Dynos to the antechamber. I shall deal with him." He spoke kindly to Cormac. "Rest. Your hard work and hasty return are greatly appreciated."

"I would rather remain to hear what Dynos says when you confront him."

"Very well. You and Gunnar wait over there. He might see you, but at least your presence won't seem too conspicuous."

In the time it took Ronan to fetch Dynos, Axel silently prayed. His mind went between great pleasure at hearing about Lexi to anger about the Bertrandians. Research proved Cormac, Ronan, and Nollen correct in their hesitation. Despite such information, he needed to proceed with firm tact. The antechamber door opened, and Ronan appeared in the threshold. Axel nodded, to which Ronan momentarily disappeared to escort Dynos into the King's presence.

The Bertrandian ambassador did not appear pleased. He bowed and made the formal obligatory greeting in a begrudging tone. "Live forever, most gracious King Axel."

Axel matched Dynos' grim demeanor. "Ambassador. I hope you have enjoyed our hospitality."

"It has been most informative, Sire."

"It has also proven informative for us. So much so, we decline the latest offer."

Dynos' posture stiffened, as he fought outrage. "A royal marriage is considered an honor. I must tell my king why Eldar chooses to insult Bertrand with this rejection."

"Take care, Ambassador!" Ronan warned.

Axel put up a hand to still Ronan's protest. Hazel eyes steely focused on Dynos. "Two words—black market." At Dynos' disturbed reaction, Axel pressed his point. "Do you truly believe Eldar would go unprepared into any negotiations?"

"As I told Lord Ronan, Bertrand never made an offer of royal marriage to an Elector."

Gunnar's impulsive cough to the statement caught attention. To divert Dynos' scrutiny of Gunnar, Ronan spoke to Axel about Dynos.

"Sire, this offer was to cover his blunder of previous failed attempts to secure a bride for Bertrand's heir apparent."

Dynos flushed red with rage. His reaction brought Gunnar to stand beside Axel, as a visible deterrent to any hasty action. Dynos clenched his fists to regain his composure.

Axel's stern voice diverted Dynos' attention from Gunnar. "Whereas, treaty negotiations require a measure of trust, a royal marriage demands the establishment of a relationship before consideration. Neither have occurred with Bertrand, as of yet. If King Rastus is serious about remaining on good terms with Eldar, he will understand why I first seek a constructive relationship." He went to his desk and picked up a piece of paper. "This list of items is a start—but legal merchandise only, no black market. Once fair trade is established, I shall consider other offers. Do I make myself clear, Ambassador?"

"Yah, Your Majesty."

"You leave tomorrow morning to deliver my response to Rastus." Axel turned his back and moved to the hearth in an abrupt act of dismissal.

Dynos bowed and left with Ronan.

Gunnar approached Axel yet did not speak until certain Dynos was gone. "Would you really agree to a foreign offer of marriage for Lexi? She is the Shield Maiden and ..."

"I said consider other offers." At Gunnar's annoyed scowl, Axel added, "No. Not after what Cormac discovered. Lexi's future is here. And we know with whom she will be happy."

"You played him well, Sire." Cormac wryly smiled.

"Hopefully well enough to convince Rastus he is not dealing with Electors anymore. Eldar is done accepting black-market goods, deceitful trade, and outright lies! Negotiations will be honest and beneficial to both or not at all!" Axel took a deep breath to calm down. "Now, I'm sure Alicia will enjoy hearing about Lexi. Goodnight, gentlemen."

Axel made his way to the royal apartment where he found Alicia already in bed. "Retiring so early?"

She stretched and yawned. "The child wearies me easily."

"Too weary to hear about Lexi?" he coyly teased.

Alicia immediately perked up. "Tell me!"

He sat on the bed. "Your advice worked out better than I hoped. She is excited and ready to learn. Once she finishes the circuit with Nollen, that is."

"Wonderful! Are they still at Mathena?"

"No, they left to follow the normal route. I reckon The Doane next, so Far Point and Gilroy."

"And?" she pressed with expectation. Her eyes gleeful.

"What?" He shrugged with impish pretense.

"Oh, don't play games. What did Cormac say about Lexi and Nollen? Lorraine and Gunnar witnessed more than a spark in the Freelands."

Axel laughed. "The spark continues. He considers himself a common trader, and unsure about being worthy of the king's sister."

"Oh, pooh! He is hardly common. Nor can I think of a more worthy man. I recognized the beginnings in Kranston. On the journey here, I noticed how he talks to her in ways different than anyone else. And she listens."

"I recognized the same at the border station, after our success against Montre. I depend upon it for this journey." He smiled with great pleasure to say, "Gott is using what we perceived early on for their good. Now, rest. I will be in later." He kissed her forehead.

In the chapel portion of the royal apartment, Axel found Gunnar seated on a bench in front of the altar. When he joined Gunnar, the First Knight spoke in a quiet tone.

"Did you tell Alicia about Rastus' offer?"

"No. As strong as she might be spiritually, the child has heightened her emotions. Besides, I refused it, so why upset her unnecessarily?"

Gunnar nodded and faced forward to stare at the altar. The action made Axel curious.

"You are not here because of that, are you?"

"No." Gunnar continued to stare straight ahead. "I'm thinking of retiring from service."

Axel momentarily balked at the statement. "Come again?"

"Age is slowing me down. I cannot act quick enough. This is proof." He pointed to the scar. "I thank Gott I survived to save others."

"Age and reflexes had nothing to with it. Sirin secretly aided Horst. Unexpected evil dealt that blow."

"Age is still a factor for any knight or soldier. I turned forty-nine last month. Fifty next year." He softly grinned. "Gott granted me a wife, and to see my childhood home again. Two things I never believed possible." His smile slightly trembled with emotion. "The farm was almost exactly as I remember. Well, at least our house remained. The guest house needed repair, while Kean laid the foundation to rebuild our grandparents' home. For me and Lorraine." He turned to Axel, the sheen of mist in his eyes. "Do you understand what I'm saying?"

Axel's arm encircled Gunnar's shoulders. "Who do think is providing the materials for repairs and rebuilding? I only hoped retirement would not be so soon."

"The construction won't be completed until the fall. Then we need to furnish it. That could take a few months."

"So, next year, when you turn fifty?"

"Aye."

Axel's arm fell from Gunnar's shoulders. "I will need help to find someone worthy to become First Knight. Although, taking your place is impossible," he said with a catch in his voice.

"The farm is only a two-day ride. It's not as if you won't see me again."

Axel took a deep breath to digest the news. "Have you told Nollen of your plans?"

"Aye, we spoke at the farm. I asked him not to tell you. It had to come from me."

"As I said, I knew the time would come, just hoped for later rather than sooner."

"Any later, and I will be too old to enjoy my wife and retirement," Gunnar teased. "Now, I should tell Lorraine. She has been anxious about me speaking with you."

When the hall door shut upon, Axel sighed, deep and long. Expectations. Changes. All concepts he dealt with since leaving Kranston four years ago. Despite the solitude, and a lingering fear of discovery, Kranston provided stability and comradery. Trying to replicate those in Eldar proved difficult. He took solace that nothing could sever the bound between him and Gunnar.

He lowly chuckled. "You and Lorraine. I never would have imagined." He then spoke to the altar. "Gott, you do work in mysterious ways. And sometimes with a sense a humor." He retired for the night.

Chapter 16

EACH NIGHT, BORKA LED SPOOR, BRYNN, AND BODIL THROUGH The Doane toward Altwald. Borka remained on foot, while the Nefal rode draft horses outfitted for long distance travel. Brynn, Spoor, and Bodil wore swords and carried longbows and a quiver.

In Nefalese, Brynn chided Spoor. "How do you know this creature is leading us in the right direction? We cannot see well enough to discern otherwise."

"I check our heading every morning. We continue east."

"One thing these mortal beasts are good for, is seeing in the dark. They have better night vision than dire-buffalos," Bodil added.

The replies did not set well with Brynn. Since leaving Nefal, she sought ways to determine the scope of Spoor's plan. Beside the fact it included the Cursians to strike back at Axel, she could not learn specific details. Her father trusted her to thwart the plan, but hardly possible until she knew the plan.

At daybreak, Borka shouted, "Stop!"

The sudden command made the Nefal abruptly rein the horses. "Why are we stopping?" demanded Spoor.

"Altwald. Leave horses here and follow me closely." Borka spoke weakly. His face showed distress while his shoulders hunched in pain.

"Why? Leaving them in the open could be dangerous," said Brynn.

"My people starve. They kill beasts for food. If you want to ride, leave them here."

"How do we know they will be safe? You look as if you would kill them," she continued her argument.

"I make promise for them. Now, come. I need to enter or soon die."

They tied the reins to low branches before following Borka into Altwald. After a hundred yards, Borka paused to take a deep refreshing breath and allow the atmosphere of Altwald to enliven him.

In contrast, the Nefal grimly frowned at the smothering air. They held their swords ready. The dim daylight made silhouettes of massive, gnarled trees. Clinging vines created an interlocking canopy that few shafts of light could penetrate. The height and breadth of the trees told of a very old forest. However, the vast majority appeared dead. Marginal light did nothing to change the bleak grayness of Altwald. A sense of uneasiness threatened to overcome Brynn and Bodil. Even Spoor's countenance showed concern.

"This place reeks of death," Bodil spoke with great apprehension.

Spoor stopped. "Borka! This is far enough. Summon your people."

Borka cupped his hands over his mouth to make a call which sounded like a cross between a bird and animal. He repeated it three times before receiving a reply. "They come," he told the Nefal.

With wariness, a handful of Cursians appear from the darkness. Wretched creatures representing male, female, and offspring. The creatures reeked more than Altwald. The Nefal balked at the odor.

Borka spoke to his people in short, clipped Cursian sentences. Mumbling came in response, yet quickly quelled by a barking order from Borka.

"Well?" Spoor asked with impatience.

"Ardon." Borka spoke a few hurried words to a male, who in turn made a harsh bird whistle.

From the overhead canopy, came the diving figure of a large bird. The echoing screech made the Nefal back away in pain. A massive black and grey bird with features that resembled a vulture and an eagle landed on a log near Ardon.

"A harpy!" Bodil exclaimed.

"I thought they were dead," said Brynn, fearful.

"There are also two jackals. They come and go. Even using them, hunting outside Altwald is dangerous. Can help Nefal and Cursian."

Spoor's warped smile showed pleasure.

Ardon spoke in a sneering tone. Borka made a sharp reply. Ardon bared his teeth in dislike of the response but quickly back down when Borka snarled louder. The Cursian leader translated for the Nefal. "Ardon ask what you give in exchange for beasts?"

"Food," replied Spoor. "We can freely hunt. This evening, we will bring meat in exchange for the harpy and jackals."

Borka told his people to a chorus of agreement. He then spoke to Spoor. "Harpy be here. Will try to find jackals."

Once back at the horses, the Nefal drank from their respective flasks to aid in recovery from the smothering effects of Altwald.

Spoor mounted. "You two hunt. I will return at sunset."

"Where are you going?" Brynn asked.

"To scout the location for our next move." He jerked the horse around to ride off.

"Why is he riding south when Sener is north?" Brynn's tone suggested irritability.

"You ask too many questions." Bodil kicked his horse to leave Altwald.

She rode after him. "I ask questions to be prepared. I cannot do so, if kept ignorant of the plan."

"Nefal warriors follow orders without question."

"This is not a military operation." She moved her horse in front of Bodil to stop him. "I am the next chief. I want to make sure the plan succeeds without harming our people. To do that, I need to know the entire plan, not what Spoor told my father."

Bodil hesitated with visible indecision.

Sensing an opportunity, she pressed her advantage. "My father trusts you. I want to trust you. Tell me everything you know."

Despite being in the middle of a meadow, Bodil lowered his voice. "I swear upon my father's memory, I know only as much as you. If using a human female will aid our people, and return our former glory, I shall do whatever is necessary to bring it about."

Brynn tried not to show surprise at the mention of a human female. A detail left out from Spoor's discussion with Maro. Rather than confront Bodil, she tactfully spoke. "Aid our people, perhaps. Former glory? Axel will not allow that. Nefal would be too much of a threat."

Bodil's ire rose. "He fears the might of Nefal, which is why he keeps us begging for scraps!"

To this criticism, her temper flared. "Take care, Bodil! We must rebuild. A wrong step will destroy everything."

"Or restore it!" He leaned forward in the saddle to stare directly at her. "Why did you come? To sow seeds of doubt?"

The bitter tone of challenge made her grip the reins tight. She needed to control her temper and not overplay her hand. She managed to keep her tone level, yet tone firm. "I told you. I want this plan to succeed without harming our people. That is my duty, both as daughter of the chief, and your future chief."

Bodil's jowls tightened. His chest puffed out, as he declared, "I have a duty to my father, who gave his life for Nefal."

Brynn's temper gave way. "You renege on the oath you swore to the chief?"

"No. I believe this is a way to honor both."

With narrow eyes of inspection, she studied him. A stubborn and brash individual, yet always sincere. At least, her father believed so. Now, she couldn't be certain after he admitted divided loyalty. Still, to uncover the full plan she needed Bodil to trust her. "Since I seek to honor my father, and Nefal, I will hold you to that same condition. Agreed?"

"Agreed."

She removed the longbow from off her shoulder. "Now, let's go hunting."

Stories of the First Ones were passed down, thus Kyros' flight into Eldar came with great wariness. He circled high above Altwald. From the dark, decaying forest below, emanated a cold sensation of death. However, that is where the Nefal went, so he must remain vigilant. Once they split, Kyros followed Spoor, since he was of primary importance.

Four hours, Spoor rode south along the River Leven tributary. Smoke rose from an area concealed by trees and brush. Spoor guided his horse toward the smoke. Kyros made a gentle, unobserved descent to land high in an evergreen for closer observation. Spoor joined the twins around a campfire. At first, the twins prepared to draw weapons then relaxed upon recognizing Spoor.

"*Salve, amicis Mateo et Marius,*" Spoor spoke in Bertrandian.

"You're late! We have been waiting two days," chided Marius

Spoor dismounted. "It could not be helped."

The brothers sat back around the fire.

"What news?" asked Mateo

"The quarry is not far. A day or two at most," replied Spoor.

"How can you be sure?"

"Once Dynos' note came, I alerted my sources. Not all are favorable to Eldar's new *king.*" Spoor picked up a stick to draw in the dirt. "You are here, and this is Altwald. It lies four hours north. Follow that bank," He used the stick to indicate the river, "to a small pool with several boulders where the tributary drops in elevation. Move there tonight and wait. We will herd the quarry into the trap. Upon arrival, act swift in capture, and leave Eldar immediately!"

"How will we identity this quarry?" inquired Marius.

"The female," Spoor replied. "Do your part, and you will be handsomely rewarded. Fail, well, the Vizier will not like that."

Mateo snarled. "Have you forgotten our father *is* Vizier?"

"Will he be less severe with his sons for failure?" Spoor rebuffed.

Marius stopped Mateo from replying. "We won't fail."

When Spoor left, Kyros took flight.

By twilight, Brynn and Bodil returned to Altwald with a doe and feral hog. They discovered Spoor waiting. He smiled with approval at their success.

"The Cursians should eat well for at least a week."

"If they are smart and do not devour these immediately," said Brynn.

"What if they do? The agreement was simply to provide meat," said Bodil.

She huffed an ironic chuckle. "I said *if they are smart*. Such creatures show little intelligence." She pulled the hog off the horse while Bodil took the doe from his mount.

Spoor led them to where they left Borka earlier. "We have returned with meat!"

The words barely uttered when the Cursians hurried to arrive, their eager faces salivating. Borka snapped for order.

Spoor placed a hand on the hilt of his sword as a warning. "The harpy and jackals first."

Ardon made the same call, and the harpy arrived.

"The jackals?"

"One returned. Ardon speak with it, and it left to fetch the other," Borka replied. He took a black sack from Ardon. "Place over harpy head when traveling. Use rope in leg clamp. See?" He pointed to a metal clamp around the harpy's leg with a ring attached.

Spoor waved at Bodil and Brynn. "Give them the meat."

They threw the hog and doe to the ground. The Cursians pounced on the carcasses.

Spoor spoke to the harpy in a language that confused Bodil and made Brynn wince. However, both became surprised when the harpy responded and took flight. Spoor motioned for them to follow and returned to the horses. To their further bewilderment, the harpy sat on Spoor's bedroll behind the saddle.

"How?" asked Brynn about the harpy.

"The Cursian did not train it. Same with the jackals," replied Spoor.

"You acted as if they did."

Spoor cocked a sarcastic grin. "To fool them. They might not be very intelligent, but not stupid. I had to pretend to believe them in order to reclaim what I left in Altwald."

"Wait? You brought the harpy and jackals to Altwald?" asked Brynn.

"All part of the plan."

"This was not—!" Brynn abruptly stopped.

"Not what I told Maro, is that what you meant to say?" Spoor demanded.

She clenched her lips in an effort to remain silent.

Spoor's good eye stared at her. "A few missing details does not alter the plan." He took a step closer. "Interference will. Do you understand?"

She boldly returned his glare. "I understand."

The battle of stubbornness only lasted a moment, when Spoor made a lopsided smile to tell Bodil, "Stay here and wait for the jackals. We will take the harpy to flush out our quarry. When we have succeeded, dispatch the jackals."

Bodil tried to mask his fearful uncertainty. "How will I get them to obey me?"

"Say, *Ad ille deus ego mandatum obedientiam.* They will become as docile as a dog."

Hearing the language again, Brynn paused in mounting. Fortunately, Bodil's question changed Spoor's focus.

"What does that mean?"

"*By the gods, I command obedience.*" Spoor placed the hood on the harpy before tying a rope through the ring and to a rear saddle ring. He mounted in such a way, as to not upset the bird.

Brynn accompanied Spoor. The incident with the Cursians brought to light some disturbing aspects of the plan. Using creatures that served the Electors showed an intent to raise rebellion. If Spoor mentioned them earlier, her father would have refused. How to thwart Spoor created a conundrum. She recalled her father's rough refusal at her suggestion to send word to Axel. *Nefal do not betray their own!* Does that leave killing Spoor as the only option?

Catching Spoor's third glance at her, Brynn sensed his suspicion, thus she spoke. "You obviously set everything in place before speaking to my father."

"Indeed."

"Then why seek his permission?"

Spoor sneered. "I do not need *permission.*" When she stiffened with outrage, he amended his tone to agreeable. "As a courtesy, to prepare him for the change. Same, as I *allowed* you to come."

She drew her horse to halt. "Allowed? You realize I will be chief!"

He reined his horse and spoke in a threatening tone. "Do not play games with me, woman. Questioning everything I do to gain information then pretend not to understand the language when I answer Bodil's question about the jackals."

Brynn gathered her courage to reply. "Naturally, I recognized it. We just returned from Sener where we met the Bertrandian ambassador. I do not understand the words, only the sound."

For another long, tense moment, they locked eyes. Spoor roughly turned his horse to continue. The barest pause occurred, as the thought flashed across Brynn's mind. *Killing him is the only option.*

Chapter 17

THE LONGER THEY TRAVELED IN HA'TAR, THE MORE UNEASY LEXI became. She slowed Sheba to place distance between them and Nollen and Alydar. She leaned down to speak her concern.

"The disturbance of this place goes deeper than what Nollen tried to explain."

"Indeed. I sense it as well."

"More clearly than Alfgar?"

"No. I would tell you if I did."

Lexi stroked Sheba's neck. "This may be something I need to sort through; to discern reality from illusion."

"You are learning, dear one."

"Axel would be pleased to hear that."

"Axel is the one who sent for me."

"He did?" Lexi's voice choked with emotion.

Sheba explained, "I came with the herd to celebrate the Son of Eldar's wedding. The first time I saw you, I felt an unusual stirring in my spirit. Somehow, I knew you, though we never met. When Axel joined us later that day, I asked who you were. At his answer, I understood the reason for the sensation. I am the Unicorn for you to ride as Shield Maiden. Axel sent for me after agreeing to this journey."

Lexi leaned down and hugged Sheba's neck. "Thank you."

"Thank you, dear one. It is an honor to be chosen by Gott as your mount."

"Is there a problem?" Nollen called. He stopped Alydar.

Lexi sat up and smiled. "No. Merely girl talk."

Sheba made a whinny laugh.

"Finish your conversation and catch up! It's almost nightfall, and a storm is brewing. We need to find shelter." Nollen faced forward to make a visual scan of the surroundings. "There!" He pointed to a large cave with an overhanging ledge a quarter mile to the west.

A loud clap of thunder sounded. Rain fell, light at first then became a downpour. The cave was large enough to ride under. Once they dismounted, Alydar, Sheba, and Callie shook off the water.

"Glad we're eating cold rations tonight. The wood would be useless for cooking," said Nollen.

"And to get warm," groused Lexi. She undid the braid to wring out her hair.

Nollen removed his saddlebag to retrieve the food. "Fortunately, rain doesn't ruin sausage or carrots."

"What about the cheese?"

"A little damp around the edges but can still be eaten." He divided the sausage in half for Lexi. He cut off a piece of his portion to offer Callie.

"No, that sausage is just big enough for you two. I will find another mouse." Callie moved to the cave opening where she stopped to tell Nollen, "Do not save me any this time."

A few moments of silence passed to eat before Lexi asked, "How much further to Far Point?"

"Five days. We rode further west to cross a shallow part of the river."

"Are there any bridges nearby?"

Nollen swallowed before he replied. "The only one is a three-day ride east, near the Great Falls. It connects The Doane to the west Freeland Road. All others were destroyed to keep the province safe from Ha'tar aggression. No one knew about the dragon riders back then, only that they helped the coup succeed."

"Why not build new bridges?"

He heaved a shrug. "Suspicion. Many in The Doane remain distrustful of the Ha'tar. When leaving Mathena, I usually return to Wyckton and take the ferry to The Doane. Bypassing Ha'tar. With you wanting to see Eldar, I'm taking you the same route I did Axel and Gunnar."

A howling yelp startled them. Even Alydar and Sheba jerked in surprise.

Nollen ran to the cave opening. "Callie!" At another yelp, he fetched his crossbow. "Stay here," he told Lexi.

"I can help!"

"No! Stay here."

His crossbow armed and ready, Nollen searched the area. He didn't raise the hood against the steady downpour. Rain made him blink and wipe his eyes. He heard the sound of flapping just before talons reached to snatch him. Sharp claws clipped the back of his head. Force of the attack knocked him face first to the ground. He rolled onto his back in time to see a large, winged bird dive at him again. He fired his crossbow. When the bird banked to avoid the dart, he recognized a grey owl. An ear-piercing screech made him recoil in pain. He glanced up in time to see the owl chase away by—

"A harpy," he fearfully muttered. The shadowy image of the harpy headed for the cave. He scrambled to his feet when another harpy screech brought him to his knees.

"Nollen!" he heard Lexi call from somewhere nearby.

He attempted to stand only forced to dodge another owl attack. He landed hard against the base of a butte.

Lexi arrived and stepped in front of Nollen. "Stop!" she shouted at the owl, her crossbow aimed.

The owl hovered and made an angry noises. It became a stare down with neither the owl nor Lexi willing to yield.

"Don't try it!" Lexi warned. Her finger encircled the trigger.

The owl moved in defiance and she loosed a shaft. The owl avoided being impaled but the dart struck its wing. It awkwardly flew away.

Anxious, Lexi knelt beside Nollen. "Are you hurt?"

Fierce growling and squawking of a fight came from nearby.

"Callie." Nollen pushed himself up. He and Lexi came upon Callie viciously shaking the owl by the neck.

Callie released the limp owl. "I made certain of the kill so it could not betray the Shield Maiden to whomever sent it."

"Who would send an owl to attack us?" asked Lexi with confusion.

"Dolus used owls as spies against the Brethren. Why now? I don't know." Nollen winced in pain and touched the back of his head.

Alydar and Sheba skidded to a halt. "What happened?" asked Alydar.

"Nollen and Callie were injured by an owl," said Lexi.

"Not just an owl." Nollen hissed in pain.

Lexi placed the crossbow over her shoulder to take his arm. "Let's return to the cave so I tend you."

"I told you to wait," he argued.

"Volker glowed red. I wasn't going to let you face danger alone."

Nollen grunted when they entered the cave and he sat. Callie laid down to lick the talon wound on her right foreleg.

From the saddlebag, Lexi fetched the apothecary medicine. Nollen hissed when she touched his head. "Sorry. There are four scratches. I'll try to be gentle with the salve."

"You said not just the owl. What did you mean?" Alydar asked.

"A harpy," Nollen angrily replied then grew unsettled in speech. "I haven't seen one in years, and certainly not at night. Its screech wracked me with such pain I couldn't move. That never happened before."

"It also rendered us unable to follow Lexi," complained Alydar.

"The harpy was the evil Volker sensed. Owls are a nuisance," said Sheba.

"Speak for yourself." Nollen pointed to his head and flinched. "Are you finished yet?"

"Aye. I hope Callie is more cooperative," Lexi wryly teased.

"What are you using?" Callie asked when Lexi knelt in front of her.

"An herbal remedy given me in Mathena. A special blend for the Shield Maiden."

"With a harpy in the area, we must move swiftly. Sheba and I will navigate Ha'tar. You two, just hold on tight," said Alydar.

Nollen nodded. "In daylight, so we can see it coming."

Outside, Kyros landed on an outcropping opposite the cave. He breathed heavy, as he avoided both the owl and harpy during his observation of the attack. The human female commanded, and at first, the owl obeyed. Strange. He became agitated and flapped to take-off when Zeta landed beside him.

"Did you follow me?" he demanded.

"I come with news."

Growling drew attention. Callie stood in the cave threshold with hackles raised.

"A white wolf!" Zeta said in stunned awe.

"Fly!" Kyros cawed and left the outcrop.

"I thought white wolves were extinct?"

"The same was said of harpys and jackals," chided Kyros. They landed on a rocky hill some distance from the cave. "What news?"

"Spyros met with Ursus and Kronus."

"Kronus?" repeated Kyros in astonishment. "I thought the great buffalo king long dead."

"Obviously not. They spoke about the plan. The main gist of the conversation—Spyros admitted he doesn't trust you."

"How did you learn this?"

"Skyron. Spyros wants him to spy on you."

"My first fledgling? I'll drop him from the sky!"

"Easy! Skyron told me because he doesn't want to, yet like you, he won't upset Spyros." She spoke with annoyed emphasis about the comparison. At his throaty grunt of anger, she added, "What example will you set for our fledglings?"

"Spyros charged me to be example of obedience. Same as I would want from Skyron."

"Then you approve of him spying on you due to mistrust?" she boldly inquired. He lowered his head at the question. Zeta grew sympathetic. "Kyros, we are mates for life, yet I cannot stand the thought of losing more fledglings. And I don't mean to Ursus. Rather Spyros' blind ambition."

Kyros moved down from Zeta, only she followed. "Spyros has been using you. Now, he wants to use Skyron!" She flapped her wings with indignation. "Do you hear me? Spyros wants to divide our flock! And for what? Tell me if you know."

"Revenge."

"Against whom? A human?"

"The First Ones. Like the white wolf we saw."

"Why, when we have lived free and peaceable for centuries?"

Kyros awkwardly shook his head. "I don't know. Yet ever since the Son of Eldar returned, Spyros and Ursus have been plotting." He stared in the direction of the cave. "I shrugged it off, believing the First Ones were only legends. The arrival of the harpy and jackals, and now the white wolf, prove they are alive."

"It still doesn't explain the depth of Spyros' desire for revenge, nor his mistrust of you."

"No." He straightened with head high. "After I complete my task, I should have earned enough to trust to learn the answers. Return to Bertrand. Try to keep Skyron from Spyros until I'm done. And, Zeta," saying her name stopped her from leaving. "Thank you."

Chapter 18

AT THE FIRST LIGHT OF DAWN, THEY LEFT THE CAVE. CALLIE TOOK the point, but soon overtaken by Alydar and Sheba in haste to leave Ha'tar. Three hours later, they reached the Leven Tributary between Ha'tar and The Doane.

Nollen jerked Alydar to a halt. Ripples and small white caps broke the surface. "The current looks swift. We should check the depth before crossing."

"We can safely swim across." Sheba lowered her head, as if to touch the water. She chomped on the bit with horse vocalizations.

From the water, rose the transparent fluid shape of two unicorns.

"Nicor," Lexi said in wonder.

"How did you know that?" asked Nollen.

Lexi shrugged with uncertainty, as she regarded the water unicorn.

One spoke. "Greetings, Shield Maiden. You may cross safely."

The water unicorns separated to ten feet apart and swam in opposite directions between the banks yet parallel to each other. This created a path of still water.

"Hold on." Sheba entered the river followed by Alydar and Nollen. Callie kept the rear.

The depth of the water rose to Sheba's chest. Lexi clutched the mane along with the reins. She nervously watched the Nicor as they swam. Angry water churned on either side of them. Lexi didn't relax until they reached the opposite shore.

Once joined by the others, Sheba lowered her head and spoke to the Nicor. The water unicorns acknowledged her before they once more became part of the river. The current returned to normal.

"Amazing," Lexi murmured in awe.

"Come. You can tell me what you sense about The Doane," said Nollen.

Lexi viewed a variety of lush trees and plant life. "Another lovely Territory. Definitely more pleasant than Ha'tar." She visibly shivered.

Nollen noticed the sudden change. "Something wrong?"

"I sense guardedness. Skepticism."

"An accurate description of many in The Doane," he said. "The Territory borders Ha'tar on the west, and Nefal on the east. The Great Falls and Takara River divides The Doane. It makes up the southern part of Eldar from border to border, with Bertrand to the south."

"I know. I studied the map," Lexi sarcastically replied. She again grew thoughtful. "Those feelings of skepticism and wariness run deep."

"Aye," Nollen soberly agreed. "During those two centuries, life depended upon viewing everything with suspicion. Four years of peace, has helped to ease some of the tension, but not completely erase long-held memories or practices." He drew rein. "It will delay our arrival at Far Point by several days, but would like to visit Heddwyn?"

She repeated the name with consideration then asked, "The forest compound?" When he nodded, she readily agreed, "Aye!"

Nollen changed course to head south. Lexi didn't need to sense his disturbance, as the brooding clearly visible. "If going to Heddwyn troubles you, we can continue to Far Point."

"I haven't ventured there since … discovery by Javan's agents."

Lexi moved Sheba in front of Alydar to stop the trek. "Nollen, we don't have to go."

"No. It is needful; for you, as Shield Maiden, and me to move past certain memories."

Lexi drew Sheba aside to continue. Nollen pointed out landmarks with commentary of how it related to a secret trek. Some stories were amusing, others poignant.

Over the course of the next two days, Lexi asked Nollen about Heddwyn and the Brethren. Hearing about his clandestine trips while riding the same trails made the stories come alive. In her spirit, she sensed everything as if experiencing the danger, tension, and wariness firsthand.

Lexi drew Sheba to rein and glanced up at the trees. "I now understand where you gained your expertise. Even the forest takes time to heal from such deep wounds."

"Everything in Eldar suffered for hundreds of years. These woods were filled with Black Jackals and harpys." Nollen's tone held an edge of anger.

"Bardolf and his pack kept Heddwyn safe," Callie reminded him.

Nollen's expression softened. "Aye." He gathered the reins. "Come. We should reach Heddwyn before sundown."

An hour later, Nollen paused beside a mound of stones with grass and weeds growing on top and around it. "This is where we buried the juvenile dragon that wounded Gunnar. He nearly died from the poison, but Gott mercifully healed him."

"Gunnar?" Lexi repeated with disturbance. "Neither he nor Axel mentioned that."

"They tend not to speak of self-sacrifice." Nollen dismounted. "We're a mile from Heddwyn. We walk from here because of the descent. It is steep and winding, and only wide enough to continue single file."

Shortly after starting the descent, Lexi slipped and fell hard on her rump. This pulled Sheba's reins and made her stumble. Sheba tossed her head to jerk free and stopped in time to not trample Lexi.

"Let us walk separately," said Sheba.

Nollen waited at the bottom with Alydar and Callie. "Are you hurt?" he asked Lexi.

She snorted an embarrassed, "No." She ignored his chuckle to glance around. "How far is the compound from here?"

"In front of you." He pointed at two towering pine trees with a strange broken vine that hung between them to reveal a narrow opening. "This is what remains of the camouflaged entrance." He led Alydar through the constricted passage.

Stalwart pines and massive oak trees formed a canopy over the compound. Six oaks formed a circle that enclosed a half-acre. Years of abandoned neglect, forest growth, and creatures, showed decay of the compound. Two spiral stairways wound around the trunks and led to an upper level where four structures were built into the trees: the roofs long gone. Broken remnants of branch bridges stretched between the structures. A longhouse dominated the lower portion of the compound. Much of the roof missing or broken.

Lexi wandered the area, to take in both ground level sights and the overhead structures. "This place is so much smaller than Kranston."

"Aye, but they made do with food from the forest, and what supplies we brought." Nollen stopped her from climbing the stairs. "It's not safe."

She crossed compound to pause at the entrance of the longhouse. She peeked inside. "This looks safe enough." She entered. "What was this used for?"

"Everything." At her curious expression, Nollen expounded, "Meals, sleeping, gatherings. This served as the center for all activities. That room was Grandfather's quarters. The opposite, for whatever was needed – like Gunnar's recovery." He made motions with each description. "A grand feast was prepared for Axel—or at least what was on hand to celebrate his arrival."

"I sense happiness and joy."

"Aye." Nollen's tone changed to thoughtful recollection. "Despite agreeing to help, I remained resistant, uncertain—fearful." He picked up a branch, the size for a good staff. "I vented my frustration on Axel during a friendly quarterstaff competition. I lost." He dropped the branch. "Humiliated, I left. Only as far as the upper-level outlook. Axel would not be put off. He confronted me and demanded to know why." His voice grew choked with emotion. "For the first time, I admitted anger because of what happened to my parents. Executed as traitors for sending the signal. I feared failing them."

Moved to tears, Lexi took hold of Nollen's hand. "Is that the memory you need to move past by coming here?"

He softly grinned. "No. Although, being here brought back emotions of the moment. I thought sharing it would help you understand the impact of Axel's return. It brought hope and excitement."

"And truth."

"Aye. His presence forced many to confront truth."

"That is an understatement. My brother is annoying with his tenacity."

"I often became irked by Ida's prodding when I wanted to be left alone. Come to think of it, our siblings are much older. Perhaps that is why we find them irritating at times. Yet, you must admit, it helps. Like now." He stared directly at her, his expression prompting.

"Aye." She moved to inspect the rest of the longhouse. "It does help to understand what he and Gunnar were doing while we waited. It goes beyond anything I could possibly conceive. Thank you for bringing me here."

He widely smiled. "You're welcome. The hearth looks stable enough for a fire. You start one while I trap something to eat." Nollen just reached the threshold when Callie appeared. The she-wolf dropped at hare at his feet. "Thought you might want it for dinner."

After Nollen prepared the hare for Lexi to cook, he unsaddled Sheba and Alydar. By the time he finished laying out the bedrolls, groomed the unicorn/horses, and fetched water, Lexi announced the hare done. They found two unbroken stools and sat at a table to eat. Even Callie partook of the hare. Once satisfied, the she-wolf yawned and laid beside the hearth.

"You're awfully quiet," Nollen commented to Lexi.

"Thinking of what life was like here compared to Kranston. Small and confining, yet similar in hiding from discovery."

"You actually experienced more freedom at Kranston."

She wryly smiled at his emphasis on *freedom*. "I can see that. Although, I sense joy and happiness from Axel's visit, I also feel anxiety and sorrow." She earnestly regarded him. "What is the memory you came here to move past?"

"Those here were captured as a result of betrayal by my cousin … Jonas."

Surprise briefly muted Lexi. "Wasn't he recently killed by traitors?"

Nollen soberly nodded. "Being family, we trusted him. He knew Heddwyn's location, and even came with me several times to deliver supplies. However, when his wife and sons were arrested for being Brethren, he became desperate. He thought to save them by leading Javan's agents here. Although, after Axel won, he repented, received forgiveness, and restored … the memories have haunted me since his death. I had to come."

"Now that you are here?" she asked with tender compassion.

"I understand everything that occurred here was for good. Axel's arrival, him confronting me, my admission, even Jonas' betrayal. It brought everyone to Sener, where they witnessed Axel's sacrifice and triumph. Something that would not have happened otherwise."

"I'm glad to hear that, but also baffled. I keep hearing references to Axel's sacrifice only I don't understand since he is king."

For a long heavy moment, Nollen regarded Lexi. When she frowned at him, he asked, "Have you not read about Oleg's Blood Oath?"

"Of course. Oleg sacrificed himself to save his people. He failed. The Electors came to power, and our family forced to flee."

Nollen's face showed his struggle to speak, thus tactful said, "It is more than that."

"Obviously. Everyone in Eldar talks about it as if a recent life and death event."

Nollen took Lexi's hand to look directly at her. "The Blood Oath did not mean Oleg. It meant his descendant—Axel's death for our lives. I witnessed Javan strike him down."

Lexi paled and gaped at him. "What? He lives," the words barely uttered.

"My blowing the horn, freed Othniel from his captivity to fulfill Gott's promise." Nollen quoted, "*The weakness of men resides in hasty words. Faithlessness results in actions that cannot save. Treachery and deceit lie behind the dealings of false men. Yet, my covenant with Oleg will remain. I do not deal foolishly like men. My word is forever.*" With tremendous passion, he described the event. "We—me, Gunnar, and Axel—went to Sener to confront Javan and Dolus to reclaim the throne. Before we arrived, Axel charged me with blowing the horn. Although Javan killed Axel, I went to do so, uncertain of how it could help. When I finished sounding the call, it fell to pieces in my hands. I felt utterly hopelessness. Othniel's unexpected arrival caused chaos. He roared so loud and fierce, the Great Hall shook. Ceiling tiles fell. Then, with great trepidation, Gunnar and I watched Othniel place a paw on Axel's fatal wound. The Great Lion breathed air onto Axel's lifeless face. A sudden audible gasp and he sat up! Everyone stunned, as we witnessed a miracle of life restored!"

Overcoming with emotions, Lexi rose from the table. She flinched when Nollen came from behind to hold her shoulders. She turned and clung to him, as she wept. "I didn't know!" She repeated it several times.

"Hush." He escorted her back to the table.

"All my life I heard those words, yet never fully grasped the meaning."

"Neither did we, until it happened."

She looked at him with new comprehension and threw her arms around his neck. "Thank you!"

"You're welcome, I suppose." He sounded a bit befuddled.

She held his face. "I suddenly realize what you meant in Miska when you spoke of a man who gave himself for others. That you could do no less than your king. I didn't know he and Axel were the same, only that you took our place to keep us safe as he charged you. It went deeper than I knew." Again, she placed her arms about his neck, and kissed him.

He returned her kiss, and they lingered in each other's embrace. Sheba made a loud whinny and stomped her hooves. Startled, they parted.

"I think we better get some sleep," Nollen awkwardly said. "I'll be near the door. You stay by the fire." He moved his bedroll and laid down with his face toward the threshold. Callie lay back-to-back with him.

Lexi didn't argue and made herself comfortable on her bedroll. She gazed up at the ceiling. Shafts of moonlight shown through the broken parts of the roof. New tears swelled, as the entire scope of prophecy became clear. All she knew is what Axel told her—that as the Son of Eldar, he would reclaim the throne for their family; stop the spread of evil; save the Brethren of Gott; and restore peace to Eldar. Her focus changed from the ceiling to Sheba when the unicorn lowered her head.

"Once again, I misjudged my brother," Lexi whispered in a voice thick with remorse.

"If you had known, what would you have done?"

Lexi sniffled back tears. "Try to stop him. Find a different way. I couldn't bear to lose him and be left alone. Though now, it sounds selfish. I didn't know anything else but Kranston."

Sheba softly muzzled Lexi's cheek. "Gott granted the Son of Eldar insight needed to realize his destiny. His silence protected you from a reality you could not understand then."

Lexi wiped her eyes. "Aye. Eldar felt like dream long hoped for, yet difficult to imagine. I have acted so cruel to him since being here."

"You are young, and just learning about the larger world."

Lexi moved in such a way to see Nollen, who remained with his back turned. Memories of the dungeon in Miska flashed through her mind. To protect the women of the group, and specifically her and Alicia from being discovered, he bravely faced Sirin. Staring into the face of pure evil, nearly cost his life. She recalled the blood streaming from his nose, his face deadly pale. Fearing he wouldn't live through the night, she asked him:

"Why did you take our place?"

Nollen licked his lips to clear the blood. "Years ago, I watched a man give himself for others. I can do no less than my king, who charged me with your safety."

Lexi rolled back on the blanket. She wiped away tears. When Alydar approached, she said, "You know what he did at Miska, and why."

Alydar lowered his head. "Nollen of Far Point is a noble-hearted human."

Lexi tenderly smiled. "Aye, he is." Her gaze passed to Sheba. "Lord Cormac was right. When finished with the trading circuit, we will return to Mathena so I can complete my training. I owe it to Axel, Gunnar, Nollen, and others."

Sheba again nuzzled Lexi. "Indeed. Now, rest, dear one."

Chapter 19

IN THE WEE HOURS OF THE MORNING, CALLIE ROSE AND CAREFULLY approached the longhouse entrance. Her ears laid back, hackles raised, and teeth bared. Sheba and Alydar quietly moved to stand beside their respective riders. Nollen and Lexi slept undisturbed.

Suddenly, four Cursian males jumped down from the ceiling. Angry whinnies woke Nollen and Lexi. Startled, Lexi cried out when grabbed. She fought the two Cursians to reach her sword. Her first defensive swiped killed one. The second used a sharp, slate-tipped spear to parry her.

Sheba bucked and knocked the Cursian into the side of the hearth. It threw a half-burnt log at Sheba then thrust out with the spear. The impact of Lexi's sword shattered the spearhead. The Cursian rammed Lexi, and both fell to the ground, with the Cursian on top. Callie leapt to take it off Lexi. When it managed to swat Callie aside, Lexi scrambled to her feet and lunged. The Cursian shrieked at being wounded. The ear-piercing noise made Lexi back away in pain. It staggered out a crack in the back wall of the longhouse. Callie went to pursue when Sheba shouted.

"No! Stay. There may be more nearby."

Nollen fought the two that jumped him. He drew his dagger and thrust it into the abdomen of one. It limped away. The other jabbed a spear at Nollen. The doublet ripped when he dodged to avoid being impaled. He clouted the Cursian with the hilt of his dagger and sent it sprawling to the ground. Alydar reared and stomped on the Cursian in a final blow. Two lay dead, while the two wounded managed to escape.

Lexi's face screwed in disgust at the creatures in animal skins that reeked of decay. "What are they?"

"Cursians. Creatures cursed by your forefather for treachery in helping the coup. I've not known them to venture out of Altwald," Nollen replied.

She noticed the tear in his doublet. "Are you wounded?"

He examined the damage. "A scrape. It didn't break the skin." He wiped off the dagger blade to sheath it. "Saddle up. We need to leave. They will bring more for revenge."

"What time is it?"

"Very early morning."

"I will scout ahead." Callie ran through the main compound entrance.

An hour later, Nollen and Lexi fought to stay awake.

"After dawn, we stop for a short nap," Nollen said. Lexi just nodded.

When they arrived at a ravine, Lexi nearly fell when she dismounted. She staggered with fatigue and sat on the ground. She didn't bother with the bedroll rather leaned against the back of the earthen ravine and fell asleep. She smelled roast meat. Maybe a dream. She gathered her cloak and turned over. Something wet touched her face. Her eyes popped open. "Callie!"

"Time for breakfast. Actually, lunch." Nollen sat by a fire over which hung a spitted fowl. "Grouse." He identified the bird.

Lexi stretched before she joined him. "Why did you let me sleep so long?"

He chuckled. "I tried to wake you twice. Callie succeeded."

After consuming half the grouse, they preserved the rest for later. With no farm or inn between Heddwyn and Far Point, they spent two nights in the open. At twilight of the third day, they emerged from a patch of woods into a meadow.

Nollen drew rein and pointed to the distance. "Two miles further, just over the rise, you can see the smoke from Far Point." He glanced at the sky. "Twilight. We feared traveling in the open this time of day because of jackals and harpys. So, we raced across."

"Like now?" Lexi merrily said. She snapped the reins for Sheba to run.

Nollen followed on Alydar. They no sooner reached a small pool with boulders when he spied them running from the woods on an intercept course!

"Jackals?" He shouted forward, "Lexi! Don't stop! Keep riding!" He released the reins to arm his crossbow. Alydar continued to gallop.

Nollen only got off one shot before something struck him. It wrapped around him, pinned his arms, loosed the crossbow, and sent him flying off the saddle. With his arms pinned, he couldn't brace for the fall, and rendered unconscious upon impact with the ground. A jackal pounced on him; teeth ready to clamp down on his neck. Callie stopped the death blow, but the jackal's fangs tore the flesh of Nollen's left shoulder and neck.

Although larger than the jackals, Callie had all she could handle with two. One jackal yelped when kicked by Alydar. Injured, it retreated into the wood. Callie and the other jackal remained in combat. Finally, it too ran off with Callie in pursuit.

Lexi saw Nollen unhorsed. Horrified, she jerked Sheba to a stop and turned around. Suddenly, an ear-piercing bird-screech echoed in the meadow. Alydar and Sheba whinnied in pain. Both reared before they fell paralyzed. Lexi managed to slip off Sheba before her leg became caught beneath Sheba's weight. Lexi collapsed to her knees, also incapacitated by the sound.

Her eyes grew wide with dread, when a harpy dove at her. She couldn't move to make defense. An eagle appeared out of the twilight rays in time to divert the harpy. Lexi could only watch the skyward battle. Unexpected hands jerked her up. She barely caught a glimpse of two men with hats pulled down over hoods before one placed a cloth over her face. He held it against her hard and suffocating. She began to feel weak, dizzy, and finally faint. The man carried her back into the cover of the trees. Shortly, they emerged on horseback with a bound and unconscious Lexi. They rode south.

At the tree line, Kyros fell from the sky. He breathed heavy. He used his beak to push himself onto his talons. He hopped in an attempt to fly. By the third hop, he took off. He barely avoided Brynn when she ran from the forest. She held her sword. A piece of cloth wrapped around her head to cover the ears. She halted to watch the men ride off.

Spoor grabbed Brynn. Angry, she broke free. "Bertrandians are taking the princess!"

"Exactly as planned. Get back before we are seen!" He talked more loudly due to the ear-coverings.

An eagle's cry drew their attention skyward. Badly injured, the harpy fluttered away. With Spoor distracted, Brynn ran in pursuit of the men. He drew his sword and overtook her. The brief exchange ended with Brynn mortally wounded.

Bodil raced from another part of the forest to join Spoor. "What happened?"

"Bertrandians." Spoor motioned to the vanishing forms of two riders heading south.

Bodil knelt to examine Brynn. "She won't survive unless we get help."

When Bodil rose, Spoor sliced open Bodil's left upper arm. Bodil backed away in pain. His cower of surprise turned to a defensive position. Instead of attacking again, Spoor sheathed his sword and removed the ear coverings.

"Why did wound me?" demanded Bodil.

"For a more convincing story."

"What?" asked Bodil, totally confused.

"Her death and your wound." Spoor returned to the forest.

Bodil hastened to catch Spoor. "You wounded me on purpose? Why?"

"All part of the plan."

Bodil rushed in front of Spoor. "I understand about the princess, but if Bertrandians murdered Brynn, we must avenge her!"

"Not if we want Maro's full cooperation." Spoor pushed past Bodil to fetch his horse.

Momentarily muted by the response, Bodil again ran after Spoor. "Shouldn't we at least bring her home for mourning and proper burial?"

"Not if we want to maintain the pretense of pursuing the kidnappers. But first ..." Spoor made whistling call. Shortly, an owl landed on a branch. He spoke to the owl in another language. It nodded and flew off. "Now, mount. We need to leave before anyone sees us."

In reluctant compliance, Bodil followed Spoor to ride southeast.

Alydar recovered by first moving his head then bolted to his feet. "Sheba?"

The she-unicorn slowly stood. She stumbled a few steps. "I am uninjured. What of Nollen and Lexi?"

Alydar saw the eagle land beside Nollen. "Ajax? Is Nollen alive?"

Ajax used his beak to nudge Nollen. He then placed his face in front of Nollen's nose. "He still breathes."

"Where is Lexi? Lexi!" Sheba pranced around the area to call. She stopped upon spying another individual lying on the ground. "Alydar! A Nefal."

"Dead or alive?"

"Unknown."

"See to the Nefal, while I tend Nollen." Alydar used his muzzle to nudge Nollen. No response. "Nollen. Please, wake up." Alydar raised his head at the sound of a wagon. The driver appeared to be making haste towards them. The mighty stallion whinnied and reared to get attention.

"Whoa!" Jarred pulled hard to stop just shy of Nollen. He jumped down from the driver's seat. Anxious, at seeing the serious wound, he fell to his knees beside Nollen. A faint moan came when he tried to rouse Nollen. "Thank Gott, you're alive." He looked up when Alydar lowered his head. "Wish you could tell me what happened."

"We were attacked by a harpy and two jackals."

Startled by Alydar's speech, Jarred sat back on his heels. "You can talk again?"

Rather than answer, Alydar asked, "How did you come by us?"

"We heard the commotion at Far Point and feared the worse." Jarred tugged at the rope with two black balls that ensnared Nollen. "Did you see the one who did this? Which way they went?"

"No. The harpy's screech was paralyzing."

"This isn't good." Jarred placed Nollen in the back of the wagon. He cut the rope to removed it then placed the rope and balls beside Nollen.

Ajax landed on the driver's seat while Sheba trotted over to join them. The she-unicorn anxious to inform Jarred, "Lexi is missing. There is a Nefal female over there. Barely alive."

Again, Jarred was taken back by speech. "Are you a former unicorn like Alydar?"

"There is no time to explain! We must find Lexi."

"Do you mean Lexi, as in the King's sister?"

"Aye!"

Jarred pursed his lips in consideration, as he surveyed the area. "First, we need to take Nollen to Far Point then determine how to find her."

"And the Nefal?" asked Sheba.

Jarred approached Brynn. He knelt to determine the extent of injury. The wound landed close to the heart. At his touch, Brynn's eyes slowly opened. Her lips moved in an attempt to speak. Hearing muted words, he leaned down with his ear near her mouth to listen. "What?" Some more muted words then a low exhale of death. He felt her neck for a pulse. "Rest in Gott's peace, or whatever the Nefal believe."

He just returned to the wagon when they heard a mournful howl.

"Sounds like Callie," said Ajax with concern.

"She pursued the jackals," said Sheba.

"Stay with Nollen. I will find her." Ajax took flight to head for the woods.

"I need to get him to Far Point." Jarred climbed onto the driver's seat.

"What about the Nefal?" asked Sheba.

"Dead." He snapped the reins for the horse to move.

Chapter 20

SEVERAL TIMES LEXI WOKE DURING THE RIDE. BOUND, GAGGED, and tightly held, prevented her from escape. Finally, they stopped. The other dragged her off the horse so the one she rode with could dismount. Unsteady on her feet, she stumbled when made to sit. Whatever they used to render her unconscious had a lingering effect. She noticed the sheath empty, so her sword gone. Hearing words, she attempted to focus and listen. Either her mind remained fuzzy, or they spoke a language she couldn't understand.

She tried to crawl away. No use. He tied her to a tree. She watched them make camp for the night. Each moment that passed, her mind became clearer. They definitely spoke another language. The firelight revealed unfamiliar clothes; long dark embroidered surcoats complete with leather belt and ornate short swords. The leather boots matched the belt. The hoods of the black cloaks were pulled up over their heads. On top of the hoods, they wore fur-trimmed caps. Perhaps, the ears being covered prevented any effects from the harpy's screech. During the conversations, she heard what she believed to be names, Mateo and Marius.

Nollen will come … A lump rose in her throat at recalling him on the ground. No. She had to find a way to escape. But how, and where could she go? She reckoned they remained in The Doane. Of course, that didn't much help since she was unfamiliar with the Territory, nor how to navigate Eldar. She glanced up to study what stars shone through the trees. She tried to recall everything he told her about using the stars at night, and landmarks during the day. *Gott, give me wisdom and courage. I pray Nollen is well and not seriously hurt or worse*—She couldn't complete the dreadful possibility.

Startled, she balked when someone jostled her arm. One of the men held a shallow bowl. He spoke and motioned to it. She shook her head in confusion. He yanked the gag from her mouth. Grateful for the relief, she moved her jaws and lips.

"Who are you? What do you want?" she demanded.

He responded in words she didn't understand. He held the bowl to her lips.

She turned her face away. "I don't know what it is."

He became insistent. When she resisted a second time, he seized her head and tried to force her to eat the gruel. Disgusted by the resistance, he roughly released her.

"Mateo!" the other called upon approach.

Mateo loudly complained to his companion, who, Lexi now believed went by the name Marius. Mateo gave Marius the bowl and left. He muttered what could be considered curses.

Marius made the same motion for eating, only scooped the gruel in his hand and ate. This time when the bowl was held to her mouth, Lexi accepted some. When he gave her too much, she gagged. Her lips screwed at the foul taste. He spoke a question about the bowl.

She shook her head. "No more."

He shrugged, replaced the gag in her mouth, and left.

Even this far south, the spring nights grew cool. Tied to a tree, prevented her from wrapping the cloak closed and laying down to get comfortable. The gag hurt. She tried to use her lips and jaws to dislodge it. At one point she bit her tongue and gasped in pain. The men turned but appeared unsympathetic. She leaned back against the tree. Tears swelled as she considered her situation. Nollen hurt, she kidnapped, and uncertain of why or how to escape.

Lexi, get a hold or yourself. Crying won't help. Besides, you are the Shield Maiden—whatever that means, her mind argued. *Sheba. Callie. They will try to find me. Maybe even tell Axel. Just survive until then.* Armed with that determination, she leaned against the tree for a few hours of sleep.

Lexi's heart raced when rudely awakened. Mateo. Darkness remained. She saw stars, but unable to determine the time. Her attention became drawn back when he spoke quick, agitated words. He untied her from the tree and jerked her up. Marius came over. In softer words, he tried to reason with his companion. Mateo spat on the ground before he shoved Lexi to Marius. He led her to the campfire. He picked up a bowl to offer her.

Lexi nodded since her stomach growled with hunger. Marius removed the gag. The gruel didn't taste much better, but she needed to eat something. After four swallows, she shook her head in decline. He set aside the bowl to offer her a cup containing a clear liquid.

"Water?" she tentatively asked.

Marius just made a motion to drink.

"If it will wash the taste from my mouth." She drank most of the water yet made a sour expression. "Doesn't taste like water," she complained. He wryly smiled. Shortly, she began to feel lethargic. "Not just water," she mumbled to herself.

In a dazed stupor, she watched them break camp, and make the area appear undisturbed. Mateo roughly helped her mount to ride with Marius. Just like last night, she sat forward in the saddle, with Marius holding her from behind. The only difference, they didn't replace the gag. Of course, in her sluggish condition she could barely speak.

Several times she nodded off, only to wake and find it still dark. Periodically, they offered her water. Twice she refused, but when she showed signs of becoming alert, Mateo forced her to drink. Once more, lethargy set in. By dawn, all she wanted to do was sleep off the effects of whatever they put in water.

They stopped after full daybreak to take shelter in a protected hollow cave. She didn't fight when Mateo fetched her down and shoved her under the ledge. The only trees nearby were outside the hollow. Too tired from whatever they used to keep her sedated, Lexi closed her eyes to sleep. She stirred to the smell of roast meat. At first, she grinned, as her mind recalled

Nollen and the grouse. Her eyes snapped open at harsh foreign words. The brief moment of reminiscing gone. She pushed herself up to sit against the hollow. They noticed her movement.

Marius spoke to Mateo. She warily watched Marius pick up a bowl and approach her. He indicated the containing of what appeared to a be a leg. He made motions with his fingers that looked like a jump then place one finger up on his head.

"Rabbit?" she asked. When he appeared puzzled, she used her bound hands to make the same movement.

"Yah! *Cunculus,*" he said of the leg on the plate. He set it down to loosen the bounds of her hands, but not completely free her. He gave her the plate.

The slack allowed her to eat by herself. Although, she cautiously sniffed the rabbit leg. He laughed and shook his head. She took a tentative bite.

"Tastes like rabbit," she said.

Again, he laughed.

She cast a wary glance to Mateo, who remained at the fire to eat. Her voice low in speaking to Marius. "Do you know who I am?" Me?" She used her fingers to tap her chest.

He frowned, as if not understanding. "*Utro cunculus!*" He left.

When Lexi finished eating, Marius returned with a flask.

"Aqua. No algea."

When she remained skeptical, he drank from the flask, and repeated the offer.

His action told her it was safe, so she drank. "Aye, just water."

When he took back the flask, she noticed Mateo lay down to nap. She flinched when the bonds were tightened. Marius spoke what sounded like words of warning. When he returned to the fire, she carefully observed the surroundings. In daylight, she could see better. However, they positioned camp in such a way that she had to pass them to escape. At least they didn't tie her to a tree.

After she woke from a nap, Lexi noticed the men appeared to be fast asleep. To test the possibility, she carefully picked up a rock in her two bound hands. The rustling sound of movement did not disturb them.

With all her might, she awkwardly threw the rock. It struck a tree, bounced, and made several sounds. The men slightly moved but remained asleep. Waiting a little longer for silent stillness, she used her hands on the back of the hollow to inch her way up to standing. No sign of activity. She took a deep breath and bolted from the hollow. Unfortunately, her action startled the horses. The animals' whinny woke the men.

Mateo immediately pursued. She dodged trees and leapt logs, but without her hands free for balance, she stumbled, and fell headlong down an incline. He pounced on her. She swung her bound arms at his face and kicked him. He fell sideways. She scrambled away. He tackled her. In anger, he slapped her face twice, which made her scream in pain.

Marius arrived and stopped further assault. They argued. Mateo remained straddled over Lexi. He cursed at Marius, and jerked Lexi to her feet. Tears of pain blurred her vision. Mateo's grip hurt her. He continued to argue with Marius. Finally, Marius yielded. Mateo pulled Lexi back to camp. He threw her to the ground where she nearly landed in the campfire. She rolled away from the flames. He grabbed her hair and forced her to drink. She gagged and coughed down the liquid. By the taste, she knew it contained the sedative. Only when satisfied that she drank enough, did he stop.

Lexi lay on the ground weeping in pain and despair at her failed attempt. "Gott, help me," she whimpered before she fainted.

From a high tree branch, Kyros observed Lexi's attempted escape. The Eldarian female showed courage against the vicious twins. He carefully descended a few branches in time to hear her call upon Gott. He only heard the name of Eldar's god spoken with disdain, never pleading for aid. Whoever she was, she bore watching.

Chapter 21

NOLLEN FELT SOMETHING WET ON HIS FACE AND NECK, YET IN his sleepy state, uncertain of what. He heard voices. One female and a several males. A dream? He recalled images of faces including Ida and Jarred. The voices became clearer the more his mind woke. He squirmed and tried to force his eyes to open. He managed to blink.

A hand seized his shoulder. He heard his name spoken. Startled, his eyes snapped open. It took a moment to recognize …"Axel?" His gaze wandered, still confused. "Ida. Where am I?"

"Far Point," she replied.

"Far Point," he muttered in consideration. "Lexi. Where is Lexi?"

"Easy." Axel sat on the bed to restrain Nollen from rising

Befuddled, Nollen asked Axel, "If I'm at Far Point, what are you doing here? And how did you get here so quickly?"

"You've been in and out of consciousness for a week. Time enough for Ajax to fly to Sener, and for us," Axel motioned to Gunnar and Cormac, "to take a ferry to The Doane."

Nollen sought to digest the news. "A week?"

"Poison from the jackal bite." Gunnar motioned to his shoulder and neck for the location of Nollen's wounds.

"Fortunately, I found Ganel medicine in the princess' saddlebags to prepare a poultice and draw out the poison," said Cormac.

"Is Lexi hurt?" Nollen's anxious gaze shifted between them. When everyone hesitated to answer, he pushed Axel's hand aside to rise on his elbows. He ignored the pain to demand, "What happened to Lexi?"

"Kidnapped," began Axel with restrained anger. "Apparently, by Bertrandians."

Stunned, Nollen fell back against the cushions. "What? How? Why?"

"We are still trying to ascertain the reasons. Jarred found Lady Brynn mortally wounded near where the attack occurred. With her drying breath, she spoke three words: Spoor, Princess, Bertrandians."

"Bertrandian involvement was confirmed by this." Jarred held up the severed rope with two balls at the ends.

"Bolas!" Nollen sneered. "That's how they took me down." With deep regret, he spoke to Axel. "I'm sorry I couldn't protect her."

"No, my friend. They laid a trap. Even Alydar and Sheba became incapacitated."

"It happened before in Ha'tar." Nollen shook his head in confused recollection. "I have never been paralyzed by a harpy's screech before. Nor seen those type of jackals."

"They also mentioned an owl scratched your head," said Gunnar.

"Sadly, there is more to tell," Axel gravely began. He held Nollen's shoulder. "Callie succumbed to multiple bite wounds for her battle with the jackals. Alas, no sign of them."

The breath caught in Nollen throat. "Callie?" he could barely speak.

Ida compassionately intervened. "Sire, he should rest. And supper is nearly ready."

"Aye," he said to Ida, then to Nollen. "We will speak again in the morning."

"Wait!" Nollen seized Axel's arm. "Is anyone pursuing the kidnappers?"

"I dispatched shield owls to the border stations to inform them of the situation. The army is on full alert, especially garrisons in The Doane. Myn assigned a dragon rider to each station, while Artair and the Eagles patrol the skies along the border."

"I hope that's enough, because there are ways to cross unnoticed."

"Trust Gott, and rest."

"I will bring you supper," Ida told Nollen. "And your shaving kit. You might consider cleaning up after so many days."

Nollen stared at the far wall in an effort to recall the attack. First, he recognized the jackals, followed by being struck then unhorsed. After that, he remembered nothing. He tried to consider any scenario based upon the limited information provided. "Bertrandians, Lady Brynn, Spoor? It doesn't make sense," he wondered aloud.

Despite soreness, his mind felt alert, while his stomach rumbled with hunger. Rather than wait for Ida, he rose and put a jerkin on over his shirt. He grimaced at discomfort in his left shoulder and neck. He slipped on his boots. Downstairs, he approached the table set for a meal. Gunnar, Jarred, Axel, and Cormac were engaged in discussion. Ida saw him when she brought drink to the table.

"Nollen, you should be bed."

"I'm fine." He waved her off to sit beside Axel.

Axel fought a smile at Nollen's tenacity. "You are a bit pale."

"I'll be fine. Especially after a good meal," Nollen said the last sentence to Ida. "What you told me doesn't make sense. Why would Bertrandians kidnap Lexi?"

Axel sent a quick concerned glance to the others before he replied. "Because I refused their marriage proposal."

"Naturally, you are already married."

Axel made muted ironic laugh to the innocent comment. "Not me. After your departure from Sener, Rastus sent a new proposal for Dynos to present—an offer of marriage between his son, Felix, and—Lexi. I refused," he assured at seeing Nollen's thunderstruck expression.

"Refused based upon the information we discovered," Cormac clarified for Nollen.

"Too bad we don't have that book now," Nollen angrily groused.

Cormac slyly grinned. "We do, along with another more important journal. And Arkin."

"Arkin? The Shield Maiden's sword? Why did you bring that? It will hardly help her now. Maybe if she had it when attacked." Nollen glowered.

"It will be of use once she is recovered," Cormac confidently spoke.

Axel nudged Nollen's arm. "Although, I do not read or speak Bertrandian, Cormac showed me the passage. It confirmed why we all felt ill-at-ease about Dynos' arrival. The marriage proposal is something I would never agree to."

"So, they kidnapped her because you refused?" chided Nollen in annoyed confusion.

"We assume so. However, the timing is puzzling. I dispatched Dynos with my refusal a few days before Ajax arrived. He could not have reached Theron in a week."

Nollen inquired of Jarred. "You said Brynn mentioned Spoor. I thought he died in battle when we disposed Javan?"

Jarred shrugged. "I simply reported what she said."

"This attack included a harpy with the unusual ability to paralyze, and two jackals with poisonous bites. None of which have been seen in Eldar these past four years," said Cormac.

"All factors indicate the likelihood of this being a planned attack separate from the proposal," said Gunnar.

"Gentlemen. Supper." Ida placed the last platter of food on the table. She joined them.

Axel offered a prayer of blessing for the meal, healing for Nollen, protection for Lexi, and wisdom to discern the situation.

Nollen's face showed deep consideration. "Planned attack," he muttered with a mouth full of food.

"What?" asked Gunnar, not understanding the mumbling.

Nollen swallowed before speaking clearly. "Just thinking you're right about a planned attack." He turned to Axel. "We may have been driven into the trap."

"How so?"

"First the surprise attack by an owl and harpy in Ha'tar followed by the Cursians—"

"Cursians? You didn't take Lexi to Altwald, did you?" demanded Axel, piqued.

"No! Heddwyn. Along the way, I showed her places where we travelled." Nollen motioned to Gunnar, Axel, and himself. "I thought seeing them would help her understand what happened during your absence."

"Did it?" asked Gunnar to aid Nollen and allow Axel to curb his ire.

"Very much so. She is determined to finish her training as Shield Maiden because, as she said: 'I thought only Axel had a destiny. Now, I see I do as well.' "

Overcome, Axel lowered his head to contain his emotions.

After allowing the king a moment, Cormac asked Nollen, "What about the Cursians?"

"They attacked us in Heddwyn. We killed two, but two escaped. We left immediately, because I knew they would return with reinforcements for revenge." His face befuddled, yet voice firm. "I have never known Cursians to venture outside Altwald, and certainly not to Heddwyn. Joined with the incident in Ha'tar, and Lexi's kidnapping, whoever is behind this drove us to the location."

"You believe the owl followed you?" asked Ida.

"Owls were spies for the enemy, remember," he curtly reminded her.

Axel's eyes narrowed in contemplation. "Spoor and Cursians would act out of revenge. Bertrandian involvement—"

"Dynos wants to cover for his past failures," Cormac said in union with Axel.

"Failure to secure a bride for Felix in previous attempts," Axel explained to a baffled Nollen. "It could be an elaborate scheme planned before presenting the terms."

"That would be bold of Rastus. It would endanger everything previously established with Eldar. Especially after Markita," Nollen countered.

"Indeed. However, you are the one who said Bertrandians always look for the advantage."

"Aye. Although, it doesn't give answer to Spoor involvement."

"The only way to learn that is to visit Nefal and speak with Maro," said Cormac.

"The Cursians first, since they are closer," replied Axel.

"We leave in the morning," Nollen declared.

"We? You are hardly recovered," said Axel in mild dispute, though he fought a smile.

"I'm well enough. Lord Cormac said he drew out the poison."

Cormac nodded to Nollen's indication. "The wounds are healing nicely. He wouldn't need a bandage in a day or two," he told Axel.

"Nollen," Ida objected, which made him glare at her interference. Jarred took gentle hold of her hand and made the barest shake of his head. She returned to eating.

During the remainder of the meal, the men discussed how to approach Maro. Would it be with or without Axel present? Should they mention Bertrandians and the kidnapping? Weighing all the arguments, Axel decided he would speak with Maro as king to chief.

While Jarred helped Ida clean-up from supper, Nollen went to the barn in search of Alydar and Sheba. Joslin and two other horses were also present. Alydar and Sheba eagerly greeted him. He became taken aback at sight of Bardolf. The White Wolf Alpha lay near Alydar. Ajax perched on a nearby beam.

"Bardolf," Nollen could barely speak.

The Alpha rose to greet him. "They told you about Callie."

Nollen could only nod, muted by grief.

"I too grieve for my youngest cub."

"Your cub?" Nollen could barely speak.

"Aye. Yet, I know she did what any of us would to protect the humans in our charge."

Too choked to speak, Nollen nodded.

Sheba lowered her head. "I failed the Shield Maiden."

"No," began Nollen in kind refute. "All the details point to a planned ambush for the purpose of kidnapping Lexi. It included using beasts of darkness in a unique way." He sat on a stool between Alydar and Sheba. "Ironic that I just told her how we once feared twilight because of harpys and jackals."

"It was no ordinary harpy. Alfgar warned us of a disturbance before we entered Ha'tar," said Alydar.

"More specific details would have helped," droned Sheba.

"He obviously did not sense anything connected to a harpy, owl, or jackals."

"If he had, I or another eagle would have accompanied you," Ajax said to Sheba.

"Markita showed us it is hard to defend against an ambush," Alydar added.

Nollen rose and stroked Sheba's neck. "You do your herd credit, so take no blame. I'm battling enough regret for both of us. I know, but," he said to Alydar in an effort to preempt a rebuff. "It is natural to feel as we do. Tomorrow, we ride to confront the Cursians then to Nefal, where we hope Maro can help us determine why his daughter was near the scene. Perhaps, we can put the pieces together, and determine a course of action."

"A pack waits nearby. With jackals reported, the King will not travel without protection," said Bardolf.

"I will watch from above," said Ajax.

After spending time in the barn to feed and tend the horses, Nollen returned to find Gunnar stood alone in front of the hearth. The small, cozy fire now reduced to coals. Gunnar held out a beckoning hand for Nollen to join him. For a moment, nothing was said, as both watched the glowing embers.

"I will miss Callie," Nollen spoke in a low thick voice.

"I know, lad."

"Lexi …" Nollen stopped when Gunnar gripped his shoulder.

"If anyone can find her, you can. You found me." Gunnar grinned.

"I think it was the other way around – you found me wounded."

"You came looking. I just happened to be nearby the last time you were ambushed."

Nollen huffed a sardonic chuckle. "I believe Lord Carl was right when he said in Miska, I have a habit of being around when trouble starts."

Gunnar tossed an arm about Nollen's shoulders. "We wouldn't have it any other way, lad. Your skills are too valuable. More importantly, we trust you implicitly." He turned Nollen to head for the stairs. "Now, let's get some sleep."

"Ha! After a week, I'm hardly tired."

Nollen let Gunnar escort him upstairs to the bedchamber. After closing the door, he listened for sounds of Gunnar retiring. He removed his boots and reclined on the bed to consider the situation. He swallowed back a twinge of disconcertion at the Bertrandian marriage proposal. Falling in love with a princess was not something he thought possible. In fact, being in love with anyone under the circumstances of oppression never entered his mind. He focused solely on survival. Yet, that is what happened. Uncertain of when his feelings for Lexi changed, yet sometime after their return from Markita. Gradually, through daily contact at Sener, visiting the market, luncheons at Wyckton, dancing lessons, this trip, and finally shared kisses.

He agreed to Axel's request about going to Markita in search of Gunnar. Whether Axel agreed now or not, he would find Lexi. With that in mind, he needed a few items from a storeroom downstairs. His saddlebags, crossbow, and quiver were placed in the room as usual. He scratched his face. No shaving. He needed more whiskers for this task. Now, to wait until certain everyone slept.

After enough time passed, Nollen put the empty saddlebag over his right shoulder. He opened the door to peek out. Nothing. He knew which boards and steps to avoid creaks, as he made his way quietly downstairs. The dim orange glow of coals provided some light. At the hearth, he placed a match against a coal for use in lighting a candle.

He cautiously crossed to a storeroom just off the kitchen. Inside a crock on a shelf, he withdrew a key ring with three keys, one of which unlocked the storeroom. A squeak began upon opening the door. He paused to listen. No sounds of footsteps from overhead. He opened it just far enough to slip inside. He placed the candle and saddlebag on the floor beside a trunk. After unlocking the trunk, he set the candle in a cubby of the upright lid. Light revealed clothes and sundry items. He rummaged as silently as possible. When finished, five pieces of clothing, a hat, and short sword lay beside the saddlebag. He just closed the packed saddlebags when —

"Nollen! What are you doing?"

Startled, Nollen sat back on his heels. "Jarred. You shouldn't sneak up me like that."

"Me? Who's the one sneaking around? And what exactly are you doing?"

Nollen drew Jarred fully into the storeroom and shut the door.

"I need some things I don't want Ida to know about. Promise not to tell her." Jarred's frown of dispute, prompted him to add, "To find Lexi."

"Very well. I'll tell her I heard a rat. A very large, noisy rat." Jarred placed a hand on Nollen's chest to prevent departure. "Let me go first, in case she comes down to see why I delayed my return."

Nollen stood behind the door to wait. Sure enough, he heard muted voices with one definitely female. He looked to the ceiling, as his eyes followed the sounds of footfalls. Once confident, Jarred took Ida back upstairs, Nollen returned to his room without anyone noticing.

Chapter 22

BY MID-MORNING, THE MEN DISMOUNTED ON THE EDGE OF ALTWALD. Axel left his horse at Far Point and rode Sheba instead.

Nollen spoke to Bardolf. "It is best you don't come with us. The Cursians looked worse than I remember. Almost emaciated."

"The King will not go unescorted," the Alpha rebuffed.

"Attacking us in Heddwyn shows they are desperate!" Nollen passionately argued.

Axel intervened. "Bardolf is coming. The rest shall wait."

With rising upset at the possibility, Nollen uttered, "I don't want to lose another!" He looked down when Bardolf licked his hand.

"Your compassion is appreciated," began the Alpha. "It is an attribute Callie greatly admired. Few humans think as highly of wolves as you. Yet, our duty is also important."

Nollen felt Gunnar place a supportive hand on his shoulder, while Ajax spoke to him.

"You know I will watch from above for signs of a harpy or jackal." Ajax took off from his perch behind the saddle.

Nollen armed his crossbow. Axel, Gunnar, and Cormac drew their swords. Axel signaled Bardolf to take the lead. Carefully, they entered Altwald. Even minimal light seemed hard to find, thus it took several moments for their eyesight to adjust to the darkness. For two hundred yards, they traveled in heavy silence. The cold gray gloom threatened to envelop them. It felt suffocating and ominous. They warily glanced around.

"I forgot how bleak and abysmal this place is," grumbled Gunnar with disturbance. He took the hilt of his sword in both hands, ready to strike at the slightest movement.

"It is worse than before." Axel also alert and poised to act in an instant.

"That is what I tried to say earlier. The Cursians' wretched state is driving them to extremes, which makes them unpredictable," insisted Nollen in a nervous whisper.

Cormac gasped for breath. His face deathly pale and covered in sweat. He dropped his sword to brace himself against a tree to keep from falling.

Concerned, Axel grabbed Cormac in support. "What's wrong?"

The Ganel shook his head in befuddlement. "I … don't … know." He weakly slid down to sit against the trunk. His eyes wide and mouth opened in a desperate attempt to breathe.

"Quickly! Get him out of here," Axel ordered Gunnar. He, Nollen, and Bardolf watched Gunnar hold up Cormac in a rush to leave.

After they disappeared into the gloomy darkness, Nollen again spoke in an anxious whisper. "Should we wait for Gunnar to return?"

Axel also breathed heavy, as he observed the surroundings. "No, I sense time is short." He waved Bardolf to continue.

Barely twenty yards further, Nollen swallowed back discomposure to ask, "What is happening? It's so hard to breathe."

Axel grabbed Nollen to stop. Instead of answering the question, he shouted, "Cursed of my forefather, show yourselves!" The effort to yell forced him to take several gulps of air for recovery. He swayed, and blinked back a sense of dizziness.

Bardolf's posture shifted between defense and cowering. Hackles raised, he growled just before the Cursians appeared with Borka in the lead.

Nollen wiped the sweat from his eyes to ready his crossbow. He fought to steady his shaking hands, not from fear, rather the growing weakness.

"What do you want, Son of Eldar? Is not our dying enough?" demanded Borka.

"Why did you attack us in Heddwyn?" Nollen demanded.

Borka sneered. "We hunt to survive. Smelled your horses."

Axel's eyes narrowed. The draining effects of Altwald visible on his now pale face. "No. More than food drove you to attack Nollen and my sister!" he stoutly declared.

Borka cocked a taunting smile at the growing weariness of the humans. "Stay in Altwald long enough, and you won't need answers. Your ancestor's curse will take you as well!"

Axel thrust his sword out toward Borka. "Speak, creature of darkness! What bargain have you with the Nefal? What did Spoor promise you?"

The Cursians behind Borka grew very agitated at the mention of Spoor.

Their reaction made Nollen forget his distress and aim at Borka. "Answer the King!"

Borka scowled with contrary anger. "You grow weaker. We could kill you both now."

"And be struck down by Gott in the process!" Axel took the hilt in both hands to contain his grip. "If you want to live, answer me."

"How will that keep us alive?"

"If you answer truthfully, I will release you to leave Eldar."

Borka listened to the Cursians murmurings then asked Axel, "Where can we go?"

"I don't care," Axel spoke through gritted teeth. "Now! What about Spoor?"

"He seeks revenge. He gave us the opportunity, and we took it."

"He forfeited on promise! Give food, but no freedom," said Ardon with disdain.

Borka stuck Ardon for speaking. Ardon argued in Cursian, to which Borka scowled, yet made no further assault. Instead, he clarified for Axel. "Spoor promised us freedom to help his plan of revenge. He used magic to convince us he could do so. Also, animals."

"What animals?"

"Owl, harpy, and jackals."

"Spoor used them?" asked Axel, a bit confused.

Borka nodded. "We thought to eat animals, but Spoor say keep safe. Ardon did. Yet when others take human female, he left us trapped here to starve!"

"Bertrandians?"

Borka shrugged with ignorance. "What is Bertrandians?"

Weary, Axel braced his posture to stay upright. This action made Nollen step forward, his crossbow ready. "How do we know you speak the truth? Spoor was killed in battle."

Borka used the spear tip to prick the palm of his hand then it up. "By my blood, I swear. Gott strike me down if I lie. Spoor survived. Face scarred and right eye covered by patch. He wants to avenge Nefal while we want to live."

Axel lowered his sword and took hold of Nollen's crossbow. "Stand down." He then spoke to Borka. "According to my word, I release you from Altwald to leave Eldar immediately. Never return, for in the day you cross the border, Gott will strike you down where you stand."

"Go! Begone, as the King says!" Bardolf snapped at the Cursians.

The creatures scrambled to leave, as the Alpha howled long and loud. Ajax's cry came from above along with brays from Alydar and Sheba.

Once assured of the Cursians departure, Axel grabbed Nollen. "We must leave quickly."

They stumbled and staggered to safety. Cormac sat on a log where Gunnar helped him drink from a flask. Upon sight of Axel and Nollen, Gunnar aided them to join sit beside Cormac. Bardolf found a nearby steam to lap up water.

"What happened? You both look as bad as Cormac."

Axel took a long drink before he handed the flask to Nollen. "The curse upon Altwald is killing the forest and everything in it."

"Why didn't you tell us before we entered?" Nollen weakly objected.

"We had to learn why they attacked you and Lexi."

"You set them free!" Nollen argued, his voice a bit stronger.

"What does he mean?" asked Gunnar.

"For the truth, I renounced my ancestor's curse to allow the Cursians to leave Eldar. With a warning of not returning or die immediately." Axel stressed the last sentence to Nollen.

"If they don't cause havoc to people while leaving. Just for spite! Not to mention, part of The Doane remains dead," Nollen continued in his surly tone.

Axel shook his head. "The curse of Altwald is directly linked to Cursians. With them gone, the forest should revive."

"I take it you learned the reason," said Cormac.

"Aye. Spoor promised them freedom if they helped his plan to avenge the Nefal by kidnapping Lexi," Nollen groused.

"A false promise," Axel stressed.

"He convinced them with some kind of magic," Nollen countered.

"Magic?" repeated Cormac with alarm.

The vehement reaction made Alex ask, "Is there something to be concerned about?"

"The Ganels always believed the Nefal possessed deep magic, or at least a dark past that involved it. We never could learn what. Yet, it would make sense based upon what Nollen reported about the harpy's new ability."

"Spoor told the Cursian to keep the owl, harpy, and jackals safe," said Nollen

Cormac's face grew hard. "Very few can control such creatures. Dolus knew the secrets. If Spoor learned, we must hope and pray he cannot widen control to other animals."

"The First Ones can resist such control. We survived the Electors, we can withstand a Nefal," said Bardolf.

"Other creatures may not be so fortunate," countered Cormac.

"How could Spoor master such control? Were any Nefal trained by Ganels at university to gain such knowledge?" asked Axel.

"No! Nor the Ha'tar. We would not dare take such a risk after they helped the coup." Cormac tried to keep the offense from his voice.

"What about Bertrandians? Could they have learned those secrets at Mathena?"

"Centuries before the coup, some Bertrandians came for learning. However, we are very particular about who we entrust with such advanced knowledge. Especially foreigners. Before we explore that possibility further, we need to establish a connection between Spoor and Bertrand."

"So, Nollen was right. They chased him and Lexi into the trap," surmised Gunnar.

"This is one time I wish I wasn't. It cost too much," Nollen murmured. "What now? Should we return to Far Point so everyone can rest?"

"No. We travel to Nefal as planned." Axel stood. He swayed with dizziness and took a deep breath. He waved Gunnar away. "I'm fine." He took an unsteady step. Gunnar caught him, and easily made him sit again.

"We will eat before proceeding. No argument," Gunnar insisted. He fetched provision then disturbed small loaves of honey bread, sausage, and apples.

Chapter 23

THE NEFAL GATHERED AROUND A FUNERAL PYRE JUST OUTSIDE OF town. Despite his attempt to remain stoic, tears streamed down Maro's face. He heard somber words of lament when the crowd dispersed. He continued to watch the diminishing flames. The future that once held promised in the form of his daughter, gone! No explanation. He received a simple note of condolence from the proprietor of Far Point about how he discovered Brynn dead.

Maro's mind warred between questions and suspicion of how it happened. One of the questions dealt with Bodil. Despite youthful impulse, Maro believed Bodil loyal—until Spoor's unexpected return. In that brief meeting, Spoor turned Bodil. Could Bodil have been involved with Brynn's death? In the pit of his being, Maro feared the answer. A treacherous nature gained Spoor a ruthless reputation that could inspire admiration from the more impressionable Nefal.

Over the years, he witnessed many clashes between Argus and Spoor at tribal meetings. As supreme chieftain, Argus held tight control on his subordinates. However, in private conversations regarding Spoor, Argus quoted a human saying: *Keep your friends close, and your enemies closer.* Now, as sole remaining tribal chieftain, Maro had the unfortunate duty to deal with Spoor. His first attempt proved to be a fatal mistake.

"May the gods greet you in paradise, and may they forgive me for the wrong I did you, my daughter," he softly spoke to the pyre.

"Lord Maro! My lord!" A Nefal raced over. Urgent excitement marked his features, as he paused to catch his breath. "The king comes to your house."

The stunning news broke Maro's dreariness. "How long has he been waiting?"

The male shrugged. "I do not know. Most everyone was here."

"Run ahead and tell him I am coming." At his age, any haste proved difficult. Still, Maro hurried as best he could. He balked at the sight of four horses in front of his house. He stopped outside the door to regain his composure. In the study, he found the male speaking with Axel.

"Sire."

"Lord Maro." Axel placed his hand over his heart and inclined his head. "My deepest condolences."

"Thank you, Sire. Please." Maro motioned to a chair.

"You first, my lord," Axel graciously offered. He sat opposite Maro.

The Nefal chief greeted the others, though Nollen had a good two-week healthy beard. "To what do I owe this honor, Sire?"

"We happened to visit Far Point when Master Jarred told us of Lady Brynn. I thought it only right to visit a fellow chieftain in a time of grief."

Touched by the sentiment, Maro momentarily regarded Axel. "Sire, I am chief of a humbled people."

"Humbled or great, all mourn the loss of a loved one."

Maro lowered his head when momentarily overcome. "None more so than a parent for a child. Something you will discover very soon."

After brief moment of heavy silence, Axel asked, "Is there anything I can do to help?"

With tear filled eyes, Maro boldly looked up. "An explanation. Master Jarred's note gave no reason or account of how it happened."

"He doesn't know. However, he found something close to her body." Axel waved to Nollen, who pulled two long pieces of rope from his satchel. Metal balls hung at the end of the rope. Axel rose to take them and hold up for view. "Do you recognize these?"

Maro stiffened and perched on the edge of the chair. His harsh reaction gave the answer before he spoke. "The bolas were near her?"

"Bolas?" Axel pretended to examine them. "How does it work?"

Maro stood and snatched them from Axel. The King made no comment to the abrupt action. Maro examined the bolas.

"The rope has been cut. The ends come together to form a weapon."

"Weapon?" repeated Axel in a commanding tone.

Maro seized both ends of the rope in his hand, so it appeared whole. The ends dangled. "It is used like this." He twirled it over his head until the balls were parallel to the ground. "Then thrown."

Everyone flinched at the motion, but Maro did not release the rope. He caught the balls, so no one was struck. "The entire bolas wrap around the target to ensnare it. If the balls strike the target, there can significant injury. Even lethal, if aimed at the head."

"Very instructive. May I?" Axel held out his hand for the bolas. He mimicked Maro in putting the end together than gave them back to Nollen.

"Sire, my daughter had no other injury save a chest wound. I do not understand how the bolas was involved."

"Again, it is unknown. Master Jarred simply found these nearby."

"Do you know who would use such a weapon?" Gunnar asked.

"Bertrandians," Maro spoke with disgust.

"Could Lady Brynn have encountered Bertrandians, fought, destroyed the bolas, only to be struck down?" Gunnar offered as a scenario.

Maro paced. He threw up his hands in frustration. "I suppose. Though for him to go to them again …"

Axel signaled the others to remain quiet at Maro's unguarded reply. The Nefal chief's back was turned, so unaware of anything until Axel spoke. "A traveler staying at Far Point, mentioned seeing another Nefal in the area."

Maro whirled about. "Nefal? Did they give a name?"

"Spoor, I think? Does that sound right?" Axel asked Nollen.

"Aye. Said he recognized Spoor," Nollen confirmed.

Maro huffed a sardonic laugh. "I hardly recognized Spoor."

"Maybe he was mistaken. Describe Spoor. For comparison," said Axel.

Maro hesitated. His heavy gaze held a hint of suspicion that passed from Axel to the others. He came back to the King when Axel spoke.

"My lord, you want an explanation. We want the same. As King, I pledge to find who is responsible, and for justice to be done."

Maro stoutly nodded. "Spoor stands a little taller than me. Younger, and stronger. His face is badly scarred from battle. It cost his right eye, and he wears a large patch."

Axel glanced to Nollen, who said, "The description matches."

Maro suddenly paled, and nearly fell into the chair. "It is all my fault," he murmured with dreadful regret. He lowered his head and softly wept.

"My lord?" asked Axel with curious concern. He sat opposite Maro and touched the Nefal chief's arm. "Why blame yourself?"

"The fate of Nefal stands in the balance between me and Spoor."

"Would he enlist foreign aid against you?"

"I don't know." Maro eyes screwed shut. "I should never have listened to him. Never sent her," he murmured with sorrow. He wept more.

Although, moved to compassion, Axel needed to ask, "Does this balance between you and Spoor threaten Eldar in any way?"

From under shrouded brows of distress, Maro barely whispered. "That is why I sent Brynn. To discover his plan and prevent it."

Axel flinched with anger but managed to tamp down his reaction. "Again, you have my pledge to find who is responsible, and defend Nefal, as I would any Territory in Eldar."

Maro nodded, unable to speak.

"May Gott comfort you." Axel left with the others.

Axel and company rode south from Ogun. Along the way, Nollen down a young doe. He hoisted it over Alydar's rump.

"Now, to find a good spot to make camp." He led them under the cover of trees to a suitable area.

Nollen and Gunnar prepared the fire and venison. Axel tended the bed rolls while Cormac fetched water from a nearby creek. An eagle's cry alerted them a moment before Ajax landed on a branch at the rim of the firelight.

"No one followed," Ajax reported.

A nearby wolf howled. Bardolf appeared. "The night watch is set. You may speak freely."

To accompany the venison, Nollen made skillet onions and potatoes. Night had fully fallen by the time the meal was ready to eat. No conversation occurred until the food was passed out, which included Bardolf and Ajax.

"Maro not only confirmed Spoor's survival, but also admitted there is great contention for Nefal leadership that could threaten the stability of Eldar," said Axel.

"With Spoor's reemergence, I am not surprised. Argus barely kept him in check. The Ganels were always wary of his ambition and ruthlessness," chided Cormac.

"I hated dealing with him when forced to trade with the Nefal," complained Nollen.

"Where has Spoor been all this time?" asked Gunnar.

Axel drank to swallow some food. "Some questions remain unanswered, so let us review what we did discover. Maro sent Brynn to thwart Spoor's plan against his leadership. He also wondered aloud about why Spoor would approach *them* again. Which assume are Bertrandians because of the bolas."

"It corroborates Brynn's last words," said Cormac.

"Unfortunately, it still leaves the question of why kidnap Lexi," said Gunnar.

"What about the jackals, owl, and harpy that attacked us?" Nollen added, then continued to asked Cormac, "You said very few can control such creatures. If Bertrandians did learn those secrets long ago, could they have helped Spoor?"

"Bertrandians have various gods, whom they believe possess powers. It is said the Vizier can tap into those powers, similar to what Dolus did."

"I believe it is time to consult the book," Axel told Cormac.

The Ganel fetched his saddlebag from which he withdrew the book brought from the university.

Nollen got a candle from his bag for ease of reading. Once the candle was lit, he sat beside Cormac. "Where do we start?"

"According to the topical index, I would say history about the Vizier." Cormac flipped to the pages. The expressions of Cormac and Nollen showed great intensity in reading.

After several moments of heavy silence, Axel prodded, "Well?"

Cormac didn't answer rather flipped back to the index. He used his finger for indication, to which Nollen agreed. He turned to a different section. At Nollen's infuriated grunt, Axel spoke more forcefully.

"What?"

"One moment, Sire," Cormac replied with distraction. He again went to the index. Only this time Nollen disagreed.

"Mecatis." Nollen used his finger to point somewhere on the index page.

"Ah! Good," Cormac flipped pages until Nollen stopped him.

"There! Mecatis."

"Excellent eyes, even in the dark." After a moment of reading, Cormac and Nollen exchanged glances of intense anger. Cormac slammed the book closed.

"I take it you found the answer," said Gunnar.

With deep regret, Cormac regarded Axel. "I wish I had known sooner. For this," he patted the cover, "is why we felt unsettled by Dynos. Not because of the trading terms, or even the marriage proposal."

"Explain!" Axel's tone suggested no further delay would be tolerated.

"Anyone appointed to the position of Vizier must be a devoted follower of Mecatis, an ancient master of dark arts. Although a mortal and long dead, he is considered a demi-god for his skill and power. The person must also be approved by the gods after completing a series of tests. Only when successful, can the Vizier properly counsel the king."

"Like Dolus influencing Javan," Nollen tersely commented

"How does this confirm Bertrandian involvement?" asked Gunnar.

When the Ganel hesitated, Nollen nudged him and urged, "Tell them!"

Cormac frowned in contrition of the obligation. "Powerful servants of Mecatis, used to enforce the will of the gods, were … the Nefal."

Axel nearly bolted up from his perch on the log. "What?"

Cormac quickly spoke in an attempt to calm Axel. "According to the book, it was towards the end of his life that the Nefal displeased Mecatis and were banished from Bertrand. It happened around the same time as when they agreed to help the coup against Oleg."

Axel stared intensely at Cormac in an effort to digest the revelation. "You believe Spoor is invoking the power of these gods as the Nefal once did with Mecatis?"

"It is a good possibility."

"Which Nefal god?" asked Gunnar.

Cormac consulted the book. "There are three primary gods often portrayed as half-human, half-animal. Same as the ones worshipped in Bertrand. A bear, raven, and buffalo. No doubt, why they rode the powerful beasts. When you ordered the beasts destroyed—"

"I severed the connection to their buffalo god," Axel concluded.

"Callie," Nollen had brief difficulty saying the name, "once mentioned bears and ravens were among the First Ones yet vanished during the coup."

Bardolf sat up to speak. "They did. The disappearance of Ursus and Spyros is what prompted Alfgar, Artair, and myself to convince Othniel to withdraw. We could not afford to lose the Great White Lion. Prophecy about the Son of Eldar depended upon his survival."

With a curious thought, Axel asked, "Did dire-buffalos exist back then or arrive with the Nefal?"

Bardolf lowered his head with a sigh of lament. "There was one such creature that bore a strong resemblance to what came with the Nefal. His name was Kronos. Gott created him to guard the sacred vault at Mathena. He is cunning with strength equal to Othniel."

The revelation caught Cormac's attention. "The vault where we hid the Horn of Kolyn?"

"Aye. However, when I and Othniel urged Oleg to remove the Six Treasures from the vault, we discovered Kronos had vanished and the vault empty."

"Ronan's great-great-grandfather anticipated the danger, and secretly smuggled the Treasures out of Mathena for dispersal. Remember the clues Ronan told you about to help recover the Horn," Cormac said to Axel.

"And Alfred's suggestion of hiding it in ladies' unmentionables and toiletries." Gunnar wryly grinned at Nollen when speaking of the young man's father.

"Did you know about Kronos?" Axel fought impatience when he questioned Cormac.

"Only as legendary guardian of the vault. Never equated to an animal."

Annoyed, Axel demanded of Bardolf, "Why did you not tell me about Kronos before?"

"Othniel told me, Alfgar, and Artair that Gott thought it best to withhold such information."

The answer did little to dissuade Axel. "Again, why? Especially after Lexi's kidnapping."

"Tell me, Son of Eldar, if you had known of Kronos and the others, what would you have done? Searched far and wide to uncover them?"

"Probably."

"And risk the wrath of neighboring kingdoms on a fool's quest."

Axel stiffed at the term fool. Gunnar's quick grip on his arm stopped Axel from making further objection.

Bardolf continued. "You would not have known where to look for such power until it became manifested. Just like Sirin remained unknown before she revealed herself. The Shield Maiden's kidnapping has exposed their whereabouts."

"Though not their intentions," Axel groused.

"Revenge. Same as Sirin," said Bardolf with a snarl.

"Against me? Since both involved Lexi?"

"Indirectly. The Shield Maiden is a symbol of Gott joining nature and men. When fully trained and endowed with special gifts, The Shield Maiden becomes their greatest threat, as she can call them out."

Axel's rapt attention shifted to Cormac. "This is why you brought Arkin and the armor only didn't tell me!"

Taken aback by the accusation, Cormac shook his head. "I didn't know the reason, only a deep sense in the spirit that I must. This revelation is just as surprising to me, as you, Sire."

Nollen's brows knitted in sudden comprehension. "Sirin wanted to know *her* identity." He looked at Gunnar. "On the plateau where you and Kean found me, and I couldn't speak of the encounter. Sirin kept demanding about *the one*. I thought she meant Alicia, as royal bride, but it's been Lexi all along," he said the last sentence to Axel.

"Truly, the scope of this is beyond what we first believed," Gunnar said.

"Indeed." Axel scratched his beard in thought. His ire turned to contemplation. "What about Ursus, and Spyros? What powers do they possess?" he asked Bardolf.

"Ursus is the bear. Although powerful, stealth is what makes him dangerous. He can almost appear out of nowhere since neither prey nor enemy can hear him coming. Spyros, the raven, is tricky. Highly intelligent, with ability to produce images using a special caw."

"What about the enhanced power of the harpy and jackals?"

"We just read about Mecatis and his dark arts," Cormac reminded Axel, to which Axel nodded in acceptance of the answer.

"Since the arrival of the dire buffalos with the Nefal, the First Ones have suspected Kronos of hiding in Bertrand. His blood mixed with Bertrandian lesser buffalos to produce a new species of mighty creatures. However, no powers were revealed to confirm our suspicions—until now," said Bardolf.

"This confirms the Bertrandians are helping Spoor," Gunnar said.

"With Lexi as a pawn!" Nollen chided.

"We won't let that happen," Axel stoutly said.

"I will go to Bertrand and bring her back!" Nollen hastily rose.

"Nollen, wait!" Axel called.

Instead of leaving, Nollen retrieved his saddle bag. "I have the means in here." He opened the bag to explain. "To gain intelligence about illegal goods, my father disguised himself as a Bertrandian trader. He did this a number of times, which helped to cleverly undercut some shady deals. Unlike Markitan, I speak Bertrandian fluently without a trace of accent. And, I have not shaved to appear more authentic."

"Now, it makes sense why you lent me your shaving kit so readily," said Gunnar with a snicker.

Axel waved for Nollen to resume his seat. "Your zeal is appreciated and will be employed. Though, you will not go to Bertrand alone."

"I don't speak Bertrandian," Gunnar objected.

"I do. Well, not fluently like Nollen, but enough to communicate," said Cormac.

Axel continued. "Once we reach Theron, the three of us will act independent of Nollen."

"You cannot go to Bertrand. A royal visit requires—" Cormac argued.

"I'm not going as king, rather, your servant."

"Come again?" asked Cormac in tone of disapproval.

"You don't speak Bertrandian either," Gunnar said pointedly to Axel.

Axel initially ignored Gunnar to tell Cormac, "You will act as special emissary to continue the negotiations with Gunnar as your companion, and me, a servant. It is unnecessary for us to speak the language," he added the last sentence to refute Gunnar.

"You cannot leave Eldar!" Cormac remained adamant, which infuriated Axel.

"Lexi is my sister! This act is directed against me, and I am responsible for her welfare."

"Along with everyone in Eldar! Leave this to us." Cormac spoke of himself, Nollen, and Gunnar.

"Hear me!" Axel commanded to still further objection. "Since Dynos arrived, you have shared my uneasiness as to the reason. It is why you returned to Mathena, where you uncovered disturbing information. Each revelation confirms the marriage proposal it is not just about trading. Spoor's actions point to something striking at the stability of Eldar. I cannot get a sense of how it all connections without being involved. I owe it to my people, my heritage, and my sister."

Although Cormac appeared to be convinced, Gunnar asked, "Why would Nollen, a Bertrandian trader, be traveling with us as foreign emissaries?"

"You got lost and needed a guide. Bertrandian traders will do anything for money. Especially, if it means fleecing Eldarians." Nollen grinned.

Axel chuckled and clapped Nollen on the shoulder. "We travel to Theron together. Once there, we separate. Nollen will use his skills and disguise among the local populous to ferret out information of Lexi's whereabouts. You," he motioned to Cormac, "will approach Rastus with Gunnar to discuss what transpired, and hopefully, forestall any hasty action by Bertrand. Servants are generally not allowed into the presence of royals; thus, I can roam the back hallways for clues …"

"You don't speak the language." Gunnar interrupted Axel

"… without running the risk of possible recognition from Dynos. He is the only Bertrandian I have met," Axel concluded.

The stalwart knight would not back down. "Calling you Axel might give it away."

"From this moment, I am Henrick. No title, no formality. Simply—Henrick."

Gunnar looked to Cormac for assistance. The Ganel heaved a hapless shrug, thus thwarted Gunnar's hope for aid.

"What about the Queen and future heir?" asked Nollen.

Axel softly smiled. "Alicia agrees for me to do what I must. Between Ronan, Irwin, and Mather, she will be well protected."

"You should know from Markita, Lorraine won't tolerate anyone coming near Alicia. She also sent for Beryl to assist her with the baby," Gunnar added.

Axel scratched his face. "To follow your lead," he said to Nollen, "I will shave. Along with new clothes more befitting a servant."

"I can help with the shave, but we need a stop for the clothes."

"How far is Milagro from here?"

"About six days normal ride, but four, if we push. Why?"

"Since it is on the way to Bertrand, I'm sure your cousin, Lady Blythe, will accommodate me with more suitable clothes."

"Aye. However, we must be careful that you are not recognized. Would not be good to go into the city looking one way and come out another."

"Shaving should help to avoid easy recognition." Axel's statement prompted Nollen to withdraw the shaving kit from the other side of his saddlebag. "Gentlemen," he spoke in such a way that Gunnar and Cormac took it for a dismissal. They moved to the bedrolls for sleeping.

Nollen arranged the items for shaving. "I usually shave in the daylight and hang the mirror on the tree. Since you will need firelight to see, let me hold the mirror."

"Water." Gunnar handed Axel a cup. The latter simply nodded, and Gunnar left.

Axel spoke while he used the brush to take water from the cup with wet the soap to mix a lather. "I wanted to talk privately. Hold it a little higher." He used the brush to indicate the mirror. "You are in love with Lexi. Do not deny it."

"I don't."

"Good." Axel tried not to grin too widely while using the razor blade.

"I don't know when it happened, only that it did." Nollen grew tentative. "I hope that doesn't complicate the situation. I wouldn't want to make things worse for you."

This time, Axel paused in shaving to smile. "The reason I refused the marriage proposal is because I know how you both feel. I will not deny my sister happiness with the man she loves."

Confused, Nollen inadvertently lowered the mirror. "I thought it was because of the Black Market?"

"That is the political reason I gave Dynos. By invoking the Black Market, I sent a message, while protecting the personal side of my refusal. You might not know the exact time your feelings changed, but those of us closest, have seen it grow since Markita. You speak to her in ways we cannot, and she responds. Soothe, you accomplished in a few short weeks what others have tried for years to show - the importance of embracing her heritage as the Shield Maiden. I will not throw that away for some shallow royal honor of a loveless marriage! Her destiny is here in Eldar—and with you."

Choked mute, Nollen couldn't respond.

"Let me finish shaving." Axel used the tip of the razor to raise the mirror for better viewing. When finished, he heartily laughed at sight of his clean-shaven face. "What a pair! I shave and you grow a beard. I look younger, while you—well, the beard doesn't make you appear too much older."

"Mine will keep growing, but you must shave every day to maintain appearances."

Axel again regarded his reflection. "I might stay this way." He heard Gunnar's muted laugh and side comment to Cormac.

"Until Alicia says otherwise."

Chapter 24

ARRIVING ON THE OUTSKIRTS OF OGUN, SPOOR AND BODIL CAME upon what remained of a funeral pyre. Disturbed by the sight, Bodil drew rein.

"Rago Tribal banner," he spoke with a tremor of lament. He balked in sudden fear. "Maro?" he asked Spoor.

"Only one way to find out." Spoor turned the horse to enter Ogun.

Small tribal banners, strips of black and red cloth, thorn and grass wreaths, and other signs of mourning filled the city. Nefal went about the day in quiet sobriety. Nobody even regarded Spoor and Bodil as they rode to Maro's home. Neither Bodil nor Spoor asked a question of any individual, mindful of the silent respect for the dead.

At the chief's house, Bodil gazed with sympathy at the door draped in black and red stripes of cloth. A place he served for years was now surrounded by sorrow. He regarded his bandaged wound then looked back at the house. Now what? he thought. His internal deliberation only lasted a moment when Spoor's approach of the door caught attention.

"Wait!" he harshly whispered in warning. He jumped down to place himself between Spoor and the door. "Let me go first."

Bodil carefully entered. Uncertainty marked his countenance, as he moved from the door to the living room. To his surprise relief, he saw Maro's profile, as the chief sat in his favorite chair before the hearth. The brief assuage turned to concern, as Bodil glanced curiously to Spoor. Before he could voice his question, Spoor boldly crossed to Maro.

"Sorrow has descended upon the city."

Startled, Maro jerked at hearing a voice. "You!" He bolted to his feet. "How dare you show you face in this house!" He launched at Spoor with hands that reached for the throat.

"My lord!" Bodil rushed to intervene. It took all his strength to aid Spoor in being free of Maro's stranglehold. Maro stumbled at the forceful separation.

"Get out! Both of you!" Maro shouted.

"My lord, please, hear us," Bodil compassionately urged.

Through a fierce snarl, Maro chided, "I once thought you loyal. Be gone, traitor!"

"I have not betrayed you. I seek to protect Nefal."

"And how did you protect Brynn?"

"So, the pyre was her," said Spoor.

Bodil swallowed back painful regret before he replied. "The Bertrandians acted before I could reach her."

"He tried to avenge her and ended up wounded." Spoor motioned to Bodil's bandaged arm. "At my arrival, they fled—with the princess."

"Princess?" Maro repeated, his ire slightly abated at the stunning revelation. "Axel's sister?"

"Yah."

Maro's brow knitted with deep consideration. "He didn't mention her."

Baffled by about the statement, Spoor asked, "Who?"

"Axel. He came to offer condolences on the day of Brynn's funeral." Maro sat, still thoughtful. His countenance again turned fierce. He pushed himself up to confront Spoor. "He said *you* were spotted nearby."

Unfazed by the accusation, Spoor casually replied, "Naturally. We three traveled together." He motioned between himself and Bodil.

Not convinced, Maro continued the interrogation. "What do you know of Bertrandians in Eldar?"

Spoor brazenly withstood Maro. "Exactly what I told you. They kidnapped the princess, killed Brynn in the process, and wounded Bodil."

Maro seized Spoor. "Do not lie to me! What part of your plan involved Bertrandians?"

Spoor flashed a lopsided grin as he knocked away Maro's hold. "I told you that striking at Axel's heart is the way to make him crumble. I just omitted how."

"You did not intervene, you aided them!" he accused Spoor then to Bodil, "And you did not protect Brynn."

"A mutually beneficial arrangement," said Spoor.

Maro flushed red with rage. Bodil stepped between Maro and Spoor only to be shoved aside for Maro to confront Spoor. "You let them kill Brynn!"

Spoor stoutly shook his head. His voice harsh and bitter in reply "She tried to stop them. Following your instruction to thwart the plan."

All the anger immediately drained from Maro's face. He staggered back and clumsily sat in his chair. "I am to blame."

"My lord," Bodil spoke sympathetically.

Maro sneered. "Out of my sight traitor!"

Spoor sneered with disdain. "Bodil is not the traitor. It is you! By showing weakness, you threaten the future of Nefal. Only with bold action can we return to our former exalted position! That is what the Bertrandians offer—an escape from human servitude!"

Maro's jowls flexed as he stared into the hearth. A few moments of heavy silence passed before he spoke. "I told Axel I had no knowledge of Bertrandians."

"You spoke truth," said Spoor.

"Then. I cannot do so if he confronts me again."

"Lying to protect Nefal is forgivable by the gods."

"The gods," scoffed Maro. "They have abandoned us."

"We allowed them to be dishonored," Bodil insisted.

"Why are you still here?" Maro made a dismissive wave at Bodil.

"The Vizier contacted me on behalf of the gods," Spoor boasted.

The revelation made Maro wary. "Why?"

"They need us again."

Maro returned his attention to the hearth. "Axel will not tolerate that."

Spoor moved to stand between the hearth and Maro. "Abdicate to me, and I will deal with Axel."

Maro huffed a sardonic chuckle. "You becoming high chief will convince him that I lied. Which I did not do."

"Use Brynn's death as a reason to retire."

The coolness of Spoor's speech set Maro's teeth on edge. "The loss of a child is not to be mocked!"

Bodil intervened. "He does not mock you, my lord. We all want the same—including Brynn—a better future for Nefal." For a moment, he held Maro's gaze. In that time, he saw the old chief struggle with the heavy burden of grief. "My lord, please," he kindly entreated.

Maro rose and shifted his attention to Spoor. "Tell me no more so I can continue to claim ignorance. Perhaps, I can give you time."

"Then you now agree to the plan?" asked Bodil, a bit uncertain.

"Agreement is of little importance. You spoke of the future. For my family, it is gone. The same will not be said of the Rago Tribe."

"A wise decision." Spoor inclined his head in salute to hide a pleased smile. He and Bodil left.

In respectful silence, Spoor and Bodil rode from Ogun. A few times, Bodil caught a glimpse of Spoor's effort to curb a smile. Not until well away from town did Bodil speak.

"Will the Bertrandians really allow Nefal to return? To resume our ancient role?"

"Yah. Once the plan succeeds." Spoor heaved an unconcerned shrug. "If not, the gods will force Cadmus from power."

"You know this for certain?"

"I received assurance from Lord Kronus himself."

Bodil gaped in astonished awe. "You spoke to a god? And lived to tell about it?"

Spoor laughed. "You have much to learn, my young friend."

Bodil smiled with admiration. "What now?"

"Part two of the plan. You know the city of Zorin?"

"It is the capital of Halvor Territory."

“Three miles northwest, at the base of the foothills, is a series of caves. There you will find the owl, and hopefully, the jackals and harpy.”

Bodil stirred uneasy in the saddle. “Why?”

“Create a disturbance to draw Axel back to Sener. A threat to his expecting queen, should keep him occupied long enough to complete the plan.”

“The queen? First the princess and now her? Bodil spoke with trepidation. “What will Maro say to that?”

“Maro left the details to me.” Spoor’s good eye stared mercilessly at Bodil. “The promised restoration of all Nefal depends upon our success. Do you jeopardize the will of the gods for some pitiful human females?”

“No. It will be done.” Bodil made the Nefal salute of obedience. “What about you?”

“I go to make certain Cadmus keeps to the bargain.”

Chapter 25

AFTER FOUR LONG DAYS OF HARD RIDING, NOLLEN DREW REIN just short of the eastern road to Milagro. Bardolf paused beside Alydar while Ajax landed on a nearby branch. Dark clouds laden with moisture showered a sheet of rain on the near horizon.

"Rain will be here shortly. If we wait until it arrives, there will be no questions of having hoods raised," he said.

"Why should that matter?" asked Cormac.

"The Milagro watch are known for efficiency. The slightest hint of something out of place, and they act."

"I think that would have changed since the coronation."

Nollen shook his head. "It still serves well, as everything imported from the south comes through The Doane. Milagro and Vanora are major centers of business. Most are on alert for anything shady or unusual. Which means Bardolf and Ajax should remain in the forest."

"How long will you be in Milagro?" asked the Alpha.

"No more than a day. Simply enough time for a change of clothes."

"Perhaps we can obtain information regarding Bertrandians in Eldar," said Axel.

"Maybe before the kidnapping, but doubtful after," countered Nollen.

A steady rain fell. Axel pulled up the hood. "Lead on," he told Nollen.

They mixed with traffic hastening to reach Milagro due to the foul weather. As mentioned, the Watch kept close eye on the arrivals. Some were stopped and pulled aside for questioning.

Within a hundred feet of the main gate, Nollen instructed the others, "Keep your hoods up. And let me speak with them." He lowered his hood and raised a hand in greeting. "Hail and good day, Friends."

"Your voice is familiar," said one guard.

"As it should be, Sergeant Loudon."

"Master Nollen. Almost didn't recognize you," said Loudon with a chuckle.

Nollen scratched his face. "Traveling whiskers."

Loudon's interest passed from Nollen to the others. "King's business, I assume."

Nollen wryly grinned. "When isn't it?"

"Let them pass," Loudon instructed the others.

Rain turned twilight dark gray as it blocked the last rays of sunshine. People rushed for shelter. Lessening crowds made for easy travel from the gate to the northern quarter beyond the city square. They dismounted before the Territorial governor's house. Nollen made three quick pulls on the bell rope. Two grooms hastened from around the corner the same time the front door opened.

"Deron, are Blythe and Ebert home?"

"Aye, Master Nollen?" replied Deron, the steward, though a bit hesitant.

Nollen led the other inside. "Tell them to come to the drawing room."

Gunnar removed his hood. "Something to chase away the chill of being wet."

"I just lit a fire in the drawing room for after dinner. You will find Gorlander sherry on the side table," said Deron.

All removed their cloaks to shake off the rain. Nollen poured the sherry while Axel, Gunnar, and Cormac went to the hearth to get warm.

"This should help." Nollen distributed the glasses.

After a sip of sherry, Axel commented, "A shame Harvey can't keep this in stock."

"Hard with such a rare commodity, but we both try," replied Nollen.

Blythe and Ebert arrived. After four years, more gray invaded Blythe's brown hair, but her smile still brightened up a room. Ebert's hair was now totally gray, and his shoulders slightly stooped, yet he too smiled.

"Nollen," Ebert began in friendly greeting then balked in curious surprise. "Sire?"

Blythe seized Axel's hand; her eyes direct on him. "Something dreadful has happened that you come to us incognito."

"Perceptive, as always, my lady."

"Is the queen well?" asked Ebert with grave concern.

"She is well. As is the baby," Axel spoke with reassurance.

"The Princess," said Blythe with certainty.

Axel returned Blythe's deep regard. "Indeed, Gott has gifted you with great insight."

"Tell us." She tugged on his hand to sit on the sofa.

Axel did most of the talking with a few comments from Gunnar and Cormac in regard to Nefal and Bertrand. Nollen stood at the hearth and stared into the flames. Blythe's attention occasionally shifted to Nollen, only to be drawn back when any of the others spoke.

At the conclusion of the tale, Blythe approached Nollen. She gently placed a hand on his shoulder. "You have not spoken a word. Why?"

Nollen lifted his eyes from the flames to meet her inquisitive gaze.

She tenderly smiled. "I see why. Have faith, dear cousin. Gott will help you in the search to find her. He has done so before."

"I always feel better when I come here." He kissed her cheek.

Blythe turned Nollen to face the others. "Dinner will be ready soon. After that, we shall find suitable clothes," she told Axel.

Later in the evening, when the house had grown quiet and servants retired, Ebert escorted Axel upstairs for a clothes fitting. While Blythe engaged Gunnar and Cormac, Nollen carefully slipped out of the drawing room. He removed his now dry cloak off a hook in the hallway and made his way to the kitchen. Believing to be successful in leaving unnoticed, he donned his cloak when—

"Where are you going?" Gunnar asked.

"Out."

"Obviously. Now tell me where."

"To try to learn if any Bertrandians have been here."

Gunnar stoutly nodded. "Good. I'll come with you."

Nollen's outstretch hand stopped Gunnar. "You might be recognized. If not your face, the uniform."

"And you won't be?"

"You saw the reaction at the gate. The beard makes me look different. Besides, I know how to blend in."

Gunnar's scowl showed annoyance. He grabbed Nollen when the young man went to leave. "You may have strong feelings for Lexi, but you are not the only one concerned. I remember the day she was born. While my sworn oath is to the entire royal family. I'm coming with you."

Nollen recanted at the heartfelt rebuke. "I'm sorry."

"I know." He clapped Nollen about the neck in a half embrace. He took a plan wool cloak off a hook near the back door. He nudged Nollen outside. "Where is the nearest tavern?"

"There are four on the square. One on each corner. The Howling Rooster is the most popular. We'll start there."

"Howling Rooster?" Gunnar repeated with a chuckle.

"Local legend from a hundred years ago of a rooster that has such an ear-piercing cry, many mistook it for a jackal's howl."

Although the rain stopped, puddles filled the streets. Remaining wetness dripped from eaves and overhangs. Inside the Howling Rooster, the dinner crowd had thinned, leaving only those who indulged in drink. Nollen and Gunnar sat at a table against a side wall away from too much light. Nollen signaled the innkeeper by holding up two fingers. Shortly, the man arrived with two tankards of ale.

Nollen placed twice as many coins on the table than the cost of drinks. He attempted to disguise his voice by speaking in a lower register. "A moment of your time, innkeeper."

"A lot of money for one minute."

"Information."

The innkeeper immediately grew wary. "Who are you? And what do you want?"

Nollen moved aside a part of Gunnar's cloak to expose the surcoat underneath complete with crest over the left breast. "Recognize the uniform?"

Gunnar coughed down a drink of ale at the action and question. "King's business then."

"Indeed." Nollen signaled for the innkeeper to bend low. "Any foreigners here lately?"

"Southern foreigners," Gunnar added.

The innkeeper huffed a wry chuckle. "They always come through here for trade. Can you be more specific?"

"Anything unusual of late?" continued Nollen. "Something that would alert the Watch."

For a moment the innkeeper pondered the question. He shook his head. "Sorry, friend. Nothing that I can recall."

Nollen pushed the coins toward the innkeeper. "Then we bid you goodnight." He rose and left without drinking.

"So much for not being recognized," Gunnar dryly groused.

Nollen cocked a sly grin. "You wanted to come. I simply took advantage of the opportunity to gain information."

"Next time, give me a warning."

"Very well. Follow my lead with the others."

Inquiry at the remaining inns on the square happened in the same manner with Nollen disguising his voice and revealing Gunnar's uniform. Upon leaving the final inn, rain returned.

"Any more places they might frequent? Perhaps off the square?" asked Gunnar.

"There are more seedier parts of town. However, word of unusual activities or strangers travels fast in Milagro. These," Nollen motioned around the square. "are the best places to learn of such things."

"Sounds like we are done for the evening."

"Aye," Nollen spoke with a disgruntled huff.

They returned to the governor's house by way of the kitchen door. To Nollen's surprise, Axel and Cormac sat at the table.

Gunnar clapped Nollen on the shoulder. "Remember, I said you weren't the only one concerned." He returned the cloak he borrowed to the hook beside the door.

Axel grinned when asking Nollen, "Learn anything during your outing?"

Nollen removed his cloak and tossed it onto one end of the table as he sat. "No. At least, not directly."

"Meaning?" asked Axel.

"Whoever these Bertrandians are, they didn't come to Eldar on any normal route."

"We suspected that due to Spoor's involvement," said Cormac.

"Tonight, confirmed our suspicions," groused Nollen. "Yet anything would have been helpful to know where to start looking in Bertrand rather than going to Theron." He looked at Axel. "Doing so can expose you to great danger. Something I hoped to avoid. For the sake of the queen and heir."

Axel gripped Nollen's arm. "Thank you for trying."

The gratitude did not allay Nollen's concern. "We can be gone for weeks. How will they explain your absence for that long?"

"While you and Gunnar were gone, we discussed a plan," Axel said of himself and Cormac. "When satisfied with the details, I dispatched Artair with letters to Alicia and Ronan apprising them of the situation. Now, ease your mind of concern for me, and concentrate on finding Lexi." He rose. "Tomorrow, we head south.

Chapter 26

Being constantly drugged, Lexi lost track of the days. She made several attempts to resist drinking or eating in hopes of avoiding the sedative. It proved unsuccessful, as Mateo seemed keen to her efforts. Thus, it became important to maintain a dazed pretense to ward off another dose as long as possible. Between her varied states of groggy and lucid, she learned to distinguish the voices of Mateo and Marius. The clothing color and facial resemblance were too similar. Attitude wise, Mateo was the more dominate, gruff, and aggressive twin. At times, Marius appeared reluctant, even sympathetic, yet always yielded to Mateo.

During more coherent times, Lexi carefully observed the surroundings. They crossed mountains, traveled through forests, and in open meadows. Weather changed from warmer days to cool temperatures in higher elevations. When they rode on what appeared to be a main road, she could only assume the brothers no longer feared being seen. In the pit of her being, she dreaded the reason—they left Eldar!

In what country did they travel freely? Between bouts of clear headedness and stupor, she fought to consider the possibilities. By maintaining the sunrise primarily to the left, and sunset to the right, she determined a southerly course. She pushed her mind to recall maps she studied of the countries surrounding Eldar. Finally, she remembered the name of the southern country—Bertrand. Of course, that only helped if she could get word back to Axel of her location. Or maybe they were passing through Bertrand to another country? Either way, she had to focus her mind to pay attention to landmarks.

One major constant to their journey along the main road, was a mighty river. The road followed its meandering course. Twice, they crossed a bridge where the river narrowed. Even though the brothers braved the open road in daylight, each night they camped in the forest. She surmised this as an effort to limit her contact with anyone. Then again, she didn't speak the language well enough to effectively communicate. She did pick up a few often-repeated words or phrases. It would not be good to let them know she gained some understanding.

After five days on the road, traffic increased to where human voices, animal grunts, and wagon noises continually invaded Lexi's sedated state. Several times, Marius shook her awake. She tried to discern why?

Near twilight, the brothers pulled off a very busy portion of the road. From the cover of budding trees, Mateo and Marius conversed. Their interest made Lexi take notice of a large city a half-mile further. It spanned both banks of the river. She blinked to bring the city into focus. Fortunately, she only had a single dose of the sedative earlier that morning. However, the lingering effects of multiple doses made staying alert more difficult. She concentrated on the cityscape. Decidedly different from Sener in being relatively flat with bold architecture, columns, and edifices. Across the river, stood a massive complex of marble and slate so striking, it must be a place of importance.

Lexi tried not to flinch or show understanding when she heard the words Eldar, Dynos, and Nefal in the discussion. She jerked in surprise when Marius vigorously shook her and spoke. She understood *phiamo* as the word for silence. His threatening tone and patting of the dagger made the lethal warning clear. She simply nodded.

Marius pulled on Lexi's doublet to keep her upright. He harshly whispered *siko, siko,* which she determined meant to sit up. When she turned her head, he forced her to face forward with a harsh command and finger pointed straight ahead. Again, she simply nodded.

While she kept her head still, her eyes shifted to take in glimpses of the city. More people crammed this city than Sener.

Riding in the lead, Mateo shouted, kicked, or clouted people out of the way. Some angrily responded while others shrank back in fear. Even those who expressed outrage, did so with wariness. At the intersection to a major thoroughfare, they turned to cross a bridge almost as large as the aqueduct of Mathena. On the other side, they headed toward the massive complex. Drawing closer, confirmed Lexi's assessment that this was a place of importance. Although the city showed its wealth with intricate archways, colored glass windows, marble, and slate, this complex exceeded what she managed to see.

About two hundred yards from the main entrance, Marius drew rein. He called to Mateo and uttered a few hurried words. Mateo obviously disagreed and they argued. They paid no attention to the traffic during their dispute. Lexi did. People, carts, and those mounted on horseback past them. If she could get on her feet—

Suddenly, she feigned difficulty breathing, wheezing, and coughing. She doubled over the horse's neck. Marius seized her. She heard his quizzical tone but kept up the distress. Mateo roughly grabbed her. She sat up, fearful and shook her head.

Marius knocked Mateo's hand away to dismount and pulled Lexi down. She pretended to stumble and fell back into a building. When Marius went to grab her, Lexi kicked him hard in the groin. He immediately collapsed to the street in agony. She bolted into the crowd. Mateo scrambled to dismount. He shouted, as he shoved people aside in pursuit.

Throngs continued unfazed by the fleeing woman and pursuing man. Lexi dodged and weaved her way through the crowd. With her hands bound in front, she could move and keep her balance when needed to brace herself. Even among the noise, she distinctly heard Mateo's shouting and cursing.

At the sight of an approaching wagon, Lexi ducked into a shadowy doorway. When the wagon passed, she carefully glanced out. She noticed the back of Mateo's head. He ran past. Across the street, she spied a narrow alleyway. Taking a deep breath, she darted between people to reach it.

Halfway down, she dared to look back. Unfortunately, she ran into someone. Both fell sideways.

Lexi pushed up to her knees to see a young woman near her age stare at her from a seat on the ground. Lexi scrambled to get up and run when the woman grabbed her. Mateo's voice echoed from nearby.

"Let me go! Please!" Lexi swung hard to jerk free. The violent action sent them again backwards into the opposite walls of the alley.

Marius joined Mateo at the alley entrance. Lexi stiffened when the woman covered her mouth and placed a finger to her own lips to signal quiet. She motioned Lexi into a deeply recessed doorway. Lexi just managed to take cover when the brothers arrived. Marius limped in pain. They accosted the young woman. She bravely withstood them. When Mateo grabbed her, her tone changed to commanding. With a snarl of reluctance, he released her. The woman's ire continued with a tongue-lashing accompanied by animated hand gestures. Marius tugged on Mateo. In a role-reversal, Mateo yielded, and the brothers left.

In wary anticipation, Lexi regarded the woman, who stood with hands on her hips and stared after the brothers' departure. Shortly, the woman entered the recess. She smiled. Her tone kind, as she gently turned Lexi to the door. After they entered a back hallway, the woman locked the door. Lexi heard activity coming from one end of the hall. Again, the woman spoke in reassuring tones. She guided Lexi away from the sounds of activity. She unlocked another door. Late afternoon light from a high exterior window, showed this to be a storeroom. It held similar sundry items to the ones at Sener.

The woman asked a question to which Lexi shrugged.

She repeated, "*Ovapa*." And pointed to herself. "Celia." Then pointed to Lexi, "*Ovapa*?"

"*Ovapa*? My name?"

"*Mi ovapa*. Celia."

Axel's warning about her identity flashed through Lexi's mind. If he wanted her to remain confidential in Eldar, surely more secrecy was needed in another country. Her consideration lasted only a moment before she decided upon a name dear to her, that of her mother. "Leizel."

Celia smiled. She noticed the bounds and held up Lexi's hand. "*Dolous.*"

Concerned at the harsh tone, Lexi attempted to back away, but Celia kept hold.

She again smiled. "Celia. *Dolous.*" She held up her hands as if bound. Then broke them apart. "*Libre*!" She undid Lexi's bounds and moved apart Lexi's hand.

"Thank you." Lexi headed for the door when Celia stopped her.

"No, no. *Dolous*!" Celia anxious spoke.

When Lexi didn't understand, Celia used her fingers as if walking fast then drew a finger across her throat to signal death.

"They will kill me if I flee." Dejected, Lexi sat on a barrel. "I can't stay here. I must get home."

"Home?" Celia stuttered over the word in confusion.

"Home. Family …"

"Ah, *familia*!" Celia said with understanding.

"Aye. Family. My brother will be worried."

They heard shouting, and someone called Celia's name. She quickly reacted and pulled Lexi into the far corner of the storeroom. Although Lexi did not fully understand, by tone and gesture she assumed Celia wanted her to hide.

Celia reached the door when an older woman entered. They exchanged a few words before Celia left with her. Lexi waited until the sounds of footsteps faded. She carefully crossed to the door only to discover it locked!

"Celia?" she harshly whispered through the keyhole. After a second call and no reply, Lexi backed away. She gazed up at the window in consideration. It contained no glass only a steel grate, and certainly not wide enough to crawl through. Still, she might be able to determine location. Twilight would soon be gone, so she used crates and barrels to climb up and look out. Even in the dim light, she recognized—cliffs! She moved down and sat on a bottom crate to consider the situation.

She was free of the brothers, but where exactly in Bertrand was she? How to leave presented new problems. Celia helped her, but could she be trusted? Not knowing the language made it difficult to understand conversations. Did Celia tell the older woman about her? Why? Celia told her to hide—twice. What does *dolous* mean?

Lexi did the motion of bound and free hands. "Free and not free … slave? That's why she warned me of being killed if I ran away." She looked up to the window. "Oh, Gott, I need wisdom and courage if I am to return home. If I am to fulfill my destiny …" Anxious, she touched the collar to feel Volker where remained hidden. She sighed in relief to say, "as Shield Maiden."

Twilight gave way to dark. Still suffering the effects of escape and lingering sedative, she grew weary. Being a storeroom of sundry items, she found nothing to eat or drink. She returned to the place Celia told her to hide. She used an empty sack as a blanket.

"Gott, protect me as I sleep."

Chapter 27

MARIUS' LIMP GREW LESS NOTICEABLE AS HE AND MATEO LED their horses through the main gate into the royal compound. His face still displayed discomfort of movement. After leaving the horses with the grooms, Marius drew Mateo aside.

"We need to consider what to tell him."

"You always say to speak the truth," Mateo chided.

Marius winced in pain when he shifted his weight from one leg to the other. "This truth won't help us. Not after last time."

"Too many people saw us chase a female!"

"Into an alley that ends—"

"At the cliffs," Mateo completed the sentence. With a large, pleased smile, he slapped Marius on the shoulder. He headed for the Vizier's residence with Marius at his heels. He snapped angry commands to the guards for admittance to the private courtyard.

They paused at the door to Cadmus' office. After a brief conferring glance with Marius, Mateo knocked. "Sir, we have returned," he announced. To his reply, they entered and bowed to Cadmus.

The Vizier sat at his desk. He looked displeased. "I expected your return two days ago."

"We were forced to travel at night until we crossed the border," said Mateo.

"Even then, we took precautions to avoid as many people as possible," added Marius.

Cadmus reclined and twirled a quill pen between his hands. "Well?"

The brothers braced themselves, as Mateo took the lead to answer. "We were successful until a few moments ago."

"Explain!"

"When we arrived, she took advantage of the crowd. Downed Marius with a swift kick." He motioned to Marius, who groaned on cue and moved in such a way to indicate the area of assault. Mateo continued, "We pursued, and nearly had her until she ran down the east alley."

With suspicious skepticism, Cadmus leaned forward. "Are you telling me she ran off the cliffs to allude you?"

"Not on purpose. Careless, and unaware of where it ended. We tried to coax her back, but when Marius reached for her, she slipped."

"Another failure!" Cadmus stood. The swift action made the chair wobble. He hastened around the desk.

"No, sir, this was not our fault," Mateo bravely countered. He stiffened to withstand Cadmus' intense stare. Any sign of wavering would reveal the falsehood.

Cadmus' gaze passed to Marius. The latter swallowed back a hint of discomposure to return the eye contact. "You both realize this places me in an awkward position."

"We tried to save her," Marius insisted. "Some things are out of our control. The gods know this." He kept his eyes on Cadmus. He noticed the barest flinch in Cadmus' face when he spoke about the gods.

Cadmus crossed to the terrace door. He spoke over his shoulder. "What about Spoor?"

Mateo shrugged. "We have not seen him since we took her."

"At one point, he was with two other Nefal," added Marius.

Irate, Cadmus whirled about to face them. "These Nefal witnessed the capture?"

Marius carefully nodded. "We noticed them prior to the trap being sprung."

"Sir, were you unaware of them?" asked Mateo, tentative.

"There was to be no other Nefal involvement! This could complicate things with Eldar."

For a long moment of heavy silence, the brothers watched an angry Cadmus pace. Finally, Mateo broke the silence. "Sir, what would you have us do now?"

"Begone!" Cadmus made a rough wave.

Leaving the private courtyard on their way to another less ornate structure, Marius grew deeply thoughtful. As if sensing the disturbance, Mateo kept glancing at Marius during their trek to an upper floor apartment. Upon shutting the door, Mateo confronted Marius.

"What troubles you?"

Befuddled, Marius sat on chest at the foot of a bed. "He didn't know we lied."

"Oh, that." Mateo nonchalantly passed off the statement. He went to a toilet stand and stripped to the waist.

Marius curiously watched his brother. "Does it not bother you?"

"No. We avoided forty lashes—or worse! It should not bother you either." He poured water into a large basin.

Marius bolted up to prevent Mateo from washing. "All our lives he threatened us with punishment from the gods for lying. That is why I always insisted on telling the truth. Today, I withstood him with a lie to protect us, and he didn't know."

Mateo huffed a laugh and shook free. "You were always naïve."

Marius grew angry. "I took many lashes for you by telling the truth, and you mock me?"

When Mateo washed rather than answer, Marius seized him. "Mateo!"

"Those were days of childhood mischief. Now, the consequences are more serious. It could mean death if we are not careful." Mateo pushed Marius aside. "You need to grow up."

Troubled, Marius stormed out of the apartment. He made his way to the north side of the compound. Near the royal shrine to the gods, he stopped to regard the elaborate structure. Through the large front opening, could be seen three statues. Each had the body of man with heads of different animals: a raven, a bear, and a buffalo. Whereas Cadmus used the gods as threats, their mother gently encouraged them to do what was right.

Marius slightly flinched when a real raven landed on the roof of the shrine. It cocked its head, as if to examine him from various angles. When it spread its wings and cawed, Marius took an impulsive step backwards. A cold shiver wracked him to the core.

Frustrated, he swore under his breath and continued to northeast spot of the compound. He climbed the rampart to gaze at the river. Memories flashed through his mind. Although, a boy of twelve when their mother died, he still felt the void left by her passing. Even as a man, he sought to do what was right, as she would have wanted. They were now neck deep in a dangerous conspiracy

What good has it done? he argued with himself. *Mateo is right. I need to grow up. What exactly that means or how …* He glanced skyward. "Mother, I have tried to endure his threats and schemes by living by what you taught. I even believed the gods reward goodness, as you said. Now, I don't know if good will help this situation. Please, if possible, ask the gods to give me a sign …" With sudden thought, he glanced back in the direction of the shrine. "Or did you already send a message with the raven?" Again, he inwardly shivered with uneasiness. "If so, why do I feel cold dread instead of the warmth of comfort?"

More frustrated than relieved, he left the rampart. He chanced to meet Celia crossing to a more spacious wing of the complex. They made eye-contact before she hastened along.

Inside, Celia paused to knock on a door before she entered. Lamplight revealed a brown-haired woman, who sat cradling a toddler. She took notice of Celia's entrance. She rose to gently place the toddler in a crib. She joined Celia at a dresser across the room.

"Did you see him?"

"Yah. I have this." Celia placed the bundle on the dresser and withdrew a folded piece of paper from a pocket of her skirt.

With a shaky smile of an anticipation, she snatched it from Celia. She moved to read by lamplight. A hand over her mouth stifled a gasp. Overcome, she sat on the edge of a bed.

"Mistress Olivia?" asked Celia with concern.

Tears highlighted Olivia's green eyes. "Did he say anything to you about this?" She indicated the letter.

"No. He simply expressed anxiety for you and little Favian."

Olivia pulled Celia to sit. She spoke low anxious words. "This confirms the rumor."

Celia seized Olivia's shaking hands. "He will not abandon you or his son. You must be strong and have faith in the gods."

Olivia sneered. "The gods have kept us apart! Or more rightly, Cadmus."

"Shh!" Celia warned. "The walls have ears. The Vizier possesses the secrets of the gods."

Olivia wiped the tears from her face. "You are right. I must be strong. If not for myself, for Favian." She crossed to the sleeping toddler. With a tender smile, she stroked the child's face. "He has his father's eyes."

Celia joined Olivia. "Mistress," she began in a tone suggesting more news.

Keen to the change, Olivia asked, "Did something happen when you met him?"

Celia led Olivia back to the bed. "We were nearly discovered by the twins," she spoke with dreaded emphasis.

"How?"

"A runaway slave. At least, I think she is a runaway. Although foreign. She fled from them, and we collided in the alley just before they followed her. Fortunately, he left a moment before it happened. They did not see him. At least, they gave no indication of it when we argued."

Olivia became perplexed. "They were pursuing a foreign slave?"

"Apparently. She was terrified and bound." She used her hands to demonstrate.

"Was she successful in escaping them?"

"With my help," replied Celia, sheepish.

Olivia frowned in disapproval. "You cannot continue to help every runaway. Especially a foreigner."

"From the twins," Celia again emphasized.

Olivia kindly touched Celia's face. "My dear Celia, you are a tenderhearted soul. Where is she now?"

"The annex storeroom. She is hungry, tired, and looks a mess. Food and a bath will help. Although, I am unsure where else to hide her or how to help her return home."

"Did you recognize her accent or dialect?"

"No. I am not allowed in the presence of foreign visitors to the royal court. You might recognize her speech."

"I may be of higher rank in the household, but not noble. You know that."

"You would risk the twins finding her?"

"You can be tiresome," began Olivia is feigned exasperation. "Why I let you talk me into helping your escapades is beyond me."

"You are also tenderhearted, Mistress. You saved me." Celia unwrapped the bundle she placed on the dresser. "I intend to give her one of my older liveries."

Olivia viewed the clothes. "No, those were when you served Natalie. If I am to help, we must keep her with us." She went to a wardrobe. "Since losing Dorothia, I am in need of a second helper." Her face grew hard-set with a twinge of pain. "One day, my fortunes will turn, and all that has happened, will be avenged." She gave Celia the clothes. "When dressed, bring her to your chamber. Meanwhile, I will send for food. You can draw the bath upon return."

Chapter 28

EXHAUSTED, LEXI FELL INTO A DEEP SLEEP. THAT WAS UNTIL SHE sensed someone trying to wake her. Reality or a dream? She could not understand the words, but at a commanding tone and rough shake, her eyes opened. She balked at a woman kneeling next to her before she recognized Celia. A single lantern sat on top of a crate to illuminate the corner.

Celia unwrapped a bundle. Lexi noticed clothes identical to those Celia wore. By the gestures and tone, Celia wanted her to change into them. There were multiple layers consisting of a white undershirt, lavender overshirt, tan pants, a lavender shift, and an embroidered blue and gold dress that flared out at the waist and ended at the ankle. The skirt was split in front from just above the knee to reveal part of the shift and pants. A large pink sash went about the waist that Celia tied to one side. There were also matching blue slipper-shoes. When Lexi kept her boots on, Celia spoke an objection.

"No. Protection." She withdrew the dagger.

"Ah!" Celia smiled with understanding. She picked up the headwear of tan brocade with gold and blue accents. A white gossamer veil hung from behind. Celia spoke with an indication for Lexi to unbraid her hair. When Lexi finished, Celia placed the headwear on her. The sheer veil reached to back of Lexi's waist. Curious, Celia asked a question regarding Volker.

Lexi carefully tucked it under the collar of the undershirt. "Family gift."

"*Familia.*"

"Aye. *Mi familia.* What about my clothes?" Lexi picked up the doublet.

Celia gathered the clothes, belt, and sheath. She used the crates Lexi left in place to climb to the window. She pushed each piece of clothing and the scabbard through the bars.

"Wait …" A stunned Lexi began to object.

"*Shhh*!" Celia commanded with a motion to the door. After she came down from the window, she spoke again. This time Lexi recognized the word *phiamo*. She repeated and used the silencing finger to her lips and nodded. Celia took the edge of her veil and placed it across her face to attach to the other side. The sheer cloth provided modest covering from the nose down though not totally obscuring features. She motioned to Lexi.

Realizing what was meant, Lexi fumbled to attach the veil. Celia helped. When satisfied at Lexi's appearance, Celia fetched the lantern. She locked the door behind them. She held Lexi's arm as they walked the halls. With the lantern casting dark shadows, Lexi could not observe much. After leaving the storeroom area, they entered a more spacious well-lit corridor. This part of the building told of wealth. Of course, various parts of Sener Castle also contained plain and elaborate corridors, along with wings for daily function of service.

Lexi heard voices, laughter, and noticed others dressed in various colored clothing. Women wore veils, but men did not. She also observed soldiers standing guard or traversing hallways. This must be a castle.

Celia made what sounded like a greeting to several people along the way, though they never paused. Finally, they reached a room where Celia locked the door. She removed the veil from her face before she used the lantern flame to light candles. The brightened room told of a personal chamber with a bed, small desk, dresser, and toilet stand with a mirror. Using both hands in a cautious manner, Celia spoke, which Lexi interpreted as wait.

After Celia left by an antechamber door, Lexi circumvented the room to inspect the surroundings. She caught a glimpse of herself in the mirror. She removed the veil. The clothes were beautifully crafted with embroidery. "At least, no corset," she wryly said to herself.

Hearing the door open, Lexi moved back to the bed where Celia left her. No need to be caught snooping. Another woman accompanied Celia. By her carriage and finer clothes, she must be someone of importance.

"Leizel," Celia introduced Lexi. "Signora Olivia." She indicated the other woman.

Lexi did a semi-courtesy. "Mistress."

Olivia asked a question that perplexed Lexi, so Celia said, "Home."

Lexi hesitated, as she recalled Axel's warning. Does she dare identify herself as Eldarian? If the brothers were looking for her, that might not be a good idea.

Olivia repeated the question, sounding a bit more impatient.

"North. Far north," Lexi discretely answered. To help them understand, she used her hands to try an illustrate compass directions.

"Ah!" When Celia understood, she translated for Olivia.

"Gorland? Eldar? Markita?" Olivia asked.

Lexi grew sheepish. How could she trust anyone without understanding what was said? She had to find a way to leave, yet safely, and not arouse suspicion or encounter the brothers.

Again, Celia spoke to Olivia. When Lexi heard the brothers' names, she said, "Aye!" which interrupted the conversation. Lexi wrapped her arms around herself in a display of fear.

Olivia kindly smiled. "No, Leizel," she mimicked the fear motion. "*Ela. Ela.*" She waved and reached to take hold of Lexi's arm. Feeling Lexi stiffen, she kindly said, "*Ela*, Leizel."

Celia added her encouragement and made a sign to eat. "*Utro.*"

"Eat?" Lexi repeated the motion.

"Yah. Eat."

The adjacent room was larger and more elaborate, which Lexi assumed belonged to Olivia. She flinched at hearing a noise then saw a toddler in a crib. Olivia spoke a word and made a cradling motion with her arms.

"Your baby," said Lexi.

"Yah. *Utro.*"

Once seated table, Lexi spoke a prayer. "Gott, thank you for hearing me." The food consisted of surprising flavors with unusually spiced meat, vegetables, and fruit combined. The bread was flat, yet hearty. She stopped eating at seeing the curious way they watched her.

"Is something wrong?"

Olivia asked, "*Ti*? Gott?"

Lexi realized they heard her prayer. "Gott." She placed her hands together as if to pray and pointed up.

"Ah. Gotts," Olivia repeated, as if she understood.

"No. One Gott." Lexi held up a single finger.

"*Uno*?" Olivia curiously mimicked.

Lexi nodded. "One."

When the toddler began to cry, Olivia moved to take care of him.

Celia sat opposite Lexi. "*Uno* Gott?" she spoke with consideration.

Lexi's answer became interrupted when Olivia spoke to Celia. The latter smiled at Lexi before she went into another room opposite of her bedchamber. Soon, Lexi heard the sound of water. When she paused to listen, Olivia encouraged her to continue eating. She might have a bellyache due to the richness of the food, but it was the best food she had eaten since Mathena. When she finished, Celia returned.

"*Ela*, Leizel." Celia waved, which made Lexi consider *ela* meant *come*.

In the other room, stood a sparkling white marble tub filled with water. Beside it, stood a small table upon which sat soap and a vial of colored oil. It must contain the wonderful scent that rose from the water. Once left alone, she undressed to bathe. It felt good to soak in warm scented water. Lexi submerged to wet her hair for washing. So, soothing and relaxing, she didn't realize she fell sleep until Celia woke her. At that moment, she sensed the water had cooled.

After getting dressed, she wrapped a towel around her wet hair. She carried the headwear with her into the other room. The toddler contently played the crib while Olivia and Celia quietly conversed. Olivia tugged on the sleeve of Lexi's dress.

"*Mi. Dolous*. Celia."

"I'm to be your slave—*dolous*—like Celia, is that it?"

"Yah." Olivia nudged Lexi toward the door to Celia's room.

Once in the chamber, Lexi sat on bench at the end of the bed. She heard Celia speaking, but more intent on considering the situation than understanding dialogue. So many questions and scenarios ran through her mind. She absentmindedly rubbed the collar of the undershirt where Volker lay beneath.

Olivia was either a noble or high-ranking household matron to have Celia as her slave. Although she recalled Celia breaking the bounds, so servant more likely than slave. How could she be a servant without understanding the language? Of course, living in Sener for months, she watched how servants behaved. How will doing that help her get home? Should she reveal her true identity? An abducted foreign princess pretending to be a servant? Who would believe such a tale? Might they consider her a spy? All scenarios led to undesirable outcomes, imprisonment or worse—death.

She faced such a dilemma before in a Markita. However, Nollen acted to save her and Alicia. Tears swelled at the thought of Nollen. She couldn't rely on anyone else.

"Oh, Gott. I don't know what to do," she lowly lamented.

"Leizel?" Celia sat beside her.

"*Familia.* Home," Lexi spoke choked words of reply.

Celia rose to fetch an opal handled brush. She removed the towel on Lexi's head. She began to brush Lexi's hair while speaking soft words.

"Thank you." Lexi took the brush to continue. She may not be able to fully comprehend Celia but did understand kindness and empathy.

Chapter 29

FOR ALMOST AN HOUR, ALICIA SAT AT HER VANITY IN THE ROYAL bedchamber re-reading Axel's letter. So much had happened in the past few months. True, she settled into her role more quickly than Lexi. She rejoiced at the encouraging news from Mathena of Lexi accepting her role as Shield Maiden. Joined with the pending arrive of their first child, life felt complete and safe. The peace and security she never experienced before became shattered at word of Lexi's kidnapping. Now this! Alicia placed a hand on her belly and sobbed.

Lorraine and Beryl waited in silence. When Alicia became emotional, Lorraine knelt beside her. "What is the matter? Is it Lexi?" she asked with anxious concern.

Alicia shook her head then nodded, giving confusing signals of affirmation and negation. Frustrated by the inability to answer, she handed Lorraine the letter. Lorraine barely began to read when the maid announced Ronan and Mather. Alicia wiped the tears away and sat up to receive them.

"My lord. General. To what do I owe this visit?"

Ronan held up a letter. "The King informed me you also received a letter from him regarding the situation."

Alicia retrieved it from Lorraine. "Indeed. A most disturbing letter."

"It can be taken as such, but also hopeful."

"How can you say that?" demanded a piqued Alicia.

"Gott works in various ways." Ronan held up letter again. "The Son of Eldar and Shield Maiden united in a common goal to thwart dangerous intentions toward the kingdom. Is that not why Axel sent Lexi with Nollen?"

"Your Ganel reasoning is cold and callous, my lord," Alicia chided.

"I do not mean it as such, Maj—"

Her rising and abrupt rebuke stopped his speech. "How are they united when Lexi is in the clutches of kidnappers somewhere unknown?"

"Majesty, please, do not upset yourself. The situation is well under control."

Lorraine gently touched Alicia's shoulder. "Listen to him. You have a child to consider."

Alicia cast an angry side glance to Lorraine. Stalwart as always, Lorraine returned a warning glare of her own while she indicated of the letter. After a tense moment, Alicia took a deep breath to calm down.

"What do you suggest be done in the King's absence?" Alicia asked.

Ronan replied, "Tomorrow morning, you, Lady Lorraine, and Mistress Beryl will be taken to Mathena to await the child's birth. It would be natural for the King to accompany you in anticipation of the happy event. As First Minister, I will conduct affairs of state. This gives ample time for the task to be completed without arousing unwanted inquiries or suspicion."

Alicia caressed her belly. "Almost five months is a long time to be away."

"Doubtful it will take that long, Majesty," said Mather.

"Let us worry about the time." Ronan flashed a genuine smile as he took hold of Alicia's hand. "After hundreds of years, all Eldar eagerly awaits the birth of an heir. Focus on your health, and that of the child. The Ganels will happily provide whatever you require."

"Lord Ronan is right," began Beryl. "The return of the royal family was much celebrated. Now, securing of the future is highly anticipated."

"Remember, Gunnar is sworn to protect Axel. While Nollen will find Lexi," Lorraine confidently said.

"Cormac took everything the Shield Maiden needs." Ronan squeezed Alicia's hand. "Place aside your fear. Gott has orchestrated everything to bring about His purposes."

Alicia swallowed emotional tears. "There remains one question about the King accompanying me. Exactly by what means will that be accomplished?"

"Simple disguise," said Ronan. "Fret not about details rather rest for the journey." He kissed her hand, bowed, and withdrew with Mather.

Once in the corridor, Mather commented, "I hope you are as confident as you tried to sound." At Ronan's rebuking glare, the general fell silent and marched at attention to the King's study.

Inside, they found Othniel, Alfgar, and Artair waiting.

"Well, how did she take the news?" asked Othniel.

"As well as a human female with child can, upset, calm, upset, calm," answered Ronan.

Mather sarcastically inquired, "Do not Ganel females experience moods swings during pregnancy?"

"No. They maintain rational minds. However, from the exchange, I gather Axel did not fully inform her of the plan."

"Would you do so if your wife didn't maintain her rational mind?"

Ronan partially scowled. "I can better answer that after I'm married."

Mather chuckled but hid his mirth at Ronan's irritation.

"What news from the troops on the southern border, General?"

"So far, all is quiet, my lord. That could change if we strengthen the garrisons. We don't want to tip our hand if we are to convince the Bertrandians that Axel is in Mathena."

A guard entered to announce, "Baron Irwin."

The tall, blond-haired Ganel stepped into the room. He carried a large old book.

"Ah, Irwin. Have you an accounting of the armory?" asked Ronan.

"More or less," Irwin gave a hesitant reply.

"Meaning?"

"We have more supplies since Markita, but less than before Markita."

The answer displeased Ronan. "How will that affect our defenses should we need to reinforce the southern border?"

"We can definitely strengthen our defenses. The question will be how quickly and for how long."

Ronan crossed to the room's large table upon which sat maps of Eldar, Bertrand, The Doane, and Nefal. Irwin, Mather, Othniel, Alfgar, and Artair joined him.

"Axel believes Maro is compromised by the return of Spoor. That does not bode well for moving troops south. It leaves the north flank exposed to Nefal." Ronan motioned to the maps.

"Nefal are too weak to even consider an uprising," Mather said.

"A perceived weakness is when the situation is most dangerous. Such as the Nefal, have nothing to lose, but all to gain should Spoor sway them," warned Othniel.

Mather remained skeptical. "I do not mean to sound dismissive, but what could the Nefal have in common with Bertrand to take such a risk?"

"General, I believe the answer is in here." Irwin placed the book on top of the maps. "I did as Cormac suggested and fetched the book to learn about Mecatis." He opened to a place marked by a piece of gold ribbon. "Part of the page is torn, yet the letters 'Mecat' are visible. The following pages speak about dark magic of the Bertrandian gods gave to Viziers. But," he said with grave emphasis, "the description of large, fierce beings who served the Viziers sound exactly like the Nefal."

"If Cormac and Axel believe the Nefal and Bertrandians are in league with each other why not simply tell us rather than send a cryptic message?" asked Mather, annoyed.

"With a harpy and jackals in Eldar, caution is required," began Artair. "Strong as I am, I too a vulnerable to a harpy attack. The letters could have been intercepted. With Gott's help, I avoided Nefal to bring them here safely."

Ronan's eyes angrily narrowed on the Bertrand map. "Each revelation shows the significance of the marriage request. A chance to control Eldar beyond favorable trade status."

Mather's ire showed in the tight grip of his sword hilt. "When Axel refused, they kidnapped Lexi to force a marriage. Did they not consider a military response to such an effrontery?"

Irwin shook his head and answered, "I do not believe they thought it a possibility after Markita. Two wars in less than six months could be devastating for us."

"My lord, the High Priest Arctander," a guard announced.

Advanced age showed on Arctander's face and in his slow gait.

Mather rushed to provide a chair for Arctander, who thanked the general, and sat.

"To what do we owe this visit, Lord High Priest?" asked Ronan.

Rather than answer Ronan, Arctander spoke to Othniel. "Gott showed me in a dream last night that it is as we feared regarding the First Ones."

The Great White Lion growled in displeasure. Artair screeched and Alfgar stomped his hoof in anger.

"The sense is unmistakable," snarled Othniel.

"We had hoped otherwise," complained Alfgar.

"That is why I must return quickly to help Bardolf guard the Son of Eldar," said Artair.

Ronan, Irwin, and Mather viewed the exchange with guarded concern. "What are you talking about?" asked Ronan.

"Ursus, Kronos, and Spyros," replied Alfgar.

"Names explain nothing," chided Ronan.

"First Ones who went missing after the coup of Oleg," said Othniel.

"That is slightly better. What do they have to do with Lexi and Bertrand?"

"Nefal worship similar gods to the Bertrandians."

"Axel ordered their idols destroyed. I carried out the assignment myself," said Mather.

"I sensed a disturbance in The Doane when we arrived at Far Point in response to Master Jarred's summons," said Artair.

"The harpy and jackals," said Irwin.

Artair's whole body moved as he shook his head. "No, an ancient manifestation beyond them. The Nefal possess no magic, while this aura felt eerily familiar."

"My dream showed the face of a crow, bear, and buffalo on the bodies of men before changing into the actual animals," said Arctander.

"So?" asked Mather, a bit confused.

"Ursus is bear, Kronos a buffalo, and Spyros a crow," said Alfgar.

The information stuck Ronan, Irwin, and Mather hard. Ronan recovered first and spoke with certainty to Mather. "The answer to why the cryptic message."

"And Axel's fear of Maro being compromised," agreed the general.

"The Queen must be taken to the safety of Mathena immediately," urged Othniel.

"She will be ready on the morrow—" began Ronan.

"No! Tonight," insisted the Great Lion.

"I can summon a herd to be here by twilight," said Alfgar.

"I will call Ottlia and a small flock to keep watch during the day. I must return to help Ajax protect the king," said Artair.

"Bardolf left the Halvor alpha-female in command. I shall speak with Rudee for wolves to scout the safest route," said Othniel.

"These First Ones are that formidable?" asked Ronan concerned.

"Nollen spoke of the harpy and jackals possessing powers beyond those vanquished when retaking the throne. Ursus, Kronos, and Spyros are the only explanation for this," said Artair.

Ronan accepted the reasoning. "Once we have formulated a defensive strategy, I will inform the Queen of the change in plan, while Artair leaves to tell Axel."

Chapter 30

IN DIM LIGHT OF THE ROYAL CHAMBER, ALICIA NERVOUSLY PACED. She wore dark traveling attire with matching cloak. Lorraine and Beryl wore similar clothing. The clock on the hearth chimed midnight. Alicia halted to regard the time.

"I thought we put secrecy and stealth behind us when we left Kranston," she complained.

"Do not equate the two," Lorraine spoke in an effort to soothe Alicia.

"How can you say that?"

"Because the circumstances are different. We are not fugitives, nor in a hostile country. This is precaution to help Axel, Gunnar, and Nollen."

Alicia flashed a kind smile. "I do know that. Although, I never experienced such conflicting emotions before."

"You're pregnant. It is natural," said Beryl.

Alicia huffed. "I can do without that aspect."

"Then use your normal level headedness as a counter, for it will be needed on this journey," Lorraine advised.

Alicia took a deep breath, closed her eyes, and made a long exhale. "Gott, help me to be strong against swaying feelings," she spoke a low, prayerful request.

Lorraine said, "He will. And we're here to remind you."

Alicia's mirth was cut short at the arrival of Ronan and Mather. Accompany them was— "Othniel." She inclined her head in a respectful greeting of the Great White lion.

"Are you ready to depart, Majesty?" asked Ronan.

"I am. Only how will we leave unnoticed?"

"The General replaced normal guards and night watch with Ganels. While I ordered the steward to divert all servants from the rear hall and courtyard. Baron Irwin prepared a nondescript carriage. All that remains is the King's double." Ronan nodded to Mather.

The General crossed to the antechamber door. From the other room, a tall, bearded man of around thirty years old emerged. He wore some of Axel's traveling clothes. "Majesty, this is Captain Darick of the Freelands," Mather introduced him.

Alicia impulsively gasped at sight of him. "Captain," she barely found her voice to reply.

"I did not mean to frighten you, Majesty," Darick kindly said.

Alicia swallowed back a lump. "Simply taken back by your striking resemblance to Axel."

Darick grinned. "The beard. Not mine own, but well done. There was no time for me to grow one." He carefully patted the whiskers.

"All the same, it is startling."

"That is the idea," said Ronan. "If any prying eyes see the departure, they will mistake Darick for the King. General."

Mather opened main chamber door. He barked a few orders then stood at attention in threshold. "All is ready, Sire," he spoke so anyone could hear.

"Very good," Darick pulled up the cloak hood to shield his face. He offered his arm to Alicia. She also raised her hood before she took his arm.

Lorraine and Beryl donned their hoods to follow Alicia and Darick. Ronan accompanied the ladies with Othniel behind them. Mather closed the chamber door before he fell in step.

In silence, they proceeded down the rear stairs and out to the courtyard. Six mounted Ganel soldiers surrounded the carriage, their harness filled with items needed for a journey. Two more Ganels sat on the carriage, one in the driver's seat, one at the rear. Every portion of the carriage packed with supplies.

Mather opened the carriage door. The window coverings were lowered for privacy. "Sire," he again spoke in a normal tone.

Darick aided Alicia first into the carriage. He began to help Lorraine when Mather roughly cleared his throat with a curt negative shake of his head. Darick entered the carriage to let Mather aid Lorraine and Beryl.

In a private tone, Mather told Alicia, "Sergeant Lamar drives the carriage, and commands the Ganel squad." He spoke in a normal tone. "Gott speed, Majesties." He shut the carriage door. "Open the gate!" he instructed the Ganel watch.

The carriage rocked slightly when it began to move and pass through the gate.

With contrition, Darick spoke to Alicia. "My apologies for a near mistake, Madam. I may look like him, but not familiar with royal protocol."

Alicia lightly tapped Darick's hand. "Neither was I upon arrival. There are times, I still feel I'm learning."

"Kind words. However, I must play my part better to avoid suspicion."

"You can start by calling me Alicia. No titles between us."

"Who can overhear us?" asked Beryl.

"Not within the confines of the carriage. Rather during stops for rest and food. Then, we could be overheard. Thus, a nondescript carriage without lights," said Darick.

Beryl groused to Alicia, "I agree with you about hoping we put all this clandestine activity behind us."

Darick flashed a reassuring smile. "No need to worry. Ganels have good eyesight at night. And we won't be traveling alone very long."

Curious, Alicia asked, "Meaning?"

He made a casual reply. "Unicorn, wolves, and eagles will join us at appointed times."

Startled by the revelation, she demanded, "What? Why?"

Alicia's reaction caught Darick by surprise. "To ensure safe travel."

Lorraine signaled Alicia to calm her visible anger. "Another detail Lord Ronan forgot to mention," she clarified for Darick.

Darick said in pointed discretion to Alicia, "He was following *my* orders. Given covertly to avoid upset." He patted the beard.

Alicia stared at Darick for a moment then nodded. "I understand."

"I don't," said Beryl.

Lorraine leaned over to whisper in Beryl's ear.

"Ah!" said Beryl upon learning of Darick's clever reference to Axel.

Despite the curtain, Alicia turned as if to stare out the window. Darick revealed all this came by way of Axel's order to alleviate some anger and anxiety … but not all. Something sinister and dreadful must lay behind the kidnapping of Lexi. Something he did not want her to know. Something that could adversely affect her and the child. She looked down and touched her belly. She heard a light cough and raised her head to meet Lorraine's gaze. Strong confidence marked Lorraine, and immediately brought to Alicia's mind the earlier encouragement. *Use your normal level headedness as a counter, for it will be needed on this journey.* This was followed by a later statement. *And we're here to remind you of it.* Alicia grinned in recollection. Yet no amount of bolstering could counter the tiring effects of darkness. Alicia fought a yawn.

Darick reached under the seat to retrieve a blanket and small pillow. "Rest. It is a long journey to Mathena." He helped Alicia get comfortable. She quickly fell asleep. "You will find pillows and blankets under that seat as well," he told Lorraine and Beryl.

Once she and Beryl were suited, Lorraine whispered. "What of you? Will you sleep?"

He grinned. "I command the night watch. I normally do not retire until mid-morning."

After all the women fell asleep, a small hatch in the roof located above Darick and Alicia opened. The rear Ganel quietly spoke. "The wolves have joined us."

"Good. Stay sharp." Darick pushed back the curtain to glance outside.

"Rudee said you won't see them," said the Ganel.

"Hopefully, no one else will either."

The Ganel shut the hatch.

Hearing voices, horses, and sounds of harness woke Alicia. She groaned and squirmed with discomfort.

"Alicia?" Darick's touch made her flinched.

"Oh, sorry," she breathed in relief. "I briefly forgot where I was." She looked perplexed at the halo of daylight around the curtain. "What time is it?"

"An hour past dawn. We stopped to rest, eat, and water the horses. I assume you want to stretch your legs."

"Among other things," she bantered.

He got out and helped her down. Beryl and Lorraine also woke to the noise and exited the carriage. They stopped at an abandoned farm.

"What is this place?" asked Alicia.

"Certainly not a proper inn," Lorraine spoke in dry humor.

"Those are to be avoided," Darick stressed. "However, we will pass a more comfortable night when we reach Zorin in three days. Discreetly, of course."

Sergeant Lamar approached. "Breakfast will be ready soon, Sire."

"Good. I shall escort the Queen on a short walk to get back circulation." He held her arm as they strolled a short distance to the house. He took careful note of their surroundings.

"I hope all our stops between here and Zorin are not so primitive. Especially when certain private necessities are required," she said.

"Why do you think I escorted you to the house?" he lightly countered.

A white wolf emerged from the building. "It is safe, Sire," she said.

"This is Rudee. Female Alpha of the Halvor pack," Darick told Alicia.

"Save the formalities until after." Alicia disappeared into the house, closely followed by Lorraine and Beryl.

Darick patiently waited for the women. He dismissed the Ganel who told him breakfast was ready—and still waited. Finally, they reappeared.

Ottlia, the eagle queen, landed on a fence post. "The skies are clear."

A beautiful chocolate brown unicorn with tan mane and tail appeared. "The perimeter is secure so all can safely rest," he reported.

"I know Ottlia, and have met Rudee, but what is your name?" Alicia asked.

"I am called Vallis, Majesty." The unicorn bowed his head.

"Welcome, Vallis, and thank you."

"Smells like breakfast is ready," said Lorraine.

The meal consisted of grains mixed with fruit and spices.

"This is delicious. What is it?" asked Beryl after finishing her portion.

"A Ganel breakfast dish, my lady. Good for energy to face the day," replied Lamar.

"I don't see many rations packed on the carriage."

Lamar chuckled. "Ganels forage when traveling."

The answer astonished Beryl. "You mean, this was foraged and cooked this morning?"

"Aye, and no." He went on to explain, "Cooked this morning, but taken from the castle kitchen last night. Before we leave here, the men will forage for ingredients to augment the grains. Perhaps, even some game should you so desire, Majesty."

"I would not offend Ganels sensibilities, Sergeant," Alicia gracious replied.

"No offense would be taken, Majesty. You must eat."

"Then perhaps a small fowl."

"Do not delay to set a trap. We shall oblige," said Rudee.

"How long before we begin again?" asked Lorraine.

"Oh, I do hope it's not all night travel," groused Beryl. "For the Queen's sake," she added at seeing Darick's wry expression.

"No, not all-night travel," began Darick. "We shall rest a couple of hours before proceeding. Then make camp for a full night's sleep."

Chapter 31

THE REMAINING THREE-DAY JOURNEY TO ZORIN PROVED uneventful. Of course, they avoided settlements in favor of making camp. A proper tent, complete with pillows and rugs, was erected for the Queen and women. They positioned a small alcove tent for Darick in such a way as to appear part of the main tent. Every precaution was taken to keep up the appearance of the royal couple traveling together.

Zorin would be the first stop where more people could glimpse Darick. In hopes of avoiding too much scrutiny of his appearance, they arrived at Mayor Lorne's home shortly after twilight.

At night, Darick needed to remove the beard to soothe skin irritation and prevent damage to the beard from sleeping. The Ganels provided everything necessary for facilitating his disguise, and aid in skincare. Just like on the road, he would not emerge the following morning until he once again resembled Axel. Darick just finished the removal skincare when there came a knock at the anteroom door.

"Axel," came Alicia's voice.

Darick carefully shielded his face to open the door. "Alicia," he said for effect.

She smiled yet waited until the door closed to speak. "I see what you mean." She motioned to her chin. "Although, there are still similarities. Same shape face and color eyes."

Conversation stopped at hearing voices in the hall. The sounds grew louder until they heard Lorne at the door.

The mayor knocked and spoke with apologetic hesitancy. "Sire. Majesty. The Aldermen are insisting upon an audience."

"Sire, I told the mayor not to disturb you," Lamar said.

Darick spoke a bit lower register, yet in firm resolve. "Mayor Lorne, tell the Aldermen it is impossible. The Queen is tired, and I will remain. Her condition comes before politics."

"Indeed, Sire. Shall I send a servant up with supper?"

"No. Sergeant Lamar will bring it."

"Aye, Sire. Please, forgive the imposition. I shall deal with the Aldermen."

"Now, enough. Away," Lamar scolded.

Darick and Alicia waited until the voices and footsteps faded.

"Lorne seems rather timid in regards to the Alderman." Darick returned to the mirror and checked his skin. Most of the redness had faded, yet a few spots needed more salve.

"Lorne is a very nice man. His timidity stems from wanting to please others. But Ax—*you* consider him very loyal," she corrected her statement.

His mirror-reflected smile faded as he finished the salve and turned to face her. "I'm beginning to wonder if stopping here was a mistake."

"Was it not part of the plan?"

"Aye. However, things can change—adapt, when needed. The insistence of Aldermen for an audience could cause a problem in leaving."

Alicia sat in a chair near the hearth. "You spoke rightly that I need rest."

He sat opposite her. "I did not mean to imply an immediate departure. Prior to dawn will be soon enough. To avoid any unwanted encounters."

She squirmed to get comfortable. "Wake me when Lamar arrives with food."

"Would you not be more comfortable in bed?" He flushed with embarrassment at realizing how his question sounded, and quickly added, "In the anteroom, I mean."

Alicia laughed. "A chair is better on my aching back for a quick nap."

Across from the Territorial mayor's house, Bodil waited in the shadows. Two Ganel soldiers stood outside the main entrance. They moved aside when three Alderman emerged, and all grumbled complaints. Bodil ducked further back from view when a watchman approached the Alderman.

"Gates will close in one hour. No departures after that unless by special order."

"We know! This always happen when he comes," one Alderman groused. They pushed past the watchman to continue.

"He could have at least seen us," chided another.

"If he was alone, perhaps. I do understand not wanting to leave the Queen during a journey. In her condition, that is," one spoke with sympathy.

"Or Lorne did not submit the petition for a new city charter," continued the first in ill-humor.

Once the way was clear of Aldermen and watch, Bodil shrank back to leave the alley by a different route. No need to alert the Ganels to his presence. Despite the fact that Axel attempted to help the races become accustomed to each other, Bodil made certain not to engage anyone. A few Zorin citizens glared at him with intense anger. Others reacted warily, and quickly avoided him. At the inn nearest the gate, he paid the teen to retrieve his horse.

Two hundred yards outside the gate, he turned northwest. Since undertaking the mission with Spoor, night travel became commonplace. Although not completely blind, he struggled to make out distinct shapes in the darkness.

"I hope you remember where to go," he spoke to the horse.

The horse grunted.

"You sound like Chago, my old dire-buffalo, when I questioned his ability."

The horse bucked slightly.

"Easy! Just get me back in one piece, and I will give you the apple I packed."

It tossed it head in a nod.

Bodil laughed. "Exactly like Chago."

After traveling two miles through woods, Bodil drew rein at the tree line of a meadow. Bright moonlight helped him see a line of caves roughly one mile on the other side. He jerked in surprise when something flew past. He pulled so hard on the reins; the horse reared. Bodil managed to stay seated when it came back down to all fours. Hooting made him look left to see an owl land on a lower branch.

"Well, if you're here, I hope the others are also."

The owl spread its wing and hooted in a tone that sounded angry.

"For that! You go first," Bodil commanded the owl.

It took flight across the clearing. Bodil kicked the horse in pursuit. He might not see clearly, but he heard the harpy screech. He quickly wrapped a piece of cloth over his head to protect his ears. Near the caves, the horse skidded to an unsteady halt at sight of growling jackals.

"Easy!" Bodil fought to get control. The horse grew more anxious, the jackals became aggressive, and the harpy screeched louder. He shouted, "*Ad ille deus ego mandatum obedientiam.*" He repeated, "By the gods, I command obedience!"

As if on cue, all the animals calmed down. The jackals stopped growling and sat. The harpy settled on the rock, and the owl landed beside the harpy.

"That's better." He dismounted. "If we cooperate, everything will go according to plan."

Chapter 32

THE ESCORT LED THE CARRIAGE THROUGH THE MAIN GATE OF Zorin shortly after sunrise. Turning northwest, they took the road leading to Ganel. Lamar's keen attention scanned the sides of the road as he drove the carriage. The sound of an eagle told him Ottlia circled overhead. When he looked back to the road, he saw Rudee emerge from the trees on the northern edge of the wood. A bright glint momentarily blinded him. He blinked to determine the reason. Vallis stood on the south side of the road. Once spotted, the unicorn disappeared into the forest. Lamar leaned back to slide open the view port behind the driver's seat. It bisected the wall six inches above the heads of Beryl and Lorraine.

"Sire. They resumed a parallel course."

"Thank you, Sergeant."

After a good night's sleep, the women appeared refreshed.

"I have not been to Mathena. Although, I heard wonderful stories about the city and aqueduct. How much further?" Alicia asked Darick.

"Another four days."

At Alicia's disappointment, Beryl said, "We have better provisions this time."

At an objecting cough from Lamar through the view port, Alicia kindly replied to Beryl. "Oh, I greatly enjoy Ganel cooking. The flavors are marvelous. I simply needed more meat since I am eating for two."

Beryl flushed with embarrassment when Lorraine indicated the view port remained open. "I meant no offense. Merely concerned for Alicia." No reply from Lamar made Beryl sigh. "I'm still adjusting to life in Eldar after the isolation of Kranston."

"You were among the returning Brethren?" asked Darick.

"Aye."

"Beryl is my sister-in-law. Wife of Sir Gunnar's brother," Lorraine emphasized with her head tilted up toward the view port.

"Apology accepted, Mistress Beryl," Lamar kindly spoke.

"Thank you, Sergeant. Although, returning to the family farm has given us focus, the larger scope of Eldar remains a bit daunting. Since coming to Sener, I have found the Ganels wonderfully elegant and charming. The Ha'tar gruff, but with a soft side." She slightly frowned with concern. "The Nefal ... well, they intimidate me."

"The Nefal intimidate many by their sheer size," said Darick.

A sudden high-pitched debilitating screech made everyone cringe in pain. Alicia cried out and doubled over. Darick caught her to stop her from falling to the carriage floor. Lorraine and Beryl came together in a protective huddle. The carriage jerked to a halt as Lamar grunted in painful anger.

At the sound of vicious growls, Darick pushed back the curtain. Two jackals attacked the lead Ganels. He called out through the view port. "Sergeant! Get us out of here!"

Lamar fought against the overwhelming noise to snap the reins. The diving harpy forced him to dodge the attack. Powerful talons ripped his right shoulder and sent him off the driver's seat. The frightened horses continued at a frantic gallop. The Ganel in the rear carriage seat, fought against the frantic ride to climb across the roof toward the driver's seat. He nearly fell off but stayed on top by grabbing a rope used to tie down the supplies.

A dun-colored unicorn appeared alongside the horses. The unicorn's bray helped the horses slowed enough for the Ganel to climb into the driver's seat and snatch the reins. Still agitated by the cacophony of noise, the horses battled against the Ganel's attempt to stop them. The dun unicorn grew more aggressive in vocalizations. The horses gradually slowed, and finally stopped. They pranced in place and chomped on the bit. A brief exchange with the unicorn made the horses toss their heads in a nod.

"Thank you," the Ganel said to the unicorn before it left to rejoin its comrades.

Darick saw Lamar hit the ground. "Stay in here!" he told Alicia before he exited the carriage.

Darick drew his sword to protect Lamar from an owl. It avoided his blade to swoop back. The second pass made Darick duck to avoid talons. As the owl looped around for another pass, Ottlia snared the tail feathers to knock it off course. Locked in combat, the owl and Ottlia rose away from the carriage. Ottlia made swift work to kill the smaller owl.

Two more eagles attacked the harpy. Being larger, the harpy managed to fend them off. When a third eagle joined the engagement, the harpy's defense began to wane. Ottlia joined the fray. Overwhelmed by four eagles, the harpy plummeted to the ground, where all four eagles landed to finish it.

From the forest, came the howl of wolves. They rushed to aid the unicorns against the jackals. The arrival of Rudee and four wolves diverted the jackals from killing the downed Ganel escort. Although the odds favored the wolves and unicorn, the enhanced jackals proved formidable. The wolves and unicorns broke into groups, each focusing on a single jackal.

One jackal made a desperate leap at Vallis, only to be skewered by another unicorn. Rudee pounced on the jackal to grab its throat and ensure the kill. One wolf lay mortally wounded by the jackals. Another wolf limped off into the woods. One unicorn suffered a severely torn front leg from savage bites. After two steps, it collapsed, dead. The rear Ganel soldiers came to aid their wounded comrades.

When all grew silent, Alicia timidly glanced out the window. "Is it over?"

"I think so—," Darick began when interrupted by the sight of a large individual fleeing on horseback. "After him!"

The rear Ganel soldiers quickly mounted in pursuit, only the eagles proved swifter in action. They swarmed the rider. The horse reared and threw the rider then galloped away. Rudee and two wolves surrounded him. He tried to rise and make defense, when Rudee leapt upon him. Another wolf aided Rudee when he fought the Alpha female.

The Ganels dismounted with swords drawn. "A Nefal!"

Bodil squirmed, though unable to get free of the wolves.

"We'll take him," a Ganel told Rudee.

When loosed from the wolves, Bodil attempted to escape. He only managed to shake off one Ganel before the wolves attacked. Viciously clawed and bitten, Bodil fell to his knees.

"Do not try it again. Or we will kill you," Rudee snarled. Her muzzle and teeth bloody from battle.

Due to the wounds, Bodil offered no further resistance to the Ganels. His left leg bled heavily, which forced him to limp. His left arm hung useless due to a deep savage bite. Blood streamed from large claw marks across his face and neck.

At the carriage, Lamar, and the other carriage Ganel, tended their comrades. Overall, the wounds did not appear life-threatening. The women also rendered aid.

Darick sheathed his sword to confront Bodil. "Nefal! What is the meaning of this?" When Bodil refused to answer, Darick seized his throat. "I asked a question. Why attack us?"

"Why do you think?"

"I cannot read your mind."

"Answer the King!" commanded Lamar.

Being so close, Bodil studied Darick. "You look different."

"How I look is immaterial. Why attack us?"

Bodil's eyes shifted when Alicia stood in such a way as to view the interrogation.

Darick noticed Bodil's interest. He jerked the Nefal's face to draw attention back to him. "To assault the queen and heir?"

"Kill one of us, destroy our gods, and Nefal will respond in kind!" Bodil spat.

Hearing declaration made Alicia back away in fear. The color drained from her face. Lorraine and Beryl escorted Alicia back to the carriage.

"Sire," Lamar began. "He should be taken back to Sener to stand trial."

"Aye! Bind him, and give Gannon charge of escorting him. Have Liron take the wounded to Zorin for treatment."

"Aye, Sire." Lamar seized Bodil.

Darick approached the women. Alicia sat on the lowered step to the carriage. "Are any of you hurt?"

Alicia could not speak due to tears, so Lorraine replied. "We are uninjured."

Darick knelt to console Alicia. "You are safe now." She simply nodded.

Vallis arrived. "She will not be completely safe until we reach Mathena."

Darick stood. "Your presence, along with the wolves and eagles, is what saved the day."

Lamar returned. "The others are proceeding as ordered. What now? We are down to just us." He motioned between himself and the carriage Ganel.

"The sooner the Queen arrives in Mathena the better," said Vallis.

"Horses can only travel thirty to forty miles in a day. Meaning, we can shorten the journey to three days instead of four," said Lamar.

"With our enhanced speed, we will arrive by sunset," Vallis boasted of himself and three other unicorns.

"You intend to pull the carriage?" Lamar wryly asked.

"No, have them to ride us to Mathena." Vallis nodded to Darick and the women.

"Ride unicorns?" Alicia finally found voice to speak.

"Majesty, your safety, and that of the future heir, depends upon it," Vallis stressed.

"If your speed is as you say, how will we hold on?"

Vallis snorted to his companions. In unison, loud whinnies echoed as they reared. Each horn sparkled in the sunlight then burst into a blinding flare that engulfed them. When hooves touched the ground, the brilliance faded to reveal the unicorns saddled and bridled with wonderfully ornate harness.

"Please, mount, Majesty," Vallis instructed.

Darick helped Alicia before he mounted. Lamar aided Beryl and Lorraine into the saddle.

"Sergeant, join Gannon in returning to Sener, and report everything to Lord Ronan," Darick said.

Chapter 33

RONAN CONDUCTED STATE BUSINESS FROM THE KING'S STUDY, just as he had done during short periods of time when Axel left Sener on various trips. Papers and maps were scattered across the table in front of him. He sat to shift through them, though primary importance given to the dispatches. He consulted the various maps in comparison to what he read.

Othniel lay beside the hearth. He lifted his head at hearing Ronan grumbling. Realizing the Ganel lord's preoccupation, Othniel relaxed. Mather entered with Lamar. The Great White Lion rose to meet them. Being so engrossed in his task, Ronan didn't notice their arrival until someone snatched a paper out of his hand. Stunned, he rocked back in the chair.

"Mather!"

"I'm glad you finally noticed me."

"Trying to sort this out takes a great deal of concentration," he groused.

"Another wrinkle just presented itself. Captain Darick sent Lamar back with a disturbing report."

Sight of Lamar brought Ronan to his feet. "Is all well with the Queen?"

"Aye, my lord. Though, just barely. Our precautions proved necessary."

"You were attacked?" asked Othniel

"By a harpy, owl, and two jackals ..." Lamar paused when Othniel made a low growl of anger. "But," he hastily added, "Vallis, Rudee, and Ottlia defeated and killed them."

Ronan appeared momentarily relieved before he questioned Lamar again. "If you are here, what about the Queen and others? They could not have reached Mathena this quickly."

Lamar replied in spellbound awe. "The unicorns suddenly wore beautiful harnesses for Her Majesty and the others to ride. They became a blur of speed and disappeared from view within a moment. Vallis claimed, they could reach Mathena by sunset that same day."

Attention became drawn to the terrace door where Ottlia pecked on the glass. Ronan hastened to admit the eagle queen. She flew from the threshold to perch on a chair at the table.

"I bring word that the Queen has arrived safely in Mathena."

"Sergeant Lamar was just telling us about the attack," said Ronan.

"The eagles have never trusted the Nefal."

"Nefal?" Ronan's curious gaze immediately shifted from Ottlia back to Lamar for an answer.

"It appears a Nefal controlled the beasts. He is in the dungeon awaiting interrogation. He refused to answer any questions enroute. Perhaps because some infection has set in due to his numerous injuries. Or just obstinance"

"Injured in the attack?" asked Mather.

"No. Rudee and the wolves prevented his escape."

"Then is it as Axel suspected." Ronan crossed back to the table to stare at the papers with deep consideration. "Does the Nefal have a name?" he asked over his shoulder.

"He would not say," answered Lamar.

"How bad are the wounds?"

"Very severe, with significant blood loss. Although he refused treatment, we bandaged the wounds so he could survive the return journey."

Ronan sent a conferring glance to Mather. "Then let us hope he can provide answers. General. Sergeant." He waved for them to join him. He paused in the threshold to speak to Othniel. "It is best you are not seen."

Mather led the way to the dungeon where he ordered the jailer to admit them. "Close the door and wait," he instructed the jailer.

Lamar held the torch for them to enter the darkened cell. Bodil lay on a cot made of leather straps. Torchlight showed his face ashen, and eyes shrouded. Ronan snatched the torch from Lamar to closely examine him.

"I know you," he declared. "You are Maro's aide … Bodil."

Bodil's eyes slowly opened at hearing his name.

"Did Maro put you up to this?"

Bodil's head fell to one side in an attempt to face the wall. His frail condition deteriorating quickly.

"Answer, and I will send for the physician before you succumb." When Bodil remained stubbornly silent, Ronan pressed. "I know the Nefal believe in an afterlife, but only when one dies in an honorable manner. Attacking women is not honorable!"

Bodil managed to look at Ronan. He spoke in a raspy voice. "Maro did not send me."

"Spoor?" Ronan demanded.

Disdain marked Bodil's weary tone. "Attacking women may not be honorable according to *your* definition. But to restore Nefal pride robbed us, it is worthy of the gods' favor." The effort to speak took all of Bodil's remaining strength. His eyes became fixed in staring up.

Mather placed a hand over Bodil's face to feel for air. He shook his head. "Dead."

Ronan began to hand the torch to Lamar, only would not release it. He spoke low and harsh. "Have the body wrapped and secretly taken at night and dumped in the lake."

"My lord?" asked Lamar, stunned by the order.

"If we are to avoid a Nefal uprising, no word of this can leave Sener. Do you understand, Sergeant?"

"Aye, my lord." Lamar held the door for Ronan and Mather to depart.

Enroute back to the study, Ronan fetched Irwin. Once returned, he told, Irwin, Othniel, and Ottlia about Bodil. He paced while speaking. Disturbance furrowed his brow.

Irwin flinched when Ronan related his order regarding Bodil. "Such action goes against our beliefs regarding treatment of the dead."

Ronan ceased pacing to reply. His face firm, yet a hint of remorse to his words. "It is not an order I give lightly. However, this attack proves

Axel's concern about Maro losing control to Spoor. Word of this reaches Maro, he may consider any movement south as hostile.

"Did Bodil confirm Spoor's involvement?" asked Irwin.

Ronan scowled. "No. The incidents may not be related, but I highly doubt it. A Nefal betraying his tribal chief is uncommon."

"Unless enticed by a more powerful chieftain or influence," chided Mather.

Ronan momentarily stared at the Freeland general. "Given our present situation, we cannot risk an internal uprising on speculation, no matter how likely the possibility. Our primary focus is the southern border, keeping the Queen safe, and hopefully, providing enough time to recover Lexi." He leaned on the table to regard the maps and papers. "We must succeed in all of these!" He looked to Irwin. "Well?"

"I provided the General with as much from the armory as possible without depleting supplies for defense of Sener."

Ronan shifted his focus to Mather. "And?"

The Freeland general approached the table to indicate the map. "To avoid suspicion, I dispatched three companies of troops to take different routes. Each left at appointed times throughout the day. One travelled the west Free Road through Nefal. Another, the east Free Road through Ha'tar, and the third took ferries."

"Only three companies?" ask Ronan asked, displeased.

"I told you our supplies are depleted," insisted Irwin.

"Alfgar took a large herd of unicorns with the first company. Two dragon riders will reinforce the border station near the main road to Bertrand. Each station can use the shield owl to alert us should the worse happen," Mather said.

"How quickly can we respond if Bertrand invades?"

Neither Mather nor Irwin immediately answered. After a long moment of deep, disturbing silence, Mather said, "We have done all we can."

"Except prayer," spoke a new voice.

"Arctander," said Ronan with a wry smile. "Always perfect timing."

"Gott's timing is always perfect, my lord, not mine. This old body can only move so fast." Arctander sat in the chair Mather provided.

Othniel approached the High Priest. "Our precautions saved the Queen and revealed the Nefal are in league with Bertrand."

"It is a shame Axel did not take my advice to banish them after the battle," chided Ronan

"He dealt with mercy," countered Arctander.

"Look where mercy has led us." Ronan spread his arms in an aggravated gesture.

Arctander rebuked Ronan. "You, of all people, question mercy? I thought Ganels regarded mercy as a godly virtue."

"We do, when properly placed. Treachery has kidnapped the Princess, made an attack upon the Queen, and left us vulnerable!"

Concerned by the unusual, unbridled passion, Irwin stepped between Ronan and Arctander. "Steady, Ronan. Arguing with Gott's High Priest will accomplish nothing, except cause division at a time we need to be united."

As if physically struck, Ronan blinked with alarm. "I didn't mean that," he began with contrition. "My lord Arctander, forgive me. I lost my head for a moment."

"That's an understatement," Mather wryly spoke.

Irwin ignored the Freelander to steer Ronan back to the table. "Truly, we have done all we can to prepare. It is up to Axel, Gunnar, Cormac, and Nollen to prevent war."

"All is in Gott's control," added Arctander. "My lords, I propose a prayer service this evening." He raised a hand when Ronan began to object. "No one need know the covert details. Only that we pray for the King, Queen, and future heir."

"To that, I agree."

When Ronan focused on the maps, Irwin spoke quietly to Mather. "Help Arctander with the arrangements." While Mather complied, Irwin came alongside Ronan. "What else troubles you?"

Stubbornly silent, Ronan only replied after Irwin gave him a hard elbow nudge. "Everything we have learned since the banquet." He slapped at the map in frustration. "Mecatis, the Viziers, and Nefal, wayward First Ones, Bertrandian lies. Everything!" He shook his head in dismay. "Gott prepared the Son of Eldar for retaking the throne, but this! I don't know if either he or Lexi are prepared for any encounter with Cadmus or their so-called gods."

"We weren't prepared for Markita."

"There is a great difference between Markita and Bertrand. And don't pretend you are ignorant of that. Also, we stood united then, and not under threat of internal strife."

"Dependence upon Gott for the outcome is the same," Irwin countered.

Othniel crossed to the table. "I will accompany Irwin to the southern border. There I shall be able to discern more clearly the presence of Kronos, Ursus, and Spyros."

"I guess I'm going south," Irwin commented to Ronan.

"Your presence will help to ease his mind," Othniel spoke in regard to Ronan. "Come. I will tell you what is needed for the journey." Othniel headed for the door with Irwin.

Chapter 34

For days, Lexi shadowed Celia in her daily routine as Olivia's maid. Being constantly together, they began to understand words, phrases, and gestures. The majority of the time, Lexi remained quiet, and took cues from Celia when needed. Regarding the veil, female household maids wore them when in public parts of the castle or outside. Cooks and scullery maids wore head scarfs, but no veils. Difficult to do around open flames and ovens of the kitchen. When among other servants, many maids removed the veils. Some didn't. Lexi only showed her face in private with Celia. No use taking chances if she should encounter the twins.

Navigating less conspicuous parts of the royal complex gave Lexi the opportunity to look for possible escape routes. She tried to observe exits other than the main gate or even the alley where she first encountered Celia. It led to the main thoroughfare, something she wanted to avoid.

One side of the complex was protected by cliffs. The lower floors had plain stone walls. The more embellished the corridor, the more important that part of the complex. Colorful tile mosaics, gold gilding, and painted murals covered plastered walls and ceilings. A series of small courtyards connected the buildings. Like the interior, individual ornamentation, and enhancements showed the level of prominence.

Interaction with other servants, also helped Lexi get a sense of the Bertrandian people, customs, and habits. Although, she wore wonderful clothes befitting a princess, the rich fabrics and elaborate details of Bertrandian attire exceeded anything in Eldar. She learned one unique fabric was called *silk.* Light, luxurious, and magnificent in accepting of vibrant dyes. Even the linen shirt she wore felt softer. Bertrandians appeared to be masters of weaving different fabrics to obtain the desired material and patterns.

The various colored livery identified the royals or nobles served. Purple and gold was for King Rastus; gold with silver accents for Prince Felix; wine accented lavender represented Princess Celeste. Cranberry with red and black embroidery belonged to Vizier Cadmus. Those in green and black livery served Lord Linux, steward of the royal household and personal aid to the King. Lady Olivia oversaw all the Princess' necessities.

Very early one morning, Celia roused Lexi. She hushed any conversation. By gestures, the need for haste was required. Lexi silently complied.

Celia carried a lantern. Once away from the room, she pulled Lexi into a private corner. She spoke in broken words. "You, Leizel," frustrated she put a finger to lips then pointed at Lexi.

"I have been quiet," Lexi replied.

Celia vigorously shook her head. Her anxious expression a cue to Lexi that this quiet was different.

"Secret?" Lexi asked.

Celia nodded. "Yah. *Secretus.*"

Lexi placed a finger to her lip in agreement. She followed Celia down flights of stairs to the lowest hallways they had yet ventured. These were dungeon like and required the lantern due to the lack of windows. Lexi rubbed her hands together to warm them from the damp, coldness of the passageways.

By the time they began an ascent, Lexi's eyes were well-adjusted to the dimness. She squinted due to the growing light. At what appeared to be an exterior door, Celia placed the lantern on a hook. She took out a key ring. Before opening it, Celia made a visible warning for quiet. Lexi again repeat an agreeing gesture. When Celia stepped out, she put up a stiff hand to stop Lexi in the threshold. Frustrated in searching for a word, Celia pointed to her eyes then pointed to Lexi's eyes.

"Watch?" Lexi mimicked the motion, to which Celia nodded. Lexi watched Celia walk a short distance down a very narrow alley to a metal gate. Lexi cranked her neck to peer out. From the direction they walked, she reckoned this to be on the opposite side of the complex from the other alley. That may put it closer to the bridge. To the left, the passage narrowed. The way Celia went bent slightly right to a gate. Most of the ornate grate visible, only the hinges obscured from view.

Celia cautiously glanced about. She flinched when the gate opened, and a hooded cloak figure arrived. She stepped back when waved aside.

"Well?" a male voice asked.

Celia reached into the pocket of her skirt. "She sends this."

Although he snatched it, his voice sounded pained. "He is getting so big. He may not know me if things do not change."

"He will. Have faith in the gods."

He produced a folded letter to give her. "We must meet. The separation is agony." He looked up when Lexi peeked out. "Who?"

"A foreigner. I helped her elude the twins. She is serving my lady, in place of Dorothia."

"Foreigner? I thought the edict stopped foreign kidnapping," he chided.

Celia shrugged ignorance. "I do not know nothing of such things, Your Grace—"

"Silence!" he snapped.

Horrified at the unintended indiscretion, she covered her mouth. Tears of regret immediately sprung to her eyes. "I'm sorry. I would do nothing—"

"Hush. I know. However, Cadmus is growing more suspicious since I continue to reject his suggestions for marriage." He gave her a nudge. "Go."

Celia returned to the door where she ushered Lexi back inside. Once the door was secure, she took down the lantern and headed in a different direction than the way they came. The hall went from plain to decorated and ended at an elaborate courtyard gate. Celia indicated for Lexi to put on the veil, as she did.

As they crossed the courtyard, Celia noticed a glow under the collar of Lexi's shirt the same time Lexi felt for Volker.

"Evil," Lexi muttered.

"*Ti*? Wh—?" Celia stopped the switch of languages when she spied him. She seized Lexi. "Cadmus! *Velo!*" She jerked Lexi down to kneel, almost prostrate. "*Thermous*, Vizier Cadmus," she formally greeted.

"Celia," Cadmus acknowledged. He spoke a few more words.

Celia timidly rose. She signaled Lexi to remain on her knees.

"*Nolos*?" he asked with a motion to Lexi.

"Leizel. *Neo dolous mi signora*."

Cadmus sneered a smile at Lexi then curtly waved Celia away so as not to be overheard. "You are just the person I was looking for."

"Me, Vizier?" Celia tried to mask nervousness.

"There are rumors concerning Lady Olivia that are most disturbing. I hope you can enlighten me to their truth or no."

"I will tell you what I can, Vizier."

"I am sure you will. The rumors regard her husband, whom most thought lost at sea. Some hinted he may have returned or was never a sailor." His tone and expression changed to severe as he spoke.

Celia clenched her fists to maintain a calm exterior. "I do not know, Vizier. My lady only speaks of him in the past tense. She is more concerned with her son, and duty to Her Highness."

Cadmus' narrow gaze shifted from Celia to Lexi then back again. "That is a shame. Dorothia's sudden departure left a void I see Leizel has filled. However, Leizel is not a Bertrandian name."

"She is foreign, Vizier."

He clicked his tongue in pretended disgust. "Against the King's edict of foreign slaves."

"Oh, no, Vizier! Leizel is willing," Celia hastily insisted.

He stared at her. "Willing? Do not deceive me. I know better."

Celia averted her eyes from him to gaze back at Lexi, who tried not to be too obvious in her curiosity of them. "While passing through Bertrand, her parents died, leaving her alone in a foreign land. Penniless, she seeks to make enough money for passage home. I found her and approached my lady for help since Dorothia left."

"How do you know this? Does she speak Bertrandian?"

"No, Vizier. It is a language I have never heard before, but—" her words hurried when he moved toward Lexi. "Through other means of communication, I pieced together her story."

Cadmus approached Lexi. "Leizel."

Lexi discretely placed a hand over Volker to hide the glow. She dared a glance up when he asked questions in several languages. She impulsively flinched at hearing Markitan.

At Lexi's reaction of recognition, Cadmus smiled. He took Celia's arm to speak confidential. "She is Markitan, which explains her presence in Bertrand."

"Yah, Vizier."

"For Leizel's sake, learn what you can about your lady's husband. You would not want Leizel to leave like Dorothia."

Celia dropped to her knees in obeisance. "No, Vizier." She anxiously watched his departure from the courtyard. She rushed Lexi into the hall from which they emerged.

"What was that all about?" Lexi asked. Celia didn't answer rather kept moving. Lexi pulled to a stop. "I asked a question. Why did I sense evil with him?"

Fearful, Celia chewed on her lower lip. She spoke in a hushed voice. "Vizier. How say …" She folded her hands and pointed upwards.

"Gott?"

Celia shook her head and counted off her fingers.

"The gods."

"Yah. Vizier like dolous. Gotts."

"He serves the gods?"

"Yah. Dorothia … poof!" She made motion with hands; the fingers spread.

"Vanished. Gone."

"Poof!" Celia insisted. "Leizel. Poof!"

Confused, Lexi murmured, "Why would he make me vanish—," In sudden realization, she asked, "Did he threaten me in some way?"

Frustrated, Celia seized Lexi's hand to continue down the back corridor. Lexi resisted and finally made Celia stop again.

"Does he know who I am? *Mi familia*?" Lexi whispered in desperation.

Celia shook her head, still anxious. "He say you … Markitan."

"Then not my family." Sympathetic to the dilemma, yet determined to have an answer, Lexi pressed. "Why did he threaten me like Dorothia?"

Celia moved close to whisper in Lexi's ear. "Olivia . . . *secretus*."

Lexi thought for a moment before surmising, "Dorothia knew this secret. You—" She was stopped when Celia covered her mouth.

"No. *Shhhh*!" This time Celia wouldn't accept any resistance to leave when she grabbed Lexi's hand.

As they went about the rest of the day, Lexi reflected on the two unusual incidents: first, the secret meeting. When the hooded head raised, she caught a glimpse of a man. Whoever he was, he must have been of importance since they went to great length to avoid being seen. As curious as she might be to the man's identity, the second encounter proved unnerving. Volker glowed the same time she felt the warm against her skin at sight of Vizier Cadmus. Celia explained that he served the gods. What evil did he possess that Volker gave warning?

The same evil that made him threaten me. But why? she wondered. All Celia revealed was it dealt with a secret concerning Olivia. A secret that cost Dorothia her life. Were the two incidents connected? Could it impact her chance of escape? So many questions swirled in her head that she followed Celia's instruction with preoccupation.

At one point later in the day, she and Celia crossed the courtyard when she spied a large statue of some kind. Lexi slowed her pace to view the open building with not one, but three statues. Man in body, yet each with the head of a different animal.

"Celia," Lexi said, a bit unnerved. "What? *Ti?*" she switched to Bertrandian.

Celia held up three fingers, placed her hand together as in prayer then pointed skyward

"Your gods." As if drawn, Lexi cautiously mounted the first step to the shrine. Overcome by a cold chill, she braced herself on a pillar to stay upright. She felt the warmth of Volker beneath the collar. She placed a hand over the glow. "You don't have to tell me, I feel it," she said, as if speaking to Volker.

"Leizel?" Celia folder prayerful hands and pointed to the statues.

Lexi adamantly shook her head. "No! They are not … No." She hastily left, with a curious Celia in pursuit.

"Leizel, no?" She made the prayer hands again.

"I do pray. But to one." She held up a single finger. "Not a half-man statue."

Celia made the prayer hands and pointed to her eyes.

"You want to see my prayer?"

Celia shook her head. "Gott." She pointed to her eyes then back to the shrine.

"What does Gott look like?"

"Yah!"

Lexi pondered a moment before answering. "Unknown. We don't have statues." She motioned back to the shrine. "He created everything." She made exaggerated motion to all around. "That is how we see him." She motioned to her eyes then skyward. "And in here." She pointed to her heart. "Them?" She again pointed to her heart.

"No!" Celia made a shivering motion.

"You fear them?"

"Yah. You—?" Celia again made the shivering motion.

"No, I don't fear Gott," said Lexi with reverence. "He is good. Merciful."

"Mer … ci … ful?" Celia repeated.

"Kind. Benevolent. *Chrestos*," Lexi spoke the Bertrandian word.

"Ah!" Celia smiled. The smile suddenly faded, and she seized Lexi in warning.

Lexi followed Celia's indication to see Cadmus across the courtyard and walking away.

Although he didn't notice them, a cold knot of nervousness struck Lexi the same time she felt Volker. She visibly shivered.

"Not *chrestos,*" Celia said to Lexi's reaction. "Come."

Toward evening, Lexi entered a large vestibule where she placed a tray on a table along the wall. She spied them almost directly across from her. The twins! Her heart raced with fear. Cadmus arrived to speak with them. Terror welled up in the pit in her being the same moment she felt Volker's warmth. She dashed around the corner and flattened herself against the wall. She clenched the shirt collar and took gulps of air to calm down. Where could she run or hide? Cadmus' presence brought evil, but the twins—they might kill her if discovered. She screwed her eyes shut.

"Leizel."

Lexi's eyes snapped open at Celia's voice. She grabbed Celia and raced away from danger. At an alcove, she paused to say, "Cadmus. The twins." She pointed back down the hall.

Sympathetic, Celia said, "Go. Room. Hide."

Lexi vehemently shook her head. "I must leave!"

"Room. Safe," Celia insisted.

Lexi rushed to Celia's room. She locked the exterior door. She flung off the headdress and veil. She collapsed on the edge of the bed, desperately fighting tears of sheer terror. "Gott, help me."

The moment she finished uttering the plea, she recalled various incidents and statements from the past, and more recent. Axel as a teenager and young adult encouraging her during practice and lessons from Gunnar. The whirlwind of emotions following Axel's departure from Kranston propelled her to learn what she could about the Shield Maiden. Her own words spoken in Mathena when seeing Arkin, echoed in her ears; Until now, I believed only Axel had a destiny. Followed immediately by Cormac saying *Sarina passed down the duties of Shield Maiden to her eldest daughter, beginning a tradition that now comes to you.* The old voice of Alwyn the Ganel apothecary declaring: *You are the Shield Maiden.*

An image came to mind of the vacant place on the Shield Maiden armor. The recollection accompanied by Axel speaking about their mother's brooch. Her hand touched the left side of her chest where the missing piece was located, as she spoke to herself in consideration. "Mama wore it at my dedication. Why? Just tradition?"

She withdrew Volker from under the collar. She paraphrased Cormac's words in regards of ruby. "This is a tool, the same as Arkin, and even the sensations. What determines success or failure, is in my heart, and mind." She released Volker to stand. Her face and voice determined. "No, she wore it because I am the Shield Maiden."

She withdrew the dagger from the boot sheath. Although the sword was her preferred weapon, she practiced the dagger drills taught her since youth. With each maneuver, she recited the statements of faith.

"Your truth is my shield. Faith is my strength. Trust is my courage."

Whether she encountered the twins again in the palace or after escape, she would be ready.

Chapter 35

THE FOLLOWING AFTERNOON, A STONE-FACED CADMUS SAT AT THE desk in his private office. Spoor waited near the terrace door. Cadmus barked a command in response to a knock. The brothers entered. Cadmus coldly regarded his sons. Marius tried to mask his worry, while Mateo appeared unconcerned. Cadmus made a silent motion to draw their attention to Spoor.

The Nefal's expression equally harsh. He held up a scabbard. "This requires an explanation."

"What is that to us?" Mateo asked, with forced disdain.

"It belongs to her. I discovered it washed up on shore a day's ride from the city."

Mateo immediately spoke to Cadmus. "We told you she fell into the river."

"What do you mean fell into the river?" Spoor interrogated.

"She managed to escape, and ran down the east alley, which ends at the cliffs. She slipped." Mateo heaved a careless shrug.

Spoor's scarred face twisted with a sneer, as he questioned Cadmus. "You believe them because of this?"

"It proves what we said is true," insisted Mateo.

Spoor confronted Mateo. His good eye stared down since he towered above the man. "There are other ways this could have gotten into the water. Tossed in to throw anyone off the trail. Or cover incompetence."

Sweat formed on Mateo's upper lip. He spoke to Cadmus in continued defense. "She fell into the river!" When Cadmus remained unconvinced, Mateo seized his brother. "Marius always tells the truth, you know that," then to Marius, "Tell him!"

Marius stiffened to comply. "She slipped."

Both Cadmus and Spoor remained stoic, which prompted Mateo to remind Cadmus, "You saw Marius' injury when we reported what happened. She escaped by downing him with a kick." He made a mimicking motion to the groin, which made Marius flinch in defense.

Spoor's sudden completion of the motion dropped Marius to the floor in agony. The move stunned Mateo while Cadmus remained impassive.

"Men are weak creatures," Spoor chided.

"He does tell the truth. A flaw instilled by his mother," Cadmus callously said.

"Flaws can be exploited," countered Spoor.

"Get out!" Cadmus dismissed the twins. When the door closed, he rose to accost Spoor. "Their explanation is reasonable. However, you need to explain about the involvement of other Nefal."

Spoor tossed the scabbard on Cadmus' desk. "Simple. Cause more trouble for Axel while preparing the Nefal to return to their proper place."

Incited, Cadmus huffed with pride. "The Nefal's proper place is where I say it is!"

Spoor's whole body went rigid with rage. "Our agreement—"

"Is based upon fulfilling your part of the bargain." Cadmus snatched up the scabbard. "The girl is dead! Do not further complicate matters by taking singular actions that will incite the gods. It will be worse for the Nefal should that happen."

Spoor bared his teeth. "You might believe your pitiful offspring, but I do not. A water-soaked scabbard does not a dead body make. As for Nefal, we do not take threats well." He snatched the scabbard from Cadmus and tore it apart with is bare hands.

Cadmus made the waving motion of a beginning incantation. Spoor seized Cadmus' hands. The Vizier struggled, but unable to free himself.

"I will start tracking from where I found the scabbard. If I discover a body, I will bring it back. If not, look to your offspring for answers. The failure lies there and not with Nefal." Spoor shoved Cadmus aside and stormed from the office.

For several moments, Cadmus stared at the tattered pieces of scabbard on the floor. They still await an answer from Eldar about the proposal. Whether the delay was good or bad remained to be determined. However, if the princess is really dead … Cadmus abruptly left his office. With long strides, he went to the shrine. He found Marius kneeling before the altar.

"Marius."

The young man struggled to stand, still sore from Spoor's assault. "Sir."

"Are you here for a reason? A guilty conscience, perhaps?" Cadmus coolly probed.

"Disturbed and wondering if it was really necessary to kidnap her—" The words were cut off when Cadmus seized his throat.

"Mind your tongue!"

"Why?" Marius struggled to speak.

"Do not question me."

"The gods," Marius forced the words, as his eyes darted to the altar.

"The gods instruct, and we obey without question." Although Marius continued to gasp for air, Cadmus did not ease his hold. "Spoor is right. You are weak." He slammed Marius into the wall in rough release.

Angry eyes glared at Cadmus before Marius staggered out of the shrine.

Spyros landed on the shoulder of the raven statue.

"My lord, Spyros." Cadmus crossed his arms over his chest and bowed at the waist.

"We are not pleased by the progress of the plan."

"There have been unforeseen complications—"

"Complications do not concern us! Obedience and success are our concern."

Cadmus made the same reverent bow at the rebuke.

"The eyes of the gods are watching. We know the girl arrived in Theron. We also know about the Nefal, harpy, and jackals. Bringing ancient enemies into Bertrand is a mistake!"

"Spoor knows the consequences of total failure."

"There is more than the future of the Nefal at stake. Inciting Eldar and the First Ones is unforgiveable. Doing so will incur retribution upon those responsible. Beginning with you!"

An expression of fear crossed Cadmus' face. He deeply bowed at the waist and spoke without looking up. "I will make certain that does not happen, my lord."

"Proceed immediately with the union. With that, we can thwart Eldar." Spyros departed the shrine.

Cadmus slowly straightened. The last statement told him Spyros was unaware of the girl's reported death. A brief moment of perplexity gave way to the realization that such ignorance would not last long. He needed to take action before Spyros learned the truth.

As Cadmus made his way from the shrine toward his apartment, he spied Felix across the grand courtyard. The Prince appeared hasty in his trek from the stable to the main palace entrance. Instead of going inside, Felix made a detour toward the far side. When Felix paused at the corner to look back, Cadmus ducked behind a wagon to avoid being seen. The Prince rounded the corner. When Cadmus stepped out, he saw Celia and Lexi reach the same corner.

"Celia!" the Vizier called.

Startled, Celia balked. Lexi held onto Celia's arm in support.

"Vizier." Celia dropped to her knees at Cadmus' approach.

Lexi mimicked the motion. She crossed her hands in customary Bertrandian oblation to grip the collar of her shirt. She lowered her head to rest her chin the knuckles of her hand.

Cadmus feigned a kind smile. "I had hoped to run into you today."

"The honor is mine, Vizier," Celia replied in a nervous voice.

"Is something amiss?"

"No, Vizier. Simple overwhelmed that you would want to meet me."

Cadmus shrugged. "Why should that be surprising after our last discussion?" He changed his focus to Lexi. "Leizel. *Dobor jutro*," he spoke *good morning* in Markitan.

Lexi forced a shaky smile, as she tilted her head to raise her eyes, yet keep her chin on the knuckles. "Vizier."

"You are looking well," he continued in Markitan.

Lexi maintained the uncertain smile. "*Efcharisto.* Thank you, Vizier."

"Ah! You are learning Bertrandian. Excellent." He returned to Celia. "She is doing well in your charge. Let us hope it stays that way." He motioned Celia to stand. He took a few steps away from Lexi to ask Celia, "Have you learned anything?"

"No, Vizier. My lady is very private in regard to her late husband. Although, I have been discrete with any inquiry," she assured him.

Cadmus casually glanced back to Lexi. "You may have to employ other means than discussion. If you understand my meaning?"

Celia pressed her lips together to contain discomfort. "I do, Vizier."

"Good. When next we meet, I expect information. You do not want Leizel to stop learning Bertrandian, now do you?"

Celia dropped to her knees. "No, Vizier."

Cadmus smugly smiled, as his eyes darted to Lexi. She quickly lowered her gaze to avoid eye contact.

Lexi didn't move until she heard Celia say, "He go."

Celia pointed to the collar of Lexi's shirt. "E–vil?" she stuttered in speaking Eldarian. When Lexi hesitated, Celia leaned close to whisper, "Vizier evil." She tugged Lexi to continue walking in the original direction.

"So, you are protecting me from him because of what happened to Dorothia—"

"*Shhh!* No, say … naa am."

"Name?"

Celia placed a finger to her lips. After they rounded the far corner, she stopped Lexi. "Here. Leizel." She used her finger to show eyes.

"You want me to stay here and watch," Lexi surmise.

"Yah." Celia again placed a finger to her lips before she moved further down the alley between buildings.

Lexi took up a surveillance position. Due to precautions at Kranston, she learned how to be discrete in observation. She positioned herself to see the courtyard and where Celia went. Once again, she saw a man, though his features obscured by shadows. His back was to her when he met Celia. Together, they walked further down the alley where the shadows grew deeper. When they paused, Lexi noticed a third person joined them. From the outline of the silhouette, the dress appeared to be female. At Celia's head turn, Lexi went back to watching the courtyard. Everything since arriving in Bertrand spoke of intrigue.

Of course, she understood the need for secrecy, it had been honed in her since birth. The word *freedom* echoed in her mind. She longed for it, sought it with all her being after arriving in Eldar. Now, she found herself disguised as a servant in a foreign country after escaping her kidnappers.

Perhaps, if I had heeded Axel and not resisted ... The thought made tears of regret blur her vision. She quickly wiped her eyes clear. Dwelling on it caused a distraction from her current situation. Once home, she would make amends.

"Home," she murmured under her breath. She took advantage of her obscure position to take in various details in the courtyard. There had to be a way to leave unobserved! "Errand," she said to herself in sudden thought. "Ask to be sent on an errand." The timing and circumstances had to be right. "Gott, grant me wisdom of when to act."

Satisfied at a possible solution, she continued her watchfulness.

Chapter 36

THE FOLLOWING DAY, RASTUS, FELIX, AND CELESTE SAT IN THE private dining room. Per the King's instructions, dinner consisted of simple food. He preferred to feast at midday and eat lighter fare in the evening. Being less formal, high-ranking servants were occasionally given the privilege of joining the royal family. This evening, the honor fell to Lord Linux and Olivia.

Celia would serve and wait upon Celeste and Olivia. Lexi's duty was to hand Celia the trays and keep everything in order on the sideboard. Olivia and Celia prepared her for the evening. Fortunately, her anxiety regarding Cadmus' presence was quickly eliminated when Olivia explained that despite the King's gracious custom, the Vizier rarely mingled with servants. Until now, Lexi had not been formally introduced to the royals or Lord Linux. She kept a shy demeanor with a bowed head and courtesy. They only gave her passing notice before proceeding with the meal.

Despite wearing the veil, Lexi hung back in the shadows at the far end of the sideboard. She may not fully understand the language, but perhaps something could help in formulating her plan to request being sent on an errand. Thus, she listened and observed.

Although reportedly the same age as Rastus, Linux appeared younger than sixty years old. Strands of auburn hair remained among the thick supple gray. He had fewer wrinkles and less jowly than Rastus. His physique trim compared to the King's rotund form. Rastus, Linux, and Felix discussed hunting and sport. At least, Lexi surmised that by what appeared to be bow-like actions.

She mainly focused her attention on Celeste and Olivia. After all, their relationship could be key in helping her leave without incident. Sometimes Olivia and Celeste giggled in private. Other times, Olivia cast longing glances to Felix. He discreetly returned her gaze. Catching one of the exchanges, Celeste whispered to Olivia. The latter flushed and made a brief nod. Celeste sent her brother an admonishing glare. Fortunately, Rastus seemed oblivious, embroiled in a lively debate with Linux.

Curious, thought Lexi. She considered Felix's profile. Something stuck her as familiar. Then she realized why. The man she saw twice at those secret meetings. Her eyes darted to Olivia. If what she suddenly suspected was true …

"Sire …"

The moment a servant spoke, Lexi felt the warmth of Volker while a sense of coldness swept over her.

"… Vizier Cadmus and Lord Dynos."

Hearing Dynos' name, Lexi stepped further back into the corner nearest the servants' entrance. Veil notwithstanding, he might recognize her! She saw Celia notice her movement.

"Ah, Dynos!" Rastus greeted.

With attention drawn to the opposite side where Rastus sat at the head of the table, Lexi slipped out the servants' door. Upon hearing Rastus mention Eldar, she kept it open enough to listen from the safety of the other room. She balked when the door opened further. Celia raised a finger for silence. She carefully joined Lexi to listen.

Lexi inadvertently flinched when Dynos spoke Axel's name. Her movement bumped Celia, which drew the maid's attention from the conversation to Lexi.

"Leizel?"

"Tell me what they are saying. It's very important … *spoudaois*," Lexi urged.

Celia translated. "King angry. No … *pantreo*." She clasped her hands together.

Lexi heard Rastus let out a string of expletives. He spoke in quick phrases hard to follow, yet the names Felix and Axel prominent.

Lexi mimicked the hand motion. "This? And what about Axel?"

Guardedly curious at the question, Celia stared at Lexi.

"Please, tell me," Lexi implored.

"King Axel no *pantreo* sister to Prince Felix." Celia again clasped hands then pulled on the ring finger of her left hand.

"Marry?" Lexi gasped in fearful understanding. She quickly covered her mouth to silence her reaction. This pressed the veil against her face. She leaned back against the wall and screwed her eyes shut to maintain her composure. Her eyes snapped open when Celia seized her arms. Tears blurred her vision. She tried to be free only Celia wouldn't yield.

"I must leave!" she urgently whispered.

"Why?"

Lexi shook her head. "*Secretus*. Like you and Dorothia with Olivia."

Celia made a curt understanding nod. "Go. Room. I shortly come."

"Thank you." Lexi gave Celia a quick embrace before she left.

A few times, Lexi was forced to slow her hurried pace due to other servants or guards. When she reached the room, she felt in command of her emotions. Now, she needed to consider what she heard. Was the startling news connected to her current situation? How could Axel even consider such a thing? Marriage? To a stranger?

The prospect of marriage seemed a distant hope when living in Kranston. Of course, if something happened to Axel, it would become her duty to carry on the royal line. Fortunately, he succeeded, and now Eldar awaited the birth of first royal heir in over two hundred years.

Again, she didn't seriously think of marriage while adjusting to life in Sener. Not until the journey and … "Nollen", she murmured in distress. Tears fell at thought of him lying motionless. She didn't know if he survived. She removed the veil to wipe her face. Now to hear about an offer of royal marriage.

She took several deep breaths to calm down. "Axel refused. He protected me because he knows where my destiny lies. He tried to tell me many times, but I wouldn't listen. In Mathena …" She bowed her head to silently pray. *Gott, I now understand how my selfishness hurt others. I stubbornly refused to see past my childish expectations of freedom.* The word freedom struck her hard, and she swallowed back rising emotions. *Nollen spoke rightly when he said I had a wrong idea of freedom. How it involves embracing responsibility without fear.* She raised her head. With tear-filled eyes, she glanced around the room. *Now, I am in a real prison. Though not of my own making, but nonetheless, a prison.* She shivered at thought of the man/beast statues. "An evil prison." She looked up. "Please, Gott, I must get home. Help me to do so …" She stopped at hearing someone at the door. She carefully reached for the dagger in her boot, yet relaxed when Celia arrived.

"Tell me everything that was said. Leave nothing out."

Celia shrugged, as she struggled with switching languages. "No marry. King angry."

"Axel is angry?"

"Rastus angry Axel for no."

"Well, I can understand Axel's refusal."

"Make trade no."

"Trade?" Lexi brief thought than asked, "You mean my … the marriage for commodities?" She righted herself in mid-sentence.

Again, Celia shrugged in her efforts to pronounce, "Com … mod …"

"Goods." Lexi plucked at her skirt and a vase. "Trade. Goods. Commodities."

"Ah! Yah. No marry. No trade. Eldar. War."

Lexi balked in fear. "War?"

"Vizier angry more. King no war."

Lexi sat on the edge of the bed to ponder the information. She muttered, "My marriage for trade or war."

"*Ti*? … What?"

Realizing her second verbal mistake, Lexi quickly waved it aside. "Nothing."

Not to be put off, Celia sat beside Lexi. "You. Not. Leizel."

Lexi took firm hold of Celia's hand, stared straight into her eyes, and firmly said, "You heard nothing. *Secretus*!"

Celia made a twisting motion over her lips and pointed up. "By gotts."

"You promise by your gods not to speak."

Celia nodded.

"Thank you. Yet, answer me one question. Why would your king make such a proposal when his son loves someone else?"

Now it became Celia's turn to look startled and anxious. The reaction made Lexi say, "That is the secret, isn't it? Those meetings …"

Anxious, Celia covered Lexi's mouth. She whispered, "King no." She pointed to her head.

Lexi removed Celia's hand from her face to quietly speak. "He doesn't know. Why?"

Celia shrugged with frightened ignorance.

Lexi murmured in agreement. "I admit, I too am unfamiliar with royal intrigue. Or, at least, I was. I'm getting a harsh lesson."

Conversation briefly paused at hearing people in the hall. Passing maids by the sound of muted female voices. The interruption brought back the urgency of Lexi's predicament. Once the voices faded, Lexi spoke.

"You must help me leave. Arrange an errand for me to go into town. Please! I cannot stay here any longer. Too dangerous … like Dorothia … Poof!" She made the open finger motion with her hands.

Celia tenderly smiled. "I help." She took Lexi's hand to stand. "Must go back. Serve."

"No!" Lexi pulled away. "I stay here. You return."

When the door closed, Lexi again considered the situation. Dynos arrived unexpectedly a day prior to Alicia's banquet. She didn't think much about it; simply another foreign dignitary seeking an audience with Axel. He acted cordial enough when they interacted at the banquet. Then she recalled Nollen mentioning something about trade items he needed to take care of before their departure. Did he know about the marriage proposal? He gave no indication. She touched her lip in remembrance of their kisses in Mathena. He pulled away and spoke about how Axel trusted him. He must have known!

"But he didn't deny feelings for me. We even kissed again at Heddwyn. Neither would have happened if he knew," she argued with herself. "Maybe it occurred after we left." She sighed with frustration. "So many questions and few answers. Too distracting." She glanced up. "Please, Gott, help me focus on what I must do, and trust the answers will come in time."

Chapter 37

EMERGING FROM A MOUNTAIN FOREST PATH, NOLLEN DREW REIN. Axel, Cormac, and Gunnar joined him. Bright morning sun revealed a vast expanse that continued for many miles. Below, the main road wound through settlements that dotted the landscape and increased in population further south. On the far horizon, an outline of spires, roofs, with rising smoke on both sides of the river.

"In the distance, is Theron. It spans the river," said Nollen. His beard a healthy month of growth.

"Looks like we should make it by midday," said Axel.

"No, we won't reach it until late tomorrow afternoon. There is another smaller valley over the next rise. So, roughly forty miles. Best to spend the night and enter with daily traffic."

"Really?" Gunnar regarded the horizon. "The city must be massive."

"It is."

"I take it, you have been there before," Axel commented to Nollen.

"Once. When I was sixteen, my father included me as a member of the annual charter delegation. He thought it time I experienced Bertrandian culture outside of trading. Also, to sharpen my language skills."

"How long were in Theron?"

"Six long weeks," Nollen complained.

"Profitable?"

Nollen scoffed a laugh. "Depends upon your point of view; Eldarian or Bertrandian." He caught sight of Gunnar fidgeting in the saddle and glancing around. "Something wrong?"

"I know you have impressive pathfinding skills, but how did you guide us this way when only visiting Theron once, and eight years ago?"

Nollen cocked a sly grin, as he reached into the saddle bag. "Remember I told you these clothes belonged to my father, who took secret trips into Bertrand disguised as trader." He held up a folded paper. "This is the map he made during those journeys."

Axel and Cormac heartily laughed.

"Lad, one of these days, I will catch you unprepared," said Gunnar, sarcastic.

"Hopefully not when it counts." Nollen replaced the map then removed another folded piece of paper. "This is the agreement that allows me safe passage in Bertrand. It has Rastus' seal." He gave it to Cormac.

"If it is specific to you, how can I use it?"

"No, a general agreement given to sanctioned travel for trade. Keep it handy, as I'm sure we will need it." Nollen gathered the reins. "From here on, we must use the main road. Keep conversation to a minimum and allow me to do most of the talking."

"I do speak Bertrandian, remember," Cormac said.

"It is best you don't until we reach Theron. Our story is of lost Eldarian travelers, not a secret envoy."

"The lad knows what he's doing," Gunnar commented.

Nollen noticed Bardolf move to the tree line. "Bardolf, you and the pack should not proceed any further. There isn't much forest between here and Theron for cover."

"You cannot continue unprotected."

"No, Bardolf. Nollen is correct," said Axel. "With Gott's help we have succeeded in alluding detection by your wayward comrades. We should keep it that way."

A sudden echoing roar made the men flinch, startled the horses, and the wolves to cower. For almost a full minute, the deafening roar sounded over the countryside. When it subsided, all took a moment for recovery.

"Ursus!" Bardolf growled.

Artair made an awkward landing on the ground beside the wolf-king. He ruffled his feathers and shook his head. "I was coming to warn you that I sighted Ursus ten miles northeast."

"Ten miles? We heard his roar from that far away?" Axel added, incredulous.

"Ursus is very dangerous. He and Kronos are equal in strength and power to Othniel," insisted Artair.

"So much for remaining undetected," groused Gunnar.

"It is not human or Ganel that Ursus senses, but us," said Bardolf of himself and Artair.

"Then continuing with us can be dangerous to the Son of Eldar," said Alydar.

Bardolf snorted in annoyance. "We are not the only ones that can be sensed."

"The loss of my horn changed my unicorn status."

"My status hasn't changed," said Sheba.

"You and Sheba must remain quiet. No human speech," Nollen chided Alydar.

"This debate only brings Ursus closer," Artair warned.

"Why do I think our part in this is irrelevant?" Cormac dryly spoke to Axel.

Bardolf ignored the comment to tell Axel, "I propose a compromise. The pack will remain here until dusk then proceed after you. This way, the distance between us will provide you safety, give us cover, and fulfill the duty of protection."

When Nollen started to voice an objection, Bardolf, spoke to the young trader. "It is not just the Son of Eldar for which I accepted responsibility. I have watched over your family since Oleg's fall. That is why I sent Callie in my stead when you went to Markita."

"Very well. We proceed as you suggest," agreed Axel.

"A further point, of which I was also going to make," said Nollen, half to Axel and half to Bardolf. "Let me take the Shield Maiden bundle. If discovered, it is more natural for a trader to have such highly valued items than lost travelers." At Cormac's visible hesitancy, he added, "Alydar retained his speed, and very capable of out running any trouble with or without me, should that be necessary."

Convinced, Cormac dismounted to make the exchange. Once all was arranged on Alydar to appear as baggage, Nollen led the descent. On the main road, he and Cormac rode ahead of Axel and Gunnar. Cormac kept glancing to and fro.

"You shouldn't be too obvious in surveillance. Act casual, especially in view of other travelers," Nollen privately said to the Ganel.

"I have never ventured this far outside Eldar," Cormac replied in the same private tone. Uneasy, the Ganel's brows furrowed. "There is a darker sense of evil here than Markita."

"Aye. We must trust Gott," said Axel.

"And keep our blades sharp," Gunnar added.

"Hush!" Nollen cocked his head to issue the harsh warning.

A group of Bertrandians came around a bend from the opposite direction. A man drove a fully loaded wagon. Two women walked beside it. A half-mile behind that group, rode four uniformed men.

Nollen casually guided Alydar to the side of the road to allow room for the wagon to pass. The others followed his lead. Axel and Gunnar closed the gap between them. No verbal exchange occurred. Instead, Nollen nodded to the driver, who returned the curt gesture.

Nollen sat up straight at the approach of the four uniformed men. When the lead rider raised his hand, Nollen stopped Alydar. Cormac, Axel, and Gunnar stopped short of Nollen.

"Citizen," the leader greeted.

"Good day, sir," Nollen returned in Bertrandian.

The leader flashed a sly grin at spying the baggage on Alydar. "Successful trading, I see."

Nollen cocked smile. "I never return empty-handed."

The leader motioned to the trio behind Nollen. "Who are they?"

"Lost travelers." Nollen leaned on the saddle bow to continue. "They paid handsomely for directions."

The leader moved to confront them. "Where are you headed?"

"They don't speak Bertrandian," Nollen said.

"What do they speak?"

"Eldarian. That is why they need my help."

"Where would Eldarians be heading?" he demanded.

"To Theron, for a ferry to the coast and then a ship to Walerian."

"Do they have papers for passage?"

"Better. Approval from King Rastus." Nollen turned in the saddle to speak to Cormac in Eldarian. "The agreement, if you please."

Cormac pulled out the paper Nollen gave him earlier. The leader snatched it to read.

"Ah. Now, I understand. Fellow traders," he said to Nollen. He folded the paper and returned it to Cormac.

"Their first trip through Bertrand." Nollen heaved a shrug. "I couldn't refuse to help. Especially, for a hefty price."

The leader huffed a sardonic question. "You fleece your own kind?"

"No, I fleece Eldarians." Nollen widely smiled.

The leader heartily laughed. "Good day, citizen." He waved for his men to continue.

"Sir." Nollen lightly kicked Alydar to continue.

When enough distance passed to freely speak, Cormac drew alongside Nollen. "*'Fleece Eldarians'*, uh?"

"I had to sound Bertrandian enough to convince them to leave."

The rest of the day pass without incident. Shortly after midday, they paused by a backwater stream to rest, eat, and water the horses. Conversation kept to directions or weather. By nightfall, they reached an inn twelve miles from Theron. The crowd of patrons forced them to dismount at a far side corral.

"Stay here. I'll arrange accommodations." Nollen left.

Axel, Cormac, and Gunnar dismounted to wait. Gunnar held Alydar's reins along with Joslin. Cautiously, they viewed the surroundings. An assorted group of travelers, and locals, patronized the inn. A few drunks staggered about while others were more interested in carousing or gambling. They shrunk back when passed by inebriated individuals or other patrons.

"What is taking him so long?" Cormac impatiently complained.

"Easy. I told you the lad knows what he is doing," Gunnar replied.

"I know. I just—" Cormac stopped when Axel clapped his shoulder.

Axel leaned close to speak confidentially. "I share your uneasiness, but we must remain calm by focusing on our task."

"It would be easier minus a certain individual," Cormac rebuffed.

Axel didn't take the slight well. His eye steady on the Ganel.

Gunnar's jab and announcement, "He comes," drew Axel's attention from Cormac to Nollen's return.

"Where are we sleeping?" Axel asked.

"Not inside. Which is good," Nollen quickly added to their frowns. He took Alydar to lead them around the back of the corral to an old shed.

"This is good?" groused Cormac.

Nollen didn't answer the terse comment. He unlocked the shed to lead them and the horses inside. After he closed the door, he replied to Cormac. "It is good we even have shelter and privacy. They don't like Eldarians. I had to convince them not to turn you away."

Gunnar laughed and patted Cormac's shoulder. The Ganel scowled at Gunnar yet asked Nollen. "I don't suppose you convinced them to provide food?" He no sooner spoke the words then there came a knock.

Nollen exchanged a few words with a sneering female before he took the tray filled with food, a pitcher, and four cups. Gunnar again chuckled, as he closed the door for Nollen. Cormac frowned, as meat dominated the tray, though accompanied with bread, potatoes, and cabbage.

Nollen placed the tray on a shelf. "I could hardly refuse meat. Bertrandians are unfamiliar with your kind thus would not understand dietary preference. You can have the cabbage and potatoes." He told Cormac. He stopped serving at hearing a sound outside the side of the shed. He shoved the plate into Gunnar's hand, which prevented Gunnar from drawing his sword. "Stay quiet," he hastily said and rushed outside.

From the doorway, Axel cautiously watched. Nollen caught the same female who delivered the tray. She tried to jerk loose but became subdue at his rebuke in Bertrandian. She spat on the ground and swore about Eldarians. Nollen did not accept her bitter attitude. Whatever angry words he spoke in reply made her shrink back in fear. She timidly nodded. When he released her, she ran around the corral and out of sight. Axel closed the door when Nollen returned to disturbing the food.

"What was that about?" he asked.

"I told you they don't like Eldarians. He father, the innkeeper, sent her to spy on you. I made certain that didn't happen."

"By saying something that frightened her? What was it?"

"Bertrandians are very superstitious. I used it to our advantage."

Annoyed, Axel stopped Nollen from disturbing the food. "That doesn't answer my question."

"I simply reminded her that she risks punishment by the gods for lying and denying hospitality."

Axel flushed with anger yet keep his voice level. "You threatened her?"

"No! I used their superstitions to save us," Nollen insisted.

Seeing Axel slow to accept the explanation, Cormac approached to take his plate of vegetables. He spoke to Axel in a voice barely above a whisper. "He's right. Bertrandians are highly superstitious to the point of idolatry. The main reason why we refused to admit many to university. Only a handful saw beyond the old misconceptions."

Gunnar gave Axel a plate of meat and bread then gently encouraged him to sit and eat.

Nollen sat on the other side of Axel. He spoke in dismay. "I would never threaten or harm a female. I'm sorry you took it that way."

"He knows that by your past actions in Markita," Gunnar gently encouraged. He sent a prompting glare to Axel.

Axel swallowed food to reply. "I do. You have proven your mettle time and again." His words came regretful. "I let concern for someone cloud my thinking."

Nollen looked directly at Axel to say, "I will find that someone."

Axel tried to curb a grin at the confident boast. "I know that too. Now, finish eating and rest. I'll take the first watch."

"Wake me after three hours to relieve you." Gunnar placed aside the empty plate to lay down.

On the opposite wall, a small window allowed in light and air. Axel sat in such a way as to view the outside. The others had settled down. In consideration, he focused on the visible night sky. Alicia spoke wisely about his need to let Lexi go and not fear for her; how Gott would take care of her. However, a tremendous fear gripped him when told of Lexi's kidnapping. He couldn't lose his sister! Not now. There was too much at stake. After speaking with Alicia, Gunnar, and Lorraine, he calmed down, and viewed the situation more rationally. Well, to a point. His mind warred between the rational and worry at what she could experience. He found it difficult to make sense of it all.

"Why Gott? Why this way? She knows little of the world," he spoke under his breath, or so he thought. He felt Gunnar squirm. He could wake at the slightest sound, believing a perceived theat. "A cat," Axel whispered. Gunnar grunted acknowledgement and went back to sleep.

All the discoveries since Lexi's kidnapping, propelled him to undertake the journey. Her importance as Shield Maiden went beyond family relations. It threatened the stability of Eldar!

His attention shifted to Nollen. Although he sensed Nollen would play a significant part in his effort to become king, the years have shown a deeper involvement. Commissary, Markita, and now Lexi. "If Gott allows, I may soon call you brother." He returned his focus to the window. "Your will be done, Lord."

Chapter 38

LEXI HELD AN EMPTY BASKET AS SHE WAITED FOR CELIA OUTSIDE Olivia's apartment. She tried hard to conceal anxiety. *Gott, please let her convince Olivia to accompany me. I don't know if or when there will another chance to leave,* she inwardly pleaded.

Although in a servants' hall, Lexi wore the veil. Other maids came and went through the corridor. She kept her head lowered and eyes shrouded. She only glanced up to see if any who passed her remained in the hall. No one paused in their course. She nearly jumped in surprise when the door opened.

"At last," she murmured at sight of Celia. "Well?"

Celia simply smiled and took hold of Lexi's arm. In the other arm, she too carried a basket. They walked to a rear exterior door. "You no talk. More coin foreigner."

Lexi lightly chuckled in relief. "Gladly."

They exited an alley gate used by servants or merchants with deliveries. Being late afternoon, commerce was well underway to and from the palace. They emerged from the alleyway into the crowded thoroughfare and mingled with the noisy throng. Lexi attempted to calm her racing heart, as the first phase of her flight to freedom was complete.

"Where?" she asked speaking into Celia's ear.

Celia pointed toward the bridge. They held tightly to each other when squeezing through the mass of people. The way became narrower on the bridge. People, wagons, and riders traversed in opposite directions. Lexi fought to keep her balance and not get knocked into the rail. At one point, her headdress was pushed forward and covered her eyes. She dropped her basket and would have fallen, save Celia pulled her to safety on the other side of the bridge.

Lexi straightened her headdress. "I hope it is easier from here."

Celia giggled. She gave Lexi the fallen basket. "*Spocho*!" She pointed to Lexi and pushed with her arms.

"Shove people?" Lexi made the same motion.

Celia nodded. "How we ..." She used her fingers in a walking motion.

"You *spocho* to walk."

"Yah." Celia again hooked arms with Lexi to continue.

Despite difficulty navigating the streets, Lexi tried to determine the best place for escape. Some alleyways or narrow streets were less crowded. A twinge of remorse struck at hearing Celia speak to a merchant. Celia helped her at great risk. If she returns alone. . . In a moment of impulse, Lexi pulled Celia into the dimness of a nearby alley.

"Come with me," she hastily said.

"*Ti?*" Celia asked, stunned.

"Come with me," she repeated.

Celia gaped in fear and shook her head. "No. *Mi senoria*. No. Poof!"

Lexi gently smiled. "I understand. Thank you." She gave Celia the basket and a quick hug. Without looking back, she ran down the alley away from the busy market street.

When the alley ended, Lexi turned left in the direction of the main road. With such massive crowds, she could blend in and leave Theron. What about after that? It would be dark in two hours. She would make the determination once safely away from the city.

Unfortunately, when she reached the main road, a group of soldiers herded the crowd back. Unsure why, Lexi tried to skirt the commotion. She didn't get far when a soldier seized her and shoved her back with the rest of the people. One soldier kept looking at her. She tried to avoid eye contact. No good. He accosted her. Using fast words and demanding tone, he scolded her. He kept making arm motions. Finally, she realized, he pointed to the palace across the river. Her manner of dress stood out from the crowd.

"Yah. Yah," she spoke in compliance. She shrunk back as if to obey.

Instead of taking the bridge, she darted across the intersection and down another street. For nearly an hour, Lexi tried various streets and alleyways with little success of reaching the main gate unnoticed. The late afternoon sun produced long shadows within the city. She sat on a stoop to catch her breath and consider her next move. She had to leave before the main gates closed for the night. A male voice from behind scolded her and waved in a shooing motion. Lexi understood and left the stoop.

She emerged onto the street to the sound of shouting, clattering hooves, and rattling harness. The noise caught her attention the same time as others. A fast-moving carriage! In the scramble to get out of the way, Lexi and three pedestrians were knocked to the ground. This time she lost her headdress. Upon standing, she noticed the headdress smashed and veil torn by the carriage wheels. The sight of how close she came to injury, made her stagger back a few steps. The grunt of a horse made her turn. She stood outside a stable.

Someone grabbed her from behind. An arm encircled her waist, while a hand covered her mouth. She struggled when he pulled her backward.

"Be easy!" a man spoke in her ears words she understood.

Still, it wasn't a command she wanted to follow. He continued to manhandle her to the rear of the stable. She stomped on his foot and broke free. A horse quickly blocked her path.

"Lexi, wait!"

Hearing her name startled her, as did seeing a black horse. "Alydar?"

"Did you doubt I would find you?" the man sarcastically asked.

She stared in confusion at the bearded man with a familiar voice. Then recognized, "Nollen!" She flung her arms around his neck. "I thought you dead."

"Hush. There's much to explain. First why are dressed like that?"

"Me? What about you? A beard and those clothes."

"All part of the plan to recover you. Have you seen the others?"

The appearance of soldiers interrupted the reunion. Alydar became agitated when the soldiers seized Nollen and Lexi.

"Run, Alydar!" Nollen commanded.

When a soldier reached for the bridle, Alydar reared and ran off.

Nollen angrily spoke to the leader soldier in Bertrandian.

"What is happening?" Lexi asked, fearful.

"Your attempt to leave was noticed," Nollen said. He argued with the soldiers, while being roughly escorted. He ignored more harsh words from the soldier to warn Lexi, "Don't answer. Say nothing."

The soldiers cleared path across the bridge. Instead of taking Nollen and Lexi through the main gate, they used the servant's gate. Once in the small courtyard, they were locked inside a building with barred windows.

"No!" Lexi clamored in angry frustration.

"Don't worry. If the others have arrived, we won't be here for long."

"What others?"

"Cormac, Gunnar, and *your* brother," he discreetly replied.

"Axe -" she began to blurt out in surprise when he covered her mouth. She gently removed his hand yet held on tight. "He came for me?" she asked in whispered wonder.

"Of course. As did I." He tenderly touched her cheek.

She hugged him. "Gott answered my prayer that you are alive. I owe my brother so many apologizes."

"He would be the first to say otherwise." He tilted her head to look at him. "Especially to the Shield Maiden."

"Some Shield Maiden," she scoffed. "I could not prevent my own kidnapping. Now, this!"

He snatched her hand to stop the gesture of futility. He pulled her close to say, "All the Shield Maiden needs is with Alydar. I told him to flee to protect the items." When she looked perplexed, he continued. "Brought with hope of finding you."

Lexi withdraw Volker from under the collar. "I managed to keep this hidden even when its glow warned me of evil."

Nollen took her hands with Volker between his hands. "Believe in Gott and trust yourself when the time comes." He felt her hands shake and saw her brows furrow in quizzical concentration. "What?"

Lexi briefly hesitated, still considering. "I … I sense Sheba nearby."

Nollen slyly spoke, "The others are here." Seeing her confusion, he added, "Your brother rode Sheba."

Alydar managed to elude the soldiers. Human crowds prevented him from running too far from the stables. A lone, riderless horse could attract attention. He had to find a way to move without being noticed.

Alydar stopped at a shop on a corner and positioned himself as if awaiting a rider. At a diagonal corner, he spied a loaded wagon pulled by two draft horses with a pack horse tethered to the rear. He carefully raised his head and began a series of low horse vocalizations. It took several attempts before one of the draft horses replied. To his further grunts and chomps, the draft horses, and tethered horse, tossed their heads in agreement. Now, he waited for the driver to return.

A few moments later, a draft horse snorted, a signal that drew Alydar's gaze. A man emerged from a building and climbed onto the driver's seat. When the wagon passed, Alydar joined the tethered horse as if part of the group. By the direction the human drove, he intended to leave the city. Not something Alydar wanted to do. However, avoiding capture was a priority.

Once through the main gate, a commotion up ahead caused a ruckus. Alydar took the opportunity to break away. He galloped west to one of the few groves of trees near Theron. He breathed heavy and stomped his front hoof more for frustration than excretion. He grew skittish at a nearby sound. He trembled, ready to bolt if necessary.

"Alydar."

He heard the whispered voice of Bardolf a moment before the alpha's nose stuck out from under a bush.

Alydar lowered his head as if to graze. "Nollen found Lexi, only they were captured by soldiers. Nollen commanded me to flee." A loud crow cawing made Alydar jerk up, and once more ready to bolt.

"Spyros," Bardolf growled.

Alydar lowered his head again to speak. "Leave before he senses you."

"What about you?"

"I will wait as long as I can. Nollen is a resourceful human. I won't abandon him. Or the others." A second caw made him snap, "Go!"

"We won't be far away." Bardolf disappeared.

Chapter 39

GUNNAR, CORMAC, AND AXEL RODE THROUGH THE MAIN GATE of the Bertrandian palace. Once in the courtyard, they were accosted by a guard. Cormac spoke enough Bertrandian to identify himself and relay his task. Gunnar and Axel closely observed the exchange.

After a few moments, the guard agreed. However, after they dismounted, the guard prevented Axel from following Cormac and Gunnar. With animated gestures, he called for others, grooms since they went to take the horse.

Cormac intervened. Although somewhat hesitant, the guard yielded and dismissed two of the three grooms. Whatever else he said, Cormac nodded in agreement.

Cormac explained by saying, "Henrick, follow Haydar to the stables and tend to the horses. I will send for you when all is settled."

"Aye, my lord." Axel made a short bow. He held the reins of the three horses to follow.

As they walked toward the rear of the palace grounds, Sheba grew agitated. She arched her neck, snorted, and began to prance. "Steady, girl," Axel tried to soothe her.

Sheba curbed some of her actions yet chomped her lips together.

At the stables, Haydar spoke and gestured to various items in the area. Axel simply nodded, more interested in Sheba. When Haydar left, Axel quietly spoke in Sheba's ear.

"You sense something?"

She lowly whinnied and slowly tossed her head in a nod.

Axel cautiously glanced around then asked in a whisper, "Danger?"

She shook her head. She began to chomp her lips when Axel touched her muzzle.

"Not aloud," he warned. "No need to alert others to our whereabouts."

She rubbed her head against his chest. He responded by scratching her cheek. When he moved to unsaddle her, Sheba turned her head and pulled on his sleeve. He moved closer to her ear again.

"I thought you said no danger."

She grunted and stomped her front hoof.

"Easy. I will remain alert."

She nipped at the saddle and shook her head.

"Very well. I won't remove them. Hay and water."

Sheba nodded.

Inside the palace, the guard escorted Cormac and Gunnar to an anteroom. Cormac agreed to the guard's instruction. After the guard left, he told Gunnar, "We wait while he informs Rastus of our arrival."

Gunnar's studious gaze scanned the room. Although beautiful in elaborate décor, his focus was not on the aesthetics. He spoke in a low cautious tone. "Not sure I like being kept in a room with one exit. Nor separated from Henrick."

"Part of the risk in diplomacy."

"Let's hope we don't have to wait too long." Gunnar's hope became realized when the guard returned ten minutes later.

Cormac cordially smiled. "Rastus will see us now," he told Gunnar.

The Bertrandian throne room dwarfed that of Sener Castle. The enormity made those coming into Rastus' presence feel small. Four stories tall, columned interior archways lined the perimeter with massive gold candelabras attached to walls between the arches. Colorful mosaic tiles broke up the polished white marble arch. On top of the interior archway, a two-story galley ran the length of the perimeter with open arched windows for light and air.

Ten marble steps led to a large, raised platform upon which sat a gold engraved throne cushioned with purple velvet. Two lesser thrones flanked the gold one, both plainer in comparison, yet also cushioned. Behind the throne rose a six-story window of colored glass. The late afternoon sun illuminated the brightly colored window. From the ceiling hung four enormous chandeliers of gold with pear-shaped crystals that reflected light. A wonderfully handcrafted carpet ran from the entrance, down the center of the room, and up the steps to the throne.

Rastus sat on the throne with Celeste and Felix also present. A rainbow effect from the window created an aura to the Bertrandian king. Other high-ranking officials, a few nobles, and even some commoners were assembled at the foot of the platform.

"We must have come during a court session," Gunnar privately told Cormac.

Cormac didn't acknowledge the comment, rather kept his focus on Rastus. Despite the dazzling magnificence surrounding them, they came for a specific purpose. When it was obvious the guard announced them, Cormac and Gunnar bowed to the Bertrandian king.

Rastus spoke to a distinguished looking middle-aged man. He wore embroidered cranberry and black robe overelaborate style clothing. By the quality of his attire, and being so near the throne, he was someone of importance. He approached Cormac and Gunnar.

He spoke Eldarian. "I am Vizier Cadmus. On behalf of King Rastus, I welcome you to Bertrand, Lord Cormac. Sir Gunnar."

"Thank you, Vizier," replied Cormac.

"Please, enlighten us as to the reason for your visit."

"My lord King Axel did not want there to be any misunderstanding between Eldar and Bertrand due to Ambassador Dynos' visit."

"The Ambassador gave a full account of his time in Eldar," said Cadmus with firmness.

Before Cormac replied, Rastus spoke in a commanding voice. Cadmus gave a lengthy response with several indications of Cormac and Gunnar. Rastus's tone and expression showed displeasure.

"I wonder who he is angry at, us or Dynos?" Gunnar quietly said to Cormac.

"I believe both. Although, he talks very fast," Cormac replied in kind.

Cadmus made a regal nod to Rastus when the king finished. He spoke to Cormac and Gunnar. "His Exalted Majesty King Rastus wishes to know how Eldar will address the insult of refusal."

Gunnar stiffened while Cormac slightly winced at the translation. The Ganel assumed a diplomatic façade to reply.

"Be assured, Your Majesty, no insult was intended. My Lord King Axel desires to first establish a mutually beneficial trade relationship before further consideration of your generous offer. Hence, why he sent myself and Sir Gunnar to reassure you of his goodwill."

Cadmus slyly grinned. "Well stated, Lord Cormac." He then informed Rastus of Cormac's statement. Rastus waved for Cadmus to return to the platform. This conversation proceeded in muted, private tones. Occasionally, Rastus cast sneering glares at the Eldarians.

Cormac and Gunnar waited, tense and uncertain.

"Can you understand them?" Gunnar asked Cormac.

"Not at this distance."

Cadmus bowed to Rastus and descended the platform. Before he could return to the Eldarians, the same lead soldier who apprehended Nollen and Lexi, intercepted him. A low hurried exchange occurred. The Vizier's face hardened, as he returned to Rastus. The King agitated by what Cadmus said. Rastus barked an order to the soldier, who saluted and withdrew.

"What now?" Gunnar asked, wary.

Cormac shook his head, a bit perplexed. "Something about a slave, I think."

Cadmus returned to them and spoke in a casual tone. "His Exalted Majesty will consider your message. For now, go with Lord Linux as our guests."

Cormac and Gunnar bowed to Rastus before joining Linux in departure. On the way out, Gunnar spied two familiar figures brought into the throne room by a side entrance. Cormac also saw them. When the Ganel paused, Gunnar touched his arm.

"Keep walking," Gunnar warned in a low harsh tone. Still, he managed to catch Nollen's eye while Lexi fought hard to conceal her notice of them.

Outside the throne room, Cormac spoke to Linux. Gunnar watched with some apprehension. Although not keen to what Cormac said, he saw Linux yielded.

"What was that about?"

Cormac tugged on Gunnar's arm. "I told him, we will fetch our things from the stable and return presently."

Chapter 40

NOLLEN HARSHLY WHISPERED TO LEXI. "EYES FORWARD," His lips barely moved. She quickly averted her gaze from Gunnar and Cormac.

With keenness of experience, Nollen sized up the surroundings in quick glances. A court session. Undoubtedly King Rastus on the throne, and he didn't look pleased. Whether due to Gunnar and Cormac's presence or he and Lexi, had yet to be determined. A soldier roughly pulled them to a halt near the base of the platform. He felt Lexi nudge him. She lowered her chin as if to look down. He followed the motion to see Volker glow underneath her collar.

"Stay calm," he again spoke out of the corner of his mouth. His attention drawn to the platform when he heard Rastus tersely aske the lead soldier;

"Is this the female runaway slave?"

"She is not a slave," Celeste said before the soldier replied.

Being so close together, Nollen felt Lexi flinch when Rastus said *dolous*, Bertrandian for slave. "Don't act as if you understand."

"Only a few words," Lexi murmured.

The conversation continued with Rastus demanding of Celeste, "How do you know?"

"Olivia employs her."

"You outlawed slavery, remember?" Felix said.

"Did she join Olivia before or after the edict?" Rastus questioned.

"Does it matter?" chided Felix.

"Of course, it matters! I did not free slaves, only outlawed any more being sold."

Cadmus intervened. "Allow me, Sire. I have encountered this female several times in the company of Lady Olivia's other maid, Celia."

The glow of Volker increased as Cadmus drew near. Lexi jerked her arm from the soldier to grab the collar. Nollen tried to step forward in an effort to shield Lexi. Cadmus waved for the solider to move Nollen aside. It took all her courage to withstand Cadmus' steady gaze.

"Leizel, what treachery is this to betray the kindness shown you by running away?" He spoke in both Markitan and Bertrandian.

Lexi clenched the collar. Her jowls tensed with lips clenched in effort to remain silent.

At her discomposure, Nollen spoke in Bertrandian. "She is not to blame. It was my idea."

Cadmus' steely eyes focused on Nollen. "Who are you?"

"Her brother."

Cadmus scoffed a laugh. "She mentioned no family other than deceased parents."

"I came to fetch her when I learned of the tragedy."

"Disguised as a Bertrandian trader? You are as duplicitous as your supposed sister." His narrow eyes focused on Lexi.

The warmth and glow of Volker increased to the point of radiating from under her hand.

Cadmus noticed. "What is this?"

Lexi attempted to shake off the soldier, but he grabbed both her arms. This abrupt action ripped the collar to expose Volker's brilliance. She braced herself when Cadmus reached toward her. Suddenly, an electrical force emanated from Volker. The Vizier cried out in pain and back away. His hand limp and useless from the shock.

"Take that off her!" he ordered the soldier.

Lexi fought to resist. Nollen struggled to break free of the soldier.

The loud caw of a raven echoed in the chamber. Spyros flew through a window of the upper galley. Everyone in the throne room thunderstruck at his appearance.

"The gods are angry!" Rastus shouted.

Spyros cawed and dove toward Lexi.

"Stop!" Lexi shouted at Spyros.

The raven king banked away with an angry caw that made people cringe. It looped around for another attack. Before it could reach Lexi, a deafening eagle's cry proceeded Artair's flight through the same window as Spyros. People scrambled to leave when the raven and eagle became locked in battle.

"Protect the king!" Cadmus ordered.

In the chaos, Nollen's hard elbow forced the soldier to release him. He helped Lexi break free of the one holding her. Together, they ran out the side door where they entered.

Commotion in the throne room alerted the rest of the castle to trouble. Sight of soldiers racing down the corridor made Lexi grab Nollen's hand.

"This way!" she hastily said.

"Do you know where you're going?"

"Aye."

At the rear courtyard stables, Cormac, Gunnar, and Axel heard the raven, then the eagle, and finally human voices of turmoil. All came in quick succession. Agitated, Sheba tossed her head and whinnied. Spyros and Artair flew overhead engaged in combat. Axel moved toward the main building when Gunnar stopped him.

"It's too dangerous. We must trust Artair. And Nollen."

"He's right. They don't know our connection to them," Cormac added.

Axel shook off Gunnar's hold but remained beside Sheba.

Lexi and Nollen emerged in an alcove of the rear courtyard. Ruckus in the throne room caused confusion outside. Soldiers and servants ran to and fro to determine the cause. Lexi and Nollen ducked behind barrels to avoid being seen. Slowing they moved forward and hid behind whatever they could in an attempt to reach the servant's gate.

Across the courtyard, Nollen spied Axel, Gunnar, and Cormac. Before they could approach, soldiers ran to the Eldarians. Nollen pulled Lexi in to the shadow of a corner to observe.

"We can't go out that way," he said.

"Why? Axel is there."

"Exactly. By doing so, we expose them. There is a rendezvous. I just need to signal them to leave. Wait here." He crouched down to inch forward behind a stack of crates.

Cormac argued with the soldiers. When one grabbed him, Gunnar knocked the soldier away and reached for his sword. Axel prevented Gunnar from drawing. Cormac scolded the soldiers. A shout from somewhere near the main building drew the soldiers from the Eldarians.

Nollen cupped hands around his mouth and made a calling sound to get attention. It worked. Gunnar spied him. In turn, Gunnar nudged Axel. Nollen continued with hand signals. Axel looked beyond Nollen to see Lexi carefully peak out from the corner of the building. He fought a smile of relief when their eyes met. Gunnar's shove made Axel join he and Cormac in mounting. In the all the activity, no one stopped the Eldarians from leaving by the servant's gate.

Nollen shrunk back to rejoin Lexi. "Now, we need to get out of here."

The soldier who captured them appeared in the rear courtyard. Nollen pushed Lexi back and flattened against the wall. "The same soldiers are looking for us. He posted one at the gate."

"There is another way out." Lexi moved down the alcove in the opposite direction.

By the damp dreariness of the path, the way was hardly used. In fact, they had to brace against the wall and squeeze through the narrow passage. When the way widened, they emerged in the back alley near the gate where Lexi stood watch while Celia met with Felix and Olivia.

"This leads to the main street," Lexi said. It was locked. "I don't have a key."

Nollen investigated. "No easy way to climb." Although detained, he still wore his pouch. He quickly looked inside. "Blast! I need something long and sharp to pick the lock."

Lexi reached down to her boot to withdraw the hidden dagger. "Will this do?" She held up the slender blade.

"Where did you get it?"

"*He* made me take it. Just in case."

"Keep watch." Nollen knelt and used the tip of the blade to jiggle the lock. It took a few moments before … *click*. He gave her back the dagger, and carefully opened the gate. He shut it to appear unaltered.

They ran down the short alley to pause at the corner. Fortunately, the commotion inside the palace had not reached the street. They quickly joined the flow of people heading to the bridge. He kept a keen eye for any signs of trouble. On her part, Lexi looked ahead. She cranked her neck to look beyond the crowd.

"I don't see them," she said, disappointed.

"That's good. We shouldn't be caught together." Nollen spied soldiers. He grabbed her arm to hurry across the bridge. He turned into an empty alley now completely in shadow from the fading sun. The alley ran alongside a city culvert. "These clothes will give us away."

"Well, I don't have anything else," she sarcastically said.

"Take off the dress."

"What?" she said with stunned incredulity.

"You have pants and a shirt underneath."

She slapped his hands when he tried to undo the sash around her waist. "I can do it. What about you?" She undressed the layers.

Nollen took the pouch and belt off to remove the long surcoat. This showed the short vest underneath. "Give me your dagger." After Lexi complied, he used the blade to cut off the surcoat sleeves and fray the bottom edge. He handed her the damaged coat. "Put this on. Along with the hat and belt. Be sure to tuck all your hair under the hat."

"Why?" she asked while following instructions.

"To look like a wayward boy." He discarded her dress by tossing it into the culvert for the water to take it downstream. He frowned when he scratched his face. "I can't shave yet. Even like this, we look too clean." He reached down to the pavement and covered his hands in dirt. He smeared his clothes and some on his face. He ruffled his hand. "Your turn to look a street urchin."

She mimicked him in smudging her clothes and face. "I hope this works."

"There's only one way to find out."

He took her hand and led her back to the main street. Once again, they entered the flow of traffic. They weaved through a mass of people, wagons, and horses to head for the main gate. A few times, they ducked into a doorway or side street to avoid soldiers. Near the gate, Nollen noticed soldiers stop and search wagons. He drew her attention to the activity.

"They might be looking for us." He glanced skyward. The colors of late twilight faded. "We need to leave before it gets dark, and the gates are closed for the night."

"What should we do?"

"Act drunk."

"What?"

"Just do it. Don't speak and keep your head down. Hopefully the shadows will fool them into believing you're a boy." He grabbed onto her, as if holding her upright. "Stagger, so I carry you," he harshly whispered.

Lexi did as instructed. As they moved, Nollen scolded her in Bertrandian. She didn't respond or even look up, rather maintained the pretense.

A soldier put his hand up. "*Stampo*!"

Nollen drew to an unsteady halt. Lexi slumped further to keep her head as low as possible. In a tone of utter annoyance, Nollen spoke to the soldier. At one time, he scolded her. Lexi made a fake burp. Nollen grimaced and waved a hand over his face.

The soldier scoffed and motioned for them to proceed.

"*Efchari*," said Nollen. He practically dragged Lexi through the gate. "Keep it up a little longer. We're almost clear of the gate," he whispered.

After a hundred yards, the road turned, and took them out of sight of the soldiers. The last rays of sun sank below the horizon.

"You can walk a bit now, but not too sober. When I say the word, we run for that grove to the right."

Lexi carefully looked to where he indicated. She felt him turn off the road.

"Now!" Nollen snapped.

Under the cover of trees, daylight had completely faded. For several hundred yards, Nollen continued at a run. Lexi struggled to see and keep up as the forest grew darker.

"Where are we going—?" She tripped and fell down a short incline.

Nollen jumped down to help her stand. "To the rendezvous."

"You made it! Thank Gott." Axel emerged from a brush to embrace Lexi.

She held on tight, and sobbed, "I'm sorry. I'm so sorry."

"It's all right. As long you're unharmed."

"You shouldn't have come for me. What about Alicia and the baby?"

"We tried that same argument. It didn't work," said Gunnar.

Lexi hugged Gunnar also.

"This is not the place for discussion. We need to leave before we are discovered," warned Cormac.

Lexi gasped and seized the collar when Volker glowed red. "It may be too late. I feel the same evil as when Volker repulsed the Vizier to stop him from taking it."

"And the large black bird, which I assume was a raven," added Nollen.

Bardolf arrived to hear Nollen. "Spyros?"

Nollen shrugged ignorance. "Maybe. Artair attacked it. The commotion helped us escape."

"It was Spyros." The voice made everyone looked to see the eagle-king settle onto a branch. "I inflicted serious injuries before he retreated. But, he will return with a flock." Artair then said the Bardolf, "Night travel is the best option."

"Why?" asked Axel.

"Ravens do not fly at night. Eagles can. Even now, Ajax circles overhead on alert for any approaching danger."

"When in Markita, Ajax told me he didn't fly at night," said Nollen.

Artair chuckled. "To divide the labor of protecting you between himself and Callie. Our preference is daylight, but we can navigate better in the dark than ravens."

"Then night travel it is," said Axel.

"Can we change clothes first? They will be looking for us. And I need to shave." Nollen said of himself and Lexi.

"I have no clothes but these," said Lexi.

"You do. On Alydar," said Cormac. "Perhaps not the whole armor right now. The under clothes will serve."

Sheba used her muzzle to nudge Lexi from behind. "It is your time, dear one."

Lexi removed the bundle from Alydar.

"When you are both ready, we leave," said Axel.

Chapter 41

FURIOUS, RASTUS PACED THE PRIVATE DRAWING ROOM. CADMUS nursed his hand by rubbing it. The Vizier's expression hard and unyielding. Felix and Celeste closely watched their father; Felix studious and determined while Celeste uncertain.

Beside Celeste stood Olivia and Celia. Both the lady-in-waiting and maid fearful. Celia clenched her hands until the knuckles turned white. Olivia's fretful gaze shifted from Celeste to Felix. He flashed a small reassuring smile, though it did little to mitigate her anxiety.

"This is all hard to accept! A Markitan orphan, whose brother suddenly appears dressed like a Bertrandian. The arrival of the gods in anger." Rastus turned upon Olivia. "Did you really think this deception would work? That the gods would be deceived?"

"I deceived no one, Sire! I too believed Leizel's story," she bravely countered.

"What of the Eldarians?" Cadmus tersely inquired.

Olivia balked with confusion. "I cannot say, my lord."

Felix intervened. "She has no dealing with foreign diplomacy. Her role is domestic. It is sheer coincidence."

"Then why did they flee during the commotion?" Cadmus challenged.

"Why stay? The entire palace is in an uproar at the sudden appearance of a raven and eagle in battle. Why would they want to become involved in Bertrandian turmoil?"

Rastus stopped Cadmus from further objection. "He is correct. This does not concern Eldar."

"I believe it does, Sire."

Rastus grunted in pain as he ceased pacing to sit. "How so?"

"Eagles are among the First Ones of Eldar. It is more than likely the eagle accompanied them."

Felix scoffed, "So? How does that prove a connection?"

"It attacked Spyros to protect their false errand from being discovered."

Felix scowled. "It doesn't explain what happened with Leizel or the injury to your hand."

"Leizel is not Markitan."

The stunning statement made everyone momentarily mute.

Celeste whispered to Olivia, "Is this true?"

"I don't know. Celia is better acquainted with her."

On the verge of fearful tears, Celia could not speak when they looked to her for an answer.

Cadmus accosted Celia. "You lied for her each time we spoke."

"No, Vizier!" Celia stammered in terror.

"You did," he stoutly confirmed.

"No. Not Dorothia!" Celia collapsed to her knees sobbing.

"Dorothia?" repeated Olivia with disconcertion. Anger welled and she confronted Cadmus, "You threatened her!"

"You employed an Eldarian spy."

Enraged, Felix stepped between Cadmus and Olivia. "Cadmus, you go too far!"

"What proof do you have to make such an accusation?" Rastus demanded.

Cadmus left a shaken Olivia and sobbing Celia to approach Rastus. "Sire, you heard Ambassador Dynos' report of his contentious audience with Axel, and the insult made to Bertrand regarding the offer of marriage between his sister, and Prince Felix." He sent a sly glance to Olivia and Felix. Olivia flinched and screwed her eyes and lips shut. Felix took hold of Olivia's arm. The action went unnoticed by Rastus as Cadmus continued. "To cover his slight, Axel further impedes Bertrand by first sending a spy then a delegation to recover the spy before Bertrand can seek redress. Unfortunately, my bumbling sons failed to secure her. They will be severely dealt with; I assure Your Majesty."

When Cadmus looked at him a second time, Felix left Olivia to engage Rastus. "He offers only speculation, no proof."

For a heavy moment of silence, Rastus considered the scenario presented. "It may be speculation, but it does fit the situation."

"To accuse Axel of such action without evidence will only lead to war! Is that what you want?"

"No!" Irate, Rastus pushed himself to stand. "What I want is for you to marry and secure the throne for Bertrand's future! If what Cadmus says proves true, then you are to blame for refusing to fulfill your duty!"

Felix stiffened with outrage.

Celeste rushed to Felix. "You must tell him! For everyone's sake. Think of Favian."

Felix glanced from Celeste to Olivia. The latter comforted Celia. When their eyes met, Felix saw Olivia's tears.

"Who is Favian?" asked Rastus.

Felix left Celeste to stand beside Olivia. "Da, you are wrong about not fulfilling my duty. I have married and produced an heir. Olivia is my wife. Favian is our son."

Rastus' expression went from shock to outrage. "And … her ?" He pointed at Celia.

"Celia kept our secret and arranged private meetings," Felix calmly replied.

Cadmus smugly smiled. "Treachery in your own house, Sire."

"Treachery? By marrying the woman, I love?" Felix hotly rebuffed. "Da, don't listen to him. I didn't tell you because I knew you would be disappointed in my choice lacking royal blood. Not as an act of treachery."

"Da, please," added Celeste. "We understand you are angry, but neither Felix nor Olivia have done anything to undermine your reign."

Rastus shook off Celeste's hold. "Everyone out!"

Felix escorted Olivia. Celia quickly followed. Celeste joined them.

Last to leave, Cadmus watched the others disappear down the corridor then headed for his office. He found Marius and Mateo conversing with Spoor. Or more rightly, Spoor giving the twins a tongue-lashing.

"Doubtful you discovered a body," Cadmus coolly told Spoor.

"No. Your offspring maintain the story of her falling into the river."

"She did not. She's alive and escaped the palace."

"What?" thundered Spoor. "Why did you not tell me before now?"

"Because I just learned her true identity!" Cadmus glared at the twins. "Leizel."

"We … we didn't know," Marius nervously stammered.

"Yah. We are ignorant of that," Mateo added.

"Ignorant is a good word for both of you!"

"Along with useless." Spoor sneered. "How will you be rid of such useless ignorance? And outright lying?" he challenged Cadmus.

The Vizier's intensity made the twins sweat with anxiety. Deadly earnest filled his words. "Leave Bertrand and never return."

"Banishment?" asked Mateo, unnerved. Marius unable to speak.

"I would kill you where you stand!" Spoor threatened.

Cadmus' gaze never left the twins. "That will happen if you ever set foot in Bertrand again. Now, go!"

Marius winced at the declaration. Mateo drew Marius from the room.

"You showed mercy," Spoor chided.

"In this case, it is warranted. I could not order their deaths when I too was fooled. I suspected something amiss with Leizel, yet even then, I did not detect her true identity until this." Cadmus held up his right hand.

"Your hand?"

"Shocked by a ruby stone she wears around her neck. Before I could touch it, a force struck me with such energy that feeling has yet to return. The arrival of Eldarians and an eagle fighting Spyros confirmed my suspicions."

"A rescue party," chided Spoor. "Have you told Rastus of the alternative plan?"

"No. It is moot since the whelp confessed he is married! To Olivia. They have a son. Telling Rastus would be a mistake now that is an heir. He needs new motivation to continue with our original purpose."

Kyros flew through the open terrace door and landed on the perch usually occupied by Spyros. "My father sends me."

The statement concerned Cadmus. "Is Lord Spyros seriously injured?"

"He will recover. The Eldarians have made a dangerous move. The plan must be altered to eliminate the First Ones and raise Bertrand as the new power in the region."

"We were just discussing that. Have the gods a suggestion?"

"Move troops to the border to meet the Eldarians."

Cadmus asked Spoor, "Has Eldar strengthened the border?"

"It would be a natural move after kidnapping the princess."

"Our scouts report an increase of troops near the main road," Kyros said.

"The news *will* anger Rastus," said Cadmus. "What of Nefal? Can you convince Maro to attack from behind?"

Spoor slyly grinned. "If Bodil successfully completes the second part of my plan then Maro is already at odds with Axel."

Cadmus' face hardened. "Your plan?"

"Do you believe I would totally trust the fate of Nefal to a human?"

"Who obeys the will of the gods!" Cadmus indicated Kyros.

"What did you do, Nefal?" Kyros demanded.

"The loss of his sister and heir will bring Axel to his knees."

"The heir was born?" asked Cadmus confused.

"No."

Cadmus stared up at Spoor, a bit unnerved by the implication of Eldar's pregnant queen. "You play a dangerous game. First you failed to secure the quarry now force our hand before we are ready."

"I did not fail. You and your pitiful offspring did not recognize her right under your noses." Spoor moved threateningly close to Cadmus. "Look to yourself, human. The Nefal will return to our rightful place whether you are ready or not." He shoved Cadmus, who rocked on his heels to stay upright. Spoor exited by way of the terrace door.

Kyros cocked his head at Cadmus. "What failure were you referring to, and why the Nefal said you did not recognize her?"

"It is immaterial since Eldar threatens invasion, which helps the ultimate plan."

Kyros cawed in anger. "Answer me truthfully or else lose your position as Vizier!"

The forceful command and threat made Cadmus swallow back a lump of discomposure. "The girl's reported death proved inaccurate. She was here all the while acting as a servant before she escaped. I only learned of it when Lord Spyros arrived and engaged the eagle. Yet, be assured, Bertrand will honor the gods' command and destroy the First Ones. I shall go immediately and convince Rastus to send troops to defend the border." He bowed to Kyros and left the office.

Kyros flew a short distance outside Theron to the grove where he left a wounded Spyros. Zeta, Skyron, Kronos, and Ursus joined Spyros. Numerous tail feathers and wing feathers were missing. A deep gouge ran from behind his left eye down his neck. Talons pierced several places on Spyros' back. Zeta used her beak to dress the numerous wounds with healing leaves and bits of bark.

"How is he?" Kyros asked Zeta in a doleful tone.

"I'll live!" Spyros groused. "Though I may not fly for quite some time. What did you learn from Cadmus?"

"Eldarians and the princess were at the palace during your battle with Artair."

"That's not good," said a growling Ursus.

"I made certain Cadmus understands the importance of executing the revised plan to engage the enemy," assured Kyros. "Since the Eldarians have moved troops to the border, Cadmus will use the bold action to convince Rastus to do the same. Battle will likely follow once both forces are gathered."

Spyros issued orders to Kyros. "At first light, take our flock and go with Ursus and Kronos. Summon the Coastland and Highland flocks to join you at the border. We shall meet the enemy with our combined strength. Skyron, find Artair. He will be near the Volker."

"What is Volker?" asked Skyron.

"An ancient source of power the eagles, unicorns, and Othniel gifted the Shield Maiden of Eldar. A female human," replied Kronos.

"Cadmus said she was the kidnapped princess," began Kyros. "Did you know beforehand she was the Shield Maiden?" he asked Spyros.

"After Sirin's demise, we became suspicious that she was among the returning Brethren. When we learned Axel's sister returned, our suspicions were confirmed. Thus, we formulated the plan to neutralize her."

"Are you certain it was Volker?" asked Ursus in a tone skepticism.

"Why else would Artair be in Bertrand?" Kronos chided.

"It was Volker," Spyros confirmed. "The draw is unmistakable. I have not felt so compelled to respond since the days of Serena. Nor to retreat when she commanded."

"She must be recaptured or destroyed before we engage the First Ones," said Ursus.

"That is precisely what I intend to do." Spoor appeared.

Ursus bared his teeth, while Kronos angrily snorted. "You are bold, Nefal!"

"Our boldness served the gods well in the past."

"He claims the Nefal have executed a plot against the Son of Eldar's heir," Kyros said.

"Successful?" asked Ursus.

Spoor flashed a conceited lopsided grin in response to the question.

"Did Cadmus authorize this without our consent?" demanded Ursus.

"No. I acted on behalf of the gods, as Nefal has done in the past." Spoor proceeded to delay the bear king's explosive anger. "To destroy the future hope along with the Shield Maiden will bring Eldar to its knees and make revenge easier. Such a move against a pregnant female is not something Cadmus would agree with. I chose to keep him ignorant rather than jeopardize the main objective. Same as I did not reveal to him the princess' identity as Shield Maiden." He heaved a careless shrug. "Men are too soft. He proved it by banishing his sons instead of executing them for failure."

Ursus made a low threatening growl, to which Kronus spoke. "The Nefal acted wisely."

"Thank you, my lord." Spoor offered a bow. "I can provide further assistance by destroying the Shield Maiden before she reaches the border. If my Lord Kronos will consent to offer me a ride."

Chapter 42

BEING SUMMONED TO HIS FATHER'S CHAMBER SO SOON AFTER THE argument, gave Felix hope for quick reconciliation. His hope became dampened upon sight of Cadmus.

"You summoned me, Sir?"

"It appears Cadmus may have been right that Axel is dealing falsely with us. Eldarian troops are amassing at the border."

The news surprised and perplexed Felix. "Why? I mean, what does he stand to gain by such an aggressive move?"

"Access to Bertrandian wealth," replied Cadmus. "Eldar has no ports for import and export of goods. By claiming ours, they gain control of the region."

Felix's brows furrowed, still unconvinced. "Our trade agreements are insurance against that."

"Axel rebuffed our offer!" Rastus declared.

"He declined the marriage, not trade," Felix countered. At Rastus' deepening frown, he added, "The trade agreement won't expire until the end of year. Invasion doesn't make sense."

"They are at the border!" Rastus thundered.

Felix would not back down. "Has that been confirmed?"

"The gods have confirmed it," Cadmus casually replied.

Felix ignored Cadmus to ask Rastus, "What about our border guards? Any word from them?"

Cadmus did not take the slight well. "You doubt the gods?"

Felix stood his ground. "I want confirmation—both divine and mortal—before committing troops to war with an otherwise peaceful neighbor."

Cadmus turned red-faced yet continued his argument to Rastus. "Sire, Eldarian troops are at the border! We must respond. By river is the quickest way. Utilizing all barges equals five thousand troops. Supply throughout the night and leave at first light. Our forces should reach the northern port in two days."

"It usually takes four days, three if the weather cooperates," Felix said in dispute. He directed attention to Rastus. "Sir, we must have confirmation from the border guards before committing to action."

Cadmus had enough and hotly confronted the prince. "Did what happened in the throne room not convince you the gods watch over us?"

"I'm convinced what I witnessed was unusual. However, I fail to agree with the leap in logic that this is all some plot by Axel to gain access to our ports."

"Enough!" Rastus snapped. "It is our duty to defend Bertrand! As crown prince, you will lead the troops to meet the enemy. Conscript extra rowers. Two days. No more."

The command forced Felix to bite back any reply. Rastus spoke the truth about his royal responsibility. For a long moment, he held his father's gaze. In a conciliatory tone, he said, "I had hoped you summoned me on another matter."

"I will speak with my son privately," Rastus dismissed Cadmus. Once alone, he spoke again, though his voice fatigued. "Security of Bertrand is of paramount importance."

"I do not dispute that, only the reason for conflict."

Rastus deeply scowled. "You will be derelict in your duty?"

"No. However, there is one condition. Hear me before you answer." Felix waited for Rastus to nod. "Battle is a deadly business, so I ask that before I leave, you publicly acknowledge Favian as my son and heir."

Rastus' jowls tightened, which prompted Felix to continue.

"You may not agree with my choice of wife, but you have what you wanted. The future of our family and throne secured through my marriage and son."

Rastus remained silent for several moments.

Weariness on his father's face concerned Felix. "Da?"

Rastus nodded with a heavy sigh. "Very well. I shall acknowledge Favian as your son, and my grandson. Heir to the throne. I shall also bestow upon Olivia the title of countess. This way, when you are king, she may assume the role of queen-consort."

Felix smiled in relief. "Thank you, Da." He grew remorseful. "I deeply apologize for not telling you sooner. If I had, perhaps this whole situation could have been avoided."

"The marriage proposal, yah. This current crisis, I'm uncertain if it matters." Rastus suddenly looked frail and swayed.

Felix seized Rastus to help him stay on his feet. "Da?"

"The chair." Rastus reached for it where Felix helped him sit. "See to your duty. Send Celeste to me."

"At once." Felix just reached the door when Rastus spoke again.

"Tell her to bring Olivia and Favian. I should meet him after all."

Felix fought a smile. He nodded and left.

In his office, Cadmus issued orders for troop departure. After which, he poured through papers and books to gain intelligence on what jewel could possess such power. Convinced it dealt with Eldar, he concentrated on that topic as recorded in Bertrandian history. The night grew late, as told by books, old journals, and worn papers stacked on his desk.

He read aloud. "'Volker, an ancient red stone of Eldar said to possess magical powers. There are reports of witnesses to its power when joined with a female."

He jerked up in surprise at a knock on the terrace door. "Come!"

Mateo and Marius entered. Both blurry eyed, unsteady in step, and wary.

Cadmus studied the twins. "Where have you two been?"

The question confused them. "You banished us," began Mateo, his words slurred.

"You're drunk."

"Something to fortify us before leaving Bertrand," chided Mateo. He reeled at Cadmus' hard slap across his face.

"Be grateful I did not order you killed!"

"We are, sir, we are!" Marius helped Mateo stand. "May I ask why you had soldiers search for us?"

"I have a task that requires no connection to anyone at the palace. By banishing you, I severed that tie. At least for now. Succeed, and you may return to my good graces."

They remained skeptical. "The task?" asked Marius, tentative.

"The barges are being prepared to ferry troops north. Felix will lead the army to meet the Eldarians. In the confusion of battle, make certain he does not return alive."

The weight of the deadly assignment clearly evident on their faces.

Mateo bravely inquired, "Since you banished us, how can we join the troops?"

Cadmus gave them two slips of paper "Report to the royal barge as conscripted rowers. Change your clothes and shave. If anyone asks, show them the papers with my seal."

Mateo slowly lowered his head in a nodded bow. "As you wish, Sir."

As they cross the compound to leave the palace, Marius spied Celia the same time she saw him. Even in the glow of torchlight, her anxiety visible.

Mateo grabbed Marius' arm. "Come. You can't approach the wench."

"It might be my last chance."

"She is a simpleton! I never understood what you saw in her."

When Celia hastened to leave, Marius broke from Mateo. Although mindful of being spotted, he caught her near a back door. He covered her mouth to stifle an outcry.

"Please. Don't scream."

She nodded and he release her. "What do you want?"

"To speak to you one last time."

She nervously looked about. "Why?"

He grew frustrated. "By the gods, Celia, I never meant to hurt you."

Angry, she drew away from him, yet the wall prevent departure.

"I know you may not believe me, but I swear by the gods." Marius caught a glimpse of Mateo, who moved closer. Marius turned his back to shield Celia and spoke in a low hurried voice. "I don't have much time. Please, tell the prince his life is in danger when he leaves. Tell only him. Do not reveal the source or it will go badly for you. I couldn't bear that."

"What—?"

To stifle her question and stop Mateo's approach, Marius took Celia in his arms and kissed her. In the same sudden move, he released her and rushed to join Mateo and leave.

Inside, Celia tried to mask her uneasiness. She fought a private battle to place aside her relationship with Marius. She believed she succeeded since he had been absent for weeks. That was until, she saw him again at the shrine. Now, this. What dangerous enterprise made him risk being seen with her and give such a warning? So, much had happened in just one day she no time to think.

Fortunately, some good came from the events. Olivia and Favian were acknowledged by the king. Word spread quickly, as Olivia would now be quartered in the royal wing. Celia helped the move. She just completed her task, and enroute back to the servants' wing when she spied Marius.

Whatever the reason, the dire message could not wait. With knowledge of hidden passageways between the wings, Celia returned to the royal apartment floor. Uncertain when the prince retired, she tip-toed toward his chamber.

"What are you doing here?"

Accosted by a guard, Celia swallowed back fear to reply. "I have a message for the Prince from Countess Olivia. His wife."

He stepped aside to let her pass.

Cautiously, Celia knocked. "Highness." She repeated the knock and call twice before the door opened.

Felix appeared in a dressing gown. "Celia? What are you doing here at this hour?"

"I have a message from her ladyship," she spoke aloud for the guards to hear.

Felix admitted her. He fought a yawn. "What now? Has Favian pitched a fit about bedtime?" he chuckled.

"No, Highness."

Her nervousness made him curious. "Is Favian ill?"

"No, Highness." She waved him from the door. Her voice so low, he bent over to listen. "I come with a warning from a source I know but cannot name for fear of reprisal. When you leave, your life will be in mortal danger."

Fire of anger rose in his eyes. "Name your source."

"Please! I cannot," she stammered in fear. "It is for your safety the person risked discovery to pass along the warning."

His attitude softened. "And placed you at risk also. Poor Celia. First Cadmus, now, this."

"I gladly do so to protect you, my lady, and Master Favian."

Felix gently smiled. "Your loyalty is greatly appreciated."

"What else can I do? I don't want to worry my lady."

"Keep this between us."

"I was instructed to only tell you."

"I am forewarned." He escorted her to the door. "Go to bed and think no more about it." He opened the door. "Tell her ladyship, I look forward to more days ahead," he spoke for the benefit of the guards.

"Of course, Highness. Good night."

Chapter 43

THE FIRST NIGHT OF TRAVEL PROCEEDED WITHOUT INCIDENT. Riding only four horses, Lexi sat double on Sheba behind Axel. Two hours after dawn, Bardolf and the wolves led them into a deep gully where a short waterfall fed a pool before continuing downstream. A large canopy of trees shaded the gully.

Gunnar walked the perimeter. "Should be safe enough for a small cooking fire. The overhang can hide the smoke if we keep it to a minimum."

"I already sent two of the pack to small hunt game. The rest will guard the area," said Bardolf.

Lexi slipped off the back of Sheba and rocked on her feet. She stretched and yawned.

"Tired?" asked Axel.

"I can barely keep my eyes open. While riding double for so long is hard on the bum."

He chuckled. "When it's safe, we'll hire another horse." He spied a very large old oak tree. "Almost looks like a bed between the tree roots. Lay down. I'll wake you when food is ready."

Lexi wrapped the cloak around her and found the spot Axel indicated.

"Here. Use this for a pillow." Nollen gave her his rolled-up cloak.

"What about you?"

"I will sit against the tree."

Within a moment, she fell asleep.

Gunnar prepared the fire near in such a way as to use the large branches for cover. Nollen Cormac and Axel sat around the fire. Lexi lay six feet behind them.

Nollen spoke low, so as not to disturb Lexi. "Something I don't understand. She was kidnapped by Bertrandians, yet Rastus believed her to be a runaway slave while Cadmus thought she was a Markitan orphan named Leizel."

Axel grinned at hearing the name Leizel. "Our mother." At Nollen's confusion, he clarified. "Her name was Leizel. Same as I took the name of our father—Henrick—to conceal my identity." He glanced at the sleeping Lexi. "She protected herself as I suggested."

"Playing the servant is what kept her alive," said Gunnar.

"Then why kidnap her?" asked Nollen.

"She couldn't learn the reason while in their midst." Axel nodded toward Lexi, who remained asleep. "It may not be a question we can answer until we reach Eldar, and safety."

"Could the book give a clue?" Nollen asked Cormac.

"Maybe." Cormac retrieved the book to search of the contents. His skimming of the pages lasted long enough for the wolves to return with a grouse and rabbit, Gunnar and Nollen to prepare it, and for cooking. The Ganel's displeased grunt drew attention.

"Find something?" asked Axel.

Cormac moved to sit beside Axel. "It could be the reason. In the past, Bertrand has resorted to marriage by force. Including kidnapping of royals or nobles."

Nollen looked over Cormac's shoulder at the indicated passage. "It doesn't explain ignorance of her identity."

Axel stared into the fire. His eyes narrow and face taut. "We are forgetting a dangerous individual. Spoor."

"If he acted on behalf of the missing First Ones, that might explain the Bertrandians' ignorance of her identity," said Cormac.

"Bardolf," Axel softly called over the alpha. "Would the missing First Ones know the prophecy about me? Or did Gott's promise to Oleg come after the coup?"

"It came after. However, since your return, word has spread."

"What about the Shield Maiden?" Nollen asked.

"Knowledge of her precedes the coup by centuries," replied Bardolf.

Artair flew down from a branch to join the conversation. "Not to mention Volker was a gift to the Shield Maiden from the First Ones."

Axel became irate; thus, his voice rose. "Then they launched the plot to kidnap her, not Bertrand!"

Gunnar seized Axel's arm to indicate Lexi when she stirred.

"I smell food," she said.

Axel assumed a neutral posture. "I was about to wake you."

In silence, they consumed the meal. Once Gunnar extinguished the fire, everyone rested. Artair perched on a branch over where they rested. He and Ajax took turns perched on guard and flight surveillance. Bardolf and the pack kept a tight patrol of the perimeter.

By late afternoon, Lexi woke. The others still slept. Nollen sat beside her with his back against the tree. Cormac reclined against another large root. Axel lay on the other side of her with Gunnar next to him.

When she stood, Bardolf became alert. She held a finger to her lips for the alpha to remain quiet. She slipped off for some privacy before she sat by the ashes of the earlier fire. Her back turned to the others. She wanted a few moments to gather her thoughts.

Although grateful for the rescue, Axel's involvement troubled her. The few times they talked during the night ride, he tried to soothe her concern. Yet nothing he said, helped alleviate the guilt she felt at rebuffing him so many times recently. The feelings became more poignant by wearing part of the Shield Maiden's uniform. She lifted Volker to admire the ruby.

"There is one thing needed for the armor to be complete."

She flinched at being drawn from her introspection when Axel spoke and sat beside her. "I not sure if I'm ready for it."

"You are more ready than you realize."

She stared along her shoulder at him. "How can you be sure of me when I'm not sure of myself?"

He smiled. "I am sure of Gott. He is the one who called you and gifted you. He wouldn't do so, if you weren't ready."

She regarded Volker again.

"Tell me, has your sense of calling deepened?"

"Aye. In Theron, all I wanted was to escape and come home. To make you proud of me." Tears rose, though her voice determined.

He placed an arm about her shoulders. "I am already proud of you." From his pouch, he withdrew something flat and round wrapped in a cloth. "This will complete your armor."

Lexi unwrapped it. Her smile trembled at seeing their mother's brooch. "This isn't a simple brooch. It's the Shield Maiden's badge. That's why Mama wore it at my dedication."

"Aye. You are the first royal daughter born in two hundred years. She let all in Kranston know the Shield Maiden has returned. You share in our family's destiny." He tenderly pushed her hair behind her ears. "That is why I came for you."

She couldn't hold back tears. "Nollen told me about the horn and the Blood Oath sacrifice." She looked at him with tears streaming down her cheeks. "If Othniel hadn't revived you …"

"He did. And by Gott's grace," Axel gently countered. "Just like Gott preserved me for my appointed time, He has called you."

Lexi wiped her face and rose. She removed the bundle from Alydar to put the badge in its place on the armor then secured everything again behind the saddle.

The others woke. Gunnar arched his back to stretch from sleeping on the rough ground. He observed the sky through the branches and leaves.

"I reckon it's five o'clock. Slept longer than I thought."

"Old bones need more rest," Nollen teased. He tried to hide a yawn.

"You slept just as long." Gunnar gave Nollen a friendly elbow as he passed on his way to Joslin. He drank some water from his flask before he refilled it at the pool. "A quick bite to eat then we should find our path before it gets dark—"

"Danger!" Lexi warned, a moment before Volker glowed and an Artair sounded a warning from overhead.

Ajax took off to join Artair. Sheba and Alydar snorted and stomped their hooves in nervousness. Bardolf and the pack growled. With hackles raised, they formed a defensive perimeter.

"I smell an ancient predator," Bardolf said.

"I sense great anger," Lexi told the alpha. She drew her sword, as did the Gunnar, Axel, and Cormac. Nollen armed his crossbow.

Three large creatures appeared on either side of the gully ridge, for a total of six. Each weighed at least seventy pounds. Striped black and white fur, fangs bared, and three-inch claws dug into the ground to propel them down the incline.

"Badgers!" Bardolf shouted. "Attack!" The wolves split to engage the badgers coming from both directions.

Overhead, the sound of a ravens joined eagles screeches.

As if by impulse, Lexi shouted, "Falcons to me!"

"They won't listen. The evil is too great," Sheba said.

Being larger and more numerous, the wolves gained the upper hand in battle. From dens in the ravine, four foxes joined the badgers. Three owls dove through the trees to help to fend off the wolves.

Axel shouted, "To horse!" He grabbed Lexi's sleeve. Both sheathed their weapons to mount. Once in the saddle, he hoisted her up behind him.

Nollen, Gunnar, and Cormac quickly responded. They pushed the horses to race downstream rather than climb out through the battle. At a break in the terrain, Axel steered Sheba north.

"What about the wolves?" Lexi asked.

"They will follow when it is safe."

After several miles, they finally stopped. Hearing noise nearby, Gunnar drew his sword while Nollen armed his crossbow. Bardolf appeared from shadows. He limped slightly. Artair landed on a lower branch.

"What news?" asked Axel.

"We dealt with the badgers and foxes. Artair and Ajax killed two of the ravens and an owl. The others flew off, wounded."

Lexi slipped off Sheba. "You're hurt." She knelt to examine Bardolf.

"A minor cut and bite."

"Still, let me tend it." Lexi reached into her pouch for the herb packets.

"We don't have time. The lead badger summoned others before succumbing. Badgers are nocturnal. They will follow."

"Then it will be difficult to allude them in the dark," groused Gunnar.

"We don't have much of a choice," said Axel.

"Alydar," began Gunnar, "Nollen said you retained your unicorn speed."

"I have. Though now confined within a normal horse body."

"Gunnar, what are you doing?" Axel asked, suspicious.

Instead of replying to Axel, Gunnar spoke to Nollen. "Escort them back to Eldar as fast as Alydar and Sheba can go. And don't look back."

"Gunnar!" Axel objected.

"I'm doing what I should have done before now. Keeping you safe!" he stoutly rebuffed. "Cormac and I will follow as quickly as possible."

"He's right," said Cormac. "The risk is too great to lose both."

"Ajax and I can keep pace with Alydar and Sheba while Bardolf and the pack remain with Gunnar and Cormac," Artair said.

Seeing Axel still not convinced, Lexi said, "Think of Alicia."

That did it. Axel reached down to help Lexi mount. He then moved Sheba alongside Joslin. For a long moment, he held Gunnar's gaze. "I expect to see you in Eldar."

"Gott willing." Gunnar than said to Nollen, "Take care of them, lad."

"I will. Gott protect you to rejoin us." Nollen put up his crossbow to gather the reins.

Chapter 44

EVEN RETAINING HIS SPEED, ALYDAR DID ALL HE COULD TO KEEP pace with Sheba. Being a full unicorn, she could call upon the herd's magic to cover more distance with blinding speed. Mindful of Alydar's reduced capacity, and feeling Axel and Lexi grow weak, Sheba eased to a lope. The moon shone brightly at its apex.

"We will stop to rest. Although, no longer than an hour," said Sheba.

Nollen, Axel, and Lexi immediately fell to the ground when dismounted beside a stream. Their legs shook from hugging the stirrups close, while arms and hands painful due to clenching the reins and mane. Each labored to catch the breath ripped from them by the powerful wind of speed.

Sheba appeared fresh and unfazed by the effort unlike Alydar. He was drenched in sweat, while his sides heaved to take in air. He greedily drank from the stream. He pounded his front hooves in the water to splash against his head and neck to cool down. Artair and Ajax landed on a fallen log.

Speech difficult, Lexi motioned to Axel for water. He stumbled to rise and fetch the flask from the saddle. He fell on his rump and gave it to her.

She sighed in relief after a long drink. "That's better. My mouth and throat were so dry."

Axel drank than handed the flask to Nollen. "How much longer?" he asked Sheba, but Artair answered.

"I can see the lights of the border station. Maybe thirty miles at most."

"What?" asked Axel, stunned.

"We can be there in a matter of minutes, but I felt Lexi nearly slip off," said Sheba.

Astonished, Nollen spoke to Alydar. “I knew you were fast, but a hundred miles in one night?”

“It will take all I have left to finish the journey,” Alydar wearily replied. His head hung low.

Nollen rose, though still unsteady. “No! I won’t risk it. You will take me at whatever speed you can manage. Let Sheba go on with Axel and Lexi.”

Grateful, Alydar pressed his head against Nollen’s chest. Nollen rubbed Alydar’s cheek.

Axel approached Alydar. “I dislike leaving people behind.”

“Under thirty miles. Even at a walk, we will be there in a day,” said Nollen. “Isn’t that right?” he asked Alydar.

“Aye. I can manage it if given an hour to rest.”

“Put the Shield Maiden armor bundle on my shoulders,” said Sheba.

“You can carry it and us?” asked Lexi.

“Dear one, I barely feel the burden of two, while this will lessen the strain for Alydar.”

Lexi and Axel transferred the bundle.

“Ajax.” Axel motioned to the eagle. Ajax landed on the back of Alydar’s saddle. With great effort, Axel mounted Sheba.

Lexi stroked Alydar’s neck. “Noble Alydar, take care of yourself and Nollen.”

“I shall, Shield Maiden.”

She kissed Nollen’s cheek. “I need a leg up.” Holding Axel’s arm, and Nollen lifting her foot, Lexi mounted behind Axel.

Artair took off the same time Sheba galloped from the stream.

Once again, Lexi held on tight to Axel. She buried her head in his back to avoid the wind whipping her eyes. She ignored the pain of cramping muscles.

Axel also lowered his head and screwed his eyes shut against the wind. He shouted back to Lexi. “Hold on just a little longer.”

She responded by increasing her grip. She grunted at the spasms which made her fingers involuntarily twitch.

Sheba spoke a different language and suddenly the wind and noise ceased. Able to open his eyes, Axel saw everything pass in a silent blur. Up ahead, the faint glow of a single light grew brighter then became multiple points of light. Artair's call made him look up. Stars appeared as trails of white light. Axel blinked and squinted in an attempt to clear his vision. He heard Sheba speak again. This time, he clearly saw Eldar's border station with an encampment of troops surrounding it. The sight made him realize Sheba no longer ran with unicorn speed rather moved at a normal pace.

"We have arrived," Sheba announced.

"Sire!" Irwin hurried over with Mather at his heels. "Princess," he happily said when Lexi peeked out from behind Axel. "We could scarcely believe it when the watch reported Artair, then you."

"Irwin," Axel wearily greeted.

Mather helped Lexi slide off Sheba. He held her up when her knees gave way. Axel managed a bit better on his feet.

Othniel and Alfgar arrived. "Greetings, Shield Maiden," said Othniel.

She simply nodded an acknowledgement. Even a short ride at unnatural unicorn speed proved exhausting for humans.

"Where are the others?" asked Irwin.

Regret filled Sheba's words. "We were forced to leave Sir Gunnar and Lord Cormac behind after a night's ride from Theron when attacked by ravens, badgers, owls, and foxes. Alydar kept pace with me until thirty miles ago. We left him and Nollen also."

Axel patted Sheba's neck. "Rest, food, and drink before more discussion." He reached for Irwin's shoulder to head for the station.

"General, my armor. The bundle on Sheba," said Lexi.

"Aye. Lieutenant! Help her inside." Mather took charge of the armor.

Artair landed on a stump beside Alfgar and Othniel to hear Sheba insist to Alfgar, "I didn't want to leave Alydar."

"Of course not. However, your first duty is to the Shield Maiden."

"Who would be devastated if anything happens to Nollen. Likewise, the King if Sir Gunnar and Lord Cormac do not return. There is a strong bond between the humans."

"Ajax is with Alydar and Nollen. Only thirty miles away," said Artair.

"The others are not so close," she countered.

"What about Bardolf?" asked Othniel.

"He and the pack remain with Gunnar and Cormac. But they barely held off the badgers and foxes." Sheba spoke to the Unicorn king in grunts and low whinnies.

"It would be dangerous to venture back into Bertrand," Alfgar said.

"You want them to die? Because that is what will happen, as they are helpless," she brazenly countered.

Alfgar angrily snorted at the rebuff.

"The sense of evil grows," said Artair.

"How is it possible for them to gain more power?" asked Alfgar, wary.

"Only if Gott allows it for His purposes," said Othniel.

"We can enhance Joslin and Valden to bring Gunnar and Cormac back faster," Sheba said to Alfgar.

"At what cost if Alydar could not maintain such speed?" argued Alfgar.

"Not in one day. Two, at most. Please! What other hope do they have against the fallen First Ones?"

Alfgar lifted his head to sniff the wind. "How far could Gunnar and Cormac have traveled since you left them?" he asked Artair.

"If unscathed, perhaps twenty-five miles in a night."

Alfgar again regarded the horizon. "It is vast terrain to cover."

"We followed the same path Nollen led along the river," said Sheba.

"I need your help to find them," Alfgar told Artair.

"Then we leave immediately?" asked an excited Sheba.

"Artair and myself. Your place is with the Shield Maiden." Alfgar then spoke to Othniel. "Tell the Son of Eldar when it is necessary."

Inside the station, the remainder of the morning was spent in consuming a hearty breakfast and explanation. Axel did most of the talking. Lexi offered a few comments on her kidnapping and subsequent time in Theron, but uncertain of the reason.

"At least, I think so," she groused. She sent an annoyed glare to Axel.

The look and sour tone prompted him to ask, "Meaning?"

"Can we speak in private?"

Axel didn't need to answer, as Irwin and Mather voluntarily left. "If you know the reason, now would be a good time to tell me."

"The marriage proposal!" she chided. "How could you?"

"I didn't agree. In fact, I sent Dynos back with a stern warning about such a bold request. How did you learn about it?"

"I overheard a conversation between Dynos and Rastus."

Axel became cross. "You don't speak Bertrandian."

"Celia translated."

"The maid who helped you?"

"Aye. How could you even consider it? You know I love Nollen." Saying his name caught in her throat.

"Of course, I know. And he loves you. Which is why I rebuffed the request. Your place is here as Shield Maiden, and with Nollen."

"So, he didn't know before we left?" she somberly asked.

"No. It happened after. An amendment to the trade proposal." At her distress, he took hold of her hands. "That is not how I hoped you would learn of it. I meant to broach the subject upon your return from the circuit."

"Sire!" Mather rushed in. "Come quickly!"

Axel and Lexi hastened from the station. They just stepped outside to join Irwin, as Nollen arrived on a galloping Alydar. Nollen barely dismounted when Alydar collapsed.

"Good Gott! What happened?" Axel asked, concerned.

Fearful, Nollen fell to his knees beside Alydar. "Badgers and a bear. Alydar insisted on fleeing at full speed."

Ajax landed on the ground. "I kept them from following."

Othniel and Sheba arrived. Tears swelled, as Nollen pleaded, "Please, Othniel. He can't die."

Sheba lowered his head to touch Alydar's muzzle. "Can you hear me?"

Alydar's lips barely moved, but no answer.

Lexi knelt on the other side. She stroked Alydar's cheek and softly spoke words in another language.

"Lexi, what are you saying?" Axel asked, perplexed.

"Ancient Ganel, Sire. Language of the Shield Maiden," said Irwin.

"How does she know that?"

When Irwin shrugged ignorance, Othniel answered, "Gott."

"Water! Quickly," Lexi said.

Nollen jerked his flask off the saddle to hand Lexi. Instead of taking it, she gave instructions.

"Be ready to pour some over his lips where I place the herbs." She reached into her pouch for the herb satchels and took a few leaves from each. She rubbed them together in her palms to crush them together. She spread the mix on Alydar's lips. "Now. Just a little at first."

Nollen carefully poured the water. At her signal, he stopped. She gently massaged the wet crushed herbs under Alydar's lips onto the gums.

"A little more water."

Nollen obliged.

"That's right, Alydar. Use your tongue to swallow," Lexi encouraged. The process of water and Alydar taking the wet herbs continued until all on his lips were consumed.

"Now what?" Nollen asked Lexi.

"We wait."

"Will it work?" Nollen could not keep anxiety from his voice.

"I … I don't know. I only did what I felt led to do."

Axel knelt to touch Nollen's shoulder. "You need food and rest."

"I won't leave him."

"I will have food brought."

Chapter 45

THE REST OF THE DAY PASSED FOR AXEL IN CONFERENCE WITH Irwin, Mather, Othniel, and various commanders. He barely contained his rage when Mather reported Bodil's attempt to harm Alicia and their unborn child. He thanked Gott for Captain Darick and the successful ploy. He could not imagine losing Lexi, Alicia, and the child. Before further talk of war readiness, he left the wardroom for fresh air to clear his mind.

On the station rampart, Axel watched the late afternoon sun sink in the west. At each corner, guards used spyglasses to watch the southern horizon along with any possible approach from the east or west. He moved away from the guards.

Below, he saw Nollen and Lexi. By their body language, she offered comfort, but he more concerned for Alydar. Now covered in blankets, the noble stallion remained on the ground where he collapsed. Alydar occasionally moved his head.

Axel reflected on his decision to allow Lexi to join Nollen on his annual trading circuit. The simple reason was for her to learn about her destiny as the Shield Maiden. However, Lexi's kidnapping brought about situations never anticipated. They uncovered a history of deception by the Bertrandians. The Nefal once served the Bertrandian gods, who are the missing First Ones. Spoor's return launched a plot against himself, Alicia, and heir. A daring rescue resulted in Gunnar and Cormac being left behind, and now the possibility of war.

Othniel approached. "You are worried, Son of Eldar."

"Aye. The scope of what we have learned is overwhelming." He again looked to Nollen and Lexi.

Othniel followed the gaze. "This would not have happened save for the emergence of the Shield Maiden. As it should be."

Annoyed, Axel asked, "How can you say that? We stand on the brink of another war."

"Where do you think the unrelenting urging in her spirit to explore Eldar came from?"

"Gott, of course."

"If she had not responded to Gott and undertaken this journey, treachery within Eldar would still be festering in secret. While a hidden danger from afar continued unabated. By being obedient, the Son of Eldar and Shield Maiden are joined, and can secure Eldar like in the old days. Long before Oleg's coup."

Axel fought a wry grin. "Our becoming united is what I hoped and prayed for, but certainly not the way I envisioned."

"Divine wisdom far exceeds human comprehension. Yet always for the good of all."

"I pray that good extends to Alydar, Gunnar, and Cormac. Their loss would mar any positive outcome." Axel returned his focus to the horizon.

"Sire." Mather arrived just as the northside watch called about an approach.

Axel ignored Mather to determine the meaning of the call.

"Nefal, Sire." A soldier pointed inland of Eldar. From a grove of trees, fifty Nefal emerged on foot. "They are not heavily armed."

Axel took the spyglass to survey the Nefal. Some carried swords, others axes, bows, or spears. All appeared in rough shape, yet weapons none the less."

"That is what I was coming to tell you, Sire. Lord Maro is here."

"For good or ill?" Axel demanded.

"He wouldn't say. Kept insisted on speaking to you only. Baron Irwin dispatched me to find you while he remains with Lord Maro."

Axel returned the spyglass and hastened to the wardroom. Irwin appeared exasperated while Maro fixed in demeaner. Upon sight of him, Maro's expression immediately changed to contrite. The Nefal chief folded his arms across his chest and deeply bowed at the waist.

"Sire." Maro voice cracked with emotion.

"My lord. What brings you here?" Axel asked, still guarded.

"A shame that is almost unbearable." Maro's eyes remained lowered, unable to meet Axel's direct gaze.

"You mean the plot against my Queen and heir?" Axel harshly asked.

Words failed him, thus Maro nodded.

"What hand did you have it?"

The startling question made Maro's head come up. "None! I swear by the gods."

"The same gods you once served in Bertrand?"

"Then by your god I swear my innocence."

"Beware of blasphemy!" Axel thundered; his temper lost.

Maro swallowed back discomposure when Othniel approached. The Great White Lion of Eldar confronted him. "The Nefal have dealt treacherously since arriving in Eldar."

Maro woefully admitted, "It is true. I do not deny past actions. Yet since the Son of Eldar dealt mercifully with us, I have sought to keep the peace and change how Nefal interact with men. Until Spoor's arrival, I believed the effort successful. Opposing him, cost me the loyalty of an aide, and my daughter's life."

Axel's eyes narrowed in respect of the Nefal chief. "Bodil, *your aide*, tried to harm the Queen and heir."

"That is the shame I cannot bear." Maro knelt. "Thus, I come before you in humility. I did not order, nor have prior knowledge of Bodil's intent. He became led astray by Spoor. Remember, Sire, I sent Brynn to discover Spoor's plan and stop him."

"How can I believe you?"

Maro looked up to the ceiling, raised his arms, and spoke in a loud voice. "I yield to divine justice. May the god of Eldar strike me down if I be not innocent."

At the declaration, Othniel lowered his head and closed his eyes. For a long moment of heavy silence, they waited. The Great Lion raised his head. "He is innocent."

"Thank you." Maro let his arms fall into his lap.

"Why come in arms?" Axel's tone changed from harsh to neutral.

"To defend Eldar. As you once said you would defend Nefal. I offer my life in battle, if necessary."

For a brief moment, Axel considered the answer. Hearing his words from their earlier visit to Ogun, spoke to Maro's intent. "Very well. General, find a place for the Nefal among the ranks."

Mather hid his displeasure and snapped to a salute. "Aye, Sire."

"You think that wise?" asked Irwin after Mather left with Maro.

"Othniel said Gott proclaimed him innocent. Besides, we need reinforcements to face Bertrand."

"Fifty more might not make a difference," Irwin groused.

"Fifty Nefal," Axel corrected. "Each is worth at least three men."

"Only if all are warriors."

Axel frowned at the continuing argument. "We don't have much of a choice!" He left the station to join Lexi, who tried to convince Nollen to eat the food delivered by a soldier. "Has he eaten anything?"

"She gave him some more herbs and water," Nollen replied.

"I meant you in my question to Lexi." Axel knelt.

"A few bites," Lexi replied to Axel.

"Making yourself sick will not help Alydar." Axel took the plate from Lexi and shoved it into Nollen's hands. "I will order a fire prepared, and blankets brought since I won't try to convince you to come inside. Eat."

While Nollen obeyed, Axel tugged on Lexi's shoulder for her to accompany him a short distance away. He grew a bit hesitant. "I have debated all day about telling you, but circumstances—"

"Nefal!"

Nollen's angry tone stopped Axel. When he stood, Axel prevented him from any rash action. He pushed Nollen to sit. Axel waved Lexi over, and also sat. At Nollen's ire, Axel said, "Hear me! I thought only to tell Lexi, but now, you too must know."

"Why are they here?"

"Listen, calmly!" Axel warned. "Eat while I explain. Eat!" he insisted when Nollen frowned to the contrary.

They listened with expressions of anger, surprise, and relief during the disclosure of the attempt on Alicia and the child by Bodil. Both became thoughtful at the retelling of Maro's willingness to be struck down by Gott and found innocent.

"Alicia, the child, Lorraine, and Beryl are safe," Axel concluded.

Lexi wiped away tears. "Thank Gott for Captain Darick and Ganels."

"Bodil betrayed Maro," Nollen murmured under this breath.

"The fault lies solely with Bodil. With Lexi recovered, and Maro declared innocent, I allowed the Nefal to join in defense, as a move toward unity. Gott knows we need that now." Axel turned to Lexi. "We have a task demanding our full attention. Can you do that?"

With staunch resolution she replied, "I am the Shield Maiden of Eldar. I stand with my brother, the king."

Axel kissed Lexi's forehead. "Make sure he finishes," he said of Nollen and left.

Chapter 46

Gunnar and Cormac carefully guided Joslin and Valden to follow Bardolf. The alpha led them through the dark forest. Gathering clouds passed over the stars and moon at various intervals, which gave intermittent light for navigation.

"Can you see Bardolf?" Cormac called in harsh whisper during a cloudy time.

"Barely. My eyes are not as keen as Nollen," Gunnar groused. He rocked in the saddle to maintain balance when Joslin suddenly stopped to avoid Bardolf. "What's wrong? Why did you startle Joslin like that?"

"To prevent her from heading to hidden cliffs beyond those bushes."

Gunnar stood in the stirrups to peer ahead.

"There is more. The scent of humans on the river."

"On the river?" repeated Cormac, confused.

"Dismount and follow me," said Bardolf.

Gunnar removed a spyglass from his saddle bag. He and Cormac crouched down to push through the bushes. The clouds passed to reveal a bright full moon. The abrupt appearance of light made Gunnar and Cormac kneel. They lay on their bellies to view the river two hundred yards below. Small lights created a dark outline that floated on the water.

"Those appear to be boats," said Cormac.

Gunnar used the spyglass. "Barges to be precise. Loaded with troops and horses." His focus changed from the spyglass to the sky. "Heading north just like we are."

"Are the breaks in the water from oars?"

Gunnar again looked through the spyglass. "Aye. Perhaps twenty on each side." He pointed the glass down river. Clouds again covered the moon. Frustrated, he lowered the glass. "Can't get a total count of barges, but by the size I estimate each can transport a thousand troops. We need to hurry and bring Axel word of this." He pushed himself up and rushed through the bushes. He replaced the glass and mounted. "This means riding day and night. I hope you're up for that."

"Never question a Ganel's stamina."

"Bardolf, take us to the main road. We need to ride as fast and far as we can for the remainder of the night."

They quickly guided their horses through the trees in pursuit of Bardolf. Once on open road, it became a full-out gallop. After three miles, they eased to a lope to allow Joslin and Valden to recoup. They repeated intervals of full gallop followed by a lope to conserve energy. By the wee hours of the morning, they covered twenty miles.

"We must leave the road to rest," Gunnar told Bardolf.

The alpha led them to a small ravine. Gunnar dismounted to splash water on his face and over his head. He sat on the bank for a breather. Joslin greedily drank before she found grub for grazing. Valden did the same, as Cormac joined Gunnar.

"How much further to the border?" asked the Ganel.

"Not sure. Bardolf?"

"Considering the amount of time since leaving Theron and the terrain, I guess roughly sixty miles."

"Blast!" Gunnar swore. "At this pace, it will take three days to reach the station. Barges will be there sooner, and Axel won't be warned!"

"I can send Javas ahead," said Bardolf of a nearby wolf.

"How long will it take him?"

"Two days."

Gunnar frowned. "That still may not be fast enough."

"You said we ride day and night," Cormac wryly reminded Gunnar.

"With at least two hours of rest in-between bouts for us and the horses. Otherwise, we'll be no good to anyone." Gunnar rose to fetch provisions from the saddlebag. He handed a piece of bread to Cormac. "Need to cut off the hard crust, but it's something to eat."

An owl sounded close.

"We may not get that rest." Cormac tossed the bread aside to grab Valden's rein. The horse protested the surprise move.

The wolves growled a mere few seconds before four badgers attacked. While the wolves engaged three badgers, one leapt upon Valden's rump. The horse reared to throw it off, but the three-inch claws dug deep to hang on. The badger climbed over the saddle to clamp down powerful jaws on Valden's neck. Shaking its head tore deeply into horse flesh.

"Leave off!" Cormac swung his sword at the badger. The animal jumped from Valden to take Cormac to the ground. The sword jarred from his grip upon impact.

In defense of Cormac, Gunnar thrust his sword into the badger's body. Engaged, it snapped at Gunnar, which forced him to retreat. Wounded, it awkwardly moved toward Gunnar. Bardolf lunged and caught the badger by the throat. This gave Gunnar another opportunity to thrust his blade into the body. The badger whimpered and went limp in Bardolf's mouth.

"Are you hurt?" Gunnar asked Cormac.

"A few scratches." He reached up for assistance to stand.

Gunnar noticed a lumbering mass move through the trees. "Get your sword!"

"What is it?" asked Cormac, wary.

Gunnar shook his head, as the creature's size grew larger the closer it came. Emerging from the darkness revealed an enormous buffalo with a rider on its back.

"Nefal!" Gunnar exclaimed in anger.

"Spoor," said Cormac in recognition. He barely uttered the name when the beast charged. He dodged Spoor's blade as the buffalo ran past.

Bardolf placed himself between them and the buffalo. "Kronos!"

The buffalo king pawed the ground. "Bardolf! Tell us where the Shield Maiden is or die where you stand."

The alpha bared his teeth and lowered his head in defiance.

A burst of brilliant blinding light engulfed the area. The badgers cried out in fear and scurried away into the darkness. The wolves cringed yet maintained their positions. Spoor shielded his eyes in an attempt to discover the source. Kronos brayed loudly in anger at the disruption.

An eagle's screech came a moment before Spoor felt powerful talons snare his shoulders. The impact knocked him off Kronos. The buffalo king stomped to charge, then cried out when a horn pierced deep into his ribs. He jerked away, which made the horn rip open his side.

A loud, echoing whinny cause Kronos to back away. He fought against the sound to stand his ground. Irate, Spoor ignored his wounded shoulder to approach Kronos.

At an eagle's summons, two nighthawks dove at Spoor and Kronos. Another loud, echoing whinny further agitated Kronos. The buffalo king retreated. Spoor grimaced in rage, yet he too, withdrew into the darkness.

The light began to fade. Gunnar and Cormac braced themselves while Joslin nervously snorted. Gunnar relaxed at seeing Artair and Alfgar.

"Well, this is a welcome sight," he said.

"We haven't much time. Kronos is wounded and likely to return any moment for revenge," warned Alfgar.

Valden's legs trembled. He fell to his front knees then to the ground. Blood poured from gaping wounds that ran along either side of Valden's neck. Cormac spoke with lament. "The wounds pierced arteries. He won't last much longer." He stroked Valden's face.

Alfgar spoke to Valden in grunts and low whinnies. Valden replied in weak horse noises.

Alfgar told Cormac. "He's sorry he failed you."

"No, my friend, you did not fail me." Cormac spoke soft words in Ganel. "Gott takes care of all creatures. Rest with Him."

Valden closed his eyes and breathed his last.

Joslin grew agitated. Alfgar spoke to her. Soon, she calmed down. After further conversation, she tossed her head in a nod. Alfgar's horn touched Joslin on the forehead. A glow radiated from her head to the tail. Joslin briefly trembled then pranced in place.

"What did you do to her?" Concerned, Gunnar held the bridle and stroked her cheek.

"Enhanced her with Unicorn strength. She is prepared to carry you non-stop to the border. I will carry Lord Cormac. Mount. We haven't much time."

"The main road is the fastest way, as there won't be much traffic until after sun-up," said Bardolf.

Chapter 47

Another day passed with little noticeable improvement in Alydar. Nollen rarely left him, and only for brief periods out of necessity. Lexi found herself called away for conferences with Axel and Othniel regarding strategy. With battle on the horizon, she wore most of her armor.

When not engaged elsewhere, she returned to help Nollen watch over Alydar. This last time, she had been gone the entire afternoon. An evening fire burned near where Alydar lay. Nollen poked at the logs.

"I hate leaving you alone with him," she complained.

"It is your duty." His voice barely above a dejected whisper.

"Do you mean that?"

He stopped poking the fire. "Of course. Why do you ask?"

"You sound disappointed."

"No. Merely concerned for Alydar." He tossed the stick into the fire. "The whole purpose of our journey was to prepare you to take your place as Shield Maiden. No one foresaw this outcome." He gazed at her and warmly smiled. "The armor suits you."

"Maybe. But am I suited for war? I certainly didn't feel prepared in Markita."

"You weren't ready then. Same as I wasn't ready years ago. When the time is right, we do what we must." He stared at Alydar.

Lexi gently touched Nollen's shoulder. "When the fighting starts, you must leave him."

He changed his focus to her. "I will stand with you."

She kissed him. They embraced to continue kissing.

"I came to inquire about Alydar. Instead, I appear to be intruding," Axel teased. He also wore parts of his armor.

"What is it about older siblings that they have uncanny timing?" Nollen wryly asked Lexi.

Alydar stirred. He grunted and raised his head.

"Alydar?" Nollen asked with wary anticipation.

Without warning, Alydar bolted to his feet. He looked to the horizon and loudly whinnied. Sheba arrived and joined Alydar in whinnying. There came a response. First one individual, then two distinct horse whinnies.

"Alfgar and Joslin," Alydar announced.

Nollen's astonishment went between a recovered Alydar and the approaching forms of Alfgar, Joslin—

"Gunnar! Cormac!" Axel hurried to meet their arrival.

Joslin breathed heavy as she pranced to a halt. Gunnar dismounted and called to a soldier. "Treat her well with a rubdown and extra feed. She deserves it." He patted Joslin's neck.

Axel heartily embraced Gunnar. "Are you hurt?"

"Sore from riding, but whole. Cormac needs a physician."

"Minor scrapes," Cormac tried to pass off the concern.

"How?" Axel examined the Ganel.

"A badger." Cormac became downcast. "It killed Valden. We were fortunate Alfgar and Artair arrived or worse could have happened."

"My herbs should help," Lexi told Cormac.

He cocked a sarcastic grin. "Indeed. Ganel herbs for a Ganel."

Though his comment made her blush with slight embarrassment, she countered. "At least, you haven't lost your sense of humor." She took his arm to head for the station.

Gunnar placed an arm about Nollen's shoulders. "I need your help, lad. I never rode so fast or far at one time. My legs can barely hold me up."

An hour later, a refreshed Gunnar and bandaged Cormac, joined the others in the wardroom. Nollen, now clean shaven, was speaking to Axel when they arrived.

"He needed a lot of rest. Along with the herbs Lexi gave him."

Gunnar sat the table. Two pitchers of ale and multiple cups were on the table. He helped himself to some ale. "Who did?"

"Alydar. He collapsed trying to keep pace with Sheba after we left you. We didn't think he would recover," said Nollen.

Thunderstruck, Gunnar paused in drinking. "I never should have asked him about unicorn speed." He then became smacked by another disturbing thought. "Alfgar gave Joslin that same speed." He rose but stopped by Axel.

"All is well. With both Alydar and Joslin."

Still disturbed, Gunnar finished the ale in a long swallow and refilled the cup.

Cormac was more in control of his drinking. "It is because of Alfgar and Artair's aid that we can report what we discovered," he told Gunnar.

"Oh?" asked Axel.

"Barges of Bertrandian troops heading north on the river," replied Gunnar. "Couldn't make an exact count since it was too dark. However, judging by the size of those I did see, I estimate three to five thousand."

Axel's displeased expression found Irwin. The Ganel baron appeared hapless, thus made Gunnar asked, "How many troops do we have?"

"Roughly two thousand," Irwin timidly replied.

"Meaning we could be outnumbered by more than two to one," groused Axel. "With those odds, our best strategy is to wait, and let Bertrand make the first move."

"Let them cross the border, Sire?" asked Mather, uncertain.

"General, this is not a war Eldar wants. We went to Bertrand for one reason – to recover my sister. That has been successful."

Cormac added his point to the convince Mather. "Gunnar and I assured Rastus that Axel's intentions were honorable toward Bertrand. We also discovered; they didn't know Lexi's true identity. We can't claim kidnapping of our princess as motive to invade."

"Moving troops here is a deterrent," Axel emphasized.

Gunnar listened with brooding countenance. "I doubt our presence will dissuade the Bertrandians. Not if Spoor has any say in it."

"Spoor? Who is he?" asked Lexi.

Gunnar confronted Axel. "You haven't told her?"

Lexi grew annoyed at Axel's reluctance. "Told me what?" she pressed her brother.

"The one behind your kidnapping. A Nefal named Spoor," he replied.

To curb her ire, Nollen intervened. "Spoor sought to undermine Maro. He nearly succeeded, save for Gott's help to unmask him."

Lexi fought to contain her temper. "Could this Spoor have helped Bodil in the attack on Alicia?"

"Unknown," began Irwin. "Bodil claimed he acted to revenge Nefal. He denied Maro had prior knowledge but died before he could reveal anything more."

"Remember, Gott declared Maro innocent," Axel reminded her.

"But you suspected Spoor because Bodil was Maro's aid," she hotly countered Axel.

Rather than rebuff her accusation, Axel calmly replied, "There is no denying Spoor's influence seems to have permeated everything, whether directly or indirectly."

"Spoor participated in the attack upon us along with Kronos, the pretended Bertrandian buffalo god." Gunnar spoke directly to Lexi, "They were after the Shield Maiden."

Unable to speak for anger, Lexi stormed from the room.

Axel seized Nollen to prevent his departure. "Leave her be. She must come to grips with this herself. To prepare to face what is her destiny. Same as I did. Same as you did." He then spoke to assembly. "Gentlemen, we keep to our strategy of non-aggression. If either Spoor, or the missing First Ones, cause the Bertrandians to set one foot in Eldar, we meet them in arms!"

Fury propelled Lexi to the walk the encampment. In Theron, she yearned to escape and set things right. She thanked Gott for making it possible. Yet in her spirit, she knew some sinister reason lay behind the kidnapping. Axel tried to convey his concerns about her welfare in regard to the kingdom. Nollen spoke similarly about the larger scheme. However, all she wanted to do was get away from Sener. Her experience in Theron showed the truth of their concern and forced her to see reality beyond herself. Now learning of Spoor's involvement, and the attempt on Alicia and the child, gave reason for her uneasiness.

During captivity, Gott used all she learned in Mathena to sharpen her discernment and confirm her destiny. Hard to believe that was scarcely two months ago. It felt like a past life, as if looking back at a different person.

She paused at the perimeter of camp. Stars and moonlight shone through intermittent clouds. Beyond the lights of Eldarian campfires lay total darkness of the Bertrandian border.

"The darkness of evil," she muttered to herself. She folded her arms across her body to steady the great chill that shook her to the core. Now visible to all, she wore Volker over the armor. Although the ruby did not glow, she touched it. Her focus remained on the black horizon. "I may sense your evil, but fear no longer has power over me. I know who I am, and my purpose." She closed her eyes to pray. "Gott, grant me the courage and strength to do what I must. What you have appointed."

"Are you troubled, dear one?"

Lexi opened her eyes at hearing Sheba. "No. My world may have been turned upside down, but now I understand why."

"Nothing has happened that wasn't meant to happen."

"It doesn't make it easy to deal with."

"No." Sheba rubbed her muzzle against Lexi's shoulder. "Gott has not left you alone. So do not bear the burden alone."

Lexi hugged Sheba's neck. "Thank you." She stroked Sheba's face. "When will your horn be revealed?"

"When you take your rightful place as Shield Maiden." Sheba's head jerked up as she felt Lexi's hard shiver. "What is wrong?"

Lexi stared intently into the darkness. Volker began to glow. "They are close. The missing First Ones. Gunnar said Kronos came looking for me."

Alfgar and Othniel arrived. "Kronos, and the others, sought to destroy you before you assumed your place. The same as Sirin tried in Markita. They know the powerful connection the Shield Maiden has to Eldar, to nature, and creatures. You unmasked them, and they want revenge," said Othniel.

"Are you willing to go to war to stop them?" asked Alfgar.

"I am the Shield Maiden. I will not allow the evil of Bertrand to invade Eldar!" Lexi staunchly declared. "Though not alone. And most grateful for that help." She patted Sheba's neck.

"Gott, the faithful First Ones, and the Son of Eldar, are with you, Shield Maiden," said Othniel.

Chapter 48

SHORTLY BEFORE DAWN, BARGES REACHED THE MOST NORTHERN town in Bertrand. Situated on the river, the Eldarian border lay three miles further north. Four miles east of the town, the road intersected with the main highway that connected Eldar to Theron.

Felix disembarked first and was met by the garrison commander and town mayor.

"Highness, this is an honor," began the mayor.

"No, honor, sir. Rather a dangerous mission," Felix roughly answered. "What is the status of your troops, Lieutenant?"

"We are ready at your command, Highness. May I ask what this is about?"

"War, Lieutenant. War with Eldar."

Both the lieutenant and mayor stood mute with surprise. The reaction displeased Felix.

"What word of Eldarian troops on the border, Lieutenant?"

"Nothing past a few companies near the station. They are well within Eldar."

Felix's brows levelled in concern. "No scouting parties or patrols?"

"None reported, Highness."

"Highness, the people will be frightened to awake and find troops in town," the mayor nervously said.

"Cannot be helped." He turned his back on the mayor to speak with the lieutenant. "When the troops are disembarked, we move inland to the main road and set up a defensive perimeter. The supplies will follow. Mayor, tell the people to prepare for invasion."

"Yah, Highness!" The mayor scurried off.

The senior officers gathered around Felix to receive orders.

Near the royal barge, Marius and Mateo worked while they kept an eye on Felix. They overheard the orders repeated.

Marius leaned close to Mateo. "They say barge crews are to wait here."

"We leave and follow discreetly." At Marius' frown of indecision, Mateo asked, "What?"

Marius hesitated before whispering, "We've never done this before ..." He paused as crew and soldiers walked past in performance of duty. "He's the prince."

Mateo pulled Marius away from the activity. "You prefer banishment?"

Marius' vacillation deepened. "I can't—kill," he whispered the deadly word.

"Fine time for an attack of conscience! Kidnapping didn't trouble you."

Marius grew irate at the rebuff. "You know it did!" Mateo scowled, so Marius continued. "When have you killed anyone?" At his brother's deepening scowl, he said with certainty, "You haven't. So, why does it not trouble you?"

"What troubles me is the thought of *me* dying."

"Banishment keeps us alive."

Now, it was Mateo's turn to waver in resolve. "It means giving up everything we know."

"Freedom from his control."

"You two! No time for laziness. Get back to work!" the barge captain scolded them.

The brothers headed back toward the royal barge. Once out of view of the captain, Mateo nudged Marius. Utilizing the busyness on the dock, they dashed away unnoticed. They paused in the shadow of a nearby building to observe the mustered troops.

"Now is our chance," said Marius, eager.

"Your chance. Not mine," droned Mateo.

"What do you mean? We can be free!"

Mateo dolefully shook his head. "I'm not brave enough to face what is out there."

Marius became dumbfounded by the statement. "You've always been the brave one."

Mateo turned from Marius. After a brief moment of hesitation, Mateo ran east.

Marius huffed with annoyance before he pursued Mateo.

"Why are you following me? Take your chance."

"I won't leave without you."

Hearing the order to march, the twins followed at a safe distance. With five thousand troops, it took until midday for all to travel the four miles to the main road. Marius and Mateo hid in the trees close enough to watch and listen.

In the near distance, lay the Eldarian border station. Felix dismounted. Handed a spyglass by an officer, he studied the Eldarian defense. Across the horizon, soldiers were encamped.

"I see dragon riders, calvary, infantry, and ..." He paused, lowered the glass to view with his own eyes then raised the spyglass again.

"What, Highness?" asked an officer.

"Nefal. I thought Axel banished them."

"You need not fear the Nefal," a deep resounding voice spoke.

Felix and the officers looked for the speaker. All stood mesmerized when an enormous buffalo emerged from the forest. On its back, sat a Nefal. The officers recovered quickly, to stand shoulder-to-shoulder in defense of Felix.

The buffalo stopped. "We are not here to harm the Prince. I am Kronos of the gods."

Astonished, Felix stepped out from behind the officers. "The gods are real?"

"You saw with your own eyes, Spyros, the raven god, chase off an eagle. An enemy from Eldar!" Kronos declared.

"Do not doubt what you see." A bear emerged from the opposite tree line. "I am Ursus." The bear king stood upright. His sheer size made the Bertrandians recoiled in apprehension

Felix swallowed back discomposure to ask, "Why are you here?"

"To aid you against Eldar," replied Kronos.

Ursus took a few steps forward, which caused Felix and the officers to retreat in fear. Ursus looked past the cringing humans to the horizon. "The Eldarians are aided by creatures you cannot fight."

"And the Nefal?" Felix tried to mask anxiety.

"Spoor is a loyal servant of the gods," said Kronos.

"But Nefal stand with Eldarians." Felix indicated the horizon.

"Part of the plan to raise rebellion within their ranks at the appointed time," said Spoor.

Felix's gaze shifted from the Eldarian army to Kronos and Ursus. Finally, he assumed a proud, regal posture. "On behalf of my father, King Rastus, I, Crown Prince Felix, gladly accept the aid of the gods. Your wisdom and strength are appreciated." He placed his arms across his chest and bowed at the waist. The officers mimicked his obeisance.

Overwhelmed by what he just witnessed; Marius' legs grew weak. He clumsily sat on the ground behind the tree. Mateo sat beside him.

"He was right. The gods are real," Mateo murmured in disturbed wonder.

"They are animals! Not men," Marius insisted, disconcerted.

"How can they speak if not possessing by the spirit of men?"

Marius shook his head, bewildered. "I don't know. Something is not right. Spoor is with them. He controlled the jackals and harpy. Could he be projecting speech?"

To this suggestion, Mateo gave thought. "An illusion?"

"Like those statues combing men and beasts. Do you see any human traits in them?"

"No," said Mateo, soberly.

Marius swallowed back confusion to continue. "I once believed what Mama told us, but lately—I have wondered. He did not know I lied about the girl. I always feared he knew and would punish me according to what the gods said." Sudden fervency brought him up to his knees. "We see for ourselves they are physical animals, not all knowing or omnipresent. What other deceptions has he put forth? Why order us to kill the prince? To appease animals? Satisfy a scheming Nefal? Or to gain power for himself?"

Beleaguered by the reasoning, Mateo could not speak.

Infuriated, Marius seized Mateo by the shoulders. "This proves that everything we believed is based upon lies and falsehood. To control us to do his bidding. We see the truth and can be free!"

"Free," Mateo weakly repeated. Eyes glazed with tears. "I don't know if I can."

"He uses fear to manipulate. Mateo! Don't let him keep us in bondage, not when we have the chance to break free! To be our own men," Marius pleaded with urgency.

"Freedom is something you always wanted." Mateo wiped his eyes.

"Mama always said freedom is in truth. Now, I understand because we see the truth. Come!" Marius pulled Mateo to his feet and turned to leave. He gasped in sudden horror at the sharp piercing between his shoulder blades. He collapsed to his knees when the blade was withdrawn.

Mateo caught Marius and eased him to the ground. Through tears, he said, "Now, you can be truly free of him. Rest with Mama." He closed Marius' dead eyes and kissed his forehead.

Chapter 49

FROM THE RAMPART, MATHER, CORMAC, AND IRWIN OBSERVED the Bertrandian array. Artair and Ajax perched on the battlement with Othniel standing beside them. Axel, Lexi, and Gunnar arrived. Gunnar wore his full uniform, minus the helmet. Axel and Lexi, partly dressed for battle.

"What news, General?" Axel accepted the spyglass from Mather.

"The Bertrandians have arrived. A mile from the border. They will send out patrols and scouts once in position."

Axel lowered the glass. "If any of their patrols wander across the border, leave them be."

"Sire?"

"Non-aggression, General."

"What if they engage our patrols?"

"Then, capture. But only if *they* start the skirmish."

Gunnar leaned close to Axel. "You are asking him to back down."

"No, I'm ordering him to use discretion."

Mather coughed. An indication he heard the discussion.

Axel began to hand the glass to Mather, only did not let go to say, "To avoid any unpleasant encounters, Artair and the eagles will make aerial reconnaissance. Agreed, General?"

"Aye, Sire."

At Axel's nod, Artair and Ajax flew off. "To deter thought of advancing, place our troops in opposite array," he told Mather. "Othniel, position the First Ones where you think best."

"In front with the Shield Maiden," said Othniel.

Lexi took a deep steadying breath at the reply.

Axel gripped her shoulder. "This is your time. I will be right beside you."

"You really expect them to attack?"

"Aye," he replied with deadly affirmation. "Now, let us finish preparing." He motioned for Gunnar to accompany them.

In the officer's quarter, they found Nollen waiting. "All supplies are distributed. I provided each quartermaster with a list of what remains. Not much, I'm afraid. Although, the Baron did well in not depleting Sener's storehouses. If I had known, I could have acquired more."

Axel patted Nollen on the back. "You were occupied elsewhere." He surveyed Nollen's appearance. "Gunnar, take him to the armory for something more suitable."

An orderly helped Axel and Lexi complete donning their respective armor. Lexi accepted the helmet to put on.

"How do I look?" she nervously asked Axel.

He proudly gazed at her. His smile slightly quivered with emotion. "Not at all like the little sister I left in Kranston." He turned her toward a half-length mirror. "What do you see?"

"An image I created in my mind as a young girl when listening to stories about the Shield Maiden. I never envisioned me in those images. I thought of her as fearless."

"No warrior is fearless on the brink of battle. Myself included," he added when she looked quizzically at him. "Overcoming fear is the key to victory. Gott has prepared us for this moment." He put on his helmet. "Time to take our place."

Outside, Othniel, Bardolf, Alfgar, and Sheba met them. "Shield Maiden," they spoke in unison and bowed their heads.

Lexi took hold of Sheba's bridle. "You still appear a horse while I am fully armored."

"Soon, dear one. Soon."

Gunnar arrived leading Joslin and Axel's horse. Nollen came with Alydar. He wore leather body armor, a dagger, his crossbow, and quiver of arrows.

"Where is your helmet?" Axel asked Nollen.

"Too cumbersome. I need clear vision to shoot." His gaze passed to Lexi. He smiled and nodded in acknowledgement. "Shield Maiden."

She blushed at his greeting. Axel nudged her to continue to the front. They led the horses rather than mount.

Mather saluted. "All forces in position, Sire. Lord Cormac is on the right. Baron Irwin on the left."

Axel looked at the respective flanks. Each group had a dragon rider, some Nefal, unicorns, wolves, and eagles.

"Sire." Mather drew Axel's attention to the Bertrandians. From this point, only a half-mile separated the armies. "They decided to move closer."

"No doubt in response to our array."

Dressed in regal armor, a man rode to the front of the Bertrandian line.

"Felix. Rastus' son," Gunnar told Axel.

"And married already," Lexi snidely added.

Axel cocked a scolding brow at her statement. "A moot point."

Felix's shout interrupted the terse sibling exchange. "Why has Eldar come against Bertrand? What further insult is to be made?" His Eldarian heavily accented.

"No insult intended," Axel shouted in response. "This was made clear to King Rastus by Lord Cormac and Sir Gunnar."

"Then why array for battle?"

"In defense of Bertrandian actions."

"Bertrand extended a generous offer only to be rebuffed."

When Lexi immediately stepped forward, Gunnar restrained Axel.

"How generous when you are already married? Did Bertrand seek to make a mockery of Eldar's princess?" Lexi boldly spoke.

Felix stirred in the saddle, obviously caught off-guard by the retort. "Who are you to question dealings between kings?"

"I am the Shield Maiden of Eldar!"

At Lexi's pronouncement, Sheba loudly whinnied and reared. A bright glow engulfed her. When the light faded, Sheba appeared splendid in red leather and silver saddle and tack. A glint of sunlight reflected off her restored horn. Even her sorrel coat, white mane, and tail seemed brighter than before.

Felix and the Bertrandian officers flinched in surprise at the display. "What dark magic is this?" demanded Felix.

Lexi held Sheba's bridle. "She belongs to the honored First Ones of Eldar. Created by Gott to defend us. Those of Bertrand are traitors to their comrades, and deceivers of men."

When Lexi mounted, the others did also. She shouted, "Kronos, Ursus, and Spyros, by Gott's authority, I command you to show yourselves!"

Othniel roared, Alfgar whinnied, Bardolf howled, and Artair screeched overhead.

Drawn forth by the irresistible summons, Kronos, and Ursus emerged from the trees. A wounded Spyros perched on Ursus' back. Each displayed fierce anger at the forced obedience.

Spoor rode Kronos. "Heed not the pitiful female!" he shouted to Felix and the Bertrandians. "Serve your gods! Attack!"

From the trees behind the Bertrandian line, came badgers and bears. Ravens and owls flew above the trees.

Lexi drew Arkin and called, "First Ones! To your Creator be true! Hawks and falcons. Wildcats and boars. To me!"

She used her sword to cut down any animal that attempted to reach her. Sheba stomped, kicked, or used her horn in battle. Alydar kept pace with Sheba while Nollen shot his crossbow to cover Lexi's charge against the Bertrandian creatures.

Artair led the eagles to battle the ravens and owls. Bardolf and the wolves divided their attention between the badgers and bears. Alfgar ordered the unicorns to support the wolves. Othniel headed straight for Kronos.

Soon, the reinforcements Lexi summoned arrived. Hawks and falcons were met by a new wave of swallow-tailed kites and vultures from Bertrand. The sky filled with aerial battles. The noise of raptors nearly deafening.

Axel shouted, "For Gott! For Eldar! Charge!" He lowered his sword.

Gunnar and Mather repeated the command for charge. At the clash of armored men, dragon riders took to the sky. To void the swarms of raptors, they flew low to the ground. Lethal flames strafed the Bertrandians troops.

Kronos lowered his head to meet Othniel. The Great Lion leapt to avoid the buffalo king's horns and take Spoor down. Rather than finish the Nefal, Othniel made ready to engage Kronos' return charge. Strength against strength fought the titans of the First Ones.

Othniel suffered several gouges from Kronos' horns while he inflicted savage bites and claw marks on the buffalo king. Each drew blood.

When Kronos withdrew to recover from the latest blow, Othniel noticed the piercing wound and gouge made by Alfgar bled heavily.

"You grow weak, Kronos," he said.

"Never!" Kronos snorted, pawed the ground, and lowered his head.

Othniel braced for the charge. The moment Kronos raced toward him, Othniel let out a mighty roar. The force made Kronos skid to a halt and snapped his head back, exposing his throat. Othniel leapt and caught Kronos by the throat; his teeth sunk deep into flesh. The force of impact sent Kronos sideways off his feet, and briefly separated from Othniel. The Great White Lion pounced before Kronos could recover. His powerful jaws one again constricted Kronos' throat. The buffalo king thrashed to be loose, but only served to worsen the wounds. Torn flesh bled profusely. He began to choke.

Othniel's front paws pinned Kronos' head when he moved to seize Kronos' muzzle in his mouth. Suffocating, and seriously wounded, Kronos could no longer fight. The buffalo king became still in death.

Bardolf fought Ursus. Although twice the size of the Alpha, Ursus could not match Bardolf's speed and agility. Other wolves joined the Alpha. Frustrated at numerous bite wounds, Ursus became desperate to flee. He stood on his hind legs and roared. He struck out with mighty claws to stay off further attacks. When Bardolf bit his leg, Ursus kicked out, and sent the Alpha sideways. Enraged, he turned to pounce on Bardolf. Ursus didn't see Alfgar until too late. The Unicorn king's horn thrust up into Ursus's chest. Ursus made a defensive swing of his paw that clipped Alfgar in the head. Alfgar's backward stagger ripped the horn from Ursus, which opened his chest open from one side to other. Ursus fell to all fours. He roared in anger. Standing again meant exposing his wound. On all fours, he could only take minor swipes at the wolves and not utilize the full force of his strength. In a uniformed attack, Bardolf and the wolves launched at Ursus. Knocked to the ground, Ursus succumbed to the pack.

Spyros could not fly and hopped off Ursus when the wolves attacked. A wounded raven on the ground became easy prey. Artair snared Spyros. He climbed high into the sky. Kyros came to his father's aid to engage Artair, but little use when Artair released Spyros. The wounded raven king plummeted helpless to his death.

Kyros became the object of Artair's attack. Try as he might, Kyros proved no match for the eagle king. Even with Zeta's help, he became wounded and forced to withdraw to the safety of the Bertrandian forest.

"We cannot survive this," Zeta spoke in desperation. She accompanied Kyros when he awkwardly landed on a branch. "You must call off the attack to save our fledglings and the flock."

Without offering an argument, Kyros sounded a call for retreat.

Spoor left Kronos to find Maro. The Nefal chieftain engaged in battle. A call from his fellow Nefal, alerted the chief to trouble. Maro parried Spoor, and the two exchanged fierce blows. Battle between Spoor and Maro confused the Nefal.

"Spoor! Capture him!" Cormac ordered a squad of infantry.

Eldarian soldiers tried to obey when several Nefal prevented them.

Maro disengaged Spoor to tell his people, "He killed Brynn!"

At this revelation, the Nefal, stepped aside. Spoor found himself surrounded by Nefal and Eldarians.

"Nefal cowards!" he spat.

Maro confronted Spoor. "You are a coward for murdering their future chief. Nefal warriors die honorably in battle. You betrayed us! Take him!" he ordered his men.

"What are you going to do with him?" asked Cormac.

"He will face Nefal justice."

"He is also responsible for the Princess' kidnapping."

Maro looked Cormac straight in the face. "She is safely returned to her family. My daughter—will never return."

Cormac gave a nod of consent and watched the Nefal leave with Spoor.

Mateo weaved his way through the chaos to find Felix. The Prince fought a Eldarian knight. Mateo picked up a fallen sword. When Felix downed the knight, Mateo went after him.

Surprised, Felix parried the attack. He kicked Mateo in the chest. Mateo landed on his rump with the wind knocked from him.

"Bertrandian! Why attack me?" Felix demanded.

Before Mateo could answer, Gunnar and five knights encircled them. Gunnar held his sword leveled at the Prince.

"Your sword, Highness," he said.

Felix stiffened with pride. "I am Felix, Crown Prince of Bertrand! I do not yield to a common soldier."

"Encase you have forgotten, I am Sir Gunnar, First Knight of Eldar. Defender of His Majesty King Axel. High Knight of the Holy Order."

"Listen to him." Axel arrived.

Felix took note of the royal armor. "You are the Eldarian King."

"Aye. When Sir Gunnar speaks, he speaks for me. Your sword."

Felix held the hilt out to Axel. Instead of taking it, Axel motioned for Felix to give it to Gunnar.

"I yield," Felix begrudgingly said. When Mateo stirred to rise, Felix snapped. "Stop him! The traitor tried to kill me."

Axel signaled the Eldarians knights to capture Mateo. He then spoke to Felix. "Tell your men to lay down their arms."

Felix issued the order that became repeated by various commanders. "Now what?"

"We need to talk. Peacefully."

Chapter 50

WHILE EACH SIDE TENDED TO THE WOUNDED AND BURIED THE dead, Axel escorted Felix to the border station. He summoned Cormac and Othniel. Once dismounted, he spied Lexi and Nollen returning. They led Sheba and Alydar. He saw no wounds.

"Take the Prince inside. I'll be along shortly," Axel told Gunnar. He smiled when Lexi and Nollen arrived. "The day is won, Shield Maiden."

She made a brief return smile, though her voice sober. "I am grateful for victory yet disturbed by the cost."

"A regretful necessity when protecting a kingdom." He gripped her shoulder, eyes direct. "Felix is inside. Keep your temper. Also, stay back and retain your helmet while I speak with him."

"Why?"

"I want to confirm whether he or Rastus had knowledge of your kidnapping."

"If they did?"

"That will change the nature of our discussion." He stopped further protest. "At the appropriate time, you can reveal your identity."

"She will comply," Nollen confirmed.

Lexi scowled at Nollen's comment but nodded in agreement.

Inside, Gunnar provided Felix with a drink. Felix tried to act calm, yet wary of the Great Lion. Othniel sat in a corner, his focus intent on Felix.

"Ah, good," began Axel at seeing Felix held a cup. "I hope you find the ale to your liking. Commissary Nollen," he spoke the title with a specific intonation, "does well to procure all trade goods."

Felix made an official nod to Nollen. "Commissary. Perhaps, if we had continued negotiations, this could have been avoided."

Axel's voice drew Felix's attention from Nollen. "It would have, if not for a certain stipulation put forth by Bertrand." When Felix squirmed, he added, "I refer to preferential trade partner. Did you take it for something else?"

Felix took a drink to cover his discomposure.

"A marriage proposal, perhaps?" Axel's tone now harsh.

"For someone already married," Lexi complained under her breath.

Felix didn't react, so he didn't hear, but Axel did. He saw Nollen nudge Lexi in warning.

Axel moved to stand in a way to blocked Felix's view of Lexi. "Well?"

"That was Cadmus' idea. I wanted no part of it."

"You didn't want to marry my sister? Princess of Eldar?"

"No." Seeing Axel's face flush with anger, Felix hastily added, "Not as an insult to Eldar or Your Majesty. I am already married."

"Really?" Axel's eyes narrowed as he folded his arms. "Help me understand this. Bertrand's Vizier convinces Rastus to propose a marriage between you and my sister, but you are already married? Are multiple marriages common in Bertrand? They are unacceptable in Eldar."

"No, it is the same of one marriage in Bertrand."

"Then why agree to the proposal?" Axel's tone suggested impatience.

Felix fidgeted as he admitted, "They didn't know! I married in secret."

Axel heard Lexi's huff, an indication her silence would not last much longer. He continued the interrogation. "Why not prevent the proposal from being sent?"

Felix sighed with humble regret. "I was afraid to."

"So, they ordered her kidnapping because you were afraid?" Lexi brashly challenged.

The new voice and question, perplexed Felix. "What kidnapping?" He tried to see passed Axel to the speaker.

Axel moved aside and motioned for Lexi to step forward. She focused harsh eyes upon Felix when speaking. "The kidnapping of Princess Lexi to force a marriage between Eldar and Bertrand."

Felix blinked in astonishment. His mouth moved several times before he could say, "I have no knowledge of that."

"Would your father or Cadmus order it?" she continued the grilling.

"Not my father. Cadmus, that is a possibility."

"I say he did. Especially when threatening Celia like Dorothia!" she roughly declared.

Curious, Felix sat forward to regard her. "How do know that?"

Lexi removed her helmet.

Felix gaped in shock. "Leizel!"

"Lexi! Princess of Eldar, kidnapped for my brother, the King's, refusal."

Thunderstruck, Felix impulsively rose to tell Axel, "I swear by the gods, I didn't know!" He said to Lexi, "I defended you when brought before my father as a runaway slave." Overcome by the implication, he collapsed into the chair.

"First a kidnapped bride and then a slave!" she chided in mockery.

Still reeling from the revelation, Felix could not respond.

"Why did you follow Spoor?" asked Axel. His patience wearing thin.

"Spoor?" repeated Felix, confused.

"The Nefal with Kronos."

Felix shook his head. "I never saw him before the gods arrived prior to battle."

"Kronos is dead! So, are Ursus and Spyros. Your so-called gods, as represented by those statues in Theron," Lexi bitterly declared.

Felix stared at her; first stunned then incredulous. "Gods can't be killed."

"Animals can. And they were animals once trusted in Eldar. The First Ones, just like Othniel." She motioned to the Great White Lion.

Felix's brows became deeply etched in unsettled consideration.

"How did they convince you to come against us?" Axel demanded.

A bit preoccupied, Felix shook his head. "Not them. Cadmus. As I said, I knew nothing of Spoor or the gods—animals—until yesterday."

Irate, Axel leaned on the table to bring his face level with Felix. "You expect us to believe you are innocent when Eldarian blood has been spilled in battle?"

A knock on the door was immediately followed by Mather's entrance.

"What is it, General?" Axel demanded, his temper short.

"You will want to see this, Sire. The translation is under the original." He gave Axel a dispatch.

Axel's expression changed to sympathetic. He held up the paper. "This changes the situation. You are now King of Bertrand."

Felix snatched the paper. "My sister requests my immediate return."

"You will be released once we have signed a treaty," said Axel, sternly.

"Draft what terms you like, and I will sign it."

"General, take the king to my quarters while we draft the treaty."

Once the door closer, Othniel approached the table. "Like Maro, he is innocent."

"That's hard to believe," Lexi groused.

"Your ordeal clouds your judgement," said Othniel.

"Maybe, yet it makes it difficult to trust Bertrand again."

"We won't," declared Axel. "The new treaty is for Eldar's protection. Including a severe demotion in Bertrand's trade status."

"Trade?" she repeated, irate.

"Much suffering in Eldar would occur should *all* trade cease," Nollen said, in an attempt to calm her.

Axel held Lexi's shoulder. "Just like what happened in Markita has worked for our advantage, so Gott will use this for our benefit. To avoid further breakdown in relations, he will agree to our terms."

Visibly disturbed, Lexi left. This time Axel didn't prevent Nollen from pursuing her. She stopped just outside the station's southern gate.

"I hope your ordeal doesn't cloud all your judgement. Especially about us," Nollen said.

She held his arm and leaned her head against his shoulder. "No. All I could do when trapped in Bertrand was pray for Gott to grant me the true *freedom* you once described. To fulfill my destiny with strength and courage. To come home to you, to Axel, to Eldar. Thankfully, Gott answered. Though in ways difficult to imagine."

"You are home now. What happened is in past."

"I feel like a different person than before we left Sener."

"You are. So, is everyone touched by this. Me. Axel. The question now is, how do we accept the experience and move forward?"

She widely smiled. "How do you think we move forward?"

His return smile mischievous. "Nothing is official without the king's approval."

"Granted!" Axel stood by the gate with Gunnar. "Arctander is waiting for our return to perform the wedding."

About the Author

Shawn Lamb is a multi-award-winning author of Christian fiction ranging from age 8 to adult. She is also an event speaker. Since 2010, Shawn has participated in homeschool conventions, book fairs, comic cons, and festivals throughout the Southeast, Midwest and Mid-Atlantic regions.

As a former screenwriter for children's television, and author of numerous books, she brings over 30 years' experience dealing with publishing and Hollywood to her speaking engagements.

For more information about Shawn's books and possible speaking engagements, visit www.allonbooks.com.